CITADEL

C. M. ALONGI

CITADEL

BLACK
STONE
PUBLISHING

Printed in the United States of America

First edition: 2023
ISBN 979-8-200-83642-0
Fiction / Science Fiction / General

Version 1

Blackstone Publishing
31 Mistletoe Rd.
Ashland, OR 97520

www.BlackstonePublishing.com

AUTHOR'S NOTE

Citadel is a sexist, classist, ableist society. This is a problem for Olivia for a number of reasons, one of the biggest being that she does not ever get a proper diagnosis. Words like "autism," "sensory overload," and "ADHD" don't exist in Citadel's vocabulary.

I've done my best to portray Olivia as a nonverbal autistic—with a possible side of ADHD—in this novel, which takes place in a world that doesn't have the words for her. And while I have worked with, have lived with, and am related to people on the spectrum and/or with ADHD—and of course ran this manuscript through an extensive community of sensitivity readers who share a similar diagnosis—I myself am neurotypical.

Neurodiversity is still taboo in our society, and my hope is that seeing more of it in media will help dismantle that stigma in real life. But such good intentions mean nothing if we miss the mark. As such, if you are autistic or have ADHD, then I encourage you to reach out after you read this book, either on social media or through the "Contact Me" page on my website (www.cmalongi.com). Reviews aren't just for other readers; they also let authors know what they got right or what they did wrong, and I'm eager to hear what you think.

The autistic community is more disabled by physical, social, and cultural barriers than by any actual disability or neurodiversity. As such, I encourage you to volunteer or donate to organizations that work to change that, such as Autistic Self Advocacy Network, Autistics for Autistics, and the Autistic Women & Nonbinary Network.

Do not donate to Autism Speaks. Fuck those guys.

Enjoy the book.

—C

PROLOGUE

Of course, the first time Elias set foot in the Flooded Forest, everything went to shit.

It started out well enough. People went in and out of the forest all the time. Hunters, fishermen, and foragers had to get food they couldn't grow at home. The iron miners made several trips to the iron bog in the spring and summer. Granted, that was less than a day's walk from the town. Where it was safe. And where no demons had been spotted in generations.

Elias was going much, *much* deeper. And rather than trying to avoid demons, he and the other soldiers were actively hunting them.

"I regret every decision I've ever made in life," he muttered, trudging through the darkness behind his commanding officer and other soldiers. The weight of his basket dug into his shoulder with leather teeth.

"Why?" asked Matthew. "We get to be heroes. Go into the deep, dark wood, hunt a few demons, bring the bodies back home. Women love that kind of story."

"My woman's already been in the woods. She's not going to be impressed."

"Oh, right, I always forget you're dating the silver frea—"

Elias punched him in the arm. Matthew chuckled, rubbing the spot.

The two had been friends for years, asking each other for dating advice and competing over grades. They even looked alike: spiky dark hair, tan skin, tall, with the only major difference being the freckles on Elias's face.

"Seriously, it's fine," Matthew said. "Most of these hunts don't work, anyway. Demons are cowards. And they may be unholy abominations, but at the end of the day, they're just animals, and animals hide from men."

Elias really hoped he was right.

They continued to march. Despite the name, the Flooded Forest was not currently flooded, as it was low tide. The blue trees of the forest were each as wide as a house, far enough apart that five men could walk abreast, and Elias felt naked in such an open space. From the safety of Citadel, the forest had seemed like a dense, dark land filled with dangers and strange plants. But once *in* the forest, there was so much space: no bushes or shrubs or even grass on the ground, no lower branches for him to climb, just the massive trunks of the trees. The biweekly sweeping tides didn't allow for anything else.

The light of the planet's rings and two dull moons poked through the leaves in slivers. The branches far above their heads intertwined with their neighbors in the other trees, and the leaves grew thick, plunging the forest floor into near-total darkness and forcing the soldiers to use lanterns. Caws and croaks of the night creatures surrounded them, but that was just background noise. What made everyone tense was the howls. First one would start, then another, and another, until it was impossible to tell how many there were or how close.

It's bad enough the demons are killing our hunters and gatherers. Do they have to be so damn noisy, too?

The group had a dozen soldiers, including the commanding officers, Lieutenant Ward and Ensign Copper, alon g with Sergeant Benson. The sergeant whistled sharply, glaring at Elias and Matthew. "Hurry up, ladies. This isn't the time to lag behind."

The two hurried to the tail of the group. Elias's foot hit a large rock, and he would've hit the ground nose first if Matthew hadn't caught him. He cursed, tapping his foot to make sure he hadn't broken any toes. "Why the fuck are we doing this at *night?*"

"Because that's when demons are awake?" Matthew replied. "Just a few hours until sunrise. You can make it."

He grumbled but followed his friend. Another hour passed in silence. He breathed into his hands, trying to warm his frozen fingers as the crisp night air cut through his military-issue coat. Every time a branch cracked or something fluttered in the leaves over their heads, the soldiers would tense, hands gripping bows and arrows. But just like the last three nights, it was just the wind or a small bird. The howls had stopped.

He knew that it was rotten of him not to want to be here. Humanity's salvation depended on destroying the demons. The priests said that humans were once angels who fell from grace and Heaven. When they landed on this planet as mortals, the Hundred-Faced God gave them just enough resources—unique crops like wheat and pears, heavenly technology known as Artifacts, and the prophet Riley Bevill—to survive. Humans would be able to return to Heaven as angels after they cleansed the world of demons. But until then they were stuck here, and everyone who died was sent to wallow in Purgatory.

Elias wasn't sure how much of that he believed. His girlfriend, Olivia, was *extremely* skeptical of everything taught by the Faith and flat-out refused to believe in God Himself. Other people whispered that the "demons" Scripture said humanity had to destroy were *inner* demons rather than the winged monsters in the forest that kept killing them.

Those people tended to be executed for heresy, so it was probably best not to think about it.

At one point, Ward called a halt, and they set the trap. The meat from Elias's and Matthew's bags went on the ground. Climbers set to work getting to the trees' lowest branches, which were some seven meters above their heads. The sound of their metal hooks and cleats digging into the dark-blue trunks felt deafening in the near silence of the woods. Once the climbers were all set—nets at the ready—everyone else got into position. Elias and Matthew ended up together, taking position behind a tree with bows and arrows out. Without the shrubs or bushes of the high ground, it was the only cover they had.

It was a simple trap, but effective. Scouts had seen evidence of demons in this area, so over the last few weeks they had left large kills for the creatures to get used to finding. The meat Elias and Matthew had carried was in the exact same spot as all the others. Only this meat was poisoned. And rather than quickly vacating the scene, the humans were staying. When the demons returned for their usual meal, they'd be ready.

Sometimes it worked. Sometimes it didn't. Sometimes it wasn't the demons who arrived for the meal, but other predators like menziva or leohiems. Sometimes the demons wouldn't show up at first, and then when the scouts checked the area a few days later they'd find a couple of their corpses near the poisoned meat. Most soldiers came home without seeing hide nor feather of the demons.

And sometimes, whole troops never returned.

Hundred-Faced God, in Your infinite wisdom, You know damn well that I am a coward. Please indulge that and don't make me kill anything tonight, Elias prayed.

The lieutenant gave the signal, and all the torches were put out, plunging the entire area into darkness. Only the silver light of the planet's rings cutting through a hole in the leaves illuminated the trap.

They waited.

This was worse than the march. At least then their blood had been moving. But sitting in the darkness behind a tree quickly cooled the body. Elias breathed into his hands again, teeth chattering.

"So," he whispered, unable to take the tense silence any longer, "your two years are almost up. What are you going to do?"

Honestly, he was amazed he was even asking that. He couldn't believe their mandatory years of military service were almost over. It seemed like they'd been going through the hell of basic training only yesterday.

"I have no idea," Matthew admitted. "Can't get a job that pays nearly as well as this, so I might just stay in service. What about you?"

"My Placement is wood carving. Christophe's agreed to take me on as an apprentice in his furniture shop after I'm discharged. It won't pay much, but . . ." He shrugged.

"That's great, El! Think you'll ask your girlfriend the Big Question?"

He gave that a bit of thought. His eyes had adjusted to the darkness enough that he could see a kuzirk—small, two-tailed lizard that made an excellent snack when grilled over a fire—scurry up their tree. The leaves rustled against each other.

"We've talked about it," he said. "But you know who her dad is. If he asks for a dowry, I won't be able to afford it."

"You could elope," Matthew pointed out.

"Then I'm fucked." Although Elias couldn't deny it wasn't the worst idea in the world. Olivia would probably like it. "Crazy" and "impulsive" were her favorite activities.

The biggest problem was that not only was her father terrifying and incredibly overprotective of his daughters, but he was also the captain of the city guard, the second most powerful man in Citadel. He could have Elias dishonorably discharged, kicked out without pay or the credit of service. That would stain him forever, possibly convince Christophe not to hire him after all.

Two sharp whistles from a scout yanked Elias out of his thoughts. He nocked an arrow on his bow, waiting. His palm was so sweaty it felt like it would slip from his fingers.

He wished he had a revolver. The small iron weapons were noisy but extremely effective and accurate. They were also incredibly hard to make and considered holy Artifacts, and thus they were reserved for officers only.

"Did you see anything?" Matthew whispered.

"I don't know. We were too busy talking!" he hissed.

He kept his attention on the trail and pile of meat, trying to peer through the darkness. *Breathe in, breathe out*, he thought, drawing back his arrow until the feathers brushed against his chin.

Nothing moved.

"False alarm?" Matthew asked.

"Maybe."

Someone shouted. Elias looked up in time to see a shadow slam into one of the climbers, shoving him off the branch high above their heads. The man screamed all the way down, until he hit the ground with a loud thud.

"Hold your fire!" Copper ordered. It was a mistake. Elias heard him shriek as something—something with claws and teeth—grabbed him, then threw his bloody body next to the scraps of meat in the center.

The torchbearers lit their lights again, the clearing bursting with almost blinding light. Men on the ground looked up, trying to find the shadows that flew among the trees.

Elias hadn't realized the demons would be so *fast*. They zoomed from branch to branch, massive wings deftly avoiding obstacles and arrows. Even with the light, it was hard for him to follow even one.

He picked a shadow at random, and he and Matthew both fired at the same time. One of the arrows managed to graze a wing, sending the beast almost into a tree before it righted itself and disappeared in the darkness.

The other climber went down, taking the nets with him. Elias cringed when he hit the ground with a sickening crack. He nocked another arrow.

That was at least three men dead, and no demons even wounded.

"If they don't sound the retreat in the next minute, I'm running," Matthew said.

Desertion was a crime punishable by death, but Elias was also thinking about rolling those dice. Another shadow flew by and he shot at it, but the arrow went wide.

"Retreat!" Ward ordered. "Everyone out—!" He cut off with a scream.

He had been stationed on the northern end of the trap. Elias and Matthew were sure to give that area a wide berth as they ran.

Screams and moans behind them, shouts and orders ahead of them, Elias sprinted as fast as he could. He tried to find a torchbearer, but the one he had his eyes on was suddenly picked up by a demon and dropped, the light going out. He and Matthew veered off into the darkness.

The emergency rendezvous point was a kilometer away. They had ten minutes to get there before they were left behind.

So this is why Peterson forced us on so many runs, Elias thought. Matthew's heavy breathing was right behind him. Neither of them dared to stop or slow down even though they could barely see their hands in front of their faces, until Elias tripped on a root and went flying.

"Son of a—" The rest of his curse was swallowed by dirt. He tumbled, rolled, and landed hard on his back, wheezing.

"The mighty soldier survives the demons, only to be felled by a tree," Matthew chuckled, catching up to him. "Are you hurt?"

Elias poked at his ankle. It stung, but there was no swelling, and it didn't feel like he'd broken any bones. "No. I think I'm all right."

Matthew grinned, offering his hand. "Lucky you."

Their palms grazed, and then something smashed into Matthew.

"Matt!" Elias yelled, scrambling to his feet.

He could hear his friend screaming as he was pulled *up* into the darkness, and then silence.

Elias swallowed. He wanted to go into that darkness. Find his friend, patch up any injuries he might have, and then get him out of this hellish place.

But the first lesson taught in training was that demons always *immediately* went for the kill. If your comrade was taken, they were dead. Didn't matter if they were still screaming, begging, or praying—they were dead, and you needed to run.

He should have left me behind, Elias thought as he ran. *He should have left me behind.*

Elias realized he'd gotten turned around when he came across a pond he had never seen before. It reflected the silver light of the planet's rings like a knife.

Lacking even the energy to swear, he decided he might as well get a drink before getting his bearings. He splashed near-frozen water on his face and hands, washing away the dirt from his fall. His *stupid* fall that had cost Matthew his life. God's Faces, why hadn't that idiot kept running like he was supposed to?

Worry about that later, said a voice in his head that sounded suspiciously like Sergeant Peterson. *Get your ass back to Citadel. Then you can wallow and cry all you want.*

Right. Get back to Citadel. Should be easy.

Except he had no idea where he was.

He buried his face in the warmth of his scarf. Olivia had made it for him during last month's Praeta festival. It was an ugly thing, lopsided and loose in some areas. But it was soft and warm and did an excellent job of absorbing his frustrated tears.

Get it together, you idiot, he scolded himself. *You went south and at one point turned east. So start going northwest.*

He looked up at the sliver of sky afforded to him by the clearing. Not being a hunter, iron digger, or experienced soldier, he'd never had to navigate by the stars before. But everyone knew the basics: the tip of the planet's rings rose in the south, and the Demon's Tail constellation pointed north. So if he followed that at an angle, then it should take him home.

He couldn't make out many constellations through his tiny window of leaves. He'd have to find a way to climb up to get a better view . . .

Something moved out of the corner of his eye.

Elias stiffened. He'd set his bow on the ground next to his leg when he drank from the pond. He slowly moved his hand toward it.

The demon smashed into him before he got close. They rolled into the shallow water. Elias gasped as claws ripped through his uniform and skin. He managed to kick the thing off him and get on a knee, pulling out his knife.

The blade looked pathetically small compared to the creature before him. Shadowed by the trees as it was, the beast was all black: fur and wings and talons, with a white patch over its eye. It bared its yellow teeth at him, most of them longer than Elias's fingers.

If he'd had his bow with him, he'd have a chance, but who knew where that was now?

Shit.

Shit.

Elias was going to lose.

He was going to die.

Well . . . fuck.

He chuckled, even as something in him broke.

The water lapped against Elias's pants, freezing his skin. Either water or blood trailed down his chest beneath his coat. He breathed in the fresh forest air that chilled his lungs.

The demon prowled closer. Elias flipped his knife and braced himself. "Let's go."

The demon lunged.

Dear Elias,

They're making me go to an execution today, hundred fucking hells. It'd be more bearable if you were here. Remember that time you pretended to be sick so we could both miss that atrocious play Evelyn wanted to see? You acted it so well that even I was fooled for a little bit! I don't think I could pull off that same stunt now. You know how bad I am at acting.

It's been almost a year since you died. Everyone keeps saying that "he's not really gone as long as we remember him," like that's useful. Memories don't keep me warm at night or go stargazing with me or mother-hen me into annoyance. All they do is remind me that you're not here.

They also say that it gets better with time. That it'll hurt less. But I don't know if I want that to happen, either. The memories hurt, but if they're all I have left of you then I don't want them to fade or dull with age.

If I ever find the demon who killed you, I'm stringing them up by their lungs.

> *Love,*
> *Olivia*

CHAPTER ONE

Olivia clenched and unclenched her bruised hand as she and Evelyn walked to the wall. Nothing was broken, but it was going to be a pain and a half to write anything for a while.

She hadn't *planned* on punching anyone today. But then a strange woman—probably a little drunk—had tugged on her silver hair while she and her sister walked by, and it had just sort of . . . happened.

The woman's nose had already been crooked; it wasn't like Olivia had made it worse.

"I still think we should let Mom see it," Evelyn said, eyeing her hand. "Just in case."

Olivia shook her head, wiggling her fingers to show that nothing was broken.

Evelyn's mouth scrunched (Disappointment? Frustration? Delayed nasty aftertaste from breakfast?), but she didn't argue further.

Placed at the very top of a hill in the middle of the forest, Citadel was a walled city that housed just over twenty thousand people, the world's entire human population. Most of the buildings were made from wood, but the wealthiest homes were made of stone. The perimeter wall itself was made of a combination of wood, scrap, and crumbling cement, the outer layer routinely fixed with waterproof materials such as animal skins and rough rubber.

They reached the bottom of the wall and had to wait in line to climb the stairs. The number of people jostling and bumping into Olivia set her teeth on edge, even through her thick sweater. She forced herself to stay still. It'd be over soon.

It'd be easier if Elias was here. He'd tuck me into his side to keep me from touching at least half as many strangers.

"Are you all right?" Evelyn asked. If she weren't standing right next to Olivia, she'd be hard to find in the crowd. Everyone wore thick, dark clothing to combat the constant chill that hung over Citadel like an obsessive ex-lover, even in the summer. Most people, and almost all the women, also wore some sort of head covering—caps, scarves, hoods—some of them for additional warmth, some for the sake of modesty. Evelyn always kept her thick, dark curls tucked into a headscarf whenever going out, spending extra money on the ones dyed brighter colors. When she opened the drawer she kept them in, it was like discovering a rainbow. But today she wore black.

Olivia shrugged, keeping her hands in the pouch of her sweater around one of her smaller sketchbooks. There was a bad feeling in her belly, like her guts had been filled with melted iron that was rapidly hardening. Nothing new there. It'd go away once this was over.

"I'm sorry about this," Evelyn said as the two teenagers moved inch by inch up the stairs. Again, carved from wood. The fact that so much of their architecture was from the indigo trees of the forest meant that most of the city was some shade of blue, and also vulnerable to fire.

"I know you usually skip these things. But you know how Dad is," she continued.

Olivia gave a tiny nod.

"You have your ear coverings, right?"

She held up the clunky things made of wool and iron that her uncle had made her.

More jostling, more trudging, and they finally managed to get to the top of the wall. They were next to one of the ballistae, a massive crossbow that shot bolts the size of spears. There were several more dotted along the wall. None of them had been used in over a century, but it still paid to be prepared.

At Olivia's back was Citadel. When she turned, she could see city hall in the center of town, where the city officials did their business. Right across the street from it was the head temple, the largest building in town, built with as much splendor and magnificence as possible with whatever the Founders could scrap together. They stood side by side at the very top of the hill that elevated the city's center above the tides.

The rest of Citadel spread out and down from there, like a massive gray-and-pale-blue target. The textile mill, the paper mill, the first-built schoolhouse, the barracks, Central Hospital, and the wealthiest homes were all in the center, clustered at the top of the hill. The farther away from the center, the smaller and more crowded the buildings became until they were leaning against each other like a group of half-dead drunks. Then suddenly there was a shocking amount of space: the Farmers' Ring. Fields of crops grew around Citadel's crowded interior, making the outermost ring of that bull's-eye the largest. It was the closest thing to open space Citadel had unless you went beyond the wall, which circled the entire city without any gaps and stood almost four stories high at the tallest.

To Olivia's front was the forest, an endless ocean of orange leaves and blue wood, with some hints of yellow and green, depending on the species. With Citadel located on top of one of the tallest hills in the area, they could see for eternity. Yesterday it had hailed, but today was a cheery blue day with a warm sun and only a slight chill breeze to temper it.

The forest didn't start for at least another half kilometer in any direction, thanks to the loggers constantly chopping trees for lumber and security. It created a field of dirt that, like most of the forest, never grew grass, and was now under a thick layer of clear water. A pit had been dug out centuries ago, lined with stone so the elements wouldn't simply move the dirt back into place, with two tall posts driven into the ground at the pit's bottom.

The wall on this side of Citadel was wider than any other part, specifically designed to allow as many people as possible to see those posts. There were even stands built so people could see over each other's heads.

Olivia never understood what was so captivating about an execution.

The man tied between the two posts in the pit was named Benjamin Novak. Olivia had only interacted with him a handful of times and could not say they were friends. But he'd never been mean to her, which was more than she could say for most people.

At this distance, she couldn't see much detail. Only that his head was just above the rising water and, per tradition, he was stripped of all clothes and shaved. He'd been there since dawn, which meant he had to have some serious sunburns by now.

At least he wasn't screaming. That always made it so much worse.

She took out her sketchbook and a pencil, wrote *Why him?* and presented it to her younger sister.

"Dad told us yesterday. Weren't you paying attention?" Evelyn asked.

If she had, she couldn't remember what was said.

Evelyn sighed—never good, it meant Olivia had done something wrong—but explained, "Ben's a heretic. A Dove. He tried to talk a bunch of soldiers into refusing to go into the forest. I've heard rumors that he even did sermons in his basement, but Dad didn't find any evidence to support that."

Olivia had to resist the urge to roll her eyes. What a stupid reason to kill someone.

"And Dad's asking us to be here because Ben was Mom's friend and, traitor or not, she's really upset about this. So we're showing our support."

Ah. That was what she needed to hear.

On the wall was a dais that had the best view, reserved for the governor and the convict's family. Benjamin only had one living relative, his mother, Bella. The older woman was clothed entirely in black, her dress covering everything from neck to wrists and ankles, her gray hair tied back in a headscarf. Her weathered face was like stone. Olivia didn't know how she could do that. When she had been on that dais, it had taken three men to restrain her.

Benjamin was the fifth "traitor" in the last month to be caught and executed. Olivia had managed to dodge seeing the other four, probably because they hadn't had any connection to the Claude family.

"There they are," Evelyn said, pointing.

If she thought she could get away with it, Olivia would slip away. Unfortunately, she was one of the few women in town who kept her hair uncovered. And while she was proud of the long, healthy locks that had turned silver when she was a toddler—a genetic anomaly passed down from her mother—right now it drew attention like a moon on fire. Especially the attention of her father.

She trudged after Evelyn to Mr. and Mrs. Claude. Olivia's stepmother, Asiya, also in a black dress but a white matron's cap, dabbed her eyes with a kerchief. Next to her was Olivia and Evelyn's father, Ormus, as stone faced as ever. He wore his dark-blue military uniform, proclaiming his rank as captain of Citadel's forces.

Evelyn hugged her mother. They both had the same short, curvy build, though Evelyn still had a ways to go, being only seventeen. Olivia and Ormus towered over both of them.

Olivia put one arm over Asiya's shoulders, ensuring that Ormus was on the other side of her. She wasn't good with comforting other people, but sometimes she enjoyed physical touch when distressed. Asiya always hugged people when they were sad. And Evelyn had hugged her first, so this was all right, right?

Asiya sniffed and gave them both a watery smile. "Thank you, girls."

Olivia quietly breathed out. She'd done it right.

"The water's rising!" a soldier with a telescope shouted.

The water had already been at Benjamin's neck by the time Olivia and Evelyn had arrived. High tide was always slow in this part of the forest, trickling in a little at a time. Some of the lowlands and valleys experienced something closer to flash floods every time the tides came in. It was why the pit had been dug, to cut the hours off an execution's already considerable time.

The soldier looked through his telescope while Asiya held her breath.

Olivia's entire body tensed, and for a second, it wasn't Benjamin Novak tied to the posts, but a woman with silver hair, much like her own.

She squeezed her eyes shut and put on her ear coverings, letting the thick wool muffle all sounds.

The bells rang on the wall. She felt the vibrations in her bones.

When the vibrations finally stopped, Olivia cracked open one eye. She couldn't see Novak through the water.

She waited five more seconds, ensuring that there was no sensation of tipping into a fall or spiraling into darkness, and then let herself relax.

Someone snapped their fingers in front of her face. She jolted.

Evelyn gave a small smile. Olivia took off the ear coverings.

"Sorry," Evelyn said. "We're going to the sermon if you want . . ."

Olivia shook her head.

"Had to ask. Maybe Dad can walk you . . ."

She shook her head again.

"Are you sure?"

A nod.

". . . All right. We'll see you at the house."

Olivia went down the stairs and away from the wall as fast as she could.

Olivia wandered the streets of Citadel, trying to clear her head. She pulled her sketchbook from her pocket and flipped to the latest page, where she saw a reminder in her barely legible writing to stop by her workplace this afternoon. With nothing else to do, she headed for the lab.

When the city of Citadel had first been built, it had been smaller. The first wall, designed to keep out both the floods and demons, had been much closer to the center of town. As the population grew over the next four hundred years, the wall was torn down and rebuilt a number of times. Olivia had once gone looking for remnants of the old walls with her mother and uncle when they'd studied history and had found the remains of three of them, some tall and obvious enough that people—especially farmers—used them as border markers for their property. She passed by the old landmarks now on her way, trying to smile at the memory.

Talk had been going around of pushing the wall out again. Every square centimeter of the city was utilized to squeeze out as much farmland and living space as possible, and there just wasn't enough for everyone. She walked along narrow dirt roads barely wide enough for a wagon. Past farmlands that were crammed with weak, wilting crops, yielded by the ground with a dying breath; even those were guarded by big men with clubs and cudgels who glared at everyone. Past buildings that had originally been built with one story centuries ago, only to have more floors stacked on top of them when it was clear they couldn't grow the population outward anymore.

The issue with building a new wall was primarily due to the tides. Citadel's weeks were six days long, which was how long it took to get from low tide to high tide, then another six days to go back down. Depending on the week, either there was only a little water available from nearby ponds ("tide pools" was the technical term), or everything below the tree branches was under water, anywhere from three to twelve meters deep. Due to the lack of available stone, Citadel's wall needed to be made from wood, and it was difficult to waterproof that much of it in a way that wouldn't let it crack and come crashing down, drowning their crops and causing another famine. They already dealt with a growing number of food shortages from the soil in the farmlands growing stale. In the marketplace, the price of pears had gone up 30 percent from last week.

Olivia passed by several people living on the street, asking for spare banknotes. She didn't have any on her and kept walking.

A man passed by the fruit stall. Olivia almost didn't see him slip a pear into his coat pocket as they passed each other. She pretended not to see.

"Stop! Thief!"

The man made it only a few paces before a city guard tackled him. Olivia cringed when a second guard elbowed him in the head, keeping him dazed and compliant as they put him in iron fetters.

She recognized the two guards and tried not to gag: the twins, Michael and Gabriel Byruk. They were just above her age—both of them twenty years old now—and the sons of Moses Byruk, a judge and one of the wealthiest men in town. They were near the end of their mandatory two years of military service, rotating between various duties such as demon hunts, wall guard, and street patrol.

Both men were her height, with the deep-tan skin common in Citadel and dark, curly hair cut close to the skull, and wore the blue military uniform, their rank of private stitched into the sleeves. The only way to tell them apart was the wine-colored birthmark over Michael's right eyebrow. He was the one hauling the thief to his feet to drag him off to jail. The man would probably have to pay a hefty fine. If he couldn't afford it, then he'd be forced to do the more dangerous menial tasks like gathering food outside the walls or iron from the bog.

Olivia kept her head down and walked past the scene, hoping to avoid attention.

"Good morning, freak. Where are you going?"

Shit.

She tried to keep moving, but a hand on her shoulder stopped her. "We need to ask you some questions about what just happened."

Olivia rolled her eyes, turning to face Gabriel. She motioned to everyone else on the street, raising an eyebrow.

"I don't want to ask them. I want to ask you," he said, lightly tugging on a strand of her silver hair.

She jerked back, away from the touch that felt like bugs crawling beneath her skull.

When she had entered the school system after her mother's death, she'd ended up in the same school as the twins. Pulling on her hair had been one of their favorite torments, in part because she would almost always respond with a shriek or a punch, and then the adults would get involved just in time to see the twins transform into rosy-cheeked little angels while she was labeled a screaming, violent "freak."

It took effort, but she did not punch or scream at Gabriel today. He smirked like he could read her inner struggle.

"Where are you going?" he asked.

She took out her sketchbook and pen.

"No, I need you to *tell* me where you're going. Like a normal person."

There was nothing wrong with Olivia's vocal cords. Several visits to the hospital had confirmed that, physically, there was nothing wrong with her. There was no reason why she shouldn't be able to take the words from her head and *say* them like everyone else. But while she could make noises, grunts, and hums, she could not form proper words. Something caught them on the way from her brain to her mouth, locking them away.

It never interfered with her writing, though, which was why she always had a sketchbook on hand.

She opened the first page of her sketchbook, which had a list of the most common words and questions she needed to say. Just as she pointed to *Work*, Gabriel snatched the book from her hands.

"Come on. Use your words," he said. "It's not that hard."

She tried to take the sketchbook back. He kept it out of reach, grinning wide enough to show the gap between his two front teeth.

Don't attack him, she reminded herself. *He's a soldier. His brother's right there. There are witnesses. Just because you* can *beat him into the ground doesn't mean you should. You'll get arrested. You'll lose your job.*

"You can do it. You'll thank me for this."

She was getting dizzy. Not the "I'm sick and nauseous" dizzy, or even the "I've spent too much time spinning around and need to take a seat" kind of dizzy. The kind of dizzy that came from looking down a tall height just before a jump.

No, no, not now! she pleaded, even though it was to be expected. Forced to watch an execution and then running into the Byruk twins? A breakdown was almost guaranteed. She had to get her sketchbook and find somewhere safe before it completely took her over.

"Shit!" Michael cried. Out of the corner of her eye, she saw him struggle to keep the thief down. "Gabe, a little help?"

Gabriel looked at him to gauge the situation, and Olivia seized her chance.

She grabbed her sketchbook, ignoring Gabriel's indignant cry, and sprinted down the street. The dizziness quickly got worse, threatening to send her into a wall. She stumbled into an alley, sliding to the ground before she fell into darkness.

CHAPTER TWO

Olivia couldn't remember most of her breakdowns. They were just a blank space in her mind. She could remember what led up to them and what happened immediately after, but the interim put her mind somewhere else. Somewhere dark, like a starless sky, and she was falling through the void until she slammed back into her body.

She blinked her eyes open in an alley. She was curled into the corner between two buildings, wrapped around her sketchbook. One was a bakery; she could smell the yeast and wheat in the stone oven. The other was a blacksmith, smelting the iron fetched from the nearby bogs. The *clang-clang* of hammers against hot metal grated against her ears. Wooden splinters caught on her sweater. A cursory check confirmed that her cheeks were wet from crying, which was perfectly normal. People who witnessed her breakdowns told her she usually crammed herself in some tight space or curled under a heavy blanket and spent anywhere from three to ten minutes sobbing. Sometimes screaming.

She hauled herself to her feet and wiped her face with her sleeve. Fucking *Gabriel*.

She had half a mind to tell Ormus about what had happened. He was the captain of the guard, essentially their boss. He could easily punish them.

She immediately dismissed the idea. During the first few weeks of being bullied by the twins at school, she'd told any and every adult in her vicinity what was happening. That was what they'd told her to do if other children picked on her.

Half of them, including Ormus, had given her a weird look and said something along the lines of, "The Byruk boys? They're so sweet! Upstanding young gentlemen. How could you lie about something like that?"

The other half, including Asiya, had shrugged and said, "Boys will be boys," and "They're just teasing you because they like you," which made *no sense* to Olivia. You didn't yank on someone's hair, call them names, and steal their things if you "liked" them.

Elias and her friend Riley had been the only ones to believe her. Riley had actually seen it happen a few times, as they'd gone to school together. But other than yelling at the boys to leave her alone, there was nothing they could do.

She wanted to go to her room, curl up under her blankets, and forget the day ever happened. But it was barely noon, she had other responsibilities, and she was an adult, damn it. She'd dealt with childish bullying all her life. She could deal with it today, too.

Making herself as decent as possible, Olivia pushed her sketchbook into her pocket and resumed walking to the labs.

Near the center of town, a block away from the main temple and right next to the hospital, was Franklin Laboratory. It was the only research facility that operated outside of the Faith, having been privately created and funded two generations ago. The modest building had been the founder's one-story house before he remodeled it to suit his needs, turning the living room into a shared office space and adding a second floor as a study space and laboratory. If Olivia looked closely enough, she could see the difference in construction style between the first and second stories, feel the subtle differences between how the wood was cut and sanded.

She heard the arguing before she stepped into the house. It came from behind a closed door near the back of the room that led to Franklin's private office, but that door might as well have not existed. She could hear every word as she passed the handful of empty desks that dominated the main room, their owners having gone to the execution and following sermon.

"Now you listen here: I have told you and all your fellow priests and nuns and even the governor himself that these labs are not for sale! They have been in my family for three generations now, and I will not be known as the Franklin who gave that up."

"You wouldn't be giving it up, Mr. Franklin. You would be contributing to the greatness of Citadel and the temple, and making a very handsome fortune besides."

"This facility is not for sale," Mr. Franklin said. "We adhere to the laws of Citadel in both letter and spirit, both of which give us the freedom to research the natural world."

"For how much longer?"

There was silence.

Olivia tried to ignore that, going to her desk near Franklin's closed office door. Franklin was always harping on her to tidy it up, but she never understood why. She could always find anything she needed on here, and he should keep his eyes and hands to himself, anyway. She only ever spent time cleaning when the piles of paperwork threatened to tip over.

She pulled her sketchbook out of her pocket and opened it to a page with a list of items she needed to get. Most were relatively standard things that other people would never think of forgetting, such as her notebook designated for field notes, extra pens, and professional sketches of their target. But writing them down was the only way to guarantee that she remembered. Such details often slipped her mind like water through her fingers.

She had half of the needed items stacked on her chair when the door to Franklin's office opened, and he stepped out with a priest. Olivia couldn't remember his name and didn't care enough to ask or write it down. He was dressed in the cream robes of an ordained priest, with three red stripes sewn into his sleeves to proclaim his rank as a high priest.

Mr. Franklin was a head shorter than him and quite a bit thicker, with beady eyes and thinning hair. He wore a dark-gray suit jacket and matching trousers, each of them with several deep pockets that always held something: extra writing utensils, little candies, a small notebook.

"I'll see you soon, Mr. Franklin," the priest said. He left the building.

Olivia couldn't read her boss's expression, so she couldn't tell if he was worried about losing his labs or not. In truth, she didn't care if Franklin lost his lab. It would serve the man right, would soothe the burning fire in the pit of her stomach that flared up every time she laid eyes on him.

But if the Faith bought the labs, then she would be out of a job within a week. They had the unfortunate requirement that each individual must possess a deep belief in the Hundred-Faced God to work for them, and she could barely muster lukewarm apathy.

Franklin met her eyes, then looked away. "Make sure you bring containers for the flowers. And the military may ask you to help them with their surveying, so be prepared for that, as well."

Olivia made a note in her sketchbook. She and Franklin were going into the forest tomorrow—with military protection—to fetch samples of the green prasina flower. Up until a month ago, it had been an unknown species until a gatherer checked himself into a hospital after eating what he thought was an edible plant but which instead had knocked him out completely. He was relatively unharmed and fully recovered, which meant he had accidentally discovered a new anesthesia that could be used in surgeries and might possibly have other benefits too.

That was their mission. The military escort was part protection, part following their own mission: they were scouting potential sites for a second city.

"And make sure you follow directions this time," Franklin continued. "You have a bad habit of wandering off during these excursions. It scares us all half to death. Stay with the group this time, or I'll find myself another assistant."

He'd made that threat twice before. One of the reasons he didn't follow through was because of Olivia's mother. She was too tired to even pretend to listen, and he wandered away.

She double-checked to make sure she'd collected everything on her list and was stashing it all into her woven wool bag when the front door opened again.

She only looked up when she heard his voice: "I thought you were leaving for a week, not a month."

Olivia grinned, shoving the last of her things into the already bulging bag. Riley stood just inside the doorway, closing it to prevent the cool summer air from stealing the house's heat. He was one year younger and four centimeters shorter than Olivia, with a mess of curly, red-brown hair that he kept a finger length long, whereas almost every other boy and man in town kept theirs cut close to the skull like soldiers, even if they weren't on active duty. He was skinny; Olivia had lifted sacks of flour heavier than him. Around his neck, peeking out over the collar of his coat, was a simple necklace with a blank, masklike face—the symbol of the Hundred-Faced God—as its only ornamentation. She had never seen him without it.

She opened the front page of her sketchbook and pointed to *Why* and *Here*.

"It's getting late," Riley said. "Thought I'd walk you home."

She gave him a look.

"Yes, yes, I've seen you beat several fully trained soldiers, while the worst I can do to someone is cough on them. But it'll make me feel better, and I haven't been to your house in ages, anyway."

The last time he'd come to the Claudes' house had been a few months ago, at Olivia's nineteenth birthday party. It had been tiny, especially compared to the lavish affairs normally thrown in their neighborhood, which Olivia hated and Ormus argued for. He hadn't argued this year, though, and it had been just her, the Claudes, her uncle, and Riley. She had tried not to notice the Elias-shaped hole in the room.

She swung her bag over her shoulder, careful not to let it pinch her hair. Riley held the door open for her. Dealing with people, trying to figure out the subtext of their speech and actions that everyone else read so easily, was exhausting. But Riley wasn't. He was one of the few people in Citadel who made talking easy.

"Are you coming to the party next month?" he asked. "I know crowds aren't your favorite . . ."

She pointed to *Where* in her book.

"My house," he said. "And yes, Dad will be there."

She grimaced.

"You don't have to go," Riley assured her, letting her breathe easy. "We can do something smaller later."

She nodded. Although it was probably bad form to miss her best—and only—friend's eighteenth birthday party and official entrance into adulthood just because she had a grudge, Riley was one of the few people she trusted to absolutely not lie to her about these things. He knew more about social rules than anyone else. It came with being the child of the governor.

Olivia flipped through her book one handed until she found the word *Placement.*

"I have no idea," he said.

She snorted. She thought *she* was bad at pushing things off to the last minute. Riley was going to be declaring what he intended to study and pursue as a career on his birthday, what he thought his Place was in this world (or what his god *thought* his Place was). That was less than two months away.

Or maybe she was just put off because she had always known what she wanted to do, ever since she was old enough to want anything. The idea that someone didn't know what path they wanted to take was almost foreign to her.

The Placement wasn't necessarily a *requirement*, but it was tradition. Especially for men. The son of one of Ormus's coworkers had gone without a Placement, and it had been the talk of the town for days, even though as a physically fit man he'd spent the next two years in the military, anyway. It was good to have that direction, to adequately prepare for how one was going to spend the rest of their life.

Riley *wasn't* physically fit. Not even the bulkiest coat could hide his wraith-thin form, and that wasn't even touching on the terrible migraines he'd been plagued with since childhood. He'd gotten a formal letter from the military excluding him from service, which had made Olivia cheer. Losing one man she cared about to the demons was bad enough.

They approached the center of town, passing by the Vaults behind the main temple. It was one of the oldest and tallest buildings in Citadel, built almost like a pyramid. The lowest level was welcome to all who made a financial contribution to the Faith, but anyone who wanted to get to the higher levels had to be a priest or nun, and only the highest-ranking clergy—and governor—were allowed access to the topmost layer.

She pointed to the Vaults and temple, wordlessly asking if he'd maybe pursue the priesthood as a career. Riley shook his head. "I considered it, and Dad wouldn't mind. But it's not for me."

She raised her eyebrows and tapped his necklace, the carved blue wood smooth against her finger.

"If every person who believed in the Hundred-Faced God became a priest, Citadel would be full of nothing *but* priests, plus you."

Fair point.

"Although it might actually get you to attend a service . . ." he said, grinning.

She gave him a flat look. He laughed. "I'm kidding. No, I'm . . . uh. I'm thinking medicine."

Olivia hummed. She could see him doing that. He'd always enjoyed helping people, and he'd spent so much time in the hospital as a child that he probably knew it as well as his own home. She knew it pretty well herself, having visited him after he got his tonsils removed, then his appendix, the four times he got the flu or a fever so bad his parents almost called a priest for last rites, the two times he got pneumonia, and the three migraines that were bad enough to call upon professional help.

They turned a corner and crossed the front of the temple. There, displayed on poles, were the bodies of two demons, so decomposed and dismembered they barely held on to their original forms. Their wings drooped so low they brushed against the ground two meters below. Insects covered them completely, creating a constant humming noise heard whenever anyone drew near. Olivia grimaced. Hopefully they'd be taken down today.

Passing the demon bodies was a procession in black. At the front was a young woman, maybe a year or two older than Olivia, carrying a clay urn. She trembled as she walked, tears dripping down her face.

"Ah, that's right," Riley said. "Joshua's funeral."

She gave him a questioning look.

"He's one of the hunters who got ambushed by demons a few days ago? His brother managed to fight them off and drag him back, but they couldn't save him."

She didn't remember hearing about it, but the news didn't surprise her. Not one month passed without someone getting killed by demons, usually more. Soldiers, hunters, and gatherers always had to have their wills up to date.

Olivia swallowed, looking away from the funeral. It left her feeling hollow, yet full of *something*. Maybe fog, or soup, or knives. Something that made it hard to breathe.

She was about to ask something else when Riley started rubbing his temples. She winced in sympathy, flipped to another page, and pointed to *Migraine*.

"I'm fine. I'll just need to go home after this."

They walked a little faster, talking all the way back to Olivia's house. Well, Riley talked. Olivia contributed with hand gestures and her sketchbook. She showed him her most recent drawings, sketches she'd done of everything she saw: plants, animals, people, buildings, household items. He whistled. "They look so real." She beamed.

"You're running out of pages, though."

She shrugged. Almost all of her paychecks went into her savings, which meant she had plenty to purchase more books of blank, blue-tinged paper made from the indigo trees of the forest.

Riley pulled something out of the inner pocket of his jacket. "Take this with you to the forest, if you can cram it in that bag."

Olivia squealed at the fresh sketchbook. It was a hardcover—durable—with several hundred pages, but was small enough to easily fit into her larger pockets. Absolutely perfect.

She squeezed him in a hug. He chuckled. "Be safe out there, Liv."

CHAPTER THREE

They had come right after lunch, when her mother Sarai was at work and Olivia was doing the reading assignment she'd given her. Sarai had made the executive decision that public schooling wasn't going to work, so Olivia was taught at home. At thirteen years old she had never set foot in one of Citadel's many schools, which was fine by her. She sat at the kitchen table, eating cherries—a rare treat, considering how expensive they were—while engrossed in a book.

She could count on one hand all the people she knew who were born out of wedlock. It was considered a sin to have sex before marriage, and difficult for single women to raise children on their own, without any financial aid from the father. If such a pregnancy did happen, the couple almost always married, saving themselves the shame and—theoretically—the hardship.

Sarai Hall stayed single, working as an assistant in Mr. Franklin's labs and part time as a seamstress to bring in a livable income. It was an open secret who Olivia's father was. Nobody had missed the young Lieutenant Ormus Claude together with the fiery silver-haired Sarai, or that they had stopped courting once Sarai became pregnant. It was apparently a huge scandal when he married Asiya rather than her.

Olivia had met him, once, when he'd come to argue with Sarai over custody a few years ago. Sarai had kicked him out of her house and told him to go back to fucking his wife.

None of that mattered now. All Olivia knew was she was reading a good book in her home. It was small, with one main room acting as both living room and kitchen, a wash closet, and a bedroom she shared with her mother. It was another one of those buildings originally built with one story, then with another stacked on later. The second floor—which had its own outdoor stairs and entrance—belonged to another family entirely, the father an old military friend of Olivia's uncle. She sat in a wooden chair with both of her feet on the table, fuzzy wool socks keeping her warm. Sarai never let her put her feet on the furniture, but she was at work.

She was so absorbed in the characters' crazy adventures that nothing short of a small army breaking down her door would have snapped her out of it.

Which was exactly what happened.

The *BANG* of the door bursting open and slamming into the wall made her jump, almost falling off the chair. In seconds, the room was filled with blue-clad soldiers, weapons out.

An ensign with *Dabral* stitched into his jacket pointed his revolver at her. "Let me see your hands. Let me see your hands!"

She dropped the book in her lap and held up her hands. She wanted to ask what was going on and where their warrant was, but the words, as always, got caught in her throat. Her sketchbook was on the kitchen table.

She moved to get it. Dabral cocked his gun at her. "I will shoot."

Olivia swallowed, frozen under the barrel of the gun. The soldiers swarmed through the house, going into every room—even opening the closet door—and tearing through their things: the kitchen cupboards, Sarai's small desk in the corner, and she could hear them turning over the bedroom.

She pointed to her sketchbook.

"All right. Go ahead."

She took the book and scribbled, *What's going on?*

Dabral finally put his gun away. "Your mother's been arrested for heresy." He pulled a piece of paper out of his jacket pocket. "This is our warrant to search her office and home. You'll be coming with us too."

Olivia took the warrant and opened it. She refused to move until she'd read through every line and made sure it was signed by a judge. The swoopy curls of Moses Byruk stained the bottom of the page.

They took her to the town jail, one of the oldest buildings in town. This was the first time Olivia had ever been to the center of town.

The jail was a long building, with interrogation rooms aboveground and a system of cages underground. No criminal ever stayed for more than a few days. Just long enough for a judge to figure out their guilt and sentence. Olivia hoped to catch a glimpse of her mother, but they didn't go underground. They put her in the interrogation room and told her to wait.

She'd had the foresight to bring her sketchbook and reading book with her, but now she couldn't concentrate. Her mind went in a million different directions. Getting arrested for heresy was the same as getting arrested for treason. But what could Sarai possibly have done to warrant that? She studied plants and animals, specializing in nutrition so that the people of Citadel might find a wider variety of food sources. And while everyone knew she wasn't the most devout person in town, she wasn't stupid enough to shout her atheism from the rooftops.

Olivia drummed her fingers against the table, staring at the blank walls. There was absolutely no decoration in this room, except for what looked suspiciously like a faded bloodstain on the floor. She started counting the cracks in the blue wood, but that got boring after a hundred, so she drew her attention back to the stain. Maybe it wasn't blood. Maybe instead it was tea or some other drink.

The door opened behind her, and her interrogator stepped into the room.

Olivia hadn't seen Ormus since his child-custody argument with Sarai. He'd trimmed his hair and grown out a short beard that made him look older than his midthirties. He tapped the cover of her book on the way to his chair. "I always loved that one."

Mom? she wrote.

"Your mother is currently being detained and questioned. You'll see her in a bit," he said. "I'm Lieutenant Ormus Claude."

It was polite to say something like *Nice to meet you* or to respond with your own name. But Olivia was in no mood to be polite. She'd asked for her mother, not her father. She underlined *Mom* three times.

Not a single muscle on his face moved. Even if Olivia had been good at reading emotions, she never would've been able to guess what he was thinking.

"I have some questions for you, first," he said. "The sooner you answer them, the sooner you can get out of here."

She gritted her teeth. That did nothing to answer her question about Sarai's fate.

"Does your mother ever talk to you about angels and demons?"

Olivia shook her head. Before he could ask another question, she wrote, *Evidence for arrest?*

He sighed, then said, "Have you heard of the *Blue Lotus*?"

She nodded. The *Blue Lotus* was a sporadic newsletter that criticized Governor Thompson, the government of Citadel, the Faith, the Vaults, and Scripture, all dicey topics. Several editions went straight into heresy territory. It was a collection of pamphlets and flyers, usually only two or three pages. But they had caused more than one riot in the streets by bringing to light evidence of priests' or politicians' wrongdoings that ended up being true. For obvious reasons, the newsletter was anonymous.

"We have reason to believe that your mother is the author," Ormus said.

She blinked, surprised and yet not, then underlined *Evidence*.

"A witness found a notebook that had an early draft of the next edition."

It's just writing, Olivia wrote. She never understood why people got so touchy about asking questions. That was human nature.

He gave her a look: flat lips, eyebrows scrunched down, nostrils flared. (Curiously studying her? Disappointed in what he saw? Feeling an itch he couldn't scratch in polite company?) "Laws are created for a reason. Without them, we fall apart. This law, the one against in-flammatory writings, is so people continue to follow the governor and the Faith. If people stop following the Faith, they stop believing in the governor, and chaos will erupt in the town, creating confusion and bloodshed, neither of which we can afford right now. We would im-plode from the inside. By crossing that line, your mother may have put the whole town at risk."

Olivia shook her head. Sarai was stubborn, but not stupid. If it was really that dangerous, she wouldn't do it.

"We're still investigating. And the sooner we gather all the necessary information, the sooner you and your mother can walk out of here."

I know nothing, she wrote. Even if she did, she wouldn't tell anyone.

"Very well," he said. "Since I'm your father, you'll be staying with me until—"

She was already writing: *Uncle Peterson.*

Ormus clenched his jaw. "That's not normally how these things go."

She didn't care. She underlined *Uncle Peterson* and added, *He's family.*

"Right," he muttered. He stood. "Well, since he's a relation and Sarai designated him as an emergency contact, I guess we can make it happen. Enjoy the book."

Sergeant Abraham Peterson was Olivia's godfather and Sarai's cousin, but they'd been raised in the same house due to the untimely death of Sarai's parents. Everyone but Sarai called him Peterson or Sergeant, so Olivia had thought Peterson was his actual name, calling him Uncle Peterson from the time she was five. He did tell her that his first name was Abe, but by then the name had stuck. The grizzled old man with salt-and-pepper hair picked Olivia up from the jailhouse and took her to his small, dilapidated house far from the center of town, close to the Farmers' Ring.

Though the house was tinier than Sarai's and had a leak in the roof, it was still familiar. Despite being a full-time sergeant, putting the fresh recruits through basic training, he usually had more free time than Sarai. This house was where a younger Olivia would spend hours while her mother went on forest expeditions with her boss, or put some extra time in her seamstress job, or took a rare night off with friends. Even now that Olivia was old enough to be safely left alone for a day or two, she still enjoyed spending time with her uncle.

But the familiarity and fond memories did nothing to help Olivia now. It felt like something was squirming in the pit of her stomach as the hours trickled by. Peterson tried to cheer her up, telling her that Sarai would be fine and it was all just some misunderstanding. But even to Olivia's poorly trained ear, he sounded fake.

Neither of them got much sleep that night.

The trial was the next day. Olivia tried on three different outfits before settling on a pale-blue dress, mostly at Peterson's urging. If they saw a lovely, rule-following daughter, they might be more likely to spare Sarai. The dress was itchy and restrictive, but Olivia wore it. She even added a headscarf, hiding her unique silver hair despite all the times Sarai had told her to be proud of it.

The courthouse was in city hall, on the second floor. It was a large, cavernous room with portraits showing the history of Citadel. It started with the angels' war against the Hundred-Faced God; Olivia couldn't recall what had triggered it. Something about questioning His authority or wanting to overthrow Him or being angry about being forced to wear inconvenient white dresses. The next painting showed the Fall, the angels losing their wings and divinity as they crashed into the Shadowlands, becoming the human Founders. The third was Riley Bevill, the prophet, following his visions of the Hundred-Faced God to lead his people out of the Shadowlands to the forest. The fourth painting was the Founders building the first temple on top of a hill, four hundred years ago.

At the front of the courthouse was a raised panel for the judge. Behind his seat was the fifth and final portrait: their faceless deity, with masklike Faces in His hands and floating around Him. The Hundred-Faced God was supposed to take up a whole new Face, identity, and personality for every situation and usually had different names for each of His identities. Olivia could never remember them all, but she knew the Faces the god held in the portrait behind the judge's seat were for two of them: Justice and Mercy.

There were enough seats for about fifty people to comfortably sit in the room, but only a handful were occupied. That didn't surprise Olivia. Sarai had always been ostracized. Genetic anomalies like premature silver hair were to be feared in the only human civilization on the planet. Maybe if she'd accepted the shame, dyed and covered her hair like a "proper" woman, she'd have more friends. But she had rejected the notion when she'd been around Olivia's age, a teenage rebellion that she had purposefully never grown out of. That was the second mark against her. The third, of course, was her illegitimate child and refusal to marry. Nobody wanted to associate with a woman of "loose morals," after all.

Dabral and Ormus sat together, both of them looking bored. Next to Ormus was a thick, dark-skinned woman in a dark dress and matron's cap that let only a bit of her curly hair show. There was a man Olivia had never seen before, with graying hair and beady eyes; a scribe who would record everything that was said and done here today; a couple of priests; and Olivia and Sarai's neighbors. A few seats away from everyone was her friend Riley Thompson.

He stood as soon as he saw her and gave her a hug. "Hi. Sorry I couldn't be by earlier."

She blinked in surprise, hugging him in return before pulling back and getting her book.

Why here? she asked.

"I heard your mom got arrested. I thought I'd come by and . . . support, I guess."

Peterson put a hand on Riley's shoulder. The boy was so small and spindly that the calloused skin almost covered him like a blanket. "We appreciate it, son," Peterson said. "Let's take a seat."

Olivia sat sandwiched between the both of them on the wooden chairs. Before long, Governor Augustus Thompson came into the room and took his seat above them all. This was unusual. Almost all cases were handled by a lower judge who'd been ordained by the governor. All misdemeanors and most felonies were overseen by them. If they passed a death sentence, it was then passed to the governor for approval. He could either approve the sentence or knock it down to something less severe. The most serious crimes, on the other hand, were handled by the governor from beginning to end.

The only physical similarities he had with his son, Riley, were the curly red-brown locks—cut regulation short—and pale skin. His face was wide and round, unlike Riley's birdlike physique, and his eyes were like chips of coal. Three people could fit in his fur coat, and he wore thick golden rings passed down from the Founders. He had a little smile on his face that Olivia couldn't decipher, but she didn't like it. People weren't supposed to smile at a trial, right?

The doors opened. Olivia jumped to her feet as soon as she saw the silver hair.

Sarai's wrists were shackled as a pair of soldiers escorted her to the floor in front of the governor. She wasn't wearing anything Olivia had ever seen her in before, not her lab coat or the cozy wool trousers or even the embroidered jacket for when she had to look fancy. Instead they'd put her in a plain white dress that was more of a smock than anything else. With her pale skin and silver hair, she looked like a wraith.

Her eyes met Olivia's and she smiled. She made three small, rapid-fire signs with her hands: *Sit down. Stay quiet. Love you.*

Olivia sat.

The soldiers stepped aside as soon as Sarai was standing where she was supposed to. Governor Thompson shuffled his papers before saying, "Sarai Hall, you are charged with blasphemy, apostasy, and the spread of misinformation. How do you plead?"

"Not guilty."

"Save us some time, woman. Confess."

She said nothing.

"Citadel calls its first witness," Thompson said.

A few feet away from Sarai, facing the governor, was a podium that acted as a witness stand. Dabral was called to present the physical evidence: they had found no copies of the *Blue Lotus* in the house or workplace, but there were some barely legal, controversial philosophical texts, and—when prompted by Thompson—there wasn't a single copy of Scripture found anywhere in the house.

Then the priests were called. They complained about the lack of Sarai's attendance in their temples, how she was continuously questioning and nitpicking the Scripture, and even "slandering our very intelligence and religion." Even their neighbors were called. They reported seeing Sarai leave the house at odd hours and how she never had anything nice to say about the Faith.

Lieutenant Claude was asked about Sarai's conduct during expeditions into the forest. Olivia held her breath.

"She follows every law and procedure during forest expeditions," he said.

Thompson held up a stack of papers. "These are all complaints against her from a wide variety of military escorts. Many of them signed by you."

He hesitated. "She does argue against military interference with scientific excursions. I believe that's more of a clash of personalities than anything else. But again, she's never broken—"

"You had a child out of wedlock with her, didn't you?" Thompson asked.

Olivia felt all eyes on her. She raised her eyebrows. *What?*

"Yes," Ormus admitted. "We did consider marriage when she found out she was pregnant, but she ultimately refused to be my wife, called me a horrible father, and has rejected all my attempts to see or speak with my daughter since then."

With every word spoken, Olivia's fists clenched tighter and tighter. Peterson had a hand on her knee, but it was shaking, the vibrations going down her leg.

"But I believe she's honestly doing what she thinks is best for her daughter," he added. "And I can't really fault her for that. Especially since she's done a fair job on her own."

Sarai gave a tight smile.

The man with the beady eyes took Ormus's place at the podium.

"What is your name and relationship with the accused?" Thompson asked.

"Elijah Franklin. I'm Sarai's boss at the labs," he said to the podium.

"Last week the military police received a tip from your office, claiming that someone had found the author of the *Blue Lotus*."

"Yes, I made that tip," Franklin said. He refused to look at Sarai. "We were working on a project together that day. She was running an errand for me, but I needed some of her notes. She's a very meticulous notetaker, writes down everything. I tried to find the right notebook, but while I was searching, I noticed something attached to the bottom of her desk: another notebook. When I opened it, I saw notes pertaining to the Scripture, but they were all . . . ah . . . none of them were positive. There was an outline of an older edition of the *Blue Lotus*, and I realized she must have written the newsletter. I turned the notebook over to the military right away."

"Thank you. You may step down," Thompson said.

Mr. Franklin went to the back of the room and sat, his eyes on the floor.

Thompson said, "The city rests its case. Is there any who would come to the defense of Ms. Sarai Hall . . ."

Both Olivia and Peterson raised their hands.

". . . who is not a member of her family?"

Olivia sputtered. Peterson swore under his breath.

By law, character witnesses could not be directly related to the accused. Which meant if Sarai was going to be defended, it'd have to be by someone else.

Olivia looked to Ormus. He did not move.

The woman next to him did. "I'll speak for the accused."

Thompson frowned but motioned her forward. She stood behind the podium.

"State your name," he said.

"Asiya Mani Claude."

"What is your relationship with the accused?"

"She's my friend," she said. "We went to school together and have known each other for many years."

"She stands accused of blasphemy and apostasy. What do you know of this?"

Asiya shook her head. "I've never seen or heard her commit those crimes, or any crime. She wouldn't dare, not when she has Olivia to look after."

"How do you explain the notebook?" Thompson asked.

She shrugged. "Someone may have planted it on her."

"Who?"

"I don't know."

"Would you say Ms. Hall is a devout woman?"

Asiya hesitated. "She's an ethical woman."

"That doesn't answer my question."

"I believe it does, Governor," she replied. Her voice sounded like iron.

He asked her a few more questions about Sarai's personal history. Asiya answered them, usually bringing up Olivia in some way, like she was reminding them that executing Sarai would deprive the young girl of her mother. Olivia decided then and there that Asiya was one of her new favorite people.

He told Asiya to step down. She did, exchanging a brief smile with Sarai.

Governor Thompson collected his papers. "At this time, I have no choice but to declare Sarai Hall guil—"

"Father."

He paused. Everyone in the room stared at Riley, who had raised his hand. "I'd also like to speak for the accused."

Thompson scowled. The room was silent.

He motioned to the stand.

At twelve years old, Riley was barely tall enough to look over the top of the podium. One of the soldiers had to bring a stepping stool for him.

"State your name," Thompson said.

"Riley Petrova Thompson."

"And what is *your* relationship with the accused?" he growled.

"She's the mother of my best friend. I see her about once or twice a week, usually at her house. She's helped me with my homework a lot and is the only reason I haven't failed math yet."

"She stands accused of blasphemy and apostasy. What do you know of this?"

Olivia had never prayed before in her life, but for the first—and last—time she prayed that whatever Riley said would convince his father to let her mother go.

"I think," he said at length, "that she's a scientist, and scientists are always looking for answers. They're always asking why. Demanding proof, looking into other opinions—it's just their nature. But they also denounce things they know are wrong. I talk about God and angels all the time at their house, and whenever I eat there, I say grace at the table, and she's never told me to stop. Has never told me to stop my faith. If she truly hated Scripture and the Faith, she would've banned me from the house.

"But if that's not enough, consider Scripture. The angel Mary tells King Leon, 'Rule with justice and *mercy*, and the Hundred-Faced God will smile on your lands. Rule with tyranny and fear, and you will only spell doom for your people, your land, and yourself.' There's no reason to kill her today. She deserves mercy."

There was a stretch of silence. Thompson clenched his jaw. "Anything else?"

Riley shook his head and stepped down.

"Thanks for trying," Peterson whispered.

Thompson left the room to deliberate alone. Sarai was also removed. Olivia wrote, *What do you think?*

Peterson shook his head.

Five minutes later, Sarai was brought back in, and the governor returned. Olivia cursed herself for being unable to read their expressions. That might have been easier, to be able to recognize what Peterson later told her was definitely satisfaction on Thompson's face.

"Sarai Hall," he said. "For the crimes of apostasy and blasphemy, I find you guilty. You are hereby sentenced to death."

Guards had to pull both Peterson and Olivia out of the courtroom. He kept swearing at the governor, and she kept trying to get to her mother. Sarai also struggled to reach her, but they never got close. Not until three days later, when Sarai was allowed final visitors before her execution.

Peterson gave them a moment alone in the underground cell where his cousin was being held. It was three stone walls and a wooden door. No window. A torch was lit so they could see. She was still in her prison smock, and it scratched against Olivia's cheek when they hugged.

Sarai brushed her hair behind her ear. "How are you doing, sweetheart?"

Olivia gave what she hoped was a look that shouted, *HOW DO YOU THINK?*

Sarai chuckled. "All right. Stupid question."

They sat in silence. Olivia heard the sound of dripping water and shuddered, thinking about the incoming tides that were going to sweep her mother away. She forced herself not to think about it.

Instead she pulled out her sketchbook and asked, *Did you do it?*

"Yes." Sarai snorted. "I suppose the bad grammar and spelling would've given me away eventually."

Olivia blinked. She had been half-convinced that Sarai was framed, that she could get the evidence to clear her name minutes before the execution. After all, Sarai had pleaded not guilty, and she rarely lied.

Should've hidden them in my books, she wrote. They could've hollowed out her thicker textbooks and hidden plenty of contraband in there. Then Sarai wouldn't have had to hide it at work and wouldn't have gotten caught.

"Then you would've ended up on the posts next to me." Sarai repositioned them so Olivia sat in her lap. By now, Olivia was as tall as her mother, but neither of them cared. This was a tradition for them, doing each other's hair. It was the main way Sarai had taught her to be proud of her appearance. She started undoing Olivia's braid. She didn't have a hairbrush, so she made do with her fingers, making sure to keep her motions firm and gentle.

"You're going to be staying with your father from now on, you understand?" she said.

Olivia frowned at her.

"I know. I'd much rather give you to Abe. But Claude has the stronger claim and already acquired judicial approval for it," she explained. "Listen to what he tells you, but take it with a grain of salt. A *hefty* grain of salt. Pay more attention to Asiya; she has a good head on her shoulders. And your uncle will still be around to give proper guidance when you need it."

Olivia's brain tried to tackle the problem from a hundred different angles. *Bribe guards?* she wrote.

"They seized my bank account and all my assets. We have nothing to bribe them with." Sarai huffed. "And they left nothing for you to inherit, the bastards."

Fight.

"There are too many. We'll die."

Uncle P can help.

"And I'd be condemning *him* to death, as well," Sarai said. She moved so she was kneeling in front of Olivia. "Even if I did escape, where would I escape *to*? They'd find me in the city in a week, and I wouldn't last a day in the forest."

She kissed Olivia's fingers, her eyes wet. "I don't want this either. I wanted to watch you grow up and use that big brain of yours to unlock mysteries I can't even dream of. To help you when you fall in love and maybe have children, and watch you take this whole planet by storm. And it kills me that I won't be there for that."

Olivia pulled her fingers free. *We find a way.*

Sarai shook her head. "Some problems don't have a solution. Or at least, not the one we want."

There really wasn't anything else to say after that. Olivia hugged her again, and didn't let go until the guards came. Sarai rocked her the whole time.

They made Olivia watch.

Peterson argued against it. *She's a child. Just have me bear witness so she can go home. She's been through enough.*

But no. She had to stand next to the platform and watch her naked, sheared mother get tied to the posts. She had to listen to the jeering and the bells ringing and the curses. She had to listen to Governor Augustus Thompson announce the sentence.

Riley tried to smile at her. She didn't know why. Smiling was for when you were happy. How was this happy? She ignored him.

"Today, we witness the execution of a heretic," Thompson said. "Let justice be swift and merciful, the waters cleanse our town as it cleanses the spirit of Sarai Hall."

Olivia imagined what it would be like to tie *him* to the posts until he drowned. She imagined it would be a warm, uplifting feeling. But he was too far away to test it.

The waters rose, sweeping in from the east, pouring into the pit. Hours passed. Olivia knew that Sarai could hold her breath for a maximum of sixty-three seconds, but would she bother?

Finally, the water reached Sarai's nose, making it impossible for her to breathe. Olivia started counting.

At twelve seconds, something in Olivia *snapped*. She surged forward, intent on jumping over the edge of the wall. It wasn't too high, and there was enough water to cushion her fall. She could untie Sarai, and they could get out of here. Live in the forest. If they went far enough, no soldiers would dare come after them.

She hadn't gone two steps before someone grabbed her arm. It was the ensign, Dabral. He yanked her back. "Don't even think about it."

Twenty-one seconds.

A couple of soldiers grabbed onto Peterson as soon as she moved, as if worried her insanity was contagious. So it was all on her.

She slammed her heel onto Dabral's foot. He howled, and she tried for the wall again, ignoring Peterson's shouts.

Thirty-six seconds.

Two other soldiers stopped her, one grabbing her left arm and twisting it, the other wrapping his arms around her torso. Ormus stepped in front of her, barring her path, and leaned forward so they were at eye level. "I need you to stop and—"

She got her right arm free and punched him in the nose. It *cracked*. Definitely broken.

Thirty-nine seconds.

Olivia had to *get to her*. She stomped on another foot and threw her weight into the soldier. He grunted but managed to stand his ground. Then a third pair of hands was on her.

Forty-eight seconds.

She bit at a forearm, hard enough to draw blood.

Fifty-one seconds.

Someone pulled her hair and she shrieked.

Sixty seconds.

She kicked at a knee, tried to twist out of their grip.

Sixty-four seconds.

Olivia dropped to the ground.

CHAPTER FOUR:
RILEY

Riley didn't fear Hell. Because Hell came to *him* every time he got a migraine.

Any smell stronger than the faintest whisper of a flower made him nauseous. Candlelight stabbed his mind with fiery daggers. The ordinary sounds of the street—people walking, talking, laughing—were like nails dragging along a steel plate inside his brain.

Augustus used to make Riley go to school when he had a migraine, saying that he was a man and, as such, had to "tough it out." Riley had very few memories of those days. The first time, when he was seven, he threw up all over his desk and passed out from the pain. He woke up in the hospital. After that, Augustus toned it down a bit but still occasionally forced him to school with a migraine. The teachers would let him go to the (dark, quiet) nurse's office and sleep through the day.

The good news was his migraines rarely lasted more than twenty-four hours, especially if he heeded the warning signs and didn't push through. On the day of Benjamin Novak's execution, he started seeing spots, pain burning in low embers behind his temples as he walked Olivia home. By the time he'd made it back home and buried himself under his blankets, nausea had arrived. He spent the rest of the day and night trying to sleep through it, the pain finally lessening enough for him to get some actual shut-eye for a couple of hours before dawn.

When Augustus hollered for him to get ready for the day, he was well enough to crawl out of bed. He still had to deal with the postmigraine "hangover" (*postdrome* was the medical term), but there were plenty of ways to mitigate that.

He tested himself by pulling open the thick curtains, letting in the morning sunlight. It burned his eyes but didn't send spikes of fiery pain into his brain so intense he was completely unable to open his eyes. Today was looking to be a good day, then.

He kept his bedroom clean and organized, everything neatly folded, dusted, and put away. In one corner of the room, opposite his bed, was a small shrine to the Hundred-Faced God, complete with wooden statuettes of Riley's favorite aspects of the city's deity: Mercy, Healer, Guardian, Hope, Justice, Life, and Death. They were each built to hold a candle, which Riley took his time lighting.

Elias had made them for Riley last year, once they'd gotten past him fearing Riley was like his father and Riley suspecting his intentions toward his best friend. Riley made sure to mention his fallen friend's soul during his morning prayers. He did a quick wash to feel slightly more human, changed his clothes, and went downstairs for the first time in almost a day.

The stone two-story house had always felt too big for Riley. It was designed for a big family and even had the rare luxury of a yard, but he was an only child. Sometimes he would catch his mother staring at one of the empty rooms, naked grief on her face. In a rare case of synchrony, he and Augustus both tried to utilize the spare bedrooms to cover that emptiness, turning them into a library, an office, a storage space, a shrine for the Hundred-Faced God. It didn't work. It didn't help that the main rooms were also much bigger than they had to be: the dining room alone had a table designed to seat twelve. That came in handy whenever the Thompsons hosted a big dinner, but for most days, it just made the three of them feel small.

The Thompsons' cook, Michelle, had already made breakfast: chicken roasted with apples for Mia and Augustus, and "migraine soup" for Riley. It consisted of broth, bacon (or whatever salty meat she had on hand), and sweet berries. It wasn't the best-tasting food in the city, but it was easy on his stomach and helped his mind recover faster, so he happily slurped it down.

Both of his parents were already at the table, Mia picking at her chicken and gulping down water as quickly as she could without ruining her makeup. She'd passed her delicate frame and features to Riley but kept the black hair and dark skin. She kept looking at the grandfather clock in the corner, a re-creation of one of the ancient Artifacts, elegantly carved from blue wood.

Augustus had a strict "no alcohol before noon" policy, which was as close as he ever came to addressing his wife's issues with drink. Though she usually found a work-around anyway, slipping some wine or liquor in the mornings her husband left for work early. Riley knew that underneath her thick makeup and bright clothing, his mother's face was wan and the bags under her eyes were almost completely violet.

She mustered a smile for him. "How are you feeling, dear?"

"Much better," he said. "Well enough to go to Scriptural study."

"That's good."

Augustus was already sitting at the head of the table, a napkin tucked into his suit collar. He snorted. "That's the sixth migraine this season. I thought those women said you were supposed to get better."

"Those women" are fully trained medics who know more about medicine than you do about executions, Riley thought.

What he calmly said was, "They said they would get better after puberty, which I'm not technically finished with."

They'd also said that migraine frequency correlated with stress, but Riley didn't mention that part.

Augustus grunted, stabbing an apple with his fork. "Find a way to control them. You can't take that many days off when you're a lawyer, never mind when you're governor."

"We don't even know if I'd be elected," Riley pointed out. "There are dozens of people more qualified than me who would, frankly, do a much better job of running the town than I could ever dream. Like Captain Claude."

The seat of governor was, unlike most positions, decided by citywide election. The winner kept the seat until death, retirement, or, in very rare cases, impeachment. It was uncommon for a governor's term to be less than a decade. Given that Augustus wanted to retire in a few years, Riley didn't see himself gaining nearly enough experience to follow in those footsteps before the next election. And that was if he ended up going into law in the first place.

"And *after* Claude?" Augustus asked. "The seat of governor has been in the Thompson clan for generations. You were born into this role."

"If you say so," Riley replied noncommittally.

"I know so. God has a plan for all of us. Yours is to continue the family legacy. Those who fail to at least *attempt* to follow their path don't even deserve to live."

Riley hid his frown with another mouthful of soup. He and his father rarely saw eye to eye on anything, including religion. He agreed that the Hundred-Faced God did have a plan for Their people, which was the origin of the idea of Placement. Pursuing that was one of the highest forms of worship.

But he *didn't* think that such Placement was determined by overbearing fathers who valued a family's reputation and legacy over the family itself.

"While we're on the subject of your future, I want to talk to Captain Claude about getting you a wife," Augustus said.

Riley stared at him. "A . . . wife?"

"Evelyn Claude is seventeen. Most girls her age already have children," he said tiredly, like he was explaining the concept to a particularly dim child. "Claude's a good man. A *powerful* man. One I need to keep in my corner. Marrying his daughter will not only ensure that but give *you* strong children."

Riley hesitated. He was pretty sure he knew what Augustus would say to his response, but hope was a funny thing, and Riley had always preferred it over resignation. "Olivia's also around my age. We know each other better. If you want me to marry a Claude girl, it should be her."

Augustus's dark, coal-like eyes pinned him in place. "I want my grandchildren to be *normal*. Not tainted with criminal blood from a convicted grandmother and whatever oddities passed on to her spawn."

So much for that idea. Riley returned to his breakfast.

To be honest, the idea of marrying Olivia had been in the back of his mind for a while now. Ormus Claude had suggested it a few years ago and had gotten a similar (if much more polite) response from Augustus. It wasn't because Riley loved her like that. Most marriages in Citadel—especially in their neighborhood—weren't about romance. They were about family connections and genetic matching: Who was going to provide both a healthy income *and* healthy children? Sometimes romantic love came out of it, like with Ormus and Asiya Claude, but it wasn't something anyone could count on.

Having said that, Riley and Olivia definitely *cared* for each other, which was more than what his parents could say. They supported each other. She was the only one he felt safe confiding in about his dream of being a medic, and he understood all of her quirks and unique traits. Successful Citadel marriages had been started with far less.

"We'll talk to Claude about it before your birthday," Augustus continued. He liked having these one-sided conversations. Riley found that it made talking to him easier, in that minimal contribution was required. They were also endlessly frustrating. "And no, your silver-haired pet isn't coming to the party."

"She doesn't want to come," Riley replied. "On account of you executing her mother."

Augustus's eyes narrowed. "Watch it, boy. I'll take no lip from a child I should've discarded for such weak blood. Or disowned for womanly tastes."

He dropped an open envelope, addressed to Riley, onto the table. *My father is going through my mail, now? Classy.*

The return address for Central Hospital caught his breath.

"Care to explain how a hospital got ahold of your exit exam scores?" Augustus asked.

The exit exams were the final tests before graduating school. A person's grades on them determined what types of careers were available. The fields of medicine, law, and science all required near-perfect scores. Riley and his classmates had their exams last month and got their scores back a couple of weeks ago. As soon as Augustus had gotten his hands on Riley's, he'd sent them to half a dozen law firms.

Riley had also, secretly, sent his scores to the best hospital in the city.

He resisted the urge to turn to his mother; she would be no help. She kept methodically drinking water and eating her breakfast like her life depended on it.

Instead, he chuckled. "Remind me to never go near the mail when I'm sick. I seriously sent that?"

"I certainly didn't," Augustus said evenly.

"I'm amazed they were able to read it. Let me guess: I got rejected? Poor Mrs. Claude probably thought I was drunk." He scooped up the envelope before Augustus could answer and pulled out the letter.

He got as far as *we are pleased to offer you a position* before his father snatched the letter back. "You think this is funny? If word got out about this—about you applying to women's work—you'd be the laughing-stock of the city."

"I'm sorry," Riley said, trying to look contrite while his heart soared. "It won't happen again. I'll look at the law firms who accepted me."

"Good." Augustus held up a meaty, bejeweled finger. "If you disgrace this family, I'll see that you're no longer a part of it."

Disownment. Riley would be completely on his own, cut off from all resources, and left to his own devices.

He swallowed and nodded. "I understand, Father."

Augustus let Michelle clear his plate and got up. On his way past Mia he said, "That new dress makes you look like a whore."

She smiled at him, like a doll. "I'll change into something more appropriate."

The second Riley's bowl was clean, he left the table.

One of the anti-Dove laws Augustus had recently passed forbade people from gathering in groups of six or more inside their homes. If a group of people had to get together, it would be outside, where everyone could see and hear them, or in a temple.

This annoyed Riley, who liked going to different households for Scriptural study. It was easy to ignore the teachings of Scripture when it was only ever talked about in a temple. But when invited into someone's home, it became more intimate and relevant.

Or maybe he just liked the variety. He honestly wasn't sure.

Either way, he walked to his local temple for Scriptural study about an hour before the sun was to set, turning the planet's rings orange. Some people thought the rings were Heaven, or at least a gateway to it. Scientific studies said the rings were just rocks floating around their planet. Either way, they were beautiful. And more importantly, their light didn't hurt his eyes the way the sun did, so he could enjoy them.

"Hey, Riley!"

He paused, biting back a sigh. "Michael. Gabriel."

The Byruk twins waved at him. They were out of uniform, probably returning home after a shift.

"Did you hear?" Gabriel called. At least, Riley was fairly certain it was Gabriel. They both wore hoods against the chill summer wind, and that obscured the wine birthmark over Michael's eyebrow. "We're going to the forest!"

"Oh? For the low-tide hunt?"

"No, tomorrow. We're going on that science trip with the freak."

A hundred damnations.

"Both of you," Riley clarified, "will be with Olivia?"

"Don't worry, we'll keep her safe for you," Michael said with a wink.

"Speak for yourself," Gabriel said. "If she annoys me, I'm throwing her off the boat."

"Her father's coming too, Gabe."

"Ah, shit."

"Why do you hate her so much?" Riley found himself asking.

"We don't hate her," Michael defended. "It's just a bunch of harmless fun."

"Harmless, huh?" Riley remembered years of Olivia crying into his shoulder after an encounter with the twins, of her raging against them, fighting them *and* the teachers who always took their side, of the true terror and dread in her eyes every day she went to school.

They rarely picked on Riley, though, which was why he'd stuck so close to Olivia until she graduated. Sometimes being Augustus's son had perks.

"She shouldn't even be alive," Gabriel argued. "Her parents should've dropped her over the wall as soon as she was born."

"Gabe," Michael scolded.

"No, really! She's an idiot. She doesn't care about anything. When she doesn't get her way, she throws a tantrum like a toddler. If she's going to keep eating our food and taking up space, the least she can do is be entertaining."

"Fascinating," Riley said. "I don't think I've ever heard someone say something so fundamentally *wrong* in my entire life."

"*I'm* wrong?" Gabriel marched right up to Riley's face, towering over him. Riley did not step back.

"People like her are why this town is fucked," Gabriel growled. "We can't eat, we can't protect our borders, we're neck deep in crime and disease, because all of our resources are going to people like *her*. I'm glad her boy toy got chomped. At least now we don't have to worry about her spreading her legs and making more freaks—"

"Gabe, Gabe, he's not going to get it." Michael gripped his coat and pulled him back. "Let's go home. I'm starving."

Riley doubted that. He'd noticed Michael looking increasingly uncomfortable with every word his brother spoke. He'd seen it before when they were children, Michael stopping Gabriel before he went too far.

"See you around, Thompson," Michael called, tugging his brother down the street.

Just over the wind, Riley could hear Gabriel mutter, "I swear, if I ever become governor, I'm making it *mandatory* to get rid of all cripples and freaks. How else are we supposed to survive out here . . ."

Riley hunched into his coat as the breeze tried to slice through him and hurried along.

The main temple—officially named the Temple of the Hundred Faces—was the oldest building in Citadel, and the one that everyone in Riley's neighborhood went to. It had two floors: the bottom for reception, casual get-togethers, and storage, the upper for sermons. He went upstairs. There were enough dark-blue pews to hold over a hundred people, all facing the podium at the far end of the room. Tables of candles lined the walls, where anyone could light one for a prayer. This late, on a day without a sermon, only a handful flickered. Riley had to light a couple of torches to properly see.

Behind the podium stood a statue of the Hundred-Faced God, carved over three meters tall. Most depictions of God showed Them as either male or with ambiguous robes, a smooth face, and two to six arms, each holding a specific Face. This statue had *eight* arms, each holding a Face: Justice, Mercy, Life, Death, Peace, War, Vengeance, and Wisdom.

Just being here calmed him, tempered the frustration that the Byruk twins had cursed him with. He was early for study, alone in the cavernous room. He set his copy of Scripture on one of the pews and started lighting candles for the dead.

Two for his grandparents. He didn't remember them particularly well, as they'd died before he was six. But he did remember his grandmother quizzing him on basic Scriptural verses and rewarding him with a sweet every time he got it right, and his grandfather carrying him on his shoulders while he laughed.

Three for his siblings, all stillborn. They hadn't even gotten names, and he didn't know if they *had* souls to pray for. He lit the candles anyway.

One for Sarai Hall. He'd met her and Olivia completely by chance, when one of his more life-threatening illnesses coincided with one of Olivia's hospital visits to try to unlock the secret of her missing voice. It had been one of the greatest blessings of his life. Not just because he'd gotten his best friend from it but because he'd gotten a mother. Where Augustus and Mia failed, Sarai stepped up. The door to her house had always been open to him, whatever the day or hour. He'd run to her when Augustus became too much, and she'd dry his tears and work to undo whatever fresh damage the governor had inflicted that day. Most days she'd have him read to her. She and Olivia would sit on the couch, one of them combing and braiding the other's hair, and Riley would sit in the other chair and read an adventure story, or a piece of classic literature, or even bits of Scripture. He got very good at doing different character voices.

One for Elias. Riley hadn't trusted him at first. He'd overheard plenty of boys and men talking about getting into the "silver-haired freak's" bed, whatever the cost or abuse. Or worse: if Elias's intentions were pure, would he really treat Olivia right, or try to force her mind to work in ways it just wouldn't, hurting her in the process?

His fears had been unfounded. Elias had adored Olivia, and had made serious efforts to be friends with Riley even though they had had very little in common. The less said about the time he tried to teach Riley how to carve wood, the better. Riley still had the scar on his thumb, and Elias had decided to keep the little wooden statue that was *supposed* to have been a person but ended up looking a little more . . . phallic.

Riley had lost a good friend last year in the forest, and Citadel was all the poorer for it.

And finally, a candle for Benjamin Novak. Executed one day ago.

Scripture said that the souls of the dead languished in Purgatory, regardless of how good or pure they'd been in life, until humans slayed all "demons" and worked their way back into the Hundred-Faced God's good graces.

Riley wasn't sure about that. He believed in God, of course. Just not what everyone *said* about God.

Yes, the Hundred-Faced God had a hundred different Faces and aspects, ranging from Mercy to Vengeance, Joy to Grief, Life to Death. But at Their core, They were the creator of humanity. Essentially, a parent. And while Riley didn't have the best experience with those, he knew that if the Hundred-Faced God was anything at all like Augustus Thompson, humanity wouldn't have made it out of the Shadowlands, never mind established a thriving city.

He had to believe that the most powerful being in the universe was kind and benevolent. That there was some sort of hope and light and *meaning* to all of this.

Maybe people like Olivia and Sarai, who didn't believe in that, were just stronger or braver than him. Because if Riley didn't have this, he knew he'd fall into the blackest despair and never crawl out.

He prayed for the comfort and happiness of the departed souls, letting himself be hypnotized by the eight flickering lights. He didn't realize that he was no longer alone in the room until something brushed against his arm.

He jumped. Markus Brown, the owner of Citadel's textile mill, smiled sheepishly at him as he reached for the matches. "Sorry, Riley. I didn't mean to scare you."

"No, it's fine," Riley chuckled, hand on his chest. "Just got lost in my own head for a moment."

Markus was almost as old as Augustus, with a big nose and one dimple on his left cheek. Behind him, sitting in the pews, was his wife, Jane. Most men married women younger than them, to maximize the number of children they could carry. Markus had done the opposite, marrying a woman not just six years his senior but also with a troubling family history of illness and stillborns. Nobody had been surprised when Jane turned out to be barren, and plenty of people had urged Markus to divorce her. He had told them all to go to Hell.

"Are the others coming?" Riley asked.

Markus's mouth thinned as he lit a couple of candles. "I don't know. Ben's execution scared a lot of them off."

"You don't think they're going to report us, do you?"

"Probably not. They'd be condemning themselves in the process. Your father isn't exactly known for his mercy."

Riley grimaced.

"Don't worry about it, dear," Jane called, motioning for Riley to join her. "They know in their hearts what's right. They'll rediscover their courage."

Riley sat next to her. She was a heavyset woman with two chins and a lovely smile, her hair neatly tucked under a matron cap. "How are you feeling, Mrs. Brown?"

"Better. And I told you to call me Jane."

"Yes, ma'am."

She slapped his arm. He chuckled. Like most of his relationships, his friendship with the Browns had started in the hospital. She had a breathing condition that sometimes grew serious enough to warrant medical attention, and had been hospitalized during one of Riley's numerous surgeries.

One thing that he always enjoyed doing whenever he was in the hospital was visiting other patients. It got lonely, sitting in those little rooms, contemplating one's mortality. Seeking out others and talking to them passed the time and turned their minds to lighter things. In the case of Jane Brown, they'd ended up talking about Scripture, its history, and the different interpretations.

Eventually, she'd invited him to a Dove meeting.

Markus had thought she was crazy, and had scolded her when he thought Riley couldn't hear: "You thought the son of Augustus Thompson would make a good member? Are you insane?"

"Not everyone acts like their parents, darling. Give him a chance."

That had been almost three years ago. Riley hadn't missed a meeting since.

"How did your exams go?" Jane asked.

He forced a smile. "Great. I'll have my pick of careers when I turn eighteen."

"That's wonderful! Work hard enough and you might even be elected governor."

"God knows we need it," Markus muttered, joining them in the pew.

And that was the only reason Riley was even considering that. Why he hadn't burned every acceptance letter from the law firms and kept only the one from Central Hospital.

Becoming governor wouldn't solve *everything*. Augustus wasn't the only one persecuting the Doves. But if Riley or any other Dove was in that seat, they could reverse a lot of the damage Augustus and the Faith had done. Change most of the town's views on the organization. It could save lives.

If Riley pursued law.

If he managed to gather enough votes to be elected governor when the time came.

And if he didn't get found out as a Dove before then and executed for treason.

"Let's review our Scriptural study for today, shall we?" Jane asked, and they each opened their copies.

"I still say we should be able to take notes," Markus grumbled, flipping the pages. "I remember things much better that way."

"That's an excellent way to get yourself killed, dear."

Riley nodded in agreement. Much like Sarai Hall, in the early days of the Dove movement it had made publications and underground pamphlets that circulated among their ranks and into the public. And like Sarai Hall, they had been easily traced and their writers executed. Now, all Dove correspondence, beliefs, and lessons were oral unless there was no other option. And even when things were written down, it was in code.

"Riley, would you like to read?" Jane asked.

"Sure." He cleared his throat. "'The stain of sin is the most difficult to remove, and impossible to remove with more sin. Two lies do not make a truth. Two murders do not save a life. A man who seeks vengeance should first seek God and—'"

Footsteps echoed up the stairs, cutting him off. The three of them looked up to see a figure in black round the corner.

Markus stood. "Mrs. Novak."

Benjamin's mother watched the three of them for a long moment before approaching the candles.

"Our deepest condolences for . . ." he tried, but Mrs. Novak cut him off:

"I always suspected my son was a Dove."

Markus's mouth closed with a click. Riley and Jane exchanged a nervous look.

Mrs. Novak lit a candle. In the soft light, dressed head to toe in flowing black, she looked like a dark wraith. "I didn't necessarily oppose it. Even sympathized with the movement. But I didn't get involved because I worried that if I was right, then I would do or say something by accident and get him turned in."

She blew out the match and finally turned to face them. Her face was set in cold fury. "Seeing as that is no longer a concern, I'd like to know just why, exactly, you killed my son."

"Are you accusing us of turning him in?" Markus demanded.

"One of you *is* the son of the man who executed him."

"Don't blame the son for the sins of the father," Jane snapped.

Riley held out his hand. "It's fine."

"It's not," she hissed.

He waved her off and stood. "Mrs. Novak, what do you know about the Doves?"

She studied him, the candlelight making fiery rings in her eyes. "You oppose the war with demons."

"Yes and no," he said. "The creatures of the forest are a problem that needs to be solved quickly, especially if we're going to be making a second town to live in. However, the Doves put more emphasis on conquering our *inner* demons, within our souls and culture: the wealth inequality that leads to over half of our people starving and sick; the housing crisis that forces the poorest to sleep in the streets; the cruelty shown to women and people with disabilities. If we don't fight *those* demons, then they're just going to continue to spread, regardless of whether or not the winged demons exist."

"The Scripture makes it quite clear that the 'demons of the Flooded Forest' are to be exterminated to grant us access to Heaven," Mrs. Novak said.

"Scripture was written by men. And while the Hundred-Faced God is infallible, humanity is not. Scripture is a collection of *some* of Riley Bevill's visions, as written by his disciple, August Byruk, our first captain, who earned a *lot* of money and personal power through his fight with the creatures. Who's to say he didn't pick and choose the visions that best suited him and write them with a slant?"

"We're not saying that all of Scripture is bad," Jane added. "But some parts of it have proved more detrimental to Citadel than helpful. If people emphasized the Books of Mercy and Charity over the others, we'd have a much happier city."

Mrs. Novak sniffed. "That's a cute fairy tale."

"Maybe it is a fairy tale," Riley said with a shrug. "But it's one worth dying for."

She gave him a withering glare.

Markus shifted his feet. Riley knew that they were taking a risk. Mrs. Novak could turn them all in and get them executed. They had all but confessed to being Doves, which was the same as committing treason.

But he meant what he said. He met her glare and didn't back down.

Mrs. Novak deflated. "He always was an idealist, the fool boy."

Riley grinned. "We all are."

"I'm not," Markus grumbled.

"No, but you are a fool boy."

"Excuse me, Mr. Thompson, I am a fool *man*."

They chuckled, and even Mrs. Novak cracked a smile.

"We were just about to discuss a passage from Scripture if you wanted to join us," Riley said. "It's from the Book of Wisdom, one of Ben's favorites."

She hesitated, then slowly sat on one of the nearby pews.

The rest of the meeting passed without any other hiccups. Mrs. Novak asked a handful of clarifying questions but otherwise didn't engage. As they finished, they invited her back to the next one.

"Perhaps," she replied.

"Did you want an escort home?" Riley asked.

"No, I'd like to stay awhile longer. Ben's ashes aren't here, but it's still the closest I've felt to him since . . ."

He nodded, and they left her alone. *When I'm governor, I'm ending that stupid rule about criminals' ashes not being buried in the temples.*

Riley paused halfway to the door. He'd started thinking about his rise to governor as *when*, not *if.* An inevitability.

It was Mrs. Novak, he realized. And Ben. And all the other Doves, and Sarai Hall, and Olivia, and everyone else who had been or was at risk of being killed for following their hearts.

He was a Thompson. That gave him power and opportunity that so many other people didn't have. He had to take it, even if it was a burden.

Dear Elias,

They're finally letting me back into the forest. They wouldn't let me go on expeditions after you died out there. I overheard them whispering about me wanting to join you. And yes, I would love to see you again. If you and the rest of the town turn out to be correct about Purgatory and the Hundred-Faced God, that would be phenomenal. But I don't believe in that. There's no scientific evidence suggesting any of that is real. So getting myself killed by demons or a menziva or anything else would be pointless.

I wonder about it, though. You never wanted to go to the forest, and I hate that they made you. That they forced you anywhere near those monsters and got you killed. I wish I'd been there with you.

Love,
Olivia

CHAPTER FIVE

"Dad, this is ridiculous," Evelyn said, as Olivia and Ormus prepared to leave the next morning. "You're the captain. You have hundreds of people whose job is to do this *for* you."

The Claude family and Olivia were in the living room of their house, one of the nicer buildings in town, with two floors (that were *not* shared between two or more families) and stone walls. Dark-blue tables and chairs gave the living room and dining room areas an ocean-like feel, and Asiya had made it look a little homier by hanging framed art on the walls. Some of it was professional, some of it was Evelyn's from when she was a child, and some of it was Olivia's. When Asiya had realized Olivia was an artist—constantly doodling and sketching—she'd asked to take some of the pictures from her books and hang them. Olivia had almost had a breakdown at the thought of tearing drawings from her sketchbooks and instead compromised by re-creating them on separate sheets of paper. They looked nicer that way, anyway.

"I need to get a feel for the dangers and potential obstacles myself," Ormus said, buttoning up his military coat. In the years since Sarai's execution and his promotion to captain, he'd shaved the beard, and the previously dark hair had slowly lightened to gray, the tight curls cut close to the skull. He also spent more and more time behind a desk, tackling all the administrative tasks that came with the title. That would've thickened his waistline considerably if he'd ever stopped his morning workouts. "The last thing I want is to sink banknotes, hours, and men into a second Citadel only to have it go belly up because someone wrote a bad report."

Olivia rolled her eyes, wishing she could tell him to stay home. But that never worked. Every time she went into the forest on an expedition, Ormus was there with the military escort, constantly over her shoulder. Half the time she dreamed about throwing him out of the boat.

Ormus kissed Evelyn on the forehead and Asiya on the mouth. She had continued to cement her place as Olivia's favorite Claude by cooking them each a loaf of metabread for the journey: a loaf of bread with meat, cheese, and spices cooked inside. It'd been invented by poorer Citadel people who needed filling, nutritious food that would last awhile, throwing whatever was in their cupboards and cold boxes into the mix.

Olivia accepted a hug from both women. She could never stand light, buglike touches that slithered atop her skin, but she loved hugs. Riley's were the best, but Asiya's were a close second. She let her stepmother double-check that she had all proper medical equipment in her bag in case something went wrong; the woman worked part time as a medic in Citadel's best hospital and had drilled proper first aid into both her and Evelyn's heads.

Finally, they left the house, loading their things into a man-drawn carriage Ormus had hired. "Carriage" was a generous term for these modes of transport, a word borrowed from Scripture that described luxurious mobile rooms pulled by angelic creatures. Citadel carriages were more like very long wagons, just big enough for two people and their luggage, the dark-blue wood only occasionally decorated with paint. The "driver" who pulled the carriage was a big, burly man, all of his days hauling his burden showing in his arms and legs.

They were silent during the long ride, which suited Olivia just fine. Ormus wasn't nearly as good at interpreting Olivia's hand signals as Riley or even Evelyn. He always had her write out everything, and since her sketchbook was buried deep in her bag, that wasn't going to happen.

As the houses went from grand two- or even three-story buildings with little gardens and wide streets, to modest one-story homes too small or unstable to add more floors, to shacks leaning against each other, to flat farmland, Olivia mentally re-counted how much money she had stored in savings. She had enough to live in a shack for a few months. The price of homes kept going up. Her mother, Sarai, had only barely afforded raising her in a shared house on a salary the laborers would envy, and that was six years ago. Now, with Citadel women only allowed to pursue a handful of lucrative careers offered to men, and paid far less than their male counterparts when they *did* get those jobs, they would've been on the streets in no time.

Last year, she had been looking forward to proposing to Elias and moving into a tiny house close to the Farmers' Ring that he had inherited from his parents. He'd been talking about saving up enough money to add a second story to loan out to other people the week before he died. But after his death, and with her being an unmarried nineteen-year-old woman with no legal claim to the property, it'd been auctioned off to someone else.

The other option was living in the forest, and there were far more efficient means of committing suicide.

One of the bags by Olivia's feet slipped. She hauled it back into place.

"I told you not to bring your bow," Ormus said.

She scowled, putting a protective hand over the weapon.

"You're not going out there alone. The whole purpose of the military escort is to protect you."

Yes, but it was *Elias's* bow. The one he had hand carved and given to her for the festival of Praeta. Ormus had scoffed at it, then, too. *Which one of you is the soldier, and which is the woman?* he'd asked.

Olivia loved it. They'd become friends when Elias had first taught her archery, lovers by the time she'd gotten good.

Do me a favor, he'd said when he'd given it to her. *Take it with you when you go into the forest, even if you have a military escort. It'll make me feel better knowing you have a way to defend yourself.*

She couldn't say she believed in spirits or souls. Not in the traditional sense, at least. Even though she wrote a letter to Elias almost every day in her sketchbook, she knew he would never read them. He was dead and gone. Sometimes, she felt dead too. Either dead and numb, or full of so much rage and sorrow and pain that it hurt to breathe. Writing those letters, holding the bow he'd given her, relieved a little bit of that pressure.

All boats were kept inside Citadel's walls and brought out as needed. During low tide, they were only brought out for fishing in the nearby tide pool, essentially a small lake left behind when the water returned to the freshwater sea. That had been the lifeblood of Citadel in the early years, providing a crucial supply of food and water. Now, though, it got fished out within hours of being replenished.

At high tide, the tide pool vanished, flooded under anywhere from a few centimeters to several meters of water, depending on the week. In those cases, the boats usually had to be carried up the stairs of the wall, and the boatmen would push off the other side, into the forest.

This tide wasn't quite high enough to reach the top of the wall, stopping halfway up, too far to safely jump. The soldiers had to lower Ormus's and Olivia's two boats to the water with rope, then roll down a ladder.

Sergeant Peterson was the one who oversaw the operation, his straight-backed form and salt-and-pepper hair easy to point out. He grinned when he saw Olivia load her bow and quiver. "You fetching us dinner, too?"

She jerked her head to Michael and Gabriel, who were loading Ormus's things onto another boat.

"Good morning, Ms. Claude," Gabriel said with a sunny smile, showing off the gap between his two front teeth. "Can I take your bags?"

She shook her head, loading the boat herself. The twins were always so careful with her around other people. They'd offer to carry her things, and then "accidentally" drop them. She'd lost a whole sketchbook to them a few years ago.

"Judge Byruk wants his boys to get some experience in the forest. With any luck, they'll be officers next month," Peterson said.

Boys from families rich enough to buy them a proper education still had to serve two years as enlisted soldiers when they turned eighteen, starting as privates just like everyone else. But as soon as that was done, they had the chance to jump into officer positions like Ormus, rather than having to crawl up the ranks like Peterson. That was because of the extra education they received as children. Public education was mandatory, but only until they were thirteen. After that, most kids stayed home to help their parents with chores and farming, or tried to get jobs at the textile mill, or *maybe* started apprenticeships as blacksmiths or ironworkers if they were very lucky. Most girls married around fifteen or sixteen.

But families with enough money to afford not to pull their kids out typically kept them in school until they turned eighteen, at which point they were legal adults. Girls in that group usually apprenticed to be medics if they weren't already married. The men did their two years of mandatory service, and then they could jump into apprentice roles for lawyers or scientists, or become ensigns in the military and begin climbing the officers' ranks.

She dreaded the day the twins had such power.

Franklin was the last to arrive, huffing up the stairs and clutching the ladder with white knuckles when it was his turn to get in the boats. He, Gabriel, and Olivia shared one boat, while Peterson, Ormus, and Michael were in the other one.

Olivia looked out at the forest. During high tide, the water created a dark reflection of the orange and yellow leaves. It looked like a world of shadows caught on fire.

Michael and Gabriel picked up the oars, and they rowed away from Citadel into the forest.

Olivia had read nearly every public account about the forest in detail, written by soldiers, scientists, and even the Founders. They always said the same thing: the forest was a dark, eerie, evil place. The Founders called its very coloring unnatural. Demon howls were heard every night, and sometimes during the day. When the demons went quiet, the only sounds were the buzz of insects, the call of birds, and the occasional splash of water from a fish. Even Elias had shied away from it, preferring to keep within Citadel's walls.

Olivia loved it.

The air was crisp and clean, free from the stench of human waste and desperation. All the people in Citadel rubbed her ears raw. The tight spaces, the *rules*, the rigid lines in which she never fit. Out here there were no rules. You lived or you died depending on your wit and preparedness. No niceties, no manners, just the raw honesty of the way things were.

The first day was spent mostly in silence, even though demons never flew this close to Citadel, so for now it was safe. Olivia spent most of her time sketching: the people in the boats, the trees, the fish swimming around the massive trees beneath them. The tree trunks were the only obstacles they had to maneuver around. All the branches were high enough to avoid the tides, and they were so thick and intertwined with each other that the boats were perpetually in shade. The sunlight that the branches missed was filtered by the orange and yellow leaves, turning the water gold. Nugzuuki—four-winged, two-tailed mammals of the sky—flew in and out of the leaves, hunting small fish and other birds. One lucky bird caught a large, amphibious snail, its shell designed to look like the blue wood or seeds of the trees it lived on. The trees reproduced through big, shelled seeds that they dropped when ripe, in the hopes that the tide would sweep them away somewhere else, where they would take root and grow. She sketched as they rowed, trying to capture the beauty around them on her paper.

Gabriel peeked over her shoulder and snorted. "I've seen more talent in toddlers, freak," he muttered. She positioned herself so he couldn't see her work and kept going.

That was the first day, with the night spent sleeping on the boats tied to a branch, the gentle rocking from the small waves lulling them to sleep, except for whoever was on guard duty. Peterson, Michael, and Gabriel all took turns. Ormus was the only one with a revolver, while the rest had bows and arrows. The metals needed for bullets were hard to come by, and guns were difficult to make and repair, so they were reserved for officers. Bows and arrows, on the other hand, were made from wood and plant fibers, while arrowheads could be carved from anything: stone, bone, scrap metal, et cetera.

Olivia fell asleep to the sound of a distant demon howling.

The next day they slowly rowed deeper into the forest, choosing stealth over speed.

"What are we looking for?" Peterson asked from the other boat.

"It's a greenish-white flower with a blue vine," Franklin said. "We think it grows above the tide, too delicate to withstand that much water."

If it's above the tidal line, how does it get any water at all? Olivia thought, putting her silver braid into a bun. *What about sunlight?*

She wrote in her sketchbook *Get higher* and showed it to Franklin.

"We're as high as we need to be," he said.

Not enough sun.

"Which one of us is in charge of this expedition?" Franklin snapped.

She pointed to Ormus.

The vein at Franklin's temple threatened to burst.

"The higher we go, the more we risk being spotted by demons," Ormus said. "And I don't want to leave the boats. Stay low, for now."

"I think I see something," Michael called, pointing. There was a thin blue vine, almost completely invisible against the blue of the tree trunk, winding its way upward.

Peterson maneuvered their boat closer so Franklin could gently pry the vine free. When he managed to free a leaf, he shook his head. "Close, but no. Just a weed."

"Seems to me Olivia had a good idea about sending someone up top," Peterson said.

"It's too dangerous. We don't need to send anyone up— *Olivia!*"

Olivia had taken the time they were bickering to make sure her pack was strapped securely to her back. Then she jumped off the boat.

"Not again," Peterson groaned.

She grabbed a branch and swung onto the tree, using the other branches as hand- and footholds to scramble up to the top before anyone could even think of coming after her.

Within seconds, she was at the very top of the tree, poking her head out of the yellow and orange leaves. She caught her breath, wishing she had brought paints to capture the scene. From this angle, the land spread out beneath her, and the leaves' colors made it look like it was all ablaze.

She saw a bit of green and climbed down. When the others saw her, she held up ten fingers and pointed southeast.

"Ten meters?" Peterson confirmed. She nodded.

"Get back in the boat," Ormus ordered.

She ignored him and went ahead to where she'd spotted the green plant.

Going from treetop to treetop—alternating between swinging, jumping, and just plain walking—was quickly becoming Olivia's favorite way to travel. The bark scratched at her palms, and she made a mental note to wear gloves next time. It was a good thing she wore long sleeves and pants, because the few times the leaves brushed against her bare skin made her shudder. Yes, gloves were definitely in order next time.

Something moved in the water. She stopped to get a better look.

It was an ingencis: a large, aquatic mammal that they were fairly sure was an herbivore, maybe an omnivore. Its body was almost as thick as the trees—in other words, as wide as a house—and five times as long. It drifted through the forest, sniffing at roots so deep in the water its snout disappeared from Olivia's sight.

They only came into the Flooded Forest in spring and summer, looking for a good place to bury and lay eggs before returning to the ocean. When they were caught, they could be completely harvested: blubber made into food or candles, bones into tools or weapons. The eggs were delicious, too. They provided so much for Citadel that the Faith even considered them a holy animal.

Too bad their two little boats weren't equipped to kill and drag this one back. She hopped onto the next branch and continued onward.

She made it to the green spot before the others did and was able to confirm that this was indeed the plant they were looking for.

She put her fingers in her mouth and gave one short whistle, one long one, and then another short one. It was a military signal: *I'm here. I'm fine.* After a beat, she heard Peterson respond with two long whistles. *On my way / reinforcements coming.*

She took out a short knife and harvested the flowers, using one of the vines to tie them all together in a bouquet. The petals were green at the edges, fading to white in the center, which made them seem delicate amid the dark blues and overpowering oranges of the rest of the forest.

By the time the others arrived, she'd spotted another green patch to the east. She told them as such through hand gestures and dropped the bouquet onto the boat, then ran off again.

It was only a couple more of the flowers, and only one of them was mature enough to take. She decided she'd try to find its source; where did it lay its roots, anyway? Within the tree, or all the way down on the ground?

She followed the vine down the tree, taking the flower itself and wrapping the vine around her hand as she went. It stopped at one of the branches, twining itself around the bark before stopping at a hard bulge embedded into the wood. Was that the original seed? How did it get so high up?

She was so absorbed in her study that she didn't notice the movement to her right. Not until she heard the growl.

She lifted her head and came face to face with a demon.

CHAPTER SIX

Most demons that were brought to Citadel were already dead, shot down by soldiers or even the odd hunter. The bodies were displayed in front of the main temple until the rot became so bad they had to be taken down and burned. Sometimes the priesthood claimed them, doing whatever studies they deemed necessary in the Vaults.

Rarely did the soldiers bring back a demon still alive, simply because they were so dangerous the soldiers were forced to kill them to protect themselves. Usually those live demons were injured, and always tangled up in nets. In those cases, the demon was killed slowly in front of the people of Citadel. Wings and ears cut off. Hot coals put in its mouth and belly, and its body hung from a rope until dead.

Olivia had seen over a dozen demon corpses and one demon tortured. Meeting one now, in the wild, without any bars, nets, or chains between them, almost caused Olivia to jump in the water.

This one was small, for a demon, but no less deadly. Its jaw could snap Olivia's arm like a twig if it was so inclined. Its body was the mythological wolf's and could grow taller than a man, but its rear legs were talons, perfect for gripping branches. Its tail was serpentine and feathered, designed for balancing in the air and on precarious treetops. The feathered wings were carefully folded against its back, but when they were spread, they would be massive.

This particular demon was cream colored, with brown markings across its fur not unlike freckles that matched his brown wings. Olivia would find it cute if it weren't for the iron grip around her lungs.

For an endless moment, they stared at each other.

Olivia had used her left hand to gather the vine, which meant her right hand was free to get her knife. But if she reached for it, she was certain the demon would charge. This close, it would be on her long before she could do any damage.

Its golden eyes went from her to the flower in her hand.

Then it dove, spreading its wings just before it hit the water and flying around one of the trees before disappearing within the orange leaves. Olivia's hand went to her knife, but it was gone before she could draw.

When she counted to ten and it still hadn't come back, she released a gust of air and slumped against the tree trunk. Her hands trembled. Her heart pounded. But most of all, her mind reeled.

Why didn't it attack me? Demons go for the kill at every opportunity, so why didn't this one?

Before she could ponder that further, the demon came back. This time she had her hand on her knife before it even landed, but she stopped when she saw what it carried in its jaws.

Flowers. Green flowers. Green prasina flowers. Just like the one in her hand.

Olivia could have swallowed a hundred bugs with how far her jaw dropped.

It's been watching me collect flowers.

It's been watching me collect flowers and did not attack.

It's been watching me collect these specific flowers and deduced that I needed them.

It then decided to get me some.

It remembered exactly where to find those exact same flowers.

It's sentient.

. . . Fuck.

A gentle woof brought her back to reality. Olivia blinked, closed her mouth, and inched closer to the demon. Peace offering or not, she was still cautious around the thing that could devour her in seconds.

She was now close enough that she could count each and every one of its "freckles." She could also see that this was a male and, as it was only as tall as her chest, was probably an adolescent.

Good to know she wasn't the only young idiot in this tree.

She carefully wrapped her fingers around the vines, about half a dozen in all. The demon's fur brushed against the underside of her hand, the softest thing she had ever felt. As soon as she had a firm grip on the plants, the demon let go, licking his chops as she pulled back.

Now that she had her present, it seemed neither of them knew what to do. There were probably some rules for what should happen when you received a peace offering from your species' mortal enemy, but even if Olivia had been normal, she probably wouldn't know what they were.

The demon slowly took one of the flowers in its mouth and ate it.

She frowned, studying the plants. These weren't poisonous to humans, and in fact, the whole reason Franklin wanted them was because they could have medical qualities, capable of knocking out a fully grown man for a few hours.

Why eat one now?

Sharp whistling made her jump. One short, one long, one short, one long. *Where are you?*

Olivia whistled back, then made a shooing motion to the demon.

He didn't need to be told twice. He jumped off the branch and flew away, disappearing into the forest.

Dear Elias,

They're sentient. It's been a day, and I still can't believe it. The demons are sentient. Or at the very least, capable of recognizing human pattern behavior and anticipating it, of giving gifts, of trying to communicate (though I'm not entirely sure of what, besides that prasina flowers can be eaten).

I'm an idiot. I know what it's like, having a mind but being unable to speak. Being judged as dumb or inferior because I can't make words come out of my mouth. The fact that I've been doing the same to demons makes me want to puke.

And yet. I am so. Angry.

Animals cannot be held accountable for their actions. They're animals. Beasts who don't know any better. But if this freckled demon is any indication, then the demons are not animals. Not completely. There is at least some level of sentience to them, if not morality (for why else would they spare me when they had every chance of killing me?).

Thus, they choose to kill humans that stray too far from Citadel. They chose to kill you.

—O

CHAPTER SEVEN

The next day, Olivia burned through a dozen pages in her sketchbook. The men around her were quiet, which was fine by her, even though she was pretty sure it was because they were angry at her. She wasn't good with facial expressions, but going by past data, it would seem to be a logical conclusion.

She didn't know why Mr. Franklin would be angry, though. He had his samples. A lot more than he thought he'd get, too.

Irrelevant. She had bigger things to worry about.

She sat in the very back of the boat so no one could sneak up behind her and see what she was drawing. That is, they couldn't see the freckled demon she'd drawn several times, putting down every tiny detail from memory, from the spots on his fur to the shape of his golden eyes.

It was the height of high tide, one of the best times to scout because they could see what parts of a potential new settlement were at risk of being regularly submerged. The only better time to survey was during a king tide, when both moons were full and the waters reached their highest point. But that only happened once every three or four months. For now, this would do.

They came across an "island," a hill tall enough that not even the king tides could touch its peak. Very similar to Citadel that way. The top of the hill didn't have the massive, sturdy trees with branches thick enough to walk on. Instead they were thinner, more tender trees that were more susceptible to drowning. Even a few *bushes* and flowers grew directly from the ground. They brought the boats up to shore, and Olivia felt almost dizzy without the water constantly swaying her back and forth.

"What do you need, Franklin?" Ormus asked.

"We need to measure the surface area, and then I'm going to need some soil samples to make sure we can farm here," he answered.

"That's it?" Peterson asked, securing his quiver on his back. "Shouldn't take too long."

"Sergeant, Michael, go with him," Ormus ordered. "The rest of us will stay here."

Olivia gave him a sharp look.

"Don't give me that. You're on probation for yesterday's stunt."

She huffed, sitting back on the boat. The three men soon disappeared in the foliage, leaving her with two of her least favorite people.

Her hand cramped from all the drawing she'd done, but she picked up her sketchbook again anyway and doodled. Because if she didn't move or at least do *something*, she would explode.

"Whoop, you've got a tail there," Gabriel said, and before Olivia could understand what that meant—she didn't have a tail; her bottom was so flat that she barely had an ass—his fingers brushed against the base of her neck. The sensation of bugs crawling under her skin was too powerful to ignore, especially when he touched her hair, and she jerked away from him.

He beamed. "All better!"

Bastard. He *knew* how much she hated being touched like that.

"Easy, Olivia," Ormus warned. "He's just trying to help. For future reference, Private, ask before you touch her."

"Sorry, sir."

That did it. She snapped her sketchbook closed and climbed out of the boat.

"Where are you going?" Ormus snapped.

She opened her book to the first page and pointed to the word

Bathroom. She didn't usually mind crouching over the edge of the boat to do her business and didn't understand why it made the men uncomfortable. They barely blinked at one of their own pulling out his penis to take a piss. Really, she should be applauded for taking their weird sensitivities into account and seeking privacy.

"Be back in two minutes."

She went into the bushes, making sure to bring her bow and quiver just in case. Walking around this part of the forest was bizarre. She had to watch her step so she wouldn't crash through the bushes or other flora on the ground. The earth was firmer, not quite as spongy. And there was less shade, as the massive blue trees around this hill were too far away to properly weave their branches together overhead.

After her business was done, she headed back to the boat, but berry bushes caught her eye.

Well. Why waste the opportunity?

They were apiberries: thick, dark-red fruit almost the size of her thumb. She popped several in her mouth, smiling around the burst of sweetness. After cherries, these had been Sarai's favorite fruit. Elias had attempted to make her an apiberry pie on Sarai's death anniversary, but while the man had had many talents, baking had not been one of them. After cleaning the burnt mess he'd made in his kitchen, he'd gone to the marketplace for one instead. She chuckled at the memory, blinking back tears.

"Olivia?" Ormus called. "Where are you?"

She wiped her eyes and whistled so they'd know she was all right. After a bit of thought, she pulled out a small leather bag from her pocket and started harvesting. Bittersweet memories notwithstanding, food was food.

The bag was half-full when movement caught the corner of Olivia's eye. It was so slight, so little, that she almost dismissed it as a bird.

She carefully scanned the trees to her right. Then scanned them again. She almost missed the black demon in the shadows.

Their eyes met. Olivia stiffened, ready to move.

The demon did nothing.

He was pitch black, fur and wings made of starless night, except for one white patch over his left eye. He was also *much* bigger than the freckled demon.

Every instinct screamed at her to take the bow from her back and fire a shot. To shriek and run away. But this demon . . . he wasn't doing anything. Just watched her from behind a pale-blue tree. She tested his patience by plucking a few more berries.

No reaction.

This was the second demon she'd run into in as many days, and so far neither had gone for her throat. That couldn't be a coincidence. Had the freckled demon talked about her, or something? She took the time to gather her thoughts before closing her bag and tying it to her belt.

The demon still hadn't moved, watching her from the shadows.

She stepped closer.

The demon pressed itself closer to the ground, flattening its ears. Olivia had no idea what that meant, but just to be safe she held up her hands to show that she wasn't holding any weapons. She didn't want to fight. She wanted to talk. She wanted to ask why they killed every human they saw, why they had killed Elias.

But as always, the words got caught in her throat.

The demon tipped his head at her, ears pointed forward.

"Olivia!"

The sound of the gun going off was like a strike of lightning. She instinctively crouched as the skinny tree next to the demon's head exploded in shards of wood from the bullet. The demon snarled and launched itself into the air, a black shadow among fiery leaves. Ormus tried to get a clear shot with his gun while Gabriel nocked an arrow beside him.

A rock flew toward the men, smacking Ormus's chest before he could fire, and a second demon flew out of the trees. Olivia hadn't even seen it.

This one was dark brown, with black-tipped wings. But what caught Olivia's attention was the fist-sized rocks floating around his neck like some sort of necklace.

Demon magic, she thought, fascinated.

Reports of demon magic were rare and had only begun surfacing a hundred years ago. It seemed some of the creatures could control objects with their minds: rocks, arrows, and even humans sometimes. Olivia had never seen it before, had almost dismissed it as stories told to scare new recruits.

"Get back to the boats!" Ormus called, dodging another rock. He needn't have bothered; the commotion had drawn the other three men toward them. Peterson grabbed Olivia's arm and they both ran. Franklin scrambled into the boat. Michael went to help his brother and his captain, drawing an arrow.

Two rocks flew at Ormus and Gabriel as they inched back, preventing them from firing. As Michael nocked an arrow, the black demon swooped down from behind.

Olivia shouted, but either Michael didn't hear her or he couldn't interpret the wordless cry. The black demon grabbed him with his talons and flew up.

"Mike!" Gabriel cried.

Michael screamed and struggled as the demon brought him higher and higher. Gabriel aimed his bow, but another well-placed rock struck him in the head, bringing him down to a knee and ruining any shot he might have had.

The demon dropped Michael.

He screamed all the way down.

The brown demon turned and flew back into the trees, quickly vanishing. Ormus fired a couple of shots at the retreating black demon, but it was too far away. He grabbed Gabriel by the scruff and pulled him toward the boats. Peterson kept his bow pointed to the sky.

The demons did not return.

Well, Olivia thought as they pushed off the shore, rowing to where they'd seen Michael drop, *I know why they attacked us* this *time.*

CHAPTER EIGHT

They recovered Michael's body from the water. Olivia didn't see why they had to drag it back to Citadel with them: whether he was rotting in the water or burned into an urn in the temple basement, dead was dead. But Ormus insisted and Gabriel cried, so she didn't write a word of protest as they covered the body and began the two-and-a-half-day journey back to town. She had never seen either of the twins shed a tear before. The sight unnerved her.

The tide began to go down, enough that they saw a few more "islands" in the water that hadn't been there before, shorter hilltops poking out of the surface. As they neared Citadel, they passed several gatherers who scoured the newly revealed land for snails and saxum mushrooms, one of the few nontree plants that survived on the ground by encasing itself in a watertight, stonelike shell that prevented it from drowning. In addition to being delicious, it was a mild narcotic when prepared a certain way, making a decent painkiller.

Olivia had never seen the gatherers go out this far. They kept having to go farther and farther from Citadel to get enough for hungry mouths and empty hospital stores.

Decicans—fist-sized crustaceans with a dozen clawlike legs—scurried across the trees, ducking in and out of the water, their mouth tentacles slipping through the tiniest cracks in the wood to get to the bugs hidden within. Peterson's hand lashed out into the water, snatching one from its feeding ground and tossing it in the cold box. He'd probably fry that for breakfast tomorrow.

They returned to Citadel at sundown. Everyone went to do their separate tasks: Ormus and the military personnel to do their reports and check in, Gabriel to tend to his brother's body, and Olivia and Mr. Franklin to store and label the samples in the lab. As soon as that was done, Olivia went to a public bathhouse. Citadel didn't have the space for internal plumbing, but the bathhouses were plentiful and clean.

When she no longer reeked of dirt and sweat, she returned home. A heavenly smell wafted through the house when she opened the door. Asiya was cooking. What it was, Olivia didn't know, but it definitely involved garlic and pork. The kitchen's oven/fireplace gave that part of the house an eerie glow.

Despite her love for cooking, Asiya didn't always make the family dinner. She had been a full-time medic at the hospital when her family had arranged her marriage with Ormus, moving to part time only after she became pregnant. Depending on the length and intensity of her shift, the family got either a home-cooked meal or leftovers. Today must have been either a day off or a light shift.

Evelyn sat on the living room rug, sewing a dress in front of the *other* fireplace, the one designed to warm the living room and Ormus's study, a small room in the corner. Her scarf, a vibrant yellow today, was pulled down to her neck, and she tucked a black curl behind her ear. She glanced up when Olivia came in before refocusing on her task. "Good to see you're still alive. Where's Dad?"

Not inclined to dig up her book, Olivia signed *B* for barracks, then put the bag of apiberries on the counter for Asiya and trudged to her room. She dropped her bag onto the bed with a relieved sigh. Unpacking after a mission was one of the few times she actually took care of her living space. It was part of the postmission ritual: sketch her discoveries on the way back, check in with Riley (if it was an appropriate time of day), wash at the bathhouse, unpack, eat, sleep.

Since she'd had to skip Riley, she took extra care in putting her things away. Tossed the dirty clothes in the large woven basket in the corner. Straightened the books on her shelf (and the ones in piles *around* her shelf). Stashed her bag in her closet with her clean clothes. Made her bed, smoothing out the quilt she and Elias had picked out together. Opened the dark drapes to let in the light from the moon and rings. Dusted the wooden figurines Elias had carved for her that decorated her window and shelves: people, pigs, flowers, trees, nugzuukis, even a very long ingencis that wound around the clutter.

She considered the sketchbook for a long moment. The drawings of demons themselves weren't illegal, but anyone who saw them would ask how she'd managed to get close enough to one, and why it'd brought her flowers. And *that* interaction—talking to a demon rather than trying to kill it—could get her tried for treason. Fraternizing with the enemy, or something. There was an entire religious minority that called themselves Doves—after the mythological creatures of peace—who argued demons were just animals, that Scripture ordered them to slay *inner* demons of pride, sin, and violence. Her reluctance to kill the freckled demon could be interpreted as her being a part of that group, like Benjamin Novak. She decided on hiding her sketchbook under her bed rather than putting it on her bookshelf with the others.

She'd just finished when Ormus came into her room.

"So," he said. "Do you want to explain your behavior during this last trip?"

She had to pull out and open a few sketchbooks before finding one with a blank page. *I got it done.*

"We would've gotten it if you'd just been patient."

More time = more danger. Ex: Michael.

"Don't try to play this as a safety thing," he scolded. "You were impatient and impulsive, and it put yourself and the entire team at risk. Do it again, and you won't be on these expeditions anymore."

Not your call.

"You really think Franklin will say no if I tell him not to bring you?"

Damn. He absolutely would agree to keep Olivia in town while he did all the fun stuff.

Ormus nodded as if he'd heard her thoughts. He pinched the bridge of his wide nose. "I'm trying to keep you safe, Olivia. You disappeared for five minutes and wound up face to face with a demon! If I hadn't been keeping an eye on you . . ."

He drifted off, just looking at her. She tipped her head, not knowing what he wanted her to say.

"Just . . . follow the damn rules next time," he finished.

The next morning, Olivia returned to her familiar home routine with ease: wake up with the sun, brush her teeth, brush and braid her hair, get dressed (trousers, shirt, jacket, *no* headscarf), eat breakfast, check her list for anything she'd forgotten or needed for work, and go.

It was hailing out, and the annoying, tiny specks of ice mixed in with the rain were needles pressed into her skin. She did her best to cover herself up completely.

She stopped by the Thompson household first, being sure to time her visit so Augustus was gone.

Like the Claudes' house, the Thompson house was a two-story building made of stone with two fireplaces: one in the kitchen for an oven, the other in the living room. Unlike most other buildings, it hadn't been one story originally and then stacked with a second to cram another family into the same space. It had been originally designed with two floors and a *lot* of empty, useless space. They even had a yard—a rare luxury in Citadel—and a small flower garden out front.

When she knocked, Mia Thompson opened the door for her and leaned against the frame. There were deep bags under her eyes that she couldn't quite hide with makeup. She took a long sip from her mug; Olivia could smell the tea leaves and rum.

Mia finally stepped aside and let her in, leading her through the large, empty house, past several professional paintings of Scripture scenes. "Riley! Your friend is here."

"I'm in the study!" he hollered back.

Olivia left Mia behind and cut through the house like a knife. The house was too big and too empty for just three people. But the study was small and cozy, with a couple of cushioned reading chairs and several bookshelves. Mostly Scriptural studies, of course.

Riley sat in the corner, huddled in a blanket, reading Scripture. He looked up as soon as she appeared in the doorway. "Hey, Liv. You're alive."

She held out her hands in a *ta-da* manner. She set a small box on his lap and sat on the other chair. It was very comfortable. Augustus was a horrible excuse for a human, a sack of sentient meat in fine clothing, but he had good taste in furniture.

Riley smiled when he opened the package. "Mr. Franklin is going to kill you."

Won't notice, she wrote in her sketchbook, and it was true. Mr. Franklin had had her log all the samples from the forest. It had been the easiest thing in the world to slip one into her pocket and adjust the ledgers accordingly.

Riley gently took the prasina flower out of the box. "This is beautiful. I'll dry it and keep it forever."

Might use it next year.

"Maybe," he admitted.

Olivia frowned. Riley looked down, away from her, and his forehead was wrinkled. That meant something. What did that mean? Was he going to be sick? Did he want to be alone? Was he contemplating breaking into song using his legs as drums?

"Olivia? Are you okay?"

The wrinkles remained. She poked them, and they deepened as Riley frowned.

"Ha!" She finally figured it out. He had a problem!

Oh, wait. Riley had a problem.

She wrote, *What's wrong?*

"Nothing," he said.

She waited.

He sighed. Oh no. Had she done something wrong?

"I sent my exit exam scores to some of the law firms, and they accepted me," he said. "I also, secretly, sent them to Central Hospital. They *also* accepted me, but they did it through my dad."

Uh-oh.

"He threatened to disown me. He says it's a woman's job, and if I did it, I'd be a disgrace to the family."

Hmm. That was a problem. Medic was one of the very few high-educated jobs in Citadel that women were allowed to do. It was actually one of Olivia's favorite stories: One of the Founders was a woman named Isabella Benson. Scripture claimed she had been an angel of healing before her fall. Either way, she was the only Founder who knew anything about medicine. As Riley Bevill and his followers preached that only men should hold positions of authority, she trained her niece and daughter to be the first medics. They then trained a handful of other women, refusing to share their practice with men despite the furious backlash. It went on for five generations, cementing the position as a feminine role. While a handful of men had since become medics throughout Citadel's history, it was still considered women's work.

How it would disgrace the Thompson family, though, Olivia didn't understand. Riley would be saving lives. That was a *good* thing!

"It would look bad on my dad," he said, as if reading her thoughts. "Which I know you would love. But it'd also look bad on Mom. And I'd have a hard time finding a wife."

Olivia snorted, writing, *Wife shouldn't care.*

"Well, most people do. And then when kids enter the picture, it's going to be harder providing for them on a medic's salary than a priest or lawyer."

Your dad help?

"He'll absolutely let me sink into poverty to 'teach me a lesson' and convince me to go with the better option."

Olivia thought for a moment, trying to work the problem. She needed more information. *Why medic?* she wrote.

"The medics always made me better whenever I was sick. Every time I got a migraine so bad I blacked out, or got so sick we all thought I would die, or needed surgery, they found a way to save me." He smiled softly, a faraway look in his dark eyes. "I want to be able to do that for someone else."

So do it, she wrote. *Or never be happy.*

He shook his head. "It's not that simple."

CHAPTER NINE:
ORMUS

"What did I miss?" Ormus asked, shaking the hail from his coat. A hundred blessings, the storm was already passing.

The military officers used to operate out of the barracks. But with the increasing surge of men in uniform, and the fact that they didn't have room within the walls to build a second barracks, most of the officers had been moved to work in city hall. Ormus's office was right across the hall from Augustus Thompson's, as the governor and captain often worked closely together. His window looked over the first temple and street, though the cloudy glass and rainy hailstorm made it difficult to see anything with clarity.

His office was nice and toasty, thanks to the fire roaring in the fireplace. He had a couple of portraits of his family decorating the walls and surfaces. Mostly Evelyn and Asiya; Olivia could never sit still long enough for a complete portrait. But other than that, he kept his space spartan: desk, chairs, and a spot on the wall for his medals of ascending rank and accomplishments. His dark-blue desk had accumulated several more files in his absence, though his men knew better than to leave it in disarray. Everything was in one of three piles: "urgent," "important," and some sarcastic soldier had labeled the third pile "nobody cares."

His second-in-command, Commander Brodsky, took the coat and

hung it on the rack. The man was a few years older than Ormus, with deep wrinkles in his dark skin and an old scar from a demon's talon peeking out of his collar. They were sometimes mistaken for brothers, having the same build and skin tone, but were actually distant cousins.

"A lot," Brodsky said. "Which do you want to hear first: the murder on a farm, or a breakthrough in the investigation of the Doves?"

"Murder."

He held up one of the files from the desk. "David Carson, forty-two years old, found by his daughter on the edge of their farm, killed with a blunt object. The farm grew carrots and turnips, some of which were pulled from the ground near the body. We've got a handful of suspects, but we've had to break up a brawl in the Ring already."

"Let me guess: No witnesses?"

"None that have come forward," he said.

Which meant that this would likely go unsolved, like half of all Farmers' Ring murders.

"Did the family have a guard?" Most farmers hired people to guard their crops from would-be thieves. It was incredibly cheap labor, with one day of work producing pocket change, but there was no shortage of people desperate enough for it.

"They had a veteran do nightly rounds. He was on the other side of the farm at the time of the incident. The guard from a neighbor's farm established his alibi."

"Could be a ruse. Make an alibi, kill the farmer, split the crops between them," Ormus muttered, thinking aloud.

"If it was more than a handful of carrots that had been taken, I would've thought the same thing. But that's not nearly enough for two grown men to split between them. Especially not if they have families."

Ormus sat at his desk and pinched the bridge of his nose. He'd bet good money that at least a dozen other reports on his desk had something to do with stealing crops or food. He couldn't wait for a second Citadel. While he was sure that would have its own bouquet of problems, hunger-based crime probably wouldn't be on the list.

"When did this happen?" he asked.

"Two nights ago, right after dusk. His daughter says he heard a noise and went out to investigate. When he didn't come back, she followed. Her screams alerted the guard."

"I thought we had a sundown curfew."

"We do, but most night patrols are focused in the center of town, where the population is thickest."

"Sink some more men into night patrols and have them fan out," Ormus said. "I want to know where everyone was that night. When we solve it and bring the killer to justice, that's one less reason for the people to turn into an angry mob. Where's the survey on a second town?"

"Right here."

Ormus skimmed the report. Though he'd been on the latest survey, most of his attention had been on his daughter and demons. That was half the reason he went. He trusted his men with the safety of Citadel and even his life. But when it was his family on the line, *he* needed to be there.

He frowned when he looked at the map and the two areas the surveyors had highlighted as the best starting points for a new town. The hill he had explored during the mission was tall enough to withstand the worst of the tides but was far from any iron bog. The other spot was much closer to a newly discovered bog but wasn't on as tall of a hill and risked floods during king tides, at least. Both spots were riddled with demon sightings.

"I need to talk to Augustus," he muttered. It was ultimately the governor's call where they decided to settle. As much as they needed iron for tools and weapons, they needed food more. He'd make a case for the hill.

"I'll schedule a meeting as soon as your calendars allow," Brodsky said. "The Byruk funeral is tomorrow, so it'll probably be after that."

Ormus grunted in the affirmative.

"What about the Doves?"

The Doves were a unique problem. They weren't violent, which was a mercy, and in any other circumstance, Ormus would leave them alone. But they threatened Scripture and, therefore, all of Citadel with their beliefs, eroding people's belief in the Faith and governor, the two pillars that held up the town. The Scripture clearly stated that humans were to slay all demons before being granted access to Heaven. The Doves argued that "demons" meant *inner* demons, humanity's propensity for sin and misbehavior.

It was a nice thought. But Ormus had been in the forest, had fought the real demons. No matter what Scripture said, those monsters had to die. There couldn't be any argument about that. Especially now.

"What did you find?" he asked.

Brodsky's eyes gleamed. "There's rumors of another circle, regularly getting together every week. Markus Brown might be involved."

"Owner of the textile mill?"

"Yes, sir."

Ormus was not going to drop his head on his desk. He was a professional. Professionals did not drop their heads on their desks. It would ruin his lovely paperwork piles.

"I sincerely hope you have proper evidence to back that claim," he said.

Before Brodsky could answer, Ormus's door burst open. He didn't recognize the panicked private who careened into the room. "Sir! You have to send men to the market. A riot's broken out!"

He jumped to his feet. "How bad?"

"Bad, sir. The entire square is a mess. Most of the food stalls are gone."

Minutes later, Ormus and half of the town's city guard were at the square, being pelted by hail. The private hadn't exaggerated: it was a mass of raging people trampling over the tattered remains of stalls through the frozen rain as they desperately tried to keep armfuls of bread or vegetables or meat, only to have the rest of the mob pull the goods from their arms—or even pull the whole arms out of their sockets. Ormus almost tripped over one such severed limb and counted two fresh corpses on the muddy ground.

He raised his pistol and fired into the air.

The deafening sound froze everyone, drawing their attention to him.

Ideally, he'd be able to arrest every single one of them. But the jails could only hold fifty, maximum.

His soldiers formed two walls behind him. The first row were all armed with batons and tall wooden shields. The second, bows and arrows.

"Everyone drop what you've stolen and return to your homes," he ordered.

A handful of people peeled away, slipping down alleys and side streets. Several people dropped whatever they were holding and sulked. Others tried to hide the food under their coats, but that was to be expected. Ormus wasn't going to be able to check all of them.

"We're starving!" a man shouted.

"Return to your homes at once," he ordered.

Someone threw a rock, smacking a soldier in the arm. Another bounced against a shield.

Ormus sighed. "Archers!"

The bowmen nocked their arrows. Much of the crowd backed up, a handful outright running away.

"Fire!"

Women screamed as the arrows rose and fell into the crowd.

The cloth arrowheads exploded upon impact, the stink bombs overpowering the smell of fresh rain and mud with the stench of feces and rotten eggs. Ormus covered his nose and mouth with a kerchief as the crowd immediately scattered, leaving behind a handful of bloody bodies and several pounds of fruit, vegetables, bread, and pungent chemicals mixed with cold mud.

He did not envy the poor privates who'd have to clean this mess.

That afternoon, back in his office, Ormus had to remind himself—again—not to bang his head against his desk. The market square still needed to be cleaned up. The families of the three people who had died and two others currently recovering in the hospital demanded justice. And given how much food had been spoiled and trampled during the mob, prices would go up *again*, so he got to look forward to another riot in the near future. And there was the Byruk funeral tomorrow.

"Sir," Brodsky called, while Ormus was nose deep in paperwork.

"What."

"Governor Thompson is here to see you, sir."

Ormus straightened. "Send him in."

The governor strolled into the office, smiling at Ormus. "Excellent. You're still in one piece."

"For now. What can I do for you, Augustus?"

Theirs was an odd relationship. Ormus didn't *like* Augustus, and he strongly suspected it was mutual. He didn't blame him for executing Sarai—she'd broken the law—but he didn't appreciate how gleefully the man had done it. Or how he constantly showed off his wealth while so many in their city wallowed in poverty.

However, they were the captain and governor. They needed to work together to lead Citadel. And they'd been doing just that for over three years.

Augustus sat with a sigh, looking around the office. The buttons of his suit gleamed against his belly. His hair had started to silver when he first got the position, and now there was very little red or brown left. Ormus sympathized.

"You really need some proper art in here," Augustus said.

"I don't like to get distracted from my work." And he rather liked his family portraits, reminding him of *why* he did this. What he was fighting for. There were even a couple of pictures by Olivia here; she couldn't sit still for a portrait, but she could create one herself. She'd done the one of Asiya knitting and another of a younger Evelyn modeling a dress, both of them prominently displayed. Ormus also had a very old drawing Evelyn had done when she was little on his desk, which he kept partially for sentimental value and partially because it produced that delightfully hilarious teenage embarrassment whenever he brought it up. Augustus sniffed at them before turning back to him.

"I think it's safe to say that Citadel is on the brink of collapse. At least until we get a second town running to better feed and spread the population."

"I hope you're coming in with some ideas?" Ormus asked.

"The Doves," he said.

Ormus blinked. "What?"

"The people need something to focus on. An outlet for their anger."

"Don't the demons do that?" he asked.

"Not well enough. And the demons aren't the biggest threat. They can only attack us from the outside. The Doves erode our authority from the *inside*. I just want to make sure that we're doing everything we can to squash them before they can incite more riots. Besides, a few executions will mean fewer mouths to feed."

Ormus raised an eyebrow. "Augustus, the Doves aren't the ones causing riots. That has to do with food shortages, lack of housing and jobs, a bad economy . . ."

Augustus waved him away. "Yes, all of them failures on our part until we can get a second town up and running. That's at least a year out. Would you like everyone angry at *us*, or the Doves?"

"I'll divert more time and resources into rooting them out. Brodsky has a decent lead. But that'll divert resources away from other crimes."

"Priorities, Ormus. If you turn your focus on the Doves, you'll produce results. But even if it doesn't, I trust you to find me some Doves anyway."

Ormus blinked. Then blinked again. Anger heated his skin. It was a struggle to keep his voice level. "You're not suggesting that I frame innocent citizens for treason, are you?"

"Innocent citizens? Heavens, no. They can be anyone you want."

"No," he growled. "I will find the *real* Doves, which you will punish to the full extent of the law. Nothing else."

Augustus held up his hands. The golden rings flared in the light of the fireplace. "Fine, fine. But make it quick. Because I intend to retire soon. And who would have a better chance at taking my place than the captain who defeated the Doves?"

The anger leaked out of Ormus. He leaned back in his chair with a groan. "You are blatantly manipulating me."

"Successfully, I hope."

He sighed, but it was tinged with a smile. "All right. I'll focus on the Doves; you focus on the bigger problem of keeping our town from eating itself."

Augustus smirked as if he'd won a game of chess. "Thank you, Ormus."

CHAPTER TEN:
RILEY

Funerals were a very common occurrence in Citadel. Riley would wager that for every birthday party he went to in any given year, he went to at least as many funerals.

The funeral service for Michael Byruk was held not in a temple but outdoors. The covered body had been placed in a small brick crematorium and set ablaze earlier that morning. Riley, Augustus, and Mia were all in attendance, as well as Ormus, Sergeant Peterson, several other families and soldiers, and of course, the Byruks. Everyone wore black.

Riley listened to the priest talk about the honor of soldiers and their glorious battle against the demons, and he wondered why he was there. He'd never really liked Michael, and he didn't get along with the rest of the family. The real reason he'd let his father drag him here was because his absence would have been noted.

". . . And as our prophet and savior Riley Bevill says, the doors of Heaven will open, and all of God's children waiting in Purgatory shall be received into Heaven by the face of Mercy. Amen," the priest concluded. Everyone else echoed the "amen."

Riley hoped that was true, or that Purgatory didn't exist and Michael was already in Heaven. He didn't like the idea of anyone in Hell, even people he didn't like. Eternal punishment for a few years of being a jerk? That just seemed . . . harsh.

The priest's acolytes carefully brushed the ashes that had once been a young man into a hole in the corner of the crematorium. It led to a short pipe that emptied out into a clay urn, which the Byruks had paid extra to have beautifully painted red and yellow, Michael's favorite colors. Once it was filled, it was given to Mrs. Byruk, and the funeral procession began.

Everyone followed the priest and Byruks not to the Temple of the Hundred Faces, where most urns were stored, but to Michael's preferred place of worship: the Temple of War. It was a slightly longer walk, down the central hill of Citadel, and it gave Riley time to seek Gabriel out.

The lone twin lagged behind his parents by several paces. Riley slipped in next to him. "Hey."

"Hm." He was unusually stone faced today, looking stoic and professional in his dress blues. Riley could see the cracks underneath.

"You've probably heard this a lot today, but I am sorry about your brother."

"Why?" Gabriel growled. "You didn't like him."

"That doesn't mean I wanted him dead. Or for you to lose someone so close to you."

The soldier snorted. "You always were too nice, Thompson."

They neared the Temple of War, the second-oldest place of worship in Citadel. Early in the city's history, as the population grew and expanded, the Founders and their descendants quickly realized that they would need more places to worship. And as different people preferred different aspects of God or turned to multiple aspects throughout their lives, later temples often centered around one Face of God, one or two books of Scripture. There was the Temple of War, the Temple of Healing right by Central Hospital, the Temple of Youth, the Temple of Justice, the Temple of Vengeance, the Temple of Love . . .

"My mother wants me to get discharged after my two years are up," Gabriel said, startling Riley. They'd been walking in silence for the last several minutes.

"Will you?" Riley asked as they drew closer to the Temple of War. It was almost as big as the original temple, with several man-sized statues of the War-Faced God lined up in front of it. Each one wore a uniform from a past era of Citadel history.

Gabriel's face darkened. "Those monsters murdered my brother. I'm not going to stop until they're all dead."

Riley hesitated. Anger was a natural reaction to death, especially that of a loved one. But that seemed extreme. And dangerous.

"Is that what Michael would've wanted?" he asked carefully.

It was the wrong thing to say. Gabriel glared at him. "Michael is dead. It doesn't matter what he would've wanted."

Riley backed off. He lingered by the statues as the rest of the procession entered the temple to place the ashes to rest and hear some final words from the priest. He refused to follow. He'd heard enough about war and bloodshed today.

"I remember when I had to wear this one."

He jumped. Sergeant Peterson had decided to join him, studying one of the latter uniforms on a War God statue. He, like Ormus and Gabriel, had worn his dress blues, the fancier uniform that included his full rank, title, medals, and other decorations. Most of those medals and honors were confined to the left side of his jacket and went down to his lower ribs.

Peterson had once told him that he attended the funeral of every soldier he trained, even the ones who died outside the line of duty, like in illness or accidents. Since he had been a drill sergeant for the last decade, that added up to dozens of funerals a year.

"It itched like hell," he continued. "And the pants never fit right, no matter what size they were. I hated it. My son always looked better in them."

Jason Peterson. Riley had never met him. He'd died before Riley had gotten the chance.

"Is he here?" Riley asked, motioning to the basement levels of the Temple of War.

Peterson shook his head. "No. I put him to rest in our own temple, near my house. Small thing. Nothing fancy. No scary statues or rich people around or anything like that." He kept his eyes on the old war uniform. "When my son died, I only ever wanted to do two things: get drunk and kill as many demons as possible. I lost five years to drink and rage."

"I'm sorry," Riley said.

"Not your fault. That was all me. Took me that long to get my head out of my ass and relearn to appreciate life now. It's not the same as it was with my boy, but it's . . . it's nice. Worth living."

He clapped a hand on Riley's shoulder. "If I could get my stubborn head screwed on right, then so can Gabriel. He'll come around."

"Michael always held him back," Riley said. "They were both bullies, but Michael at least knew when to stop. Gabriel doesn't."

"He'll learn," Peterson promised.

Riley prayed he was right.

CHAPTER ELEVEN

Olivia spent the next several days running tests on the prasina flower with Mr. Franklin. It was difficult to focus on taking her notes, even during the more interesting human trials. They paid all subjects a handful of banknotes, so they had no shortage of volunteers. She doodled as she worked in an effort to clear her mind and burned the drawings when they ultimately turned into the freckled demon.

The good news was she was able to skip out on Michael's funeral. He hadn't deserved to die, but not so deep down she was glad at least one of the Byruks was gone.

Finally, it was the day of rest and worship, and her day off from work. Asiya tutted at her as the Claudes got ready to go to the temple in the morning. "Were you up all night *again*?"

Olivia hummed an affirmative, not looking up from her book. She hadn't even attempted sleep last night, knowing by now when she'd be able to get a fitful rest and when she'd end up staring out the window all night, counting the planet's rings. Rather than suffer through that, she'd gathered every single book in the house that pertained to demons—most of them Citadel's history, some of them commentary on Scripture—lit several candles on the kitchen table, and read.

"Maybe I should bring this up with the other medics," Asiya said, clearing up the candleholders that now only held stubs of wax. "This isn't healthy."

Olivia shrugged, still reading. Sarai had taken her to the hospital several times when she was little, trying to find a cure for her lack of sleep *and* lack of speech, the two aspects of her oddity that had most concerned her. All that had done was get a bunch of medics scolding her for being such a "difficult" child and worrying her mother.

Ormus took one of the books and raised an eyebrow. "Anything in particular you're researching?"

She didn't respond.

"Olivia."

She had to dig for her sketchbook beneath the mountains of paper around her to write, *No sleep. Demons are interesting.*

"We're going to be late," Evelyn warned, tucking her hair into a light-green headscarf.

Almost every family in Citadel attended sermons at least once a week. When Olivia had moved in, Ormus and Asiya had tried to make her go with them. They said it was good for Ormus's career, having his whole family attend service. They said she might find something there that would help her deal with the grief of losing her mother.

She let them take her to one service. The priest had talked about a passage in the Scripture that taught unconditional forgiveness.

She'd laughed herself out of the temple and never went back.

Ormus set the book down. "Be sure to clean all this up when you're done. And remember to eat."

Olivia hummed to let him know she'd heard him and returned to her history of Citadel, although it read a bit like Scripture at the beginning:

After the angels were cast out of Heaven for rebelling against the Hundred-Faced God, they were stripped of their divinity and immortality, and crashed into the icy wastes of the Shadowlands. In this way, humanity came to the planet. But the Hundred-Faced God is as merciful as He is wrathful. According to Scripture, He sent a vision to the most devout and remorseful of the new humans, Riley Bevill, showing him the way to the forest, where his people would survive and have a chance at redemption. After weeks of travel, during which untold numbers of humans died in the cold darkness, Bevill led them out of the Shadowlands, into sunlight and the Flooded Forest. He immediately ordered the first temple to be built to honor the Hundred-Faced God . . .

She flipped ahead, looking for specific references to demons.

The first demon attack on Citadel happened within a year of the town's creation. They came without warning, pulling children and adults into the sky and dropping them from great heights . . .

. . . Bevill received a vision from the Hundred-Faced God, who, according to Scripture, ordered humanity to cleanse the Flooded Forest of all demons in order to cleanse their souls of sin . . .

. . . the young man secured his place as the governor's successor by bringing back a total of thirteen demon bodies, still a record at the date of this book's publication . . .

She closed the book and sighed. Nothing new. She needed more information, anything that might give her something about the demons' intelligence.

She grabbed her coat and bag, only just remembering to leave a note for the Claudes:

Gone to the Vaults.

—O

As captain of Citadel's military forces, Ormus had access to the first three levels of the Vaults. But he also made frequent donations to the Faith, enough that anyone in his family could enter the first level of the Vaults if they chose to. Evelyn used the access for some of her bigger school projects, and Asiya came whenever something new about medicine or the human body was published.

Olivia avoided the place on principle. Too many priests. Too much of the information that she wanted was off limits, and she never understood why. Why was it accessible only to those the Faith and governor deemed worthy? Shouldn't knowledge be shared by everyone?

She was taken aback when she stepped into the first floor and saw so many tall bookshelves. It was all she could see. There must be *hundreds* of books in this room alone!

The priest manning the front desk raised an eyebrow when he saw her. "Ms. Claude. Never expected to see you here."

The name made her grit her teeth. After gaining custody, Ormus had gone to legally change Olivia's name from Hall to Claude. She had torn up the papers as soon as she saw them and still signed everything with her mother's name.

There were three red stripes on the priest's sleeve, making him highly ranked. Olivia tried to put a name to the wrinkled face but came up blank. She doubted she'd written it down anywhere, either.

She opened her sketchbook and wrote, *I need everything you have on demons.*

He read the note and pointed. "Near the back corner there. And cover your hair while you're here. This is a place of holiness. You'll find extra scarves in the closet."

Olivia resisted the urge to roll her eyes and got a damn scarf. It wrapped around her head and neck like a noose. She kept it on just long enough to find the books that looked like the ones she needed and found a secluded spot in a cushioned chair in the corner. Then she tore it off.

She skimmed through one book, then two. The third was *The Origin of Demons*, and after some more skimming, she found something relevant:

Though most priests would have you believe that Riley Bevill wrote the Scripture exactly as it is written today, this is not the case. Bevill didn't even compose it. That honor went to his successor, Citadel's first captain, August Byruk, who took all of Bevill's teachings and fragmented writings and turned them into the beloved holy book of the Hundred-Faced God. As such, many of

Bevill's writings got left out *of the Scripture, including the exact origins of the demons.*

Accordingly, after creating the Heavens and the earth, the Hundred-Faced God created several distinct classes of angels: the archangels, who directly serve God and each rule over legions of seraphim; seraphim, who are the "standard" angels—many of these eventually became human; and the mera. The mera were not angels per se, but holy beasts of burden. Though all life is created to serve the Hundred-Faced God, the mera were supposed to serve the higher classes of angels to make their tasks easier. Though it's unclear what exactly their tasks were to be, Bevill refers to them as "the guard dogs of Heaven" and "Heaven's hounds," so it was likely a guardian position of sorts.

However, some dogs bite, and even the Hundred-Faced God can make a miscalculation. The mera had hardly been created before they turned on their masters. According to Bevill, they "tore through Heaven with tooth and claw, the skies turned gold with immortal blood, until the forces of the Hundred-Faced God triumphed."

The mera were stripped of their divinity and cast out of Heaven, crashing into the Shadowlands. There, they became demons and flew to the Flooded Forest to spend the rest of their wretched days.

I find it ironic that humans, as former angels, have more in common with the demons than the Hundred-Faced God. Both of us were cast from Heaven for rebelling against authority. Perhaps this is why the Hundred-Faced God has tasked us with hunting these creatures. By purging them from the world, we purge the shared sin from our souls, thus proving that we are worthy of being welcomed back into Heaven as angels. Other critics believe that—

"There you are!"

Olivia looked up. Evelyn walked through the bookshelves toward her. "Liv, put your scarf back on," she hissed. "This is the *Vaults.*"

No, I hadn't noticed, Olivia thought but didn't write. She didn't get the scarf, either.

Evelyn sighed. She looked at the books. "Are you still reading about demons?"

Olivia nodded and wrote, *Time?*

"Just after lunch. You forgot to clean up the table when you left. Dad is *not* happy."

Olivia sank into her chair, hiding behind the book.

"Well, he doesn't want you walking home alone, with the riots and crime."

She sank farther.

Evelyn huffed and left. Olivia expected her to leave the building and was surprised when she returned with a book herself. She settled into the chair opposite Olivia. "Let me know when you're ready to go."

Olivia smiled. But it was short lived. She couldn't sink back into her research, such as it was. The idea that demons had once been citizens of Heaven like humans was new, but not a surprise, and ultimately useless in the face of her atheism. The fact that they were categorized as beasts of burden—therefore possessing no more intelligence than an animal—didn't bode well. Maybe her encounter with the freckled demon had just been a fluke.

She got up, almost falling to the floor as her stiff muscles shrieked in protest. After some stretches and several interesting pops, she meandered to Evelyn's chair and peeked over her shoulder.

Evelyn showed her the cover: *History of Artifacts.*

"I'm thinking of being a nun," she said.

Olivia's eyes almost bulged out of her skull. She didn't even have to write her question, as Evelyn chuckled and explained, "I want to do more of what you do. Not natural science. I want to be able to *create* things, but also discover stuff. And study the stars. Maybe find a more accurate method of predicting the height of the tides."

Olivia was going to write that Franklin might be able to help her out with that, but she'd only gotten as far as the *A* in his name when Evelyn shook her head. "I want to study the Artifacts and re-create them."

Olivia whistled. According to Scripture, the Artifacts were pieces of technology that humanity managed to bring with them when they were banished from Heaven. The *true* story behind them was a mystery, as far as Olivia knew, but even she could admit that they were very old, advanced forms of technology that benefited Citadel greatly. The originals were all stored in the highest levels of the Vaults for study and, hopefully, re-creation. Things like clocks, revolvers, and textile machines. The Claudes had a massive clock in their living room, a sign of their wealth. Even without the Artifacts, almost all of Citadel's inventions came from the people working in the Vaults.

And almost all of those people were men.

OK, she wrote.

Evelyn narrowed her eyes. "No long lecture about how I should get married and have children, first? Fulfill my duty as a woman to become a wife and mother?"

Olivia shook her head, then wrote, *Whose ass(es) do I need to kick?*

Evelyn burst out laughing, immediately clamping down on it so they wouldn't draw attention. "It's just the usual reaction." She squeezed Olivia's hand. "Thank you."

Olivia beamed. She didn't know what she'd done to deserve thanks, but it seemed one problem, at least, had been solved today.

"So what *are* you reading about, anyway?" Evelyn asked. "Find anything useful?"

Olivia shook her head, then reconsidered.

I need the 2nd level, she wrote.

"Of . . . the Vaults?" Evelyn asked. "Laymen like us only get access to the first floor. Even low-level nuns can't get much higher without special permission."

Olivia scowled.

Evelyn studied her. "This . . . thing . . . you're looking into. Is it really that important?"

Olivia nodded.

Evelyn stood. "Well, we can ask. Put on your scarf and pretend you don't hate everything for two minutes."

Olivia did as she was told, properly hiding her silver hair even as something inside of her squirmed. It had always been one of the biggest reasons other children had made fun of her. Sarai had faced the same problem when *she* was a child, and had taught Olivia to wear her difference with pride. Elias had been the first man to call it beautiful. Hiding it felt like giving up, giving *in*. Like she was letting them both down.

It's only for two minutes, she thought as they approached the priest's desk. *Only two minutes.*

"Father Gabriel," Evelyn greeted with a warm smile. "I know this is a little unorthodox, but my sister and I were wondering if we could go up one level just for a little bit."

The priest—Olivia already forgot his name—shook his head. "Not possible, Ms. Claude. The second floor is for ordained priests and nuns only. Perhaps in a few years, if you two wish to join the sisterhood, then you can go."

"Please?" Evelyn asked. She leaned closer, lowering her voice so that they probably thought Olivia couldn't hear: "She's hoping to find some medical information. Something to help with her . . . ah, oddities. I'm sure our father will be able to make up for this little breach of conduct."

Damn, Ev, Olivia thought. *I was just going to sneak up the stairs.*

The priest wavered before reluctantly nodding. He wrote something on a piece of paper and gave it to her. "This is a temporary invitation to the second level. You will be allowed one hour. You may *not* bring anything out."

Evelyn took the paper with a little bow. "Thank you so much. Hundred blessings to you, Father."

"A hundred blessings, my child."

The stairs were guarded by a soldier. He'd been close enough to overhear the conversation and waved them on, leaning against the wall the whole time and barely giving them a glance.

Halfway up the stone steps, Evelyn suddenly let out a gusty breath and clutched her chest. "God's Faces, I've never done anything like this before. We could get in so much trouble!"

Olivia grabbed her hand, squeezed it, and gave what she hoped was an encouraging smile.

"How are you not terrified?" Evelyn hissed.

Olivia grinned.

"Right. You're insane. I forgot."

Giggling, she pulled Evelyn up the stairs.

The second floor had less space (obviously; the building was built like a pyramid) but roughly the same amount of books. The spaces between the shelves were barely enough for the girls to squeeze through. There was one spot in the middle with tables and chairs, currently occupied by one person. For a second, Olivia thought it was a priest. But the robes were slightly different, and this person had a headscarf that covered everything but her face.

The elderly nun looked up from her pen and paper and frowned. "Who are you? What are you doing here?"

Evelyn gasped. "You're Sister Mira! I've read all your articles on Artifacts. Are you working on one now? What's it about? Wait, sorry. I'm being terribly rude."

The nun's face softened. She even chuckled. "Thrilled as I am to meet you, Ms. Claude"—Olivia was pretty sure Evelyn would have fainted if they hadn't been holding hands—"this area is off limits."

"Oh!" Evelyn produced the priest's note and gave it to her. "My sister needs to research something really important, so he gave us an hour."

The nun looked at the note, then at Olivia. "I see. Do you need any help?"

Olivia shook her head, heading for the shelves while Evelyn started chatting again. "Was the pocket watch you invented an Artifact already, or did you just downsize from the clock?"

"It was its own Artifact," Sister Mira replied. "What most people don't realize about re-creating them is that it's not the knowledge itself that's difficult but getting the right supplies . . ."

As soon as they were out of sight, Olivia tugged off her scarf so it rested around her shoulders and set out to find something pertaining to demons.

As is obvious from Father Anjali's research on demon behavior, there is still much about them that we don't know, and though this essay focuses on the demons' anatomy and physiology, we should bear in mind that there are likely several functions that we are simply not privy to without studying the demons live in the wild . . .

Olivia noted the book title by Father Anjali and looked for it on the shelves. When she found nothing, she went back to the table in the center, pulling up her scarf.

". . .thinking about becoming a nun?" Sister Mira asked.

"Absolutely! But every time I bring it up to my friends and family, they say, 'No, you should wait until after you've had kids and your husband passes away.' But you have to be a *matron* to study Artifacts, and that takes *decades.*"

"I know. And believe me, most people you meet are going to react that way. But if you truly believe that this is the path the Hundred-Faced God meant for you to take, then face those sneers with a smile. He will open a path for you."

Olivia rounded the bend and caught Sister Mira's eye.

"Something I can help you with?"

She showed the older woman the note. Sister Mira grimaced. "Ah, yes. That's on the third floor. Most demon research and everything pertaining to the military is up there. In the Boys' Club, as I like to call it."

Damn. So close, Olivia thought.

"Why are you researching that?" Sister Mira asked.

"Olivia works in natural sciences, for Mr. Franklin," Evelyn explained before Olivia could write something.

"Oh, that's right. I had heard that. It's hard for an atheist to wear a habit."

Olivia couldn't decipher the nun's face or tone, but it made Evelyn frown. Her sister quickly hid it with a smile. "I've been thinking about architecture, too. I know you can't really tell me much about the Artifacts, but are there any that might help with that?"

Sister Mira brightened considerably. "Absolutely! I'll tell you a secret:

Most of the original Artifacts aren't actually physical objects. Rather they're blueprints that we do our best to follow . . ."

Olivia left them again, making sure they lost track of her in the bookshelves before going for the stairs. She crept up to the third floor without a sound. Unlike the bottom level, this narrow hall didn't have its own guard. Probably because no priest or nun would dare risk their career like this. A layman or woman would probably be risking charges of heresy.

There *was*, however, a lock on the door.

She considered her options. She never wore hairpins; they pinched and pulled and it always felt like someone was raking their nails over her head.

The lock was quite large. Clunky. Maybe she didn't need something as delicate as a hairpin.

A quick dig at her pockets produced a pen and a pencil. She knelt and peeked through the keyhole. Through the bookshelves, she could barely make out a priest with his nose in a book. She could also see the mechanisms within the lock.

After a bit of tricky maneuvering, she heard the deafening click of it unlocking.

She peeked through the keyhole again. The priest turned a page.

She opened the door and slipped inside, pressing herself against the wall. There were fewer shelves, a couple more tables, and three priests. They sat at the same table, all reading, one of them writing notes. Small windows cast sunlight into the room, letting them work without the use of candles.

None of the priests looked up. Olivia silently moved along the wall, trying to find the right shelf. Everything was organized by subject, then author. She passed the *Ms, Ls, Js, Fs* . . .

A book closed like a gunshot. One of the priests stood.

Olivia ducked behind a shelf as he came down the aisle. He brushed his finger against the spines of all the books he passed. *Thwump-thwump-thwump-thwump.*

He stopped a meter away from her, putting the book back. Olivia dropped to a crouch and half crawled, half walked back to the end of the previous shelf, pressing herself against the smooth blue wood.

The priest searched the shelves before he continued walking closer to her. Olivia ducked around the bookshelf so the books hid her as he turned the corner, biting her lip.

He turned into the aisle next to her, running his eyes and fingers over more book spines. They were less than a meter apart, nothing but paper between them. Olivia wanted to move to a farther aisle but feared the movement would draw his attention.

The book spines dug into her back. She held her breath, hoping he didn't come her way.

The priest pulled a book from the shelf and flipped through a few pages. After a long moment, he went back to the table.

Olivia let out a long, silent breath, sagging against the shelf. She kept close to the wall as she moved forward, down three more aisles before finding the right one. Father Anjali's book was a skinny thing, too tall to cram into a pocket. She stuffed it down the front of her shirt and snuck back down the stairs.

"You didn't," Evelyn gasped.

Olivia grimaced. She had hoped to keep the book hidden so that Evelyn wouldn't have to lie or otherwise risk herself. But after leaving the Vaults, Evelyn had tripped. Olivia caught her but dropped the book she'd hidden under her shirt. Evelyn saw the title.

"Liv, that was the *third floor*. You could land on the posts for that," she hissed.

Olivia shrugged.

Evelyn groaned, dropping her face in her hands. "I'd ask why we just stole from the most revered building on the planet, but honestly the less I know, the better. You're on your own returning that."

Olivia returned the book to her shirt, and they walked home in silence.

Ormus had her clear her mess on the kitchen table, which she did, and then she went to her room and locked the door.

The book was just shy of seventy pages. Olivia read it in under an hour, her heart stopping near the end:

While any farmer can tell you that an animal is capable of learn-
ing—provided a good trainer—this is something else. The behav-
ior displayed by demons mirrors that of humans in many ways.
Predators may be naturally stealthy to sneak up on their prey,
but no creature with merely animal intelligence can set large-scale
traps for their prey the way humans do to demons and, I believe,
vice versa. The testimonies of surviving soldiers I've quoted in this
essay allude to demons luring *humans into the woods, drawing*
our soldiers deeper and deeper so they lose every possible advan-
tage. This is not typical animal behavior, as most predators will
attack any intruder as soon as they are sniffing their borders. This
shows the very real possibility of demons implementing strategy
and tactics, beyond the means of simple animal intelligence . . .

Olivia dropped the book. Her entire body trembled, and she shoved her face into her pillow because it felt like she was going to scream.

She laughed. Big-bellied laughs that could have been heard from the moons if she hadn't muffled herself in time.

When she finally got herself under control, she looked out the window. The sun was setting, the planet's rings gold against the reddening sky. One moon was a crescent, a sliver of silver-gray in the pink sky. The other was half-full and half-hidden behind the swoop of the planet's rings.

If the Faith and Governor Thompson were hiding the mere possibility of higher intelligence in demons from the people, what else was hidden in those Vaults? She was half-tempted to sneak back in, but she'd used up all of her luck just getting this much. Anything else could end up in a variety of bad ways: her kicked out of the house, Ormus stripped of his rank, Evelyn and Asiya blacklisted . . .

And for what? What could possibly be worth all of this? Why was Citadel so hell bent on destroying the demons? And if Olivia and the now-long-dead priest were right and demons *were* intelligent, then why did the demons continue to attack them, even the noncombatants like hunters and gatherers?

Olivia looked beyond the walls of Citadel, to the forest. The orange leaves gradually turned the color of blood in the fading sunlight.

Why did Elias have to die?

There was only one way to find out.

Dear Elias,

You'd probably call me an idiot for doing this. Or insane. But with a lot more swearing. God's Faces, you really could swear, especially when you were scared. But I don't care. I need to do this. I need to know why you died. And the wishes of the dead matter little against the needs of the living.

Does that make me a bad person? A bad girlfriend? Ignoring what would be your arguments and desires to pursue what I want?

Love,
Olivia

CHAPTER TWELVE

"You're distracted," Peterson said, pinning Olivia to the ground of the sparring ring. "Something I need to know about?"

She dropped her forehead to the dirt and groaned. Every week for the last several years, the two would meet at the yard behind the barracks, turned barren after four hundred years of young men's boots and bodies dragging against it. It had started as basic self-defense lessons and evolved into something Olivia truly enjoyed, and only partly because it let her spend time with her uncle. A few soldiers who passed stopped to watch them grapple each other, or shout a quick "hello" to Sergeant Peterson, but by now, everybody knew not to interrupt. And the ring's location behind the barracks sheltered them from most gawkers, though not from the elements. The air still nipped at them, and it was a good thing it wasn't raining, because that turned the ground to slush.

It was actually how she'd met Elias. Sometimes Peterson conscripted his privates if he wanted to do a two-on-one scenario, and Elias had needed extra combat training. A *lot* of extra training. He hadn't cared that he learned best from a woman and the town "freak." After he'd passed basic training, he'd offered to teach Olivia how to use a bow.

"I promise, I'm a *lot* better with archery than hand-to-hand," he'd said with a toothy smile. "This way, I can teach *you* something."

These days, Olivia could sometimes win a spar with Sergeant Peterson. He had been in the military for decades and had experience in every branch: hunt, wall guard, city police, and now training. Even when she didn't win, she could make him work for it.

Today, he'd won the last three rounds without breaking a sweat.

He rolled off her and brushed the dirt from his workout clothes: military-issue gray shirt and pants. "Come on. Get your sketchbook and tell me what's going on."

Rubbing the spot on her wrist where he'd twisted her arm behind her back, Olivia slowly approached her bag. She wasn't great at predicting people's responses, but she had a pretty good idea of how Peterson would react if she wrote, *I'm planning on running off into the forest to talk to demons, which I believe may have higher intelligence—possibly even a moral code. How do I know this? Because I broke into the Vaults.*

That . . . probably wouldn't go over well.

But she hated lying to Uncle Peterson. He was her godfather, the man she had thought *was* her father until she was six. After Sarai's death, he'd spent a week arguing with Ormus—then a lieutenant, but still outranking him—and a judge over custody of Olivia. And she had run away from the Claudes over a dozen times, most of them in her first year living with them. She usually found her way to Peterson's house. He always gave her a cup of tea, a plate of food, and a place to spend the night, then walked her back the next morning. Whenever he heard about something setting off a breakdown, he gave something to the Claudes to help prevent them: a stack of wooden flatware that wouldn't cause the god-awful scraping sound that iron silverware did, heavy blankets that felt like a warm hug, a new set of ear covers after the old ones broke and Ormus refused to get new ones because "she needs to learn to function without crutches."

To which Peterson had replied, "Crutches don't limit people with broken legs, sir. They let them walk."

So lying to Peterson, hiding things from him, always left a bad taste in Olivia's mouth. But if she told him about her plans to go into the forest—alone, because the last time Franklin and the military had been with her, they'd shot at the demons before she could get any more data—he'd try to stop her.

She compromised by writing *Elias*.

"Ah," Peterson said. "You've been thinking about him a lot?"

She nodded.

He gave her a gentle hug. "Do you want some advice on it?"

She nodded again.

"Sometimes, it helps to focus on the good things the dead have left behind," he said. "My son, Jason, was excellent at building repairs. He'd fix up leaky rooftops and broken doors all around town for extra money, and every time I pass by those houses, I can see his handiwork. It makes me glad to see the good impact he's had on people, to know that they're living a little better for having known him."

Olivia considered that. Elias had been an excellent wood-worker. He had wanted to open his own shop after his mandatory two years of service and an apprenticeship but had hesitated because it didn't guarantee a steady income. In addition to her bow and arrows, he had constantly made little wooden toys that he kept in his pockets to give to children, and home decorations to give as presents for his friends. Riley had gotten a whole collection of stat-uettes of his favorite aspects of the Hundred-Faced God for his birthday . . .

Oh shit!

Olivia pulled out of the hug and scrambled for her book.

"Problem?" Peterson asked.

Riley's b-day, she wrote.

"It's not for another couple of weeks. You have time to get him a gift."

No, she didn't. She intended to be in the forest by then. And since she had no idea when she'd be coming back, she needed to get him his present *now*.

Peterson sighed. "All right, go on. We'll pick this up again next week. You let me know if you need anything, all right?"

Olivia nodded, cramming her book into her bag and leaving. At the wooden fence marking the border of the barracks' training grounds, she stopped. She went back to Peterson to kiss him on the scratchy, grizzled cheek before leaving again.

The Vaults had a choke hold on any and all information related to Scripture, Artifacts, and demons. But every other book could legally be bought and sold anywhere else. Mr. Franklin usually published his findings in a bookstore—John's Books—down the street from his lab.

John's Books was a tiny shop on the very edge of the market square, no more than a single room and a broom closet. It had been in business for a solid eighty-seven years. Olivia came through the door and was immediately wrapped in the smell of paper, leather, and ink.

"Ms. Hall," cheered the elderly shopkeeper, John (not to be confused with his grandfather and the founder of the store, also named John). "Always a pleasure to see you. Come for more sketchbooks already?"

They were the only two here, and John had always been patient with her. So she took her time writing out her request and giving it to him: *Riley's 18th b-day. He's interested in medicine. Need gift(s).*

If John had any qualms about a man being interested in healing, he didn't show it. Instead he gave her a toothless grin and said, "I can definitely help you. Come with me."

They passed the shelves on astronomy, natural science, and physics, straight to anatomy, physiology, and medicine. He pointed out several texts that were good for beginners, landmark discoveries done by great scientists and medics of the past, and a very thick tome with illustrated details on every aspect of the human body, from the skin to the bones.

Olivia knew he was setting her up for a large sale, but she could never resist big, pretty books. And it was for Riley. After putting up with her for so many years, he deserved a special treat.

She purchased the anatomy tome, along with a notebook and set of pens, as every student should have.

She also got a book on herbology and the medicinal uses of plants. Everyone should know that, not just medics.

And a sketchbook for herself. To save a trip for later.

She *almost* got one on the history of a measles outbreak in the year 217 and how it was ultimately solved and mostly cured, but even she had to admit that her pile of purchases was getting a little ridiculous.

John tallied up the total and Olivia wrote a check. There was no physical currency in Citadel. Half of the economy was an unofficial barter system, or "women's currency," since they were the ones doing most of it. Had Olivia been a homemaker like Asiya, she might have paid in handmade clothing, or an offer to repair any leaks in the roof if she were married to a handyman, or food if she were a farmer.

The other half of the economy was run by the bank, which ran on banknotes and was backed by wheat. Needless to say, famines were bad for both Citadel's stomachs and economy. Everyone had an account at the bank, though many opted for an immediate payout of wheat as soon as the numbers were tallied. Others, like Olivia, preferred using checkbooks to make transactions, relying on the shaky faith that those numbers on a page would be good for a while yet.

She shoved her purchases in her bag, and even though she was carrying a considerably heavier load, she felt several pounds lighter as she started the walk back to the Claudes' house.

It was just late enough to no longer be considered midday, and the dirt streets were crowded. To avoid all the people brushing against her, Olivia took the back way, cutting through alleys and more rugged neighborhoods. There was the faint scent of something sour, but it beat getting jostled and bumped along in a crowd. Most beggars would be where the people were, at various populous market squares, so she didn't see many of those. She did see a couple of back-alley women, their heads uncovered and their necklines showing as much skin as they could handle in the chill. One of them made out with a paying customer against an alley wall, lifting her skirts as Olivia hurried by. Funny how Citadel outlawed that, yet every man who hired such a woman had served—or was currently serving—as city guard.

As she walked, she thought about her plan to leave for the forest.

Almost everything was in place; she just needed a few more items. She had snuck out of her house a few nights ago to leave the book she'd stolen from the Vaults by the door, making sure nobody saw her.

The real question was when, exactly, she should leave: High tide or low tide? High tide gave her the advantages of an easier exit and plenty of fresh water, but it hindered travel unless she stole a boat. Low tide allowed her to walk on the forest floor for the first week, but the guards would stop her when she left, since she clearly wasn't a hunter or gatherer. And she would have to start out carrying more water.

"Give me your bag!"

Olivia groaned. She'd gone down one of the narrower alleys, and now her path was blocked by a tall, skinny man in ragged clothing with a large knife pointed at her nose.

A quick glance at his stance confirmed that he'd gone through basic military training and probably the full mandatory two years of service. But his hair was beginning to silver, and there was hardly any meat on his bones. That training was likely decades ago. He must've been discharged and now couldn't find a proper job. A very common problem among veterans.

"I mean it!" he said, waving the knife. "Give me your bag. I don't want to hurt you."

The bag did hinder her movement. Too much weight pulling at her right shoulder. She set it down behind her and put up her fists.

"Don't say I didn't warn you," he said and charged.

For all his gusto, he lost in about two seconds. Olivia pivoted as he charged her, caught his wrist, and elbowed him in the face.

He went down.

Pathetic.

Olivia studied the blade. It was sharp, with a sturdy handle designed for outdoor use. After a quick check of her unconscious attacker, she found the sheath. She added it to her bag and resumed walking.

High tide it is, she thought, leaving the man in the alley.

The thing about running away from Citadel was that no one ever did it. There was nowhere for them to go. To the north were the Shadowlands, frozen wastes of perpetual darkness, thanks to the planet's rings blocking all sunlight. Supposedly humans had crash-landed there after losing their war against God and being turned from angels to mortals. East was the freshwater sea, where the tides came from. A few attempts had been made to search the ocean for more land, but they had all come up empty, even during low tide. The Flooded Forest stretched so far west and south that no human had ever gone far enough to learn what lay beyond.

She packed everything in a waterproof animal-skin bag (specifically the massive ingencis) used by hunters and soldiers. It also held several days' worth of food, a length of rope, some medical supplies, and a water canteen. At her belt was the mugger's knife hidden beneath her jacket, and at her back were her bow and quiver. She tied iron cleats to the bottoms of her shoes, having almost gagged when she'd had to write the check for their obscene price. And this time she had leather gloves. She left her present for Riley on her bed, along with a note:

Testing a theory in the forest. Estimated return date one month. Make sure Riley gets these.

—O

She'd probably get yelled at when she returned, even though there wasn't actually a rule against leaving Citadel. Ah well. Ormus yelled at her for a lot of things; he'd probably enjoy the month to rest his vocal cords.

The sun had set, and the lights in the neighbors' houses had gone out. By now, the Claudes should be in bed. Evelyn's bedroom door was closed. Asiya had used the washroom an hour ago before going to bed. There was no sound, no movement.

Olivia crept down the hall and got halfway down the stairs before she saw the light. She bit back a sigh. The study light was on, which meant Ormus was up. Curse the man's perpetual need to complete paperwork on time.

She had to pass the open door of his study to get to the front door. That wasn't going to happen.

Back up the stairs, Olivia went to her window.

Though it was two stories up with no ladder, the house was old, made of brick and wood. It took quite a bit of finger strength and a couple of splinters, but Olivia climbed halfway down and jumped the rest of the way. She shook out her hands, adjusted the straps of her bag, and walked to the wall.

The planet's rings glowed silver against the night sky, making the two moons seem gray in comparison. Demon howls echoed in the distance, just beyond the safety of the walls.

In an attempt to keep the levels of crime down, Ormus had suggested—and Governor Thompson had approved—a strict curfew. Guards patrolled every street, so Olivia kept to the shadows and back alleys, stopping at each intersection and moving only when she was certain the coast was clear. Most of the guards she passed either chatted with each other or chased sleeping homeless people off the streets. One loudly complained that all the shelters were full, the argument escalated into a fight, and the guard cuffed and dragged the man to jail.

The patrols died down a bit when she reached the Farmers' Ring, mostly replaced with privately hired guards to watch the crops. The land here was so flat she couldn't hide behind anything, but while a few of the private guards spotted her, they didn't approach. Just watched her with clubs in hand. Maybe it was her imagination, but it seemed that there were far more private guards out tonight than the last time she'd been out here two weeks ago.

She climbed up the wall's stairs, poking her head out to make sure no city guards were walking along this section yet. The high tide had come in a few days ago and reached its peak, the surface of the water about three meters below the top of the wall. When both moons were full, the surface of the water was much closer to the top. Last double-full moon it had also stormed, meaning several gallons had splashed over the edge, flooding the outermost streets and farms. That might explain the excess guards: the flooding had ruined some of those crops, meaning even less food was going to be harvested. They really needed that second city, or at least a second spot to plant crops.

Beyond the wall and reflective water, the Flooded Forest waited. The endless mass of trees swallowed all light, casting everything beneath the leaves in perpetual darkness. Like a creature with its maw open.

She found a rope ladder and unfurled it over the edge, wincing at the light splash the bottom made.

Nobody shouted or rushed over. They must have thought it was a fish.

She climbed down, slipped soundlessly into the cold water, and swam to the trees.

CHAPTER THIRTEEN:
ORMUS

Ormus banged on the door of the Thompson house, not stopping until it opened. Governor Augustus yawned, a thick robe hiding his sleep clothes. "Ormus? What's going on?"

"I need to talk to your son. Now!"

Forehead furrowed, Augustus let him in. Ormus should have probably apologized for the early hour, rudeness, inconvenience, and his own ruffled appearance (he was still in the plain pants and shirt he'd worn to bed, plus untied boots) but didn't bother. He ran up the stairs, heedless of the heavy weight in his arms. "Riley! I need to talk to you!"

The boy stumbled out of his bedroom, reddish-brown curls a tangled mess around his head. Honestly, could the boy never get a proper cut?

He rubbed his eyes. "Cap'n Claude? Wha's going on?"

"Olivia's gone. She left this for you." He shoved the books and note in Riley's hands.

"Did she go to Peterson's again?" he asked. His pale skin went almost deathly white as he read the note. "What is she doing in the forest?"

"Did she say anything to you? Any indication of where she's going?" Ormus demanded.

"No, sir. Nothing." He looked at the books. "She must have meant these as an early birthday present."

"Why did she give you medical books?" Augustus asked.

Ormus jumped, not having realized the other man had followed him so closely. He'd wondered the same thing, as everyone knew only women were medics. That was why he'd thought this was some sort of code or clue as to Olivia's true whereabouts.

Although, given the low, dangerous tone of Augustus's voice, he had a completely different concern.

Riley's eyes glanced around the hall, like he was a cornered animal looking for an escape. "It's just a personal interest. Don't worry, I already did a few tours of some law firms."

"She should've gotten you something useful."

"Dad, it's the crack of dawn. I'm not having this argument before breakfast. Captain Claude, do you want something to eat while we figure this out? Maybe she left a note in here?" He flipped through one of the books, as if Ormus hadn't already done that twice.

"No, that's quite all right. I need to go," Ormus said, swallowing his disappointment at the dead end.

Augustus put a hand on Ormus's shoulder. "Riley, go eat. I need to talk to the captain."

Riley stashed the books in his room and sped down the stairs. Augustus and Ormus stayed in the hall.

"I know this must be hard for you," Augustus said. "As . . . ah, *difficult* . . . as your daughter was, I know you loved her. But if she's in the forest . . .well, I don't want you to get your hopes up."

Ormus pulled his shoulder away. "It's been less than twelve hours. I'm sending search parties in every direction. They'll find her."

Please let them find her.

"Captain!"

Ormus paused just outside his home and had to blink because he almost didn't recognize Sergeant Peterson in civilian clothes, riding a man-drawn carriage. It must have been his day off, as he was wearing plain cotton pants and a shirt rather than his blues. Asiya was with him. The elder man jumped out of the carriage before it even stopped moving, leaving her to pay the fare.

"Your wife told me what happened," he said. "Did you try Riley?"

"I just came from there. He knows nothing."

Peterson cursed, then grimaced as Asiya joined them. "Pardon, ma'am."

"I've heard much worse," she assured him.

He straightened. "Sir, I ask that you assign me to one of your search parties."

"Done," Ormus said. Few soldiers had a better track record or more field experience than the sergeant. "You leave immediately."

Peterson saluted, nodded to Asiya, and ran off.

She hugged Ormus. He let himself sag into her arms for five deep breaths, letting himself feel the worry and the edges of panic. He pulled back with a straight face. "I better get to the office, make sure they don't bungle those search parties."

"Of course. I'll fix us something quick for breakfast."

"I'll eat at the office."

"That's a lie," she scolded. "You're not doing this on an empty stomach. Five minutes, Ormus."

They went in, Ormus literally bumping into Evelyn in the living room. Her arms were crossed so tightly he was half-afraid she'd break a rib. Like the rest of them, she was still in her sleep clothes; in her case, a pale nightgown, dark-brown curls free. "I have to tell you something."

"What is it?" he asked, tone gentle.

She winced. "Remember when Olivia went to the Vaults last week and I went after her and we spent the afternoon there together? She was there researching demons and wanted to go to the higher levels . . ."

Ormus's stomach dropped. "You didn't."

"I talked to the priest and convinced him to give us temporary access to the second floor. He said it was all right!" she said, holding up her hands. "But then I turned my back to talk to Sister Mira, and when we left the Vaults, Olivia had taken a book from the *third* floor, and . . . it was about demons too."

Ormus pinched the bridge of his nose, remembering the report he'd gotten of a potential break-in of the Vaults. A priest had found a classified document innocently sitting on the front step. Thompson had thought the Doves were involved, but since nothing else had been missing, the priests and nuns had thought perhaps one of them had taken the book with them only to have it fall out of their bag, and some thoughtful citizen had returned it. Ultimately it was dismissed.

Asiya covered her mouth with both hands. "Oh, Evelyn. Why didn't you tell us sooner?"

"I didn't want her to get in trouble again!" she cried. "You know how she is. I didn't think anything serious would happen. I didn't think she'd go into the Flooded Forest like this!"

"Continue to keep quiet about it," Ormus decided. "Breaking into the higher levels of the Vaults is a serious offense."

"I know. I'm sorry."

"We're going to get through this," he said. "No more secrets, no more crimes. We're going to find your sister, and everything will go back to normal."

CHAPTER FOURTEEN:
RILEY

Seven days passed with no sign of Olivia.

Riley sat at the kitchen table carved from blue wood, a copy of Scripture open in front of him. He usually read in the study, but no food or drinks were allowed there, and he'd grown hungry. He chewed and swallowed a cherry tart, not tasting it, eyes never leaving the book lit by candlelight.

It was the Book of Light, the first book of Scripture. The first several passages detailed humanity's fall from Heaven, turning from angels into mortals, but Riley ignored that. Instead, he focused on the passage describing the visions God had sent his namesake, Riley Bevill. How the Hundred-Faced God had given him the visions and knowledge needed to lead his people out of the Shadowlands and into the relative safety of the Flooded Forest. How God had kept him and his people safe in the wilderness. How, against all odds, they had survived an impossible situation.

Of course, this was after Riley Bevill had spent several cold, miserable days praying to the Hundred-Faced God, beseeching Their forgiveness and mercy. Riley didn't think Olivia had prayed a day in her life.

I'll just have to pray for her, he thought, turning the page.

"Riley? It's almost midnight."

He jumped at his mother's voice. Mia drifted into the kitchen like a wraith without her makeup and jewels, wearing a pretty pale-blue nightgown.

"I'll go to bed soon," he promised, finishing the last of his tart.

Mia hummed. She went straight for the cupboard in the corner, where her drinks were stored. It was more of a show than anything. Augustus had once tried to cut Mia off completely, a punishment for not being polite to one of his political allies a couple of years ago. It hadn't disrupted her drinking one whit. She had bottles stashed all over the house, in the yard, and probably in the nearby temples too.

Riley wasn't surprised until she poured two glasses instead of one. She slid the other across the wooden table, in front of him. "It'll help."

He studied the golden liquid. Sauvib cider, one of her favorites. He took a tiny sip. It was overwhelmingly bitter, with only a hint of the fruit's trademark salty-sweetness.

Mia took the chair next to him. They sat in silence for a long moment. This was new. Usually Mia took her vice somewhere private, pretending that none of them knew she was drunk when she came out to speak with them. Now she drained half of her glass an arm's length from Riley.

"Your father probably wouldn't mind if you decided to become a priest," she said. "He won't be *thrilled*. You'll get some grumbling. But he could always use more allies among the Faith."

She knows, Riley realized. His mother knew that he didn't want to be a lawyer or go anywhere near politics.

Being a priest would be fine. It'd certainly be more enjoyable than being a lawyer.

But it wouldn't offer any of that much-needed protection for the other Doves.

It wouldn't be like being a medic.

"That's not my Placement," he said dully, taking another tiny sip of cider. It went down a little easier.

Mia finished her glass and refilled it. "Your friend's sister, Evelyn. She's probably just as worried as you are."

The sudden change in conversation didn't throw Riley. Olivia often did the same thing, sharing random thoughts, then dropping them and picking up a different thread midconversation. It was like riding in a boat: sometimes you just let the water decide where to take you.

The change to *this* topic, however, made him pause. He huffed a weak smile. "Is this you trying to make me feel better?"

This was also new. Sad, but kind of adorable.

"You two could help each other," Mia said, studying the golden liquid in her glass. "Your father's idea of bringing you two together isn't the worst one."

"No, it's not. I just . . . I'm not ready. And when I am, I want it to be for more than just 'Dad told me to.'"

Mia gave him a flat look. "Drink."

"Why?" he demanded, no longer amused.

"It makes it bearable." She gripped his hand, her thin fingers surprisingly strong. "You don't want to go against your father. You'll lose. Accept it now. Drink. Try to enjoy the good parts."

She smiled then. That fake, doll-like smile that Riley had seen all his life.

"I hate seeing you drunk," he said. "You're not you."

The smile dropped. She took the bottle with her when she left.

Riley dropped his head on the Scripture, smooth pages kissing his forehead. He could count on one hand all the days he'd seen his mother sober, and most of them were old and blurry enough that he couldn't truly rely on them.

He could see why. Augustus ordered them around like puppets, used them like tools rather than treating them as people. It was easier to handle that with a bit of liquid courage. So what if it drained your soul a bit more every day?

He picked up the full glass of cider she'd left him and poured it down the drain.

Dear Elias,

I think you would hate me for this, but I love being out in the forest. I shouldn't, right? I shouldn't do a lot of things, but preferring to be in the place where my lover was killed is probably one of the big ones.

It's just so much easier. Yes, it's hard. I have to forage for food and keep an eye out for predators and hope the demons don't tear me apart. But there are no people to disappoint or invisible social rules I don't know. Maybe it's just because I've always been so miserable in Citadel, but the forest, for all its dangers, has always been a safe place for me.

Sometimes, when I'm walking, I'll wonder if I'll chance upon where you died. Maybe find your body. I know that's impossible. The tides would have swept you away within a week. But the thought is there. You're there. You're a ghost that won't leave me be. Aestus starts tomorrow, and I remember how you would sneak snacks into all of your pockets—and my purse!—when everyone else was fasting, and you'd bribe me with them so I wouldn't tell. (I wouldn't have told anyone anyway. You know that, right?) I had to sew up a hole in my shirt yesterday, and all I could think of is how horrible you were at it. Give you a bit of wood to whittle and you'd make a masterpiece in an hour. Ask you to do some very basic sewing that everyone else mastered by the time they were eight, and you'd prick your finger a dozen times and swear every time.

There's a demon howling right now. I wonder if that's the one that killed you.

Love,
Olivia

CHAPTER FIFTEEN

Olivia tore off a piece of metabread and ate, listening to birds twitter and watching the clouds drift overhead. After she and Elias had been dating for a couple of months, they would lie on the roof of her house or a quiet patch of farmland and watch the sky. If it was daytime, Elias would describe what he saw in the clouds while she tried to draw it in her sketchbook: mystical serpents and wolves and doves. At night, Olivia would tell him about the constellations. She'd had a brief infatuation with astronomy when she was fourteen, so she'd read everything she could get her hands on and, years later, told Elias. They would make up ridiculous stories about the Demon Tail, the Great Archer, the Celestial Carriage, and all the others.

Now, she sat on one of the branches of the Flooded Forest. The water stretched beneath her, reflecting the shadows and orange leaves above. The surface was so close that if she dangled one of her legs over the side of the branch, she could dip her toes in. A gap in the trees over her head provided her with a clear view of the sky, a cheerful bright blue. She'd been walking for hours and had kept going long after the sun rose to get herself a head start before stopping to eat.

She considered setting up camp here, then decided against it. She didn't think anyone would bother coming after her to retrieve the "town freak," but it was safer to put as much distance between herself and Citadel as possible before letting her guard down. She finished her meal and kept going, traveling from tree to tree until sundown.

The tent she set up on a thick branch was tiny, not even big enough for Olivia to stretch out. She had to bend her knees at least ninety degrees and keep her arms close to her chest. Part of it was to limit the amount of animal skin needed to make a tent, and the other part was to force the body to curl up and conserve heat. Add a blanket, position the camp so the body of the tree blocked the wind completely, and it was downright cozy, if a little cramped.

She kept to a strict schedule: wake up at dawn, take down the tent, tend to her hair, eat a bit of breakfast, walk for six hours, eat lunch, walk another six hours (possibly with a snack break), set up camp, eat dinner, sketch, go to sleep. If at any point she saw a potential meal like wild berries, snails, or birds to hunt, she would pursue it. As she was essentially going in blind, following the sound of howls, there wasn't much of a specific direction she had to go, except perhaps toward the general area where she'd encountered the freckled demon. The water gradually receded throughout the week, slowly revealing more and more of the forest floor until it was dry enough to walk on the ground.

With it being midsummer, it was warm and temperate, a slight chill in the breeze the only thing encouraging people to wear long sleeves. But that was in Citadel. With almost every inch of the forest shaded, it was a few degrees chillier. Olivia was glad she'd brought gloves and extra layers.

Life in the forest was brutal in its simplicity. For all of her preparation and training, she knew she was running on a lot of luck. She had to find the friendly demon before something else found her.

On the seventh morning, she rolled up her tent, which she'd set up at the base of a tree. The first three days, when she'd traveled by branch, she'd had access to the fruits that grew up there. But while walking on the ground was safer when it was dry, she didn't have easy access to that food. She'd considered staying in the branches all the time, but even if she didn't factor in the risk of taking a wrong step and plummeting to her death—or at least painful injury—it was slower and more difficult than just walking on the ground.

She was just about to open a jar of preserved sauvibs—a salty-sweet fruit that was one of her favorite foods—when she felt a prickle on the back of her neck.

Instincts keep you alive, Peterson had told her once. *If you get the sense that something's wrong, then chances are, something's wrong. Don't argue with it. Just get out.*

She set the jar in her bag and picked up her bow.

She slowly scanned the area, looking for anything amiss. Nothing but open space and massive tree trunks. Insects buzzed near her ear. Birds chirped, hidden in the leaves. Somewhere in the distance, a demon howled.

Olivia looked up.

With a startled shriek, she dove out of the way of the charging demon that had tried to drop on her like an avenging angel. It snarled when it missed. Olivia hit the ground shoulder first, rolling with the movement and jumping back on her feet.

It wasn't the freckled demon. This one was much larger, and older given the specks of white around its muzzle. Its fur was slate gray and its wings were tipped with black. It was such a simple, beautiful gray-scaled design that Olivia's fingers itched for her sketchbook.

The demon spread its wings and growled, stepping closer.

Wait a minute, she thought. *This is perfect!*

Olivia dropped her bow.

The demon paused, regarding her with narrowed eyes.

Hm. She really hadn't thought this through.

She looked to her pack, next to her sleeping roll. Her sketchbook was in there.

She took a step.

The demon lunged.

Olivia jumped out of the way, hitting the dirt hard. The demon pivoted, wings spread for balance as it turned on her, teeth bared, primed to rip and rend her flesh.

Olivia pulled the knife from her sheath and threw it.

The blade hit the demon's front leg. It didn't sink into the flesh, but it was enough to get the demon to yowl and skitter back, enough time for Olivia to grab her bow.

The demon shot into the air, broke through the leaves, and was gone.

It makes sense, Olivia thought grumpily, double-checking to make sure everything was packed away.

Of all the humans in Citadel, she was the minority who wanted to talk to demons. It made sense that the demons had a similar mix of attitudes. Besides, every time humans came this deep into the forest, it was with the express intention of murdering them. Why *wouldn't* they attack first?

Despite her understanding, there was a heavy feeling in her chest, like her diaphragm had been replaced with stones. She'd thought—hoped—that with the freckled and black demons' attitude, finding them or another demon willing to talk to her would be easy.

Olivia hoisted her bag onto her back. Yesterday and today were the lowest point in the tides. The water would begin trickling back in sometime tomorrow, gradually filling the eastern areas and lowlands with water over the course of days, forcing her back into the trees. She could turn around now, before anything else—another demon or a different type of predator—ran into her.

Or she could go deeper into the forest and hope that the next demon she met gave her a chance to ask her questions.

Elias used to say that she never knew how to quit. Olivia's mouth twitched toward a smile as she kept going.

CHAPTER SIXTEEN

After setting up her tent high in the branches and catching two small ruzina—red fish with tentacles in their mouths for catching prey in the trees—Olivia tried to sketch. She'd found and plucked a new type of flower. But every time she tried to capture its thorny, pink petals, it turned into Riley reading. Or Elias laughing. Or Uncle Peterson sharpening his arrows. Or Evelyn modeling a new scarf.

She leaned against the tree with a sigh, watching the ruzina cook over the open fire. Starting a fire in a tree was risky and a bit difficult but doable. The trick was preparation. Olivia had filled one of her bags with dirt during low tide last week and used it to cover part of the branch after dousing the wood with water. Then she made the fire on the dirt and kept it small to limit the amount of sparks that could land on the wood. She'd carefully chosen her fuel so it wouldn't cause as much smoke. The demons might see it, but since she was actively trying to find them, she considered that a bonus.

It was much preferable to have a fire on the *ground*, but that wasn't an option right now. The water was at its highest tide again, meaning it had been two weeks—twelve days—since she had left Citadel. She was almost completely out of the food she'd brought, having to rely more and more on what she caught and found. And while she was good enough at hunting and fishing—thanks again to Peterson's training—more than once she'd gone to bed with an empty stomach.

But more than that, she . . . missed home. Not Citadel, but her friends. It was like the ache she had for Elias and Sarai, but for people who were still alive. Riley, Peterson, Evelyn, Asiya—God's Faces, she was even starting to miss *Ormus*. She wasn't used to being alone for so long, and she found herself longing for the days when she would spar with Peterson, or walk with Riley, or even sit in the Claudes' living room, listening to the others talk as she sketched or studied.

It was so tempting to turn around and go back home. Declare the experiment a failure. Try again later. But she couldn't do that. It had taken her months to be able to look at her old sketches of Elias without crying. Even after all this time, every time she thought of him, she felt like she was breathing through a hurricane of glass. She couldn't go back to Citadel without knowing *why*.

She turned the sizzling ruzina. It looked like they were almost done. If only she had some spices to add . . .

The ruzina moved.

She frowned. Was she just imagining things, or . . .

No, now the stick spearing both fish through floated in the air.

With a cry, Olivia grabbed it, just before whatever force was levitating it tried to yank it into the darkness. It tugged on Olivia, but apparently she was too heavy. She pulled the fish free from its grasp, tossing it to the tree branch and stepping on the stick. She grabbed her bow, having an arrow nocked and aimed in less than two seconds.

Something growled at her from the shadows.

She aimed in its general direction, straight ahead of her, but couldn't see anything in the dark.

The water lapped against the trees. Bugs buzzed near Olivia's skin. A bird flew.

It growled again. This time much closer, and to Olivia's right. She whipped around, trying to find something to aim at. Damn, the thing was *quiet* when it moved.

After another beat, it came into the light.

Olivia blinked. This wasn't the freckled demon, but probably around his age: adolescent. Female. Her fur was dusky white, with one pale-blue ear, and dark wings that were just a shade too dark to be sapphire.

She was also much skinnier than the others Olivia had seen. Her ribs pressed against her fur.

She snarled, showing her yellowed teeth, but now Olivia could think.

The other demon had gone after *her*. This one went after her food.

This one also clearly demonstrated being able to use demon magic, but wasn't using it to attack her.

Maybe she just wanted to eat.

Slowly, Olivia lowered her bow.

The demon stopped snarling at her and looked pointedly at the ruzina, still pinned to the branch by her foot.

Olivia couldn't talk, couldn't ask her any questions. But that didn't mean she couldn't communicate.

She took the stick of ruzina and removed one of the fish, holding it out.

It flew from her fingers and into the demon's mouth. In two bites, it was gone.

The she-demon licked her chops, then looked expectantly at the second ruzina.

Olivia shook her head, holding it closer to her chest. She needed to eat, too.

The she-demon made a noise like a huff.

The ruzina and stick were yanked from Olivia's fingers. She yelled, but the she-demon was too quick, snatching the fish in her jaws and then diving into the inky sky.

Bitch, Olivia thought, dropping onto her sleeping roll. She had one small jar of preserved berries and a handful of nugzuuki jerky. Her stomach gave a pointed rumble, reminding her that she hadn't eaten since breakfast. She could eat the nugzuuki for dinner and save the rest for tomorrow . . .

The blue-eared she-demon dropped back on her camp, so silent and sudden that Olivia had to strangle a scream before it could escape.

Floating around the demon's head were five sauvibs.

It was hard to tell in the firelight, but two of the fist-sized fruit looked a little too yellow from being underripe. Olivia didn't care. She almost cried.

The she-demon floated the sauvibs to Olivia's lap. She immediately grabbed one and took a big bite, moaning at the sweet-salty taste exploding on her tongue.

The blue-eared demon wagged her tail once. As silently as she came, she vanished.

CHAPTER SEVENTEEN:
ORMUS

Two weeks.

Two weeks had gone by, and not a word from Olivia.

Ormus had sent as many search parties as he could, with strict orders to detain her without injury. But with the tides lowering and revealing the ground, they hadn't been able to use the boats, losing their advantage of speed and distance. No one had seen her since.

It had been bad enough when Olivia jumped ship—*again*—during their last expedition, swinging from branch to branch and wandering out of sight of the others. She'd all but vanished for a few minutes, and Ormus had been convinced that a demon or some other creature had found her and killed her. That he'd failed to protect her. But then she'd been fine, coming back with an entire bouquet of green flowers.

He could only hope that she'd return to him again, no worse for wear.

The people of Citadel had been gentler to the Claudes, but not overly sympathetic. Ormus wasn't sure if it was because Olivia wasn't confirmed dead, or because death and misery were simply a part of the town. Everyone had lost at least one person to the forest, usually more. Time didn't stop for it. You moved on.

He didn't want to think about an equally likely possibility: that

Olivia simply wasn't liked in Citadel. That while no one was necessarily glad to see her go, only a select few were truly worried about her.

The Thompsons had extended an invitation to a late-night dinner, which Ormus accepted. They had to host it after sundown, as the monthlong holiday of Aestus had just begun. A quiet, reflective time to pray and conserve resources. No food was eaten or water drunk during daylight hours. It was one of the few religious holidays that Olivia observed without issue, because it actively preserved their resources, and Ormus was not going to think about that right now.

Asiya was unable to come, thanks to a hospital shift. She'd had to take more and more of those lately. More people starving meant they were more likely to succumb to illness, to say nothing of the increase in hunting and gathering accidents as people grew more desperate to bring in food.

Ormus explained this to their hosts with an apologetic smile. Augustus waved it away as he took their coats. "She's doing her duty to the town, as we all must do. Miss Claude, you're looking radiant."

"Thank you," Evelyn replied primly. She wore one of her best dresses and headscarves, the pastel-pink wrap complimenting her dark skin. The latest fashion among girls and women these days was apparently adding a belt to the waist, offering something of an hourglass silhouette. Many priests and conservatives disapproved, since it hinted at temptation, but Ormus and Asiya saw no harm in it. Evelyn's patterned cloth belt was also pink, vibrant against her black dress, and she'd added the subtlest hint of makeup.

Ormus had just put on his dress blues and called it a day.

After the initial panic of her sister's disappearance, Evelyn had pulled herself together and been a pillar of strength, just like her mother. Ormus wasn't normally a praying man, but he thanked the Hundred-Faced God for them both. Without them, he would have fallen apart days ago.

"We're just setting up the table," Augustus said, gesturing for them to follow him. Something sizzled in the kitchen as they passed, and Ormus caught a whiff of roasting pork loin.

In the dining room, Riley finished putting down the plates and silverware while his mother, Mia, drank a glass of wine. She, unlike Evelyn, wore something more conservative, more billowy, and covering more skin. She still wore far more makeup and jewelry: a golden necklace, jeweled rings, and bangles. All passed down from the Founders, kept in the Thompson family for generations. She was similar to Augustus that way, who never missed an opportunity to show his inherited wealth.

Meanwhile their son wore a black, long-sleeved shirt and his usual Hundred-Faced God wooden amulet. The family was two violent splashes of color and gold next to a plain black canvas.

Mia smiled as they came in. "Captain. Evelyn, you're looking beautiful."

"New dress," she said, now looking just a tiny bit uncomfortable. "Hey, Riley."

"Ev," he replied, somewhat stiffly.

Out of the corner of his eye, Ormus saw Augustus frown at his son. Riley caught the look and cleared his throat. "How are you handling everything?"

She shrugged. "I'm not too worried. Olivia's too stubborn to die."

That pulled a genuine chuckle from the boy. Evelyn took her seat, looking quite pleased with herself.

A hired cook brought their meal into the dining room. Several wealthy families hired help to assist in their household. Part of it was old-fashioned class pride: *Look at us. We don't have to do menial labor. We can just pay someone else to do it.* But Ormus liked to think he was helping with Citadel's struggling economy by hiring help, at least in a small way. The cleaner, gardener, and—when Evelyn was little—babysitter he hired were all paid as generously as he and Asiya could spare, so that they could make their own purchases and keep the money circulating.

But they'd never hired a cook. The one time he'd floated the idea to Asiya, she'd shot it down. "Some people stretch their bodies to relax. Others pray. I cook," she'd explained. "Don't take that away from me."

They took their seats as the dishes were brought out: roasted pork loin garnished with a cherry sauce, carrots and peas cooked with garlic, and mashed potatoes half-buried under spices and ingencis oil. Their hunters had been lucky enough to catch one of the massive beasts and drag its corpse back to town, which *everyone* celebrated because it alleviated some of the food shortage. At least for a few days.

"Shall we say grace?" Augustus asked. Barely waiting for everyone to lower their heads, he began, "Hundred-Faced God, we thank You for Your great bounty and ask for Your help in serving You in whatever way we can. Give us the wisdom to see the path You've laid before us, and the strength to follow it. Amen."

Ormus watched Augustus and Riley both during the prayer, noticing how Augustus gave a side-eyed glare to his son. Riley kept his eyes on his empty plate.

Curious.

They loaded their plates, and the conversation drifted to safe topics. The sound of scraping cutlery startled Ormus. He was so used to using wooden utensils that he'd almost forgotten the sound of iron. He didn't mind, but it wasn't entirely pleasant, either. No wonder this was one of Olivia's breakdown triggers. Evelyn was prodded about school, Riley about his exit exam scores and future job prospects. Augustus and Ormus commiserated about the growing amount of paperwork on their desks. Mia went through two glasses of wine while explaining some of the work they were doing for Riley's eighteenth birthday.

At the mention of the upcoming date, Augustus put down his silverware. "That's something we wanted to talk to you about. Especially you, Evelyn."

Her forehead wrinkled. "Me?"

Augustus smiled. "As you know, Riley is physically unfit for military service. The good news is that this will let him jump right into whatever lucrative career he chooses. Law, most likely."

Riley stiffened but didn't interrupt his father.

"And of course, a man of his own household will find himself in need of a wife."

Ormus's heart soared. He'd been the first to suggest this idea to Augustus years ago, when Olivia was first put under his care. Who better to provide for his daughter than the son of the governor? Augustus had shot it down but said they could revisit the idea later when Evelyn was of age.

His good mood vanished as soon as he saw Evelyn's frown.

Riley noticed it, too, and said, "I think this is something Evelyn and I should discuss first, Dad."

Augustus waved him away. "It's a family decision, as you know. And how could you possibly do better than this little angel, hmm?"

Ormus was just opening his mouth to agree with Riley—*that's a great suggestion that Evelyn and I need to discuss with her mother*—when Evelyn beat him to it: "Thank you anyway, Mr. Thompson, but I'm going to be a nun."

A beat of silence as everyone absorbed the words.

Augustus laughed. "No need to rush to the nunnery, my dear! Women don't do that until they're widows."

"Those women never make it beyond the second tier of the Vaults," she replied. "I want to work on Artifacts, and I can only do that if I'm a matron, which takes ten years. So if I join the convent after my education's done, I'll be a matron when I'm twenty-eight. That gives me the *whole* rest of my life to study and re-create Artifacts! Plus astronomy, engineering, mathematics . . ."

This wasn't the first time she'd expressed an interest in Artifacts, or science in general. But it *was* the first time Ormus had heard her lay out a plan to achieve that goal in a step-by-step process.

"That sounds amazing," Riley cut in, giving a real, genuine smile for the first time tonight.

"It sounds like a waste," Augustus grumbled.

"Don't you want children?" Mia asked.

"No," Evelyn said.

She gave no further explanation. Ormus resisted the urge to turn his head to the ceiling and beseech God as to why *both* of his daughters had to be so difficult.

"Then we *definitely* shouldn't get married," Riley laughed. "Because I want several. Three at least, plus grandbabies."

"Ask Olivia. She's always wanted children," Evelyn said, the smirk on her face saying she was half-kidding.

"Not in this lifetime," Augustus snapped.

Ormus cleared his throat. He might have lost control of the conversation a while ago, but he was *not* going to stand by and let a member of his family be insulted, governor or no.

Augustus calmed and smiled. "No offense, Ormus, but your eldest inherited some . . . problematic blood from her mother. I wouldn't want my grandchildren to be subjected to the same issues."

"The biggest problem with Olivia is that she's still grieving her dead lover," Ormus replied frostily.

"Yeah," Evelyn added. "And your grandchildren would be *lucky* to have half as much of a spine as her."

There was a long, awkward pause as they all tried to stare each other down. Mia downed the rest of her wine and said, "Dessert?"

Though Ormus desperately wanted to leave the Thompsons after the extremely awkward dinner conversation, that would be the height of rudeness. They stayed through dessert. Then Ormus unfortunately *very much* had to use the restroom.

As he finished washing his hands, he overhead hissed whispers. Curiosity had always been a fault of his, so he pressed himself against the closed door to hear—

". . . hell do you think you were *doing*?" That was Augustus.

"I told you, I don't have any interest in Evelyn," Riley replied. "And she clearly doesn't have any interest in me."

"That doesn't matter. You'll be lucky to make it to your thirties. The least you could do before dying is give your mother and me some grandchildren."

"And I will. With the right woman."

"The right woman is the one I choose for you."

"It's *my* life. I should get a say in it."

"You get a say when you've earned it."

There was a pause, long enough that Ormus thought that he should stop acting like a teenager and open the damn door already, until Augustus spoke again, "We're getting you married within a year, after you've started your career in law."

"We do have a shortage of medics—"

"I will not have my boy sully the family name by acting as a woman," Augustus snapped. "Law, then marriage, then you continue our line. Or I remove you from this family like I should've done when you were born."

Carpeted footsteps faded away, eventually followed by a quieter set.

Schooling his expression, Ormus finally emerged from the bathroom. He could see where Augustus was coming from: lawyers earned more than medics, and medicine was a woman's job, anyway. The right marriage ensured both economic safety and healthy heirs. And it was humanity's sacred duty to reproduce, as well as push the demons out of the forest.

But the man went too far.

It's an empty threat, he told himself. *Riley's all he has. He's not going to kick him out. He certainly won't* discard him *at this age.*

Mia chatted with Evelyn as the girl put on her coat and boots, the woman's words only slightly slurred by drink. Augustus put on a pleasant smile as he shook Ormus's hand. Riley echoed it, but Ormus could tell his heart wasn't in it.

He and Evelyn didn't hire a carriage, despite the fact that the sun had gone down over two hours ago and the streets were lit by torches. Their house was only a couple of blocks away, and he wanted the extra time to talk to her.

"So," he began. "A nun?"

Evelyn's spine stiffened. "I love astronomy, technology, and Artifacts. And devoting myself to the Hundred-Faced God is very honorable."

"No one said it isn't," Ormus said, holding up a hand. "But breaking the vow of celibacy *is* shameful."

"Good thing I don't want to get married, then."

"Oh, Evelyn. You're young. You don't know what you want."

"I know what I *don't* want," she snapped. "I've tried, Dad! Everyone says that getting married and having children is the best thing that can happen to a person, to a woman. But every time I think of that happening to me, I don't feel happy or excited. I feel . . . trapped."

"You're nervous. I was, too, when I found out I was going to be a father." He hesitated, then decided to continue, "Even though I did propose to her, I was relieved when Sarai turned me down and decided to raise Olivia on her own. I thought, 'I'll just send her some of my pay so they're provided for, and she can do all the heavy lifting.' But then Olivia was born, and you soon after, and I realized I wanted both of my children with me. That I could never give up either of you. And for all the difficulties that come with being a parent, it's also one of life's greatest blessings."

Back then, the sudden surge of protectiveness had shocked even *him*. He'd buried his feelings for Sarai after her rejection and at that time hadn't developed anything more than lukewarm compassion for Asiya. But as soon as Evelyn had been born, as soon as he'd seen Olivia toddle along the city streets, he'd wanted them both under his roof, under his care. He hadn't wanted to miss a minute of their lives.

"I'm not saying that having a family is bad," Evelyn said after a brief pause. "I'm saying it's not for *me*. Everyone else my age has had crushes or been in love or had sex or *wanted* all of that. I don't. Even when I was little and all my friends talked about getting married and played 'house,' that was never what I wanted. I want to create and explore! And children . . ." She grimaced. "They'd get in the way. I'd love them, but I'd also hate them for that. That's not a good way to grow up."

Ormus sighed as they reached their house. "You're just a late bloomer. At least wait until you're an adult before you make a decision."

"I've made it," she growled, running to her room before even taking off her boots.

He pinched the bridge of his nose. Asiya wasn't home yet, which was a shame because he would have loved to talk to her about all of this. He stumbled in the dark to light their candles and lamps.

Evelyn was seventeen. She had another year before adulthood, during which anything could happen. As much as he'd be thrilled if she married someone like Riley, he'd be happy with *anyone* who loved and provided for his daughter. He'd eventually approved of Elias, even though he'd been as poor as a farmer, because he had been devoted to Olivia in every way that mattered.

But while the laws of Citadel provided him quite a bit of power as a man and father, there was nothing he could do to stop a woman—even a member of his own family—from joining the convent.

He'd just have to hope and pray that Evelyn found a man before that year was up, and didn't lose him to demons.

CHAPTER EIGHTEEN:
RILEY

"That girl is an idiot," Augustus grumbled as soon as the door closed behind the Claudes. "Joining the convent before marriage. What a joke. And *you*. You should've tried harder."

Riley didn't say anything in his defense. He couldn't. This whole evening had been exhausting—the last two *weeks* had been exhausting—and he just wanted to go to bed. But moving would draw attention to himself. He stayed put, standing awkwardly by the fireplace in the living room.

"There are other girls out there," Mia pointed out, refilling her wineglass from the sofa. Her rings clinked against the glass. Expensive stuff; normally even the Thompsons had to drink from ceramics instead of actual glassware. "He'll have his pick of the lot when he's a lawyer."

Augustus's shoulders relaxed, just a little. "I'd rather have Claude secured. He's a good man, but ambitious. That can be dangerous."

She shrugged. "I'm sure you'll think of something. So what if that girl's an idiot? Riley has options."

Thanks for trying to defend me, Mom, he thought, clamping down on a smile.

Augustus turned to Riley. "Those books that Olivia gave to you. You still have them?"

Surprised at the sudden change in conversation, Riley said, "Yes."

"Bring them to me."

Confused, Riley did as he was told. He'd skimmed all of them, hoping that Olivia had left some sort of note or message in their pages. But there was nothing. They were genuine gifts. Her way of supporting his dream of being a medic, which became less and less likely the closer he got to eighteen. He still read them every night by candlelight, trying to absorb the knowledge. But reading had never been his strength. He learned best by *doing*.

It was nice to dream, though.

He handed the heavy stack to his father. Augustus grunted as he took the weight.

Then he went to the fireplace.

Riley's eyes widened. "Wait—"

Augustus dumped all of them into the fire.

Riley watched the paper blacken and burn. A little piece of him died with it.

Don't cry, he ordered himself. *You'll just make it worse. Don't cry, don't cry, don't cry.*

He turned to his mother for help. Mia had forgone the glass entirely and drank straight from the bottle.

Augustus wiped his hands. "Go to bed, Riley."

He did, feeling numb as he changed into his sleepwear and blew out the candles. Except for the one in front of the Guardian statuette. His prayer for Olivia's safety fell from numb lips.

He lay in bed, staring at the black ceiling, numbness slowly giving way to grief. And then cold anger. He'd already decided to become a lawyer. What right did Augustus have to tread on him like this?

The moons rose in the sky, their grayish-silver light reflecting the dry green flower hanging on the opposite wall. It was the one Olivia had given him, which he'd dried and pressed into a frame.

He got out of bed and took the frame off the wall, his knuckles white around the blue wood.

So do it. Or never be happy.

He hadn't really understood how Olivia could just do whatever she wanted so blatantly and openly, knowing full well that people would hate her for it. Even though Riley had always been something of an outcast, too—being a sickly boy with "girly" interests—he'd at least tried to be likable. All of his acts of rebellion were little or secret. He kept his hair just a bit longer so it didn't look like a military cut. Only a handful of people knew he was a Dove. Even fewer knew of his career dreams.

But now he understood. Maybe only a precious few people—if anyone—could truly accept Olivia for who and what she was. But she accepted *herself* and lived her life accordingly. That made her, if not happy, at least content. And now Riley faced the same decision.

If he became a medic, the whole town would condemn him.

If he became a lawyer, he condemned himself.

He knew he'd only be able to live with one of those choices.

CHAPTER NINETEEN

Over the next few days, Olivia conducted an experiment. Whenever she caught a creature—a ruzina fish, a serpentine conchek, a shelled decican—she would cook and eat or preserve half of it, then leave out the other half a little ways from her camp. It went against everything Peterson had taught her, as such practices attracted dangerous predators, demons included.

But it seemed this attracted exactly the predator Olivia wanted. Because every morning, without fail, she would go to where she had left her offering and find fruit. Sauvibs, uvam berries, apiberries. Even though Olivia hadn't seen the demon since that night with the ruzina, she had to be following her. Olivia took to calling her Blue in her sketchbook.

Dear Elias, it's day 17, and I left half a fish last night. Came back to two sauvibs, she wrote. *None of the plants Blue has given me have been poisonous, which means she knows—in general, at least—what humans can and cannot eat, and is not attempting to poison me. The fact that she initiated the trade at all, when she could have just as easily stolen from me, indicates that she has at least some sort of moral code. Maybe she's an outlier, but I doubt it. We're well past the spot where I met the freckled demon. Perhaps they know each other? I still don't know how I'm going to communicate with these creatures. You once told me that figuring out how to hear me was like learning a new dialect, if not an entirely different* *language. We don't have that sort of time. But I think if I can get closer to* *Blue, I can find a way to—*

A sharp *yipe* caught her attention. Olivia looked up, trying to see through the orange and yellow leaves above her. It was one of the sounds the demons made when they were being tortured to death in Citadel.

There was a distant snarl and the sound of bodies smashing through leaves. Olivia dropped her book, grabbed her bow, and ran.

It was her third week in the woods, and the tide was almost down completely. But these were the lowlands; much of the ground was still covered in several meters of water and would remain that way as tide pools, which forced Olivia to set up camp in a tree last night. She kept to the branches, scrambling over blue wood, trying to follow the sounds of fighting.

Something splashed. Something else growled. Olivia jumped onto another tree, wove around the trunk, and finally saw it.

Blue had fallen into the water. She flapped her wings and landed on a low-hanging branch, snarling up at another demon. This one, Olivia didn't recognize. Unlike Blue, he was an adult, with plenty of meat and muscle on his bones. His fur was deep brown and his wings a dark red. He bared his teeth.

Blue growled again, wings slightly spread, hackles and feathers raised. *Aggression*, Olivia recalled from her lessons. *She wants to attack.*

But she didn't, and the reason was clearly written on the talon that she kept raised instead of using it to grab the branch. Blood slid down a slash on the leg, dripping into the water below. Olivia was too far away to tell, but she could guess that the injury came from the male demon's talons or teeth.

Demons fought each other? Why?

Should Olivia intervene? She didn't know Blue, not really. She didn't know why the red demon saw fit to attack her. Had Blue done something wrong?

The red demon dove down, grabbed Blue by the scruff of her neck with his talons, and dragged her off the branch.

He didn't get far. Blue tore herself free, leaving behind a fair bit of fur and skin. She wavered as she flew, landing on another branch. She stumbled, putting too much weight on her bad leg, and managed a quasi-graceful fall onto a small bit of dry land, a tiny island in the middle of the Flooded Forest.

The red demon flew back around.

All right, that's enough, Olivia thought, nocking an arrow. Wherever this demon was trying to take Blue, she obviously didn't want to go. Olivia couldn't stand by like a good little scientist and just observe. She had to *do* something, or Blue would end up far more seriously hurt.

The red demon dove down to Blue, talons out.

Olivia fired.

The arrow flew in front of the demon's nose, forcing him off course as he veered away from Blue to the trees.

Exactly what Olivia wanted.

He snarled, loud enough that it echoed. Olivia nocked another arrow and revealed herself, keeping it aimed at the demon. Blue managed to pull herself off the ground, flying up to Olivia's tree. The red demon barked. She ignored him, landing behind Olivia.

Olivia was bad enough at reading human expressions, never mind demonic ones. Peterson had said that raised hackles, spread wings, and bared teeth all indicated aggression, though.

Her arms trembled with the effort of holding the arrow back. Killing or even hurting this demon could damage her odds of success, but if he tried to attack Blue again, she didn't see any other choice.

The red demon glided down toward the water, turned, and flew away into the forest.

Olivia put her arrow back, shook out her arms, and turned to Blue.

The gash on her leg had almost certainly been from a talon, and the back of her neck was bleeding from where the red demon had tried to drag her. Olivia grimaced, examining the injuries as best she could without actually touching her. They weren't bad themselves, but they could easily get infected. She had a basic medical kit, but it was back at camp. They could conceivably go there together, but given Blue's injuries, that was less than ideal. Better for Olivia to go and bring her things back here.

Now, how to communicate that to Blue.

After a moment of thought, Olivia took one of her arrows out of her quiver.

Blue gave a low growl. Probably didn't like the idea of a human holding a weapon around her.

Olivia drove the arrowhead into the wood between them. Blue stopped growling, tilting her head to the side. Olivia pointed down to the arrow. Blue looked at it.

Maybe a demonstration, Olivia thought. She got down on her belly and pointed down again.

This time Blue got it. She lay down, careful of her leg.

Olivia stood but motioned for Blue to stay there, right by the arrow. Blue put her head on her paws.

Olivia grinned. They could communicate! At least a little.

She ran across the tree branches, grateful that they were wide enough that she could do it without too much fear of stumbling. She made it back to camp, packed all of her things in record time, and returned to find Blue exactly where she had left her. The young she-demon had re-moved the arrow from the wood with her magic and was floating it in the air, spinning it. The arrow dropped as soon as Blue saw her.

Olivia returned the arrow to her quiver and got her medical kit, specifically a healing salve that prevented infection and some bandages.

Both injuries got cleaned with water and slathered in salve. Olivia lightly smacked Blue's snout when she tried to lick it. She bandaged the leg, hoping nothing needed stitches. She had needle and thread, but the fur would be a problem.

Riley would know what to do, Olivia thought, finishing with the bandage. After Sarai's death, Ormus had sent Olivia to public school rather than try to homeschool her. The same school Michael and Gabriel attended, as well as several other teenagers who had thought bullying the silver-haired freak was a fun pastime. Olivia got into several fights.

Riley got good at patching her up. Yet another reason he would make an excellent medic.

When Olivia finished, she reached into her bag to retrieve some fish meat she'd dried a couple of days ago and fed it to Blue. The she-demon ate and licked Olivia's cheek. She giggled. It was a strange situation for both of them, but that was all right, because she was pretty sure she'd just made a friend.

CHAPTER TWENTY

Demons, Olivia quickly learned, were nocturnal creatures.

It was a common theory in Citadel already, given that the frequency of howls from the forest went up as soon as the sun went down. Now, Olivia called it a tentative fact.

Blue and Olivia only traveled far enough to make it difficult for the red demon to track them down, at which point Blue lay down on a branch and closed her eyes. It was midafternoon. Olivia itched to move—this broke her routine, but so did getting into a fight with another demon—and quelled it by putting a few fishing lines in the water and sketching. She had a new subject, after all.

As the sun set, Blue woke. She tried to nibble at her bandages, but Olivia's sharp "uh-uh!" stopped her. Her lines had caught a fish, which she gave to Blue. It was gone in two bites.

Blue spent some time cleaning herself, which was difficult with the bandages. She preened her wings with her teeth and talons and licked some of the stray blood from her fur. Olivia watched as she reeled in her fishing lines. She wondered how often demons had to clean their wings for them to be functional.

Blue stretched her wings and flew to the damp ground. Olivia scrambled after her, almost slipping on her cleats. As soon as she caught up,

Blue started walking. Olivia winced at the she-demon's limp, but they didn't go far. Blue led her to a hilltop, tall enough to rival Citadel's height. Olivia could immediately see that the top of this hill had never been touched by the tides: the few trees here were skinny and small, not built to withstand the twice-monthly onslaught of water. But Olivia barely paid attention to them, as her eyes were immediately pulled to the small field of berry bushes.

Uvam berries were dark and tart and could grow to the size of a person's thumb. Because they grew on bushes on the ground and had no protection from floods, they were very difficult to find in the wild but relatively easy to grow domestically. One of the first agricultural products ever grown in Citadel, if not *the* first, was uvam berries.

Olivia squealed and immediately began harvesting. It was a little difficult; even with the light of the planet's rings and moons, it was still pitch-black night. She fixed the problem by making a small torch with a piece of wood, shredded cloth, and alcohol from her medical kit. The berries weren't officially in season yet, most of them too pale to be ripe. But several still found their way into Olivia's bag and mouth. Blue left her alone, lying on the edge of the berry bushes to rest her leg, half-hidden in darkness.

Until she suddenly shot to her paws, spread her wings, and *snarled*.

Olivia froze, berry halfway to her mouth, hand holding a torch. She immediately put it out—it wouldn't help much against demonic senses, but there was no need to advertise her location—and reached for her bow.

Two shapes flew from the sky, landing several meters away from Blue. Olivia waited for them to charge, to attack, to snarl back at her.

They did not.

It was hard to make out their features in the dark. One of them was roughly the same size (and age?) as Blue, the other twice that size. The larger one had fur and feathers so dark it blended with the shadows behind him, while the muted light from the rings lit the smaller's lighter fur.

After a while Olivia realized that if the newcomers were going to attack, they would have done it already, especially with Blue being injured. Cautiously, with her bow in hand (but no arrow), she came out of the bushes, standing next to Blue.

The smaller demon barked and darted forward, heedless of Blue's intensifying growls. He came close enough for Olivia to see the freckle-like spots on his fur.

With a whoop, Olivia dropped her bow and approached the freckled demon that had given her the green flowers, all those weeks ago. Through the euphoria of finally finishing her search, she decided then and there to name him Freckles.

Freckles wagged his tail and, when she got close enough, gently headbutted her chest. Olivia staggered a little to keep her balance. Why he did that, she had no idea. It was either a demon thing or something she'd need Riley or Asiya to explain to her. But it didn't matter because *she'd found him*!

Blue snarled. Olivia and Freckles both turned to see that the larger demon had slowly approached her. He retreated, putting plenty of space between them. His feathers and fur were all completely black, except for a single pale patch over his eye barely visible in the darkness.

I know you too, Olivia thought. It was the demon Ormus had shot at, who had killed Michael Byruk. The memory probably should have scared her, but he had only gotten violent *after* the soldiers attacked. It had been self-defense.

I'll call you Patch, she decided.

Blue kept snarling at Patch until he flew away.

Freckles stayed behind. Blue narrowed her golden eyes at him. He lay down at Olivia's feet, every muscle loose and relaxed.

It occurred to Olivia that Blue *really* didn't like these other demons all that much, but she couldn't figure out why. (Scared of Patch? Just didn't like demons? She didn't like Freckles's adorable spots?) But . . . perhaps she could ask.

Sitting down in front of Freckles, Olivia started a new torch so they could properly see each other. Then she pulled her sketchbook out of her bag and wrote on a new page, *Can you read this?*

Freckles tipped his head at the book. He whined.

Olivia sighed, dropping the book in her lap. So much for that plan.

A flutter of wings heralded Patch's return. That more than anything surprised Olivia. Demons were silent when they traveled, their prey unknowing of their presence until teeth and talons pierced their flesh.

He landed a safe distance away from Blue and dropped a decican carcass he'd been carrying in his jaws. In the dark, the fist-sized crustacean looked like a rock with legs. He used his snout to push the dead decican forward.

Blue licked her chops. At her silent command, the meal lifted in the air and floated to her before dropping near her paws.

Patch jerked his head at Freckles, who whined. He gave a low growl. Freckles dragged himself to his paws and talons.

As he walked to Patch, Olivia realized that they were about to leave. She opened her mouth but, as usual, couldn't force any actual words out. Just a long sound.

Freckles paused. After a brief moment when he looked at Patch, he grabbed a fallen branch with his teeth and drew in the dirt.

He started with a line going east to west. Then added two circles and several half circles to it, which Olivia realized was the planet's moons and rings. Finally, he drew a half circle on the western end of the line.

The first thing Olivia thought was, *If there's ever confirmation that these beings are sentient, it's this.*

Her second thought was, *What the fuck does it mean?*

After a few beats, she got it. She took out her book and did a rough sketch of the uvam berry field they were standing in, silhouettes of herself and Blue on the ground, and silhouettes of Patch and Freckles in the air, about to land. She added the sun setting in the west, making sure the shadows were right, and then presented it to Freckles.

We will all meet back here at sundown.

Freckles wagged his tail once (that was good?), and then he and Patch flew off.

Dear Elias,

I've got Freckles learning how to read. First I tried teaching him "sunset," re-creating his sign for the time and then writing the word beneath it. He didn't get that, so I wrote "fire" in the dirt next to the firepit. Then "Blue" next to Blue, then "Olivia" at my own feet. It took him three more words to get it, but he got there. He had to use a stick in his jaws, and his handwriting was atrocious—worse even than yours! But it works. We're getting somewhere.

Patch came the first couple of evenings, never joining us in the field but staying in the trees to watch us. Blue liked to growl at him. He wasn't there the third night, but I'm pretty sure he was still watching us. Just not somewhere I could see him. Demons are pack creatures after all, and Freckles seems pretty young. I don't mind having him around, though. Neither he nor Freckles have tried to take a bite out of me, yet.

The only thing that's frustrating is how slow the reading lessons are going. Freckles always has to leave early, after barely an hour. At this rate, it'll be years before he can understand and answer such a complex question as "How do you justify the murder of humans?" or "Why are you fighting us?"

We just learned "food" and "eat."

It's probably for the best that I never became a teacher. The frustration and impatience are eating me up inside.

Love,
Olivia

CHAPTER TWENTY-ONE

Freckles came every sunset as the tides rose and lowered again, bringing food for both of them: a serpentine conchek, the leg of a menziva, or an avitio bird. They always had something missing: a wing or tentacle would be torn off by the time it reached her camp. But the rest would be intact, and Olivia couldn't fault Freckles for helping himself to a snack en route. After they ate, it was time for reading lessons.

Blue stayed far away from them both whenever Freckles arrived, often flying to the other end of the berry field with her share of the meat. Olivia was disappointed she didn't want to share in the reading lessons, but the she-demon's leg did need to heal.

Five weeks—thirty-one days—after Olivia left Citadel, she went hunting and brought back a spiven. Blue's leg was healed, and she'd helped by sniffing out and helping her track down the spike-shooting creature.

Olivia accidentally burned her share of the spiven meat but swallowed it down anyway. Blue gnawed on the animal's meaty bone. Whatever filled their bellies was a good meal.

She looked across the berry field and empty forest beyond. Five weeks. She'd estimated that she'd be back in Citadel by now, and it didn't surprise her that she'd been wrong. Timekeeping had always been her weakness. Part of her still longed for the city, for the Claudes and Peterson and Riley. But it had been mitigated somewhat by Blue and Freckles's company. She wondered what Elias would have thought of them.

A lump caught in her throat at the thought. Her grief was a constant companion, but it still caught her off guard. She took another bite of burned spiven to help her swallow her tears.

A few hours later, at sundown, Freckles returned. This time, instead of bringing meat, he brought a small bouquet of green prasina flowers.

He put one in front of Olivia and three in front of Blue. Blue bared her teeth but didn't growl. Progress? Yeah, Olivia was calling that progress.

Freckles took up his stick in his mouth and wrote, *eat*.

Eat flowers? Really?

Olivia examined hers but didn't eat it. It wouldn't kill or hurt her—probably—but when she'd left Citadel, she and Franklin hadn't been able to categorize every side effect, dosage, or how to synthesize it into a proper anesthetic. How many would it take to knock someone out? How much was too much? What they did know for certain was that it wasn't nutritious and didn't taste very good.

Freckles huffed, took one of the flowers he'd given Blue, and ate it. Blue looked at Olivia.

With a shrug, Olivia popped hers in her mouth, grimacing at the sour taste. Blue followed suit. One flower probably wouldn't affect her too much.

Halfway through the writing lesson with Freckles, Olivia realized eating the flower had been a mistake. Her insides churned. It wasn't *painful*, but it wasn't pleasant, either.

The bigger problem was the headache building behind her eyes, and the fact that her brain felt like it floated in a fish tank that was her skull. Blue snarled, stumbling toward Freckles, and almost fell over. He backed away, easily evading her.

Olivia tried to think. Freckles had eaten a flower—twice now—and had been all right. But he'd also fed twice as much to Blue, which was probably why she experienced symptoms while he didn't. But why? And why did she have a headache? That was a new symptom, never reported by their test subjects.

She couldn't figure it out. Everything felt bendy, even her thoughts. The headache grew worse, pressure building up in her frontal lobe.

That's my favorite part of my brain. It'd better not break, she thought.

Blue staggered forward again, snapping at Freckles. He barely managed to dodge that one, having to spread his wings and fly back.

Olivia tried to stand, to get Blue to *stop*, because didn't she know that they couldn't kill each other until after they'd answered Olivia's questions? She fell back on her bottom.

She glared at Blue, who was still stubbornly on all fours. *Not fair that she's so scary when I'm . . . I'm . . .*

The headache was getting worse. Something was clawing at her brain, sinking talons into the gray matter and ripping out entire chunks. Olivia put her head in her lap, squeezing her skull.

Patch emerged from the darkness above, landing next to Freckles. Another demon joined them. Deep-gray fur with a blue tinge to the wings. She couldn't call the new one Blue, though. Then what would she call first Blue?

Someone howled, a triumphant sound.

Something in Olivia's head broke, and everything went blessedly black.

CHAPTER TWENTY-TWO:
ORMUS

Asiya smoothed Ormus's jacket and mustered up a smile. "Are you sure you want to go? No one will blame you if we stay home."

Riley's eighteenth birthday had finally arrived, held at sundown to honor the fasting month of Aestus. But the Thompsons would probably ignore the part where they were all supposed to limit the amount of food they ate even after the sun went down. The party was more of a social networking event than an actual celebration of the young man in question, but that was the way it was in their circles. Ormus was expected to make an appearance. Even though Olivia had said "estimated return four weeks" and they were now on week six. Everyone in Citadel had their own personal tragedy, and the world didn't stop for it.

"We can't stay holed up in here forever," he said. "If you or Evelyn want to stay, though—"

"No, no, we'll go."

He kissed her forehead. "Thank you, my sweet."

The three of them walked the two blocks to the Thompson household. Asiya was in a dark dress, clothing worn for mourning. Evelyn, in sharp contrast, had a pale-blue-green and patterned headscarf and matching belt, as if her sister hadn't been missing and probably dead for a month and a half. Ormus had just gone in his dress uniform, as had Commander Brodsky and the other officers who arrived.

A couple of long tables had been set up in the Thompson yard and filled with food. The risk of famine, decreased food supply, and deteriorating economic situation never touched the governor's family. Chairs were scattered throughout the yard, but most people stood and mingled. A dozen freestanding torches gave the yard a warm glow. Ormus saw the Brown family across the way.

"Why don't you go greet Riley?" he suggested to the girls. "I need to talk to some of my officers."

Evelyn and Asiya went to the buffet tables. Ormus made his way to Markus Brown, who owned the lucrative textile mill and, according to Brodsky, might be their biggest lead on the Doves. He wore a deep-green suit and matching hat, and smiled at one of the other guests, showing the dimple in his left cheek.

"Mr. Brown," Ormus greeted, shaking his hand. "How's your wife?"

"Not the best," Markus admitted. "She had a rather nasty asthma attack a few days ago. Your wife saw to her; she's an angel. Oh, sorry about your daughter."

Ormus fought a grimace. He wanted to make himself appear as a friend in case he'd have to wring out a confession from the other man. Which, since Commander Brodsky had noticed him going to the temples but not *donating*, as well as talking to other known malcontents, was looking more and more likely.

But Markus gave him the same look so many others had for the last five weeks, the one full of polite pity that got under his skin.

He said his thanks and left. He had no appetite, yet he wandered over to the food anyway. A woman gnawed on a spiced nugzuuki wing; he didn't recognize her until he saw her face. "Mrs. Thompson?"

"Hello, Captain," Mia grumbled. Her hands trembled, yet she sweated through her pale dress. Even Ormus could tell that her makeup needed refreshing. A single black hair had broken free from the matron cap, curling around her right ear.

"Are you all right?" he asked.

"I'm fine. Planning parties is stressful work."

Someone snorted. Ormus raised an eyebrow when he saw Sergeant Peterson's salt-and-pepper head. The older man crossed his arms and leaned against the table. "What'll hold you over, ma'am?"

She frowned. "I'm sorry?"

"You've gone at least a day without a drink. Let me guess: Riley asked you to be sober for his birthday."

Ormus winced. Mia Thompson's alcoholism was one of Citadel's worst-kept secrets. It was hardly a source of scandal. Many people fell to drink in these dark times, and Mia had the good grace to keep her habit out of the public eye.

So why Peterson was deliberately poking at the issue was beyond him.

"What do you know about it?" she snapped.

Peterson chuckled without humor. "I lost five years to the bottom of the bottle. Now I'm asking you, with no judgment, in honor of your son's wish: What's going to get you through the day?"

Mia tossed the half-eaten wing into the bushes and rubbed her arms. "Cigarettes. I know, I know it's a bad habit, lung cancer and tooth rot, it stinks, it's a fire hazard . . ."

Peterson held out a plain pack of cigarettes: dried red rebrum leaves wrapped in pale-blue paper. The poisonous plant grew above the tide line in the wild and was notoriously addictive and hard to find. She stared at them for half a second, like staring at a hypnotizing jewel, before snatching them from his hands and storming off.

"First day's always the worst," he said, joining the captain. They were both in their dress blues, though Ormus's jacket had significantly more stripes and medals.

"How did you get in here?" Ormus asked. Peterson was a good man, but hardly a pillar of elite society. He should've been turned away at the property line.

"The boy invited me. Some of us see a party as a party, not an investigation or networking event or whatever the hell you rich folk do when you're supposed to have fun," he teased. His smile slipped away. "No news on Olivia?"

"Nothing."

The sergeant grunted. Ormus found himself irrationally envying the old man. His son, Jason, had been killed in a demon hunt over a decade ago, a sweet young man Ormus had met a handful of times in his early days with Sarai. The boy's death had been tragic but, in the end, just another military casualty. At least it'd been certain. Everyone knew for a fact that Jason Peterson was dead; his ashes were in the basement of a temple like the rest.

But with Olivia, nothing was certain. No body had been found. No documented demon attack. Nothing. Despite the fact that only a handful of the most experienced hunters had lasted more than a week on their own in the forest, there was that niggling hope in the back of Ormus's mind that whispered, *She might still be alive.*

"You said you had an alcohol problem?" he asked. Mentally, he cringed. He'd hoped to find a safer topic than his missing daughter, and *that* was what he settled on?

Peterson laughed. "Right! We did a spectacular job avoiding each other after you left Sarai. You must have missed it." He shrugged. "It seemed better than dealing with Jason's death. Sarai wouldn't let me anywhere near Olivia until I pulled myself out of it."

"I didn't know that," Ormus admitted.

"Not your fault." Peterson studied him for a moment, then apparently came to some sort of decision. "What happened between you and Sarai, anyway? She never told me. Just that you were finished and she wanted you to have no contact with her child. I only pushed hard enough to confirm that you didn't hurt her."

Ormus thought about what he wanted to say. He and Sarai had never been serious, despite how captivating she'd been in their youth. Her recklessness and ambition had presented as courage and confidence, back then. His parents had warned him away from her, pushing him toward the match they'd arranged with Asiya. The medic had good genes, they said. No history of weak immune systems, genetic disorders, or mental abnormalities for five generations. They'd have strong, healthy children and be an ideal match.

But he'd been young and stupid, and convinced himself he'd been in love with the silver-haired vixen.

"I proposed to her," he said. "After she told me she was pregnant."

Peterson stared at him. "I thought you left her after getting the news."

"No!" Ormus snapped. "I'd never dishonor her like that."

Peterson held up his hands. "All right, all right. So you proposed and she turned you down? That sounds right."

Ormus pinched the bridge of his nose. "She asked me what marriage looked like. What I expected her to be as a wife."

Peterson looked like he was watching his favorite drama unfold in the theater.

"I expected her to act like any good wife: stay home, raise the children, support me."

"And what about her career in science?" Peterson asked.

Ormus glared at him. "You sound exactly like her."

"And you sound like a hypocrite, sir. You let Asiya do her job as a medic."

"Part time. The girls are her first priority. Sarai was pregnant, and all she could think of was how it would affect *her job*."

Peterson laughed. "You're an idiot if you think Sarai's first priority wasn't Olivia. She adored her. She just wanted her own life too. Like you. She wanted to know that you would support her, not hold her back. Or her daughter."

"Well, look where that got her. And now . . ." He swallowed. "Now, it looks like Olivia's thrown her own life away."

Peterson shook his head. "No. I have faith that she's still alive, and that I'll get to kill her when she comes back." He patted Ormus on the arm. "Let me know if you need anything, Captain."

Ormus watched his salt-and-pepper head disappear into the crowd. He never was sure what to make of Peterson. He outranked the man by leagues, thanks to coming from a good family and being able to afford the extra education. Everyone knew that the old sergeant was never going to see another promotion. He'd hit his ceiling. And yet, Peterson never let himself get cowed. He'd follow orders, sure, and do it better than almost anyone else, with one exception: if he thought an order would cause the unnecessary deaths of or harm to his men, he would not follow it. He'd danced the line of getting court-martialed more than once. It was one of the reasons he was now training sergeant rather than still in the field.

Would things have worked out between Ormus and Sarai? Probably not. Their relationship had already begun to fade by the time she announced her pregnancy, and they'd been dancing the on-again-off-again tune for a long time before even that. But something Peterson had said, *She wanted to know you would support her, not hold her back,* stuck in his head.

What did he expect Ormus to do? Sacrifice his *own* career to be a househusband?

Someone whistled, loud and shrill enough to get everyone's attention. All eyes turned to Augustus and Riley, standing side by side. They couldn't look *less* like father and son. Augustus's huge girth just made Riley look smaller, even if the boy's back was straight. While the governor wore one of his richest suits, every finger adorned with rings, Riley had only a simple shirt and jacket. Nice and high quality, but nothing flashy. Ormus didn't think he'd *ever* seen Riley wear anything flashy.

Augustus smiled, holding up a glass. "Thank you all for coming. Today's a big day. For today, Citadel gets a new man."

Everyone clapped. Riley smiled politely, but it seemed to Ormus that he was stiffer than usual. Maybe he was sick again.

Asiya slipped her hand through Ormus's arm, letting him take it in his own. She didn't seem worried about the boy, and nothing got past her sharp medic's eye, so he let himself relax. Evelyn joined them, munching on a bit of bread with a meat spread on top.

"As is tradition, our new man has found his Placement," Augustus continued, gripping Riley's shoulders. "As you all know, his health unfortunately keeps him from the honor of military service. But where the Hundred-Faced God closes a door, He opens a window. This time next year, we'll have a new lawyer."

More clapping. Until Riley cleared his throat and said, "Medic, actually."

Ormus raised an eyebrow. Several people looked confused while more chuckled. Augustus laughed. "Good joke, Riley."

Riley slipped out of his father's grasp. "No. I told you I wanted to be a medic, and you threatened to disown me unless I chose something else. Well, I'm not choosing something else. Definitely not something as dull and corrupt as law."

"Oh no," Asiya whispered.

Augustus's smile slipped. "You're not a woman, Riley."

"We have no law forbidding me from practicing medicine," he challenged. "And I'd hardly be the first male medic in history."

Augustus's face twisted into a cold glare. "Riley, consider your next words carefully. Let's not make this any more of a scene."

The governor was a large man any day, but with the torchlight casting deep shadows, he looked particularly tall and menacing. Especially compared to his son, who was a whole head shorter and so much frailer than him.

Riley gave him a sunny smile. "Good thing I've already packed."

He left a ripple of murmurs and whispers as he went into the house. Evelyn gaped. "They're bluffing, right? Mr. Thompson isn't really kicking his son out, is he?"

Ormus kept his face neutral. "He never bluffs."

Asiya gripped his arm. "We should take him."

"What?"

"Riley. He's going to be out on the streets."

He loved his wife. Really, he did. But she was blinded by compassion sometimes. "If we take in Riley, we put ourselves in direct opposition with the governor. We don't need that thorn in our side."

She glared at him. "You can't mean to go along with this."

"Riley's a smart boy. He'll come around before he gets hurt."

Honestly, Ormus thought that Riley would come out any minute, apologize to the crowd, and accept his fate.

Instead, Riley came out with a bag and his mother. Mia shrieked at him, lit cigarette in hand: "After everything we've done for you, you're going to be a *sissy*? Are you going to start bedding men, too? I'm talking to you!"

Riley grimaced. "You've made your point, Mom. I'm done."

Mia stopped dogging him and sniffled, tears running down her face. She immediately went to one of the opened bottles of cider on the table and took a long swallow.

"You're breaking your mother's heart, Riley," Augustus scolded.

He gave his father a sarcastic bow. "I learned from the best."

"Get off my property."

Riley didn't run, but he did move fast, the crowd parting before him. He wasn't cowed. He didn't slink off. He walked taller and prouder than any soldier Ormus had met.

Peterson caught up to him at the edge of the property line. Ormus couldn't hear what they said, but Riley's face lit up.

Well, he thought, *at least the idiot won't be sleeping on the street.*

CHAPTER TWENTY-THREE:
RILEY

Riley was seven the first time Augustus said that he'd tried to kill him.

He'd been born a month early, and it was Mia's first pregnancy. They hadn't known that the following attempts would lead to a string of stillbirths and tears, at least on Mia's side. So as far as Augustus knew, he'd have plenty of other opportunities for a perfect son.

"You were frail, puny, and sickly," Augustus had said. "You didn't even look human. More like a fish trying to pass as one. I wanted to take you to the wall during high tide and drop you into the water."

Riley wished that he could've believed his father was lying. That parents didn't really do that. But as Citadel's resources grew slimmer over the years, and families had more and more mouths to feed, infanticide became more common. It was rare in upper circles, much more common closer to the wall and Farmers' Ring. Elias had been able to list several families who'd had to make the difficult decision between sacrificing a newborn and seeing the rest of their children starve. Sometimes it wasn't a newborn but a child or adult with a physical or mental impairment. Suicide was usually frowned upon, but when a father couldn't find work because he had a shattered leg, or a grandmother's mind was fading fast and she knew her caregivers couldn't afford to tend to her at all times, they would go to the wall. And not come back.

No arrests were ever made, and nobody talked about it except to their priests.

"Unfortunately, your mother has a weak heart," Augustus had said. "One look at you, and she couldn't bear to part with you. She said if I threw you over the wall, she'd do the same to herself. Remember that the next time you think about disobeying either one of us."

That memory plagued him during the carriage ride to Sergeant Peterson's house. Which was *very* inconsiderate of his mind, since the old soldier was laying out the rules of the place.

"I don't have much. A sergeant's salary doesn't get a man what it used to. Ask before you eat anything, and if you need something like extra clothing, you're on your own. My only truly unbreakable rule is don't bring any alcohol under my roof. I don't need that temptation in my life. If you decide to bring a lady companion, just give me fair warning."

Riley choked, soundly knocked out of his own head. "I'm not— That's not . . . It shouldn't be an issue." It had barely been an issue when he'd been a Thompson set to become governor. Now . . . now he seriously doubted any girl would so much as look at him.

Which was fine by him, because he had enough on his plate.

Peterson gave him a little smirk.

"I can pay for rent," Riley offered. "Once I get my salary."

He waved it off. "We'll talk about that later. Let's just focus on getting you settled."

The city changed around them. He hadn't been to this part of town since Sarai died. It had been rough then, and the last six years hadn't made it any kinder. The buildings shrank and grew rougher around the edges. Streets became narrower and more crowded, the smell of slop and filth of human waste getting more and more powerful. More beggars, more prostitutes, more guards.

The carriage dropped them off at a small wooden house mostly distinguished from the others by the fact that it was only one story, not stacked with more on top and shared with multiple families. Peterson paid the carrier while Riley examined his new home for the foreseeable future. The houses here didn't have yards, the buildings so close together the edges of the rooftops almost kissed. But there was still a little space between the front door and the street that people could use for decorations. Riley was surprised to see that Peterson had a small garden. No food—that would likely be stolen. Instead, there were a half dozen different types of flowers and herbs, two of which Riley recognized from Olivia's medical books, though he couldn't recall what they did.

"No second story?" Riley asked, thinking about Sarai's old place. "Housemates?"

"Nah. The people who built this place did a shit job. Walls and foundation aren't strong enough to add another spot on top of it," Peterson explained. "A couple of other houses have the same problem. The city's thinking of tearing it down and building something better, giving me a payout for my trouble. As if they'll actually pay us enough to put those new roofs over our heads."

The inside of the house was even smaller than the outside promised: one main room that was both living room and kitchen, a large fireplace, a washroom, and a bedroom. The wooden walls were decorated with framed portraits of Olivia's art, some medals for valor, and a surprisingly large collection of antique knives and axes that used to be standard issue for soldiers throughout Citadel's history. The oldest was dated at least three hundred years and would probably fetch a good price if sold to the Vaults. A fresh patch of wood in the corner of the ceiling spoke of a recently fixed leak. Everything was neat, cleaned, and put away. Riley would have expected nothing else from a military man.

"The way I figure, you can take the sofa," Peterson said, motioning to the hay-filled couch against the wall. "I've got some extra blankets and pillows you can use."

"That'll work," Riley said, setting down his bag. "Thank you, Sergeant. Really."

He shrugged. "Just doing what everyone else at that party should have done. Your father's an ass."

"Yeah . . ."

You're breaking your mother's heart, Riley.

He swallowed.

She said if I threw you over the wall, she'd do the same to herself. Remember that.

"Mom's going to be so drunk tonight." He hadn't asked her to be sober today. That had come as a pleasant surprise, along with her grumbled explanation: *You hate seeing me drunk, but sober me is no fun for anyone.*

He'd ruined that today.

"That's her responsibility, not yours," Peterson said firmly.

"I'm not exactly helping."

"You've been in that house for eighteen years. If she didn't stay sober then, she's not going to start now."

Riley bit his lip, looking away.

Peterson put a hand on his shoulder. "Take it from me, son: You can be the brightest angel to someone caught in drink. But if they don't choose to help themselves, not even the Hundred-Faced God can help them. That journey doesn't start with you. It starts with *her.*

"If and when she decides to give up the drink, you'll be there for her. She knows that. Until that happens, there's nothing you can do. And the only person you owe or need to look after is yourself. You hear?"

Riley nodded, blinking the blurriness from his vision. Peterson squeezed him in a half hug. "You get yourself settled while I make us some dinner. If there's one mistake you made today, it's that you made your announcement *before* we got to the food."

Riley managed a weak laugh. "Sorry. And thank you again, for supporting me."

Peterson opened the cupboards, looking for something to eat. "We need more medics than lawyers in this town, no matter what the sex. People who say there are only 'girly' and 'manly' things in this world haven't had to cook for themselves in the middle of the forest, or stitch up the claw wounds in their friends."

"Soldiers get medical training?"

"A little. Enough to keep us alive long enough to get back here. And every time I train a new batch of recruits, there's always at least one idiot who says they shouldn't have to learn that stuff because it's 'womanly.' They stop complaining the first time one of them gets hurt out there."

Riley opened his bag. He had been fully prepared to sleep on the streets tonight and make for a shelter tomorrow, so he had a couple of blankets, a change of clothes, and the small wooden statuettes of God Elias had made for him. They weren't, strictly speaking, necessary for prayers. But it made him feel better. These days, he couldn't go to sleep without lighting a candle to the Guardian for Olivia.

He also had a wallet full of banknotes. One of Augustus's better parenting moves had been to give Riley an allowance and teach him how to budget.

"Peterson," Riley called, holding up the wallet. "We can cook tomorrow. Let's celebrate tonight."

Peterson closed the cupboards. "Well, damn. You should've led with that."

There were a handful of restaurants and a large number of mobile food carts all along the streets of Peterson's neighborhood. Not nearly as elegant as the places Augustus used to take Riley and Mia, but the air was much more casual, and Riley felt like he could finally relax. He didn't have the pressure to be the perfect governor's son, to put on a show for his town and parents.

Peterson took him to a large, crowded restaurant with splintered blue walls and a slanted roof. A group of musicians played drums and flutes in the corner while servers handed out bowls of stew and plates of charred metabread. Peterson knew almost all of them by name, and the minute he mentioned that it was Riley's birthday, they got a steep discount.

With their stomachs pleasantly full, Peterson then took Riley on a nighttime tour of his part of the city. Despite the fact that the sun had set hours ago, the streets bustled with activity. That was common during the month of Aestus. People fasted during the day, then went out with friends and family at night, huddled in their summer coats and laughing.

"Where's your temple?" Riley asked.

"There are three around here," Peterson said. "The one I go to is right down this street."

Riley followed, curious. While religion didn't define a person by any means, you could still learn a lot based on what temple they chose to go to. Augustus had bounced back and forth between the first temple and the Temple of War. Riley himself usually preferred the Temple of Healing by Central Hospital, where he'd often, surprisingly, bumped into the entire Claude family, sans Olivia. Asiya had convinced her husband to switch from the Temple of Justice, though he was still seen there during certain holidays.

The temple Peterson took him to was just a little bigger than the homes around it. It had no words or sign, but next to the doors was a carving of the Face of Mercy.

"Father Victor served in my unit a while back," Peterson explained. "He was a miserable soldier. Makes for a much better priest."

The inside was as simple and plain as the outside: candles along the walls for light and prayer, enough pews for a small congregation, and a wooden statue of God in front of the altar. They were carved in a distinctly feminine form, a rarity in Citadel, with four arms that each held a Face. Mercy was held directly in front of the head, but the other three were Healing, Justice, and Humility.

Riley knew that he was going to really like this place.

A teenage girl sat in the front pew, praying, her hair covered in a tight brown scarf. The priest tended to the candles, looking up when Riley and Peterson closed the doors behind them.

The priest smiled, walking over with a slight limp. He was maybe a decade younger than the sergeant, with a soft belly sticking out under his robes. He grew his hair long, a rarity among Citadel men, and twisted into dreadlocks. "Abe."

"Father Victor." Peterson clasped Riley on the shoulder. "You might have a new addition to your temple."

"Is that so? What's your name?"

"Riley," he replied, leaving out his last name for now.

The Doves were a fraction of Citadel's population, but they were spread out. Riley honestly didn't know every single member, and neither did any of the others. It ensured their safety whenever one of them was caught and questioned. But they all *did* know the small, subtle hand signal used to identify each other.

Riley used the middle three fingers of his right hand to scratch at his upper left arm.

Victor's mouth twitched, and he gave a slight nod. "It's an honor to meet you, Riley."

Yes! Another Dove!

"Do you mind if I borrow the washroom?" Peterson asked. "Dinner isn't sitting right with me."

"Of course."

Victor and Riley waited until he was gone before smiling to each other. "Mary," Victor called. "Come meet our new friend."

The girl from the front joined them. Riley could have sworn he recognized her. The round cheeks made her look even younger than she was—maybe fifteen?

She definitely recognized him. "Thompson?"

He snapped his fingers, remembering. "You work at the bathhouse. Mary, was it?"

"Right." She glanced nervously at Victor.

The priest looked shocked. "You're Riley *Thompson?*"

"And a Dove for three years," he said with a grin. A thought occurred to him. "Is Peterson . . ."

"No," Victor said. "I've been trying to decide whether or not to approach him. Military men make us wary."

"Well, I can get a feel for him, since we're living together."

He frowned. "What?"

Riley explained what had happened at his birthday party. Mary snickered. "All right, I was worried before, but I would've paid good money to see that."

"Yeah . . ." Riley grimaced, the fears and doubts he'd fought back clawing their way up his throat. "I just don't know if I made the right choice. I don't like law—it bores me to tears and doesn't seem to do much to actually help the people who need it. But I could've stuck it out and become governor, and . . . we could've really used that. Maybe I'm just being selfish."

"Perhaps," Victor admitted. "But the Hundred-Faced God gives everyone a purpose. We each have our place in the world. If your faith is strong and you truly believe that yours is medicine, then nobody, not even us, has any right to tell you otherwise."

"Exactly," Mary added. "It's weird for a man to want to be in medicine, but not unheard of. Besides, if you keep converting, one of *those* people might become governor someday, so it all works out."

Riley felt his tension fade, just a little.

The priest wrapped an arm around the girl's shoulder. "Mary is one of our most prolific converters. Half of my congregation is here because of her."

She blushed. "I just talk to people."

"How many have you switched?" Riley asked.

"Eight."

He smirked. "Nine."

She returned the smirk. "First person to twenty buys the other lunch."

"Deal!"

"Children," Victor sighed. "It's not a contest. Don't rush things."

The back door opening cut off whatever Mary was about to say. Peterson returned. "Sorry about that. Everyone getting along here?"

"Absolutely," Riley said. "Father Victor was just about to give me the temple schedule."

"Of course, of course. Let me get you a copy . . ." The priest limped away.

Riley nudged Mary. "All bets aside, if you ever need an escort or help, let me know," he murmured.

She beamed. "Thank you."

CHAPTER TWENTY-FOUR

When Olivia woke up, it felt like someone had taken a spoon to her skull and scooped everything out.

She sat up and bumped her head against rough animal skin. She had been moved into her tent. Poking her head out, she saw they were still in the uvam field. Blue lay on her side with her dark-sapphire wings facing Olivia, probably sleeping. There was no sign of Freckles, Patch, or the new demon.

What little water had remained in the lowlands from the tides had disappeared. She must've been out for a day or two.

Olivia put a hand on her head. The headache was still there, now down to a mere throbbing, and the sunlight did *not* help. She wondered if this was what Riley felt like during or after one of his migraines; how did that man function?

But there was a new sensation, like a petal stuck to the back of her head. When she ran her fingers through her hair, there was nothing. Just her imagination, then?

She wanted to crawl back into her tent and go to sleep. But she also wanted to clean up, and should probably eat something. She wished it were high tide or that they had a tide pool closer than a kilometer away so she could properly wash up. Instead she settled for using her canteen to rinse out her mouth and wash her face.

Blue sat up, a little more quickly than Olivia had, and stretched her wings. The sticky petal feeling intensified, and Olivia heard a girl's voice speak in her mind as clear as day:

"*Still hurt?*"

Olivia blinked.

"*Do you still hurt?*" the girl's voice repeated.

Olivia shot to her feet with a yelp.

The dizziness returned with a vengeance, forcing her back to the ground.

Blue made a huffing sound. Olivia suddenly saw, in her mind's eye, Freckles and the gray demon scrambling backward as she—no, as *Blue*—snapped at them and beat her wings, only to succumb to dizziness and crumble to the ground.

She blinked, and she was back in the present.

That had been a memory. *Blue's* memory.

And she was hearing Blue's voice in her head.

Have I officially gone mad? she wondered. Half of Citadel thought she was already insane. She didn't like proving those people right, but in the face of overwhelming evidence . . .

"*Silver! Is'hav!*" a boy called.

Freckles flew down and landed next to them, a dead nugzuuki in his jaws. As usual, one part—in this case, a wing—was missing, while everything else remained intact.

Blue snarled. Though her mouth didn't move beyond that, her voice cut clear through Olivia's head. As if a knife had spoken. "*You do not call me Is'hav!*"

Freckles hunched his shoulders and wings. "*Not Is'hav.*" He perked up, his mental voice like a child leaking sunshine. "*Food!*"

He dropped the nugzuuki at Olivia's feet. She blinked, and she saw herself, from Freckles's eyes this time, making a fire and cooking a fish a few nights ago before eating it. With the memory came a burning sense of curiosity. *Why do humans burn food?*

Olivia narrowed her eyes. Now that the headache had started to wear off, she could think more clearly. She focused on that sticky sensation in the back of her mind, the one that got stronger every time one of them "spoke."

Freckles drooped, giving a low whine. "*Do you still not hear?*"

She focused harder. It felt less like a petal now, more like a rope. Two ropes, one connecting to Freckles, the other to Blue. She pulled on them both.

"*What is this?*"

Freckles's mind exploded with sunshine and cheer. He jumped into the air, did a flip, and landed with a howl. "*Silver hears! She hears!*"

Olivia looked between the two of them. Blue didn't move, other than to tip her head at her.

She did it again. "*This . . . is me?*"

Freckles replied with a barrage of images and memories, of watching humans from the shadows of the trees. The humans whispered in the dark, trying to be quiet. But to a demon's ears, it was the same as shouting. So noisy and ridiculous. What was worse was they were mind deaf. No matter how many times he and his packmates tried to form a bond with them, connect with them the way he connected to his friends and pack, it was like flying into a tree. Until he saw the silver human. She never used her mouth to talk and shout; she might have mind-speak. So he followed her as she left her group and gave her the pale flowers that opened the mind. He even ate one so she knew what to do, but obviously that didn't work. So when she came back into the forest, he tried again, and this time it worked! And now they could finally talk and—

Olivia reeled back, shaking her head to help separate her thoughts from Freckles's. He retreated into his own mind, letting her wrap her head around what was happening.

"*You can hear me?*" she clarified, using words instead of blocks of memories. "*You understand what I'm saying to you?*"

"*Our minds are not broken,*" Blue said. She looked at Freckles, who was still bouncing on his paws. "*Well, his is.*"

He nipped in her direction. Demons didn't chuckle, but Blue's mind took on the flavor of someone who was, like children making bubbles in the water. Olivia barely registered the wonder of hearing demons talk and make fun, through telepathy of all things. She still struggled with the wonder that she could now *speak*. That people could *hear her*.

Freckles bounced to her, whining. "*Your eyes bleed! Do you hurt? Where do you hurt?*"

Olivia burst out laughing, tears streaming down her face. "*I CAN TALK!*"

Freckles tipped his head. Blue huffed. "*She is happy, you slug-mind. Can you not feel it?*"

"*I feel it. She still bleeds water,*" he said.

"*That happens sometimes,*" Olivia replied, wiping her face. "*Usually when we're hurt, but sometimes when we're really, REALLY happy. And I can talk now!*"

Freckles tipped his head the other way and shared another memory: Olivia teaching him her squiggles, showing him how she communicated. It wasn't as elegant as mind-speak, of course, but humans had to make do when they were mind deaf, and it clearly got the job done. But now she was telling him that other humans didn't use squiggles?

Olivia winced, thinking of all the times Gabriel had torn up her sketchbooks while Michael laughed, of people walking away from her when she was halfway through writing because they didn't want to waste any more time, of people telling her to "just talk; it's not that hard." With some concentration, she sent those memories down the rope.

He whined and bumped the top of his head against her chest. "*I like the squiggles.*"

She grabbed her sketchbook from her bag. "*I'll show you some more! You don't have a written language, I take it?*"

She felt a third rope being added to the others, and she froze as a new mind pushed the image of Olivia and Blue sleeping, with the command, "*Rest.*"

Blue's hackles went up, but she didn't snarl or attack the old gray demon with blue wings who landed next to Freckles. He held a bouquet of plants in his jaws, and Olivia recognized several herbs used to soothe pain and headaches back in Citadel.

"*This is Ukurf,*" Freckles said. "*He is* sif'tep."

"*He's a what?*" Olivia asked.

The memory that Ukurf shared was different from Freckles's. Age had blurred the edges. But she could still make out a demon with dark-brown wings and fur finding herbs to help with sickness, using his teeth to wrap bandages around bleeding flesh, comforting those too broken to fix . . .

"*Oh, you're a medic,*" she realized. And male. Riley would be thrilled.

He set the herbs on the ground in front of Olivia and Blue. "*Eat.*"

"*More plants,*" Blue growled, the prasina flower blooming in her memory.

"*I know these ones. They'll be fine,*" Olivia promised. She gave two-thirds of them to Blue to account for her extra mass and got to preparing the others for herself. Her medical kit included a small iron bowl for making teas out of these exact herbs.

Images of other demons with various injuries and illnesses flashed through her mind from Ukurf. Olivia nodded; he had others to tend to.

"*Cyrij stays with you,*" he said.

"*Cyrij?*" she asked.

"*Me,*" Freckles said.

"*Oh. I've been calling you Freckles.*"

He tipped his head. "*What is 'freckles'?*"

She pictured the freckles dotted across Evelyn's, Asiya's, and Elias's faces and sent them to the others.

Ukurf's tongue lolled. His mind went bubbly, similar to Olivia's when she was about to laugh. "*Cyrij means 'spots.'*"

Cyrij preened. "*I like my spots.*"

"*Why does he stay?*" Blue demanded.

His light-brown wings drooped, and he tucked his tail between his legs. "*Pale flower makes you sick. I do not know this until after I give you pale flower. I just want to hear you.*" He nudged the nugzuuki to them. "*So I give you meat and fight predators until you are better.*"

Blue bared her teeth. "*I fight predators better than you.*"

"*Yes, but you still hurt,*" he said gently.

"*Free food,*" Olivia pointed out, taking the animal.

Blue huffed. *"Free food."*

Ukurf left. Olivia built a fire. Cyrij cleaned his feathers with his tongue and talons.

"So this is how demons communicate?" she asked.

"Demons?" Cyrij echoed. *"We are chimera."*

"Okay. But this is how you talk to each other?"

"Of course!"

"And the prasina flower helps activate the telepathy?" she clarified.

"Pale flower helps open chimera's mind if it is closed. Like . . . um, what do I call you, if not Is'hav?" Cyrij asked Blue.

She made a motion that might have been a shrug.

"I've been calling you Blue," Olivia suggested, motioning to her single pale-blue ear.

"Blue is good," she said.

"Good!" Cyrij said happily. *"Before, Blue's mind is closed. So I give her pale flower to open her mind, and make bond so we can mind-speak. Then I think, 'Maybe humans can also get open minds,' and give Silver pale flower, too!"* His ears and wings drooped. *"But I do not know that pale flower also makes you sick until you get sick and Ukurf tells me and yells at me."*

"Worth it!" Olivia cheered.

Blue growled low in her throat. *"I like mind-speak. I do not like dizziness and sleep."*

"Sorry," Cyrij said. *"I do not know it comes with that."*

Olivia held up the nugzuuki. *"Blue, you want this raw or cooked?"*

"Do not burn it."

They split it. The chimera tore into her meal while Olivia cooked her portion. *"So how come your mind was 'closed,' like mine?"*

Blue growled again, her mind darkening and twisting in a way that was so familiar. It was like whenever someone brought up Sarai or Elias.

"I do not talk about it," she said.

Olivia shrugged and went back to her meal. She was far too happy to care.

CHAPTER TWENTY-FIVE

Olivia wrote in her sketchbook while she rested, waiting for the lingering side effects of the prasina flower to run their course. She jotted down the entire experience under the heading *Day 32*, not leaving out a single detail.

Dear Elias,

Chimera don't seem to understand much of the concept of time. They communicate only through present tense. Usually it's with memories of personal experiences, but sometimes they'll say "before" or "after" to reference a vague point of time in the past or future. I'm not sure how I feel about that. On one hand, I appreciate Citadel's calendar and timekeeping to help me stay on top of chores and events. On the other hand, everyone's insistence that I must be at this place by that time, God forbid I be late, grates on my skin like a rusty knife. That doesn't exist here.

I don't think I'll ever get used to this telepathy. Even though Cyrij is currently out hunting, I can still feel him in the back of my mind. If I concentrate on the bond between us, I can feel what he's feeling. The same with Blue.

"*I am better. We leave now,*" Blue said, spreading her wings.

"*What? No!*" Olivia protested, looking up from her book. It was almost noon. Cyrij was due back from hunting soon. "*I haven't asked my questions yet.*"

Blue growled, suspicion darkening her mind. "*Packs are bad.*"

Olivia frowned. "*Why? What do packs look like?*"

Huffing with impatience, Blue sent Olivia a memory. Or rather, a blurry group of memories: several chimera sleeping together, flying together, eating together. It was foggy around the edges, more of a sensation of feelings, of safety and home and grief. Most of them featured a large female chimera with blue fur and white wings.

"*That doesn't seem too bad,*" Olivia said, once she'd blinked back to the present. It felt like when she had lived with Sarai.

"*Good packs are dead,*" Blue said. "*We leave now.*"

"*Why aren't you a part of a pack anymore?*"

Blue's mind closed in on itself, like all the doors of a house closing at once.

Cyrij returned, the leg of a serovim—a large migrating herbivore—in his jaws. He flew in and landed on the edge of the berry field, tail wagging. "*Food!*"

Olivia barely glanced at the severed limb in the dirt. "*How many packs are there in the forest?*"

"*Many.*"

"*But how many? Five? Ten?*"

"*Many,*" Cyrij repeated. "*Six-and-ten? Ten-and-ten?*"

"*And who's in charge of them all?*"

He tipped his head. "*All?*"

"*Yeah, who's in charge? Your governor or leader.*"

"Iyi'ke," Cyrij corrected. "*One iyi'ke, one pack.*"

Olivia blinked. A pit formed in her stomach. "*So . . . there are anywhere from fifteen—er, five-and-ten to ten-and-ten 'iyi'kes,' each one with their own pack?*"

"*Yes.*"

Fuck.

She'd assumed, once realizing that demons were sentient, that they would have a social or government structure similar to Citadel. Now she realized that had been stupid. These were entirely different creatures, with a lot more space than what humans had access to, and probably very different needs and values.

There was no central authority figure for her to talk to, to tell them to stop killing humans, to demand justice for Elias.

"*Who's your iyi'ke?*" she asked. Better start somewhere.

"*Mek'tay,*" he said, providing an image of Patch.

"*Take me to him.*"

"*No!*" Blue snarled. "*No more packs! We leave now.*"

Cyrij whined. "*Is'hav, why—*"

"*NOT IS'HAV. YOU DO NOT CALL ME IS'HAV!*"

The twigs, leaves, and even small stones on the ground around Blue blasted away, smacking against Olivia's and Cyrij's skin. Her mind was like a pot of water overboiled, spreading fire through the link to both of them, and with it came the memories. The blue-furred, white-winged chimera Olivia had seen earlier was covered in blood. The ground and trees of this memory were soaked red as chimera tore each other apart. The aggressors, the horrible victors, all used telekinesis, working together to throw torso-sized rocks that smashed bones, and branches sharpened to spearpoints that impaled wings.

"*You run, Is'hav,*" the white-winged chimera ordered, tearing into a telekinetic even as one of her beautiful, cloudlike wings dangled bloody and broken from her back. "*Follow no chimera. Go!*"

Olivia gasped and almost fell over, back in the present. "*What the fuck was* that?"

Blue looked away, the barbed coils of regret curling around the link between them. "*I do not want you to see that.*"

Cyrij whined, shaking his head against the dirt as if it would wipe the memory away. "*That is not my pack. That is Mulo pack.*"

"*Not true.*"

"*THAT IS NOT MY PACK,*" Cyrij snarled, baring his teeth. His mind had gone from the pleasant warmth of sunlight to sticking one's hand directly into a firepit. "*Isilna pack is good! Isilna pack only defends! Isilna pack does not kill cubs and nonwarriors to steal* kizaba*!*"

Olivia felt like she was missing 90 percent of this conversation. It happened a lot in Citadel, when the people around her would somehow silently communicate just through facial expressions and body language. She hated feeling that way.

"*What is Isilna, what is Mulo, and what is kizaba?*" she asked.

"*Isilna is my pack, with Mek'tay as iyi'ke. Mulo is bad pack. This is* kizaba," he said, showing a memory of a dark-brown, black-winged chimera moving a couple of crudely made dolls with his mind before a small group of cubs. A telekinetic.

"*Kizaba are special. Only one in many, many cubs is born kizaba. Mulo pack have many kizaba. They kill nonkizaba and steal others. When a kizaba is born outside Mulo pack, Mulo demands kizaba cub be given to them. Some packs give. Some packs do not. Blue's pack does not. Some packs are strong enough to fight Mulo. Some packs are not.*"

"All *packs take kizaba,*" Blue growled. Memories of the red chimera she and Olivia had fought appeared in all three of their minds, as well as a few others Blue had had to fight off herself.

"*Some packs take kizaba,*" Cyrij admitted. "*Some packs just worry. You are alone. No chimera should be alone.*"

"*I like alone. Alone is safe.*"

Cyrij pointedly looked at the fresh scar on her back leg.

"*Better blood than a tied mind,*" she said, her exact fear bleeding through their bond, echoes of her mother's warnings whispering in Olivia's ears. That she would become chained to a pack, unable to roam free. Forced to use her gift to cater to the whims of her masters.

"*Chimera are free,*" Cyrij soothed. "*Chimera join any pack they want. Chimera leave any pack they want. But in pack, chimera are safe.*"

Blue's words dripped venom: "*That is why you and Mek'tay give me food? To join Isilna pack?*"

"*Maybe after, we ask you to join,*" he admitted. "*But we give food to chimera outside Isilna pack, too. Friends.*" He shared a memory of following Mek'tay—Patch—through the forest. The black-furred leader and several other chimera carried half of an ingencis corpse to another group of chimera on the edge of their border. They could just barely see the lights of Citadel in the distance. *"Humans chase away prey. We feed our friends until they find new territory. That is how I meet Silver!"*

The dark cloud of suspicion around Blue's mind stayed.

"Your whole pack was killed?" Olivia clarified. *"You've been out here by yourself since then?"*

"Yes," Blue said.

"How long ago was that?"

She sent confusion down their link.

"Um . . . how many years?"

That got confusion from both of them.

"How old were you when it happened?"

"I just learn flying," Blue said. Olivia could feel a memory rush to the surface, quickly squashed by Blue, as if she were stuffing it back in a box before it could be seen. *"I just learn to stay in the sky. Then Mulo attacks."*

Cyrij whined. *"What a little cub."*

Olivia stared at her. She didn't know how long it took chimera to reach adulthood, but given Blue's adolescence *now*, that was the same as dropping a young child in the middle of the forest, alone, with no guidance or resources. *"How did you survive this long?"*

More confusion, flavored with fluffiness. It took Olivia a second to find the real word for that emotion: embarrassment. *"I just . . . know,"* Blue said, shuffling her paws in the dirt. *"I know what meat is good, how to make a den, how to hunt . . ."*

"Pack memory," Cyrij explained.

"What?" Olivia asked.

"When chimera is born, they get their father's and mother's wings. Father's and mother's eyes. And father's and mother's memories. And their fathers' and mothers' memories. And theirs. All the way up."

Olivia put her head in her hands. *"You have ancestral memory."*

"Humans do not?" he asked.

If she had been speaking aloud, her voice would have been weak. *"Just one set of memories per brain."*

Cyrij's tongue lolled out of his mouth in a goofy grin, mind bubbly. *"Some have better memory than others. Blue has good memory. Very good memory. I do not."*

One small part of Olivia's mind reeled with the possibilities, vibrating with excitement. How much history was locked away in the minds of chimera? They'd been here since before humans; how much did they remember about the planet? And that was only the ancestral memory! They had different communities and governments; how did any of those work? What happened when an iyi'ke died or stepped down or became unfit?

But it was all background noise. She only had one real question.

"Why do you keep killing humans?"

Cyrij tipped his head. *"Humans start it."*

"We did not," Olivia said, fiery rage building in her chest, making it hard to breathe. *"We came in from the Shadowlands and had barely finished building the first temple before you attacked us."*

"Humans start it," Cyrij snapped, his mind boiling over like Blue's. Through his mind, Olivia saw another young chimera with the same cream coloring as him, only without the spots. The memory hurt.

"Bullshit. We don't have 'pack memory,' but we have historical accounts. Written documents from the founding of Citadel. And every single report I read, every historical account, every diary entry, they all say the same thing: humans came to the forest, and before we even knew you existed, you chimera immediately attacked. You've been attacking for four hundred years."

"You send warriors to kill us in our dens," he growled.

"And what about our hunters? Our gatherers? The earliest accounts have you killing our women and children!"

"You come into our den. You chase away our food. You kill our cubs. You kill our packs. AND YOU ASK WHY WE KILL HUMANS?"

He turned his back to them and spread his wings. *"You leave now."*

He shot into the air, disappearing before Olivia could even process what had just happened.

Blue insisted they move camp after Cyrij left, and Olivia couldn't find an argument against it. They moved a couple of kilometers away from the uvam berry field, setting up the tent at the base of a tree, and ate the serovim limb for dinner. Since Cyrij wasn't going to be bringing them food anytime soon, Olivia went hunting the next morning while Blue slept.

It was at the point of lowest tide, the ground as dry as it got in the Flooded Forest. As she kept her eyes open for tracks or movement in the darkened, empty woods, she thought about Cyrij. The good thing about telepathy was that she no longer had to guess what someone was feeling. She had felt his rage during their conversation; there was no doubt about that. What telepathy didn't tell her was *why*. She had gotten heated in that conversation, too, but hadn't ordered the chimera to leave her presence. War made idiots of everyone, but Cyrij had seemed personally offended. What was with that?

Ugh. People were so exhausting.

She squinted at a set of tracks in the mud. Big, round, at least four legs. A spiven, perhaps. She followed them.

If Cyrij wasn't going to answer her questions properly, then she'd need to ask someone else. Blue simply didn't know, and when Olivia had asked if she could tap into her ancestral memory, she had said she didn't know how to do that either. It was just instinct for her. She couldn't consciously call upon it. So that left Mek'tay, Cyrij's pack leader, or their healer, Ukurf.

Unless Cyrij had told them not to talk to Olivia because of their argument. In that case, Olivia would just have to keep wandering the woods until she found another chimera. With her new telepathy, she might have more success than last—

A growl yanked her out of her thoughts. Olivia cursed herself.

She'd gotten so deep inside her own head she hadn't noticed that she'd come across the owner of the tracks she'd been following.

It wasn't a spiven. It was a menziva.

Unlike the spiven, menziva were predators, with six powerful legs that ended in six-inch claws. The massive amphibian had platelike muscles along its back and legs that could extend into fins when it was in water. Outside of water, the plate acted like armor.

The menziva bared its teeth at her. Olivia strung an arrow but didn't pull it back, choosing instead to slowly back away.

I won't be able to penetrate its armor, she thought. *The eyes, the inside of the mouth, and its lower neck and belly are the only weak points. But I'm not going to be able to aim for the latter unless it stands on its hind legs.*

She glanced at the nearby massive trees. None of the branches were low enough for her to climb. And like an idiot, she'd left her cleats back at the camp.

If she ran, it would chase her. Menziva were deadly in the water but could also run faster than a man on the ground. Several hunters had been eaten alive making the mistake of running.

Her best chance was to keep moving slowly and hope that it wasn't hungry.

The menziva hissed at her. She took another step back.

It charged.

She pulled back her arrow and fired.

The arrow—barely—missed its mark, hitting the nose instead of the eye. The menziva hesitated half a beat before continuing to charge.

Olivia dropped her bow and sprinted for the nearest tree. She whipped out her knife and ran as far *up* the tree as her boots would allow. As soon as gravity began to pull on her, she stabbed the wood with her knife. The metal couldn't cut farther than the thick bark and threatened to slip. She used her free hand to grab on, and with all of her core strength she pulled her legs up so she was a tiny ball.

The menziva jumped, snapping at her. She could feel the wind of its snout breeze against her bottom, but it couldn't reach her.

It dropped back to the ground, hissing again.

Olivia swallowed, looking down. She wouldn't be able to hold this position forever. Already her abdominal muscles cramped, and if her hand or knife slipped, she would fall. Maybe she could climb up?

She carefully set her shoes against the bark, struggling to find purchase, then slowly let go of the wood with the hand that wasn't holding the knife.

Immediately, the knife slipped. She scrambled to keep her hold. The menziva took its chance and jumped again. Its teeth nipped at her pants leg, ripping the fabric. It dropped to the ground.

This is not how I thought I'd die. She looked up at the cover of the orange leaves, wondering if she'd be able to hold on to the tree long enough to pull her knife out and stab higher to climb. Probably not.

The menziva jumped again.

A mass of black fur and feathers slammed into it, teeth and claws ripping into the exposed neck and belly. The menziva was dead seconds later, without ever being able to strike back.

Olivia pulled her knife free and dropped. She landed on her feet and only stayed that way because she was able to lean against the tree for support.

Mek'tay stood over the menziva's corpse, licking his bloody chops. "*Do you hurt?*" he asked.

"*No,*" she replied. Maybe it was the gallons of adrenaline rushing through her veins, but she still felt giddy at the ability to talk. "*Thank you.*"

He tore into the menziva's body but didn't eat right away. Instead, with the first chunk of meat still in his mouth, he dug a shallow hole. He dropped the mouthful, buried it, *then* began eating.

"*What was that for?*" Olivia asked.

"*Gift to Edalide.*"

"*Edalide?*"

Mek'tay flooded her mind with images of the forest, tides, streams, sky, creatures, Shadowlands, rings. Olivia had to lean back against the tree when she got dizzy.

"*Edalide,*" he repeated when the images finally stopped.

"*You mean . . . the planet?*"

"*Yes. Do you want meat?*" He motioned to the menziva.

"*I'd need to cook it first, or I'll get sick.*"

"*Cook?*"

She thought for a minute, remembering the day Asiya had enlisted

her and Evelyn's help in making dinner. They'd just bought enough ingencis meat to last several weeks. Asiya had cut it in the middle while
frying it on a skillet, showing them the pink innards. "You can see it's still
raw in the middle. We need to let it cook for another few minutes before
it's safe to eat; otherwise you'll spend the night in front of the toilet."

Olivia shared the memory with Mek'tay. He made a sound that
might've been a huff but didn't argue.

"*Take two legs*," he instructed. "*Go to Blue. Stay. We talk.*"

Olivia brightened and immediately set to work severing a couple
of menziva legs.

CHAPTER TWENTY-SIX:
RILEY

Riley stood in front of the hospital, his acceptance letter in the notebook in his hands. The letter had specifically stated to bring study materials, so he'd brought the notebook Olivia had gotten for him, the only part of her gift that his father hadn't been able to burn.

Like its temples, Citadel had multiple hospitals, all varying in size and quality. The ones near the wall barely counted as hospitals, acting more as places for sick people to die. Others actually did the work to try to cure illnesses and mend injuries. Central Hospital, which was built by the Founders in the center of town, was the largest and most respected.

They all took in medics to train, although where one trained usually determined what type of work one could expect. It was very rare for a "wall-trained" medic to find work in Central Hospital. Being trained in Central Hospital, on the other hand, guaranteed that a medic could find work anywhere.

Which was where Riley now stood.

Taking a deep breath (and whispering a prayer to the Face of Courage), Riley went in.

He was very familiar with this building, but it took on a new light now that he would be working here. It was one of Citadel's very few three-story structures, and built like a cross, each wing pointing to a cardinal direction. The hallways were wide enough for multiple people to run around without bumping into each other, the blue wood smoothed with age. One side of the walls had large windows of impure, cloudy glass that let in the sunlight and showed off the hospital's ridiculous wealth, while the other side had professional paintings of Scriptural scenes, history, and famous medics.

He approached the front desk, where an older woman scribbled through a pile of paperwork. She wore a white shirt—signifying her rank as a fully trained medic—and hid her graying hair under a full headscarf. Riley smiled when he realized he knew her. "Good morning, Mrs. Princops."

She looked up, then back down at her papers. "I sincerely hope you're here for treatment."

"No, I have my acceptance letter to begin medical training." He placed it on the desk.

Mrs. Princops didn't take it. "This is in poor taste, boy."

He frowned. "I'm sorry?"

"Riley!"

Asiya Claude speed-walked toward them, big smile on her face. She wore the same white medic shirt as Mrs. Princops, her usual matron cap over her thick black curls. A long skirt flowed around her legs and was tied tight around her waist, emphasizing her curves. "You made it. We're waiting for you in the training room. Do you have your letter?"

He gave it to her. She skimmed it as she wrapped a thick arm around his shoulders and steered them away from the glaring Mrs. Princops. "Excellent. Now, normally training would take a couple of weeks, but given how understaffed we are, we've crammed that down to a few days and more hands-on work."

"All right," Riley said. His heart gave a nervous thrill at the thought of doing hands-on work so soon. He knew he learned better that way. But now, suddenly, this was *real*.

She squeezed him, squishing his arm against her soft side. "Don't worry about Mrs. Princops. She's . . . well, a bit of a traditionalist. Many of the women are."

He grimaced. He'd suspected as such, but it was still disappointing to hear it confirmed.

"It's nothing I'm not already used to," he assured her. *I didn't come here to make friends.*

Asiya led him to a large meeting room of some kind, tucked out of the way of medics and patients. A handful of medics glared at Riley as they passed. Asiya glared right back at them, like a puffed-up spiven in a matron's cap. He had to remind himself that he had every right to be here.

The meeting room felt like a classroom, which Riley guessed was its intended purpose. There were two rows of long tables with chairs, all facing the front. At the front was a smaller table, a cloth dummy, and several medical supplies.

"Go and take a seat, dear," Asiya said, nudging Riley toward one of the few empty chairs. There were over a dozen other new medics in the room, all of them girls. Riley recognized several from school and waved. Only a couple acknowledged him. The others turned away and whispered to each other.

"All right, trainees," Asiya called, making her way to the front. The whispering stopped. "Now that we're all here, let's get started. Today we're going over the basics of first aid and cardiopulmonary resuscitation. Our hope is that we can get you all treating minor injuries and ailments within the next couple of days. You'll also be given books on human anatomy and physiology that you will be expected to study and memorize the contents of as quickly as possible. This will make it easier for you to learn our procedures on the job. Now, who can tell me . . ."

The morning passed as a lecture. Riley took detailed notes, though he was pleasantly surprised to realize that he already knew some of what Asiya talked about. She gave everyone a copy of an anatomy book and told them which chapters they'd need to read for tomorrow before they broke for lunch.

The hospital had a large cafeteria for its staff, divided by a long counter. A woman served stew behind it, while another handed out slices of metabread, and a third gave drinks. A fourth medic, still in training given her gray shirt, made notations in a ledger of who took what.

"You're welcome to take anything from the cafeteria," Asiya said. "But it will be docked from your pay. Alternatively, you can bring your own food from home."

Riley glanced at the prices and winced. He was *definitely* bringing food from home.

"Today, however, your meals are free."

"Thank God," one of the girls grumbled. Gabrielle, whose family owned and operated the town's paper mill. "This food looks like it came from the slums."

"I know," her friend replied. "They're *charging* us for this?"

"I'm just annoyed they have us doing schoolwork," a third muttered.

Ignoring them, Riley selected a slice of metabread and salted it within an inch of its life. He and Olivia had once done an experiment, after hearing that some sicknesses were linked to certain diets, and had found that if he ate salty foods, his migraines became less common.

He checked out first and took a seat at one of the cafeteria's tables. The other medics in training came later. None of them sat by him.

Wow. I thought we all outgrew this, he thought with a chuckle. He opened his anatomy book. Might as well get some studying done.

Asiya sat across from him with a bowl of stew. She gave the other trainees a disappointed look. "How are you doing?"

"Reliving my early school days."

She frowned. "You're the governor's son. Surely . . ."

"I also suffer from chronic migraines—a sure sign of 'weak blood'—wasn't ever into sports, and preferred the company of the town's atheists to almost everyone else." He motioned to the tables. "This was pretty standard."

"That's hardly fair."

"I can't complain. When I left home, I honestly thought I'd be spending the night on the street. Instead I have a roof over my head and Sergeant Peterson's couch. That's a hundred blessings right there."

"I tried to convince my husband to take you in at the party," she said. "He didn't want to get on the wrong side of your father."

Riley nodded. "That's probably for the best. Peterson has the luxury of not giving a darn. You and your husband do not."

"Oh, he cares. He's just too cautious sometimes."

He shrugged, deciding to switch topics. "How's Evelyn?"

Lunch passed much more pleasantly than he expected. Afterward, Asiya took them all to get their training uniforms: loose cotton shirts dyed black.

"Once you finish your training, you'll get the gray ones," Asiya explained, digging through the pile of fabric to find the right sizes for her charges. "And when you've completed one year of work after that, you will officially be deemed medics and given your white uniforms."

Some of the girls, Gabrielle included, made faces at the shirts. Others put them on without complaint. Riley did, too, then looked down. "Uh, Mrs. Claude. I don't mean to complain, but . . ."

Gabrielle laughed at him. He didn't blame her. He giggled at himself, his entire frame swallowed by an ocean of black fabric. It looked more like a dress, going all the way down to his knees.

Asiya chuckled an apology and went digging for a smaller size. Riley examined himself. "I don't know, girls. You think if I get the right accessories I can make it work?"

"Thompson, I think I speak for all of us when I say, take that ridiculous thing off," Gabrielle laughed.

He pulled it off, red-brown hair sticking up with static, which didn't help his image. But he didn't care, and there was a certain freedom in that. His image was going to be tarnished anyway, so why not enjoy it? Asiya found him a smaller shirt, which was still a bit too big, but at least he could tuck it into his pants.

To his surprise, some of the ice seemed to have thawed as they left the closet. Gabrielle walked alongside him. "We heard your parents kicked you out the minute they heard you wanted to be a medic. That's not true, is it?"

"It is," he sighed. "I'm staying with a friend."

She gaped at him. "You let yourself get kicked out of the *governor's house*, for bad food, itchy clothes, and boring lectures?"

"Yes."

She shook her head. Then smiled sweetly at him. "So, did you happen to take notes? Because I forgot my notebook at home."

"I'll let you copy mine," he said.

She rubbed his head, smoothing out his staticky hair. "You're a doll."

"Not every day in the hospital is spent tending to the wounded," Asiya instructed, bringing everyone's attention to the front. "There are a host of day-to-day activities that keep this place running: administrative, delivering medicines to our outpatients, and cleaning."

That last one got several groans. Even Riley couldn't hide a grimace.

"Don't take that tone with me. We all do it. If a hospital isn't clean, it leads to greater infections and illnesses in our patients, which leads to more death. Believe it or not, cleaning saves lives."

She divided them up into groups for the rest of the day: one for cleaning, one to help with administration, and one for medicines. Riley found himself in that last group with a girl named Bella. Not to be confused with Bella Novak, the mother of the executed Dove Benjamin; Bella Carter was a distant cousin of Riley's.

"Lots of patients require ongoing medications," Asiya explained, leading the two of them to a different pocket of the hospital. It was in a different wing than surgeries and emergencies, so Riley wasn't as familiar with this part. It was quieter here, the medics not moving quite as fast. Almost every room was still full, though, usually with two to three patients.

"Sometimes it's only for a few weeks, other times for the rest of their lives," she continued. "It used to be that you had to come into the hospital for a full checkup before getting your medicine refilled. But with recent complications, that's no longer possible. We've started delivering. You'll likely take up that duty at some point in the next few days, but for now, you'll be stationed here."

She motioned to a desk in front of a closet with an open door. It was filled with shelves stacked with bottles and boxes of medicines.

A gray-shirted medic sat behind the desk, talking with an older man. She made a few notes on a piece of paper, went into the closet, and came back with a vial.

"When a patient—or their spouse, parent, or adult child—comes to pick up their medicine, you'll ask them these questions," Asiya explained, holding up one of the pieces of paper. Riley skimmed the questionnaire. "You'll then find their medicines in the closet by last name. Put the completed form in the envelope under the desk, making sure to mark their name. We put them with the rest of the patient's information to keep track of how their treatment is progressing."

"What if someone comes up and says they're not seeing any improvement, or dealing with side effects?" Riley asked.

"If they're serious enough, call a fully trained medic. We'll see to it," Asiya said.

Someone down the hall called, "Asiya! Emergency room needs us! Carriage accident!"

The gray-shirt looked up at the call too. Asiya plopped Riley and Bella behind the desk, said, "I'll be back when I can," collected the gray-shirt, and jogged away.

Riley and Bella shared a slightly terrified look before getting settled.

"So, do you prefer men?"

The question caught Riley completely off guard. Especially since he and Bella had been sitting in relative silence for the last hour. Only two patients had come to collect their medicines, and it had been very straightforward, minus the odd looks they both gave Riley.

"What makes you say that?" he asked.

Bella shrugged. "You're here. Obviously you're not . . . well, not the manliest person in town. Why else would you pursue women's work?"

"The same reason some women pursue men's work. It's their Placement," he said, a defensive edge to his voice. He forced himself to take a deep breath and be calm. Wouldn't do to get into an argument on his first day.

"If you say so," she said. "But you didn't answer my question."

He rolled his eyes. "No, I do not prefer men. The few times I have liked someone like that, they've all been girls."

"Sure."

He caught the disbelief in her voice and didn't care. Such accusations of "sexual deviancy" had led to executions before, but they were incredibly hard to prove. And like most of his father's policies, Riley honestly didn't see the point in pursuing this one. That was how the Hundred-Faced God made them, and some had joined the Doves specifically because of it. Just because he didn't see the appeal of the same sex didn't mean he was going to persecute those who did.

A tall, big-nosed figure strode up to the desk. Riley straightened. "Markus! Good to see you."

Markus blinked at him. "So it's true."

Riley bit back a sigh. *Hundred hells, can we have a single conversation today that doesn't revolve around this?*

"Getting medicine for your wife?" he asked.

"Yes," Markus said, somewhat stiffly.

Bella excused herself to use the restroom, leaving the two of them alone in the hall.

"I'm disappointed in you, Riley," Markus said. "You could've been governor. We needed that."

"Even if that did happen, that would've taken *years*," Riley pointed out. "Help me fill out this form so we can keep track of your wife's treatment."

They did, very awkwardly. Riley noticed that Markus was dressed in one of his best suits and frowned. "I thought you worked during the day."

"I do. But Jane was too weak to leave the house today, so I took a break."

Riley went back into the closet to fetch the medicine, searching through rows and rows of glass and wood. While he was there, he came to a decision.

"You know," he said, coming back out, medicine in hand, "we do deliver."

"We prefer not to do that," Markus said. Under his breath, he added, "Too dangerous."

"I can ask Asiya if I can take you on specifically. Everyone knows

Jane and I are friends." He set the medicine on the desk between them. "God knows I could use the exercise."

Markus opened and closed his mouth, then nodded. "You know, that would be very nice. Thank you, Riley."

He smiled, watching Markus leave.

Let them whisper. Let them laugh. Let them hate his guts. He was going to be the best medic Citadel had ever seen.

CHAPTER TWENTY-SEVEN

After an hour or so of hacking at the corpse Mek'tay had provided—and realizing that she was in desperate need of a bath if she wanted to not smell like menziva guts for the next year—Olivia hauled the two limbs to her and Blue's camp. It was a few minutes away from a tide pool, but not right next to it so as to avoid predators coming for a drink.

Halfway there, Olivia felt a poke at the back of her brain, followed by Blue's sharp voice: "*Cyrij is here.*"

Olivia stiffened. "*Is that good or bad?*"

Blue sent an image of Cyrij before her, on his back, exposing his belly. "*Good? He says leaving us before is bad.*"

"*Well, it was a jerk move,*" Olivia grumbled. "*I'll be there soon.*"

When she got there, Cyrij was no longer on his back, instead lying on his belly a safe distance away from Blue. He perked up when Olivia arrived and tossed a menziva limb to Blue. She'd skin and smoke the other so she could eat it and save the leftovers. "*I'm taking a bath.*"

Blue dug into her meal. "*Cyrij protects you.*"

Olivia shrugged, heading for the pond. After a beat, Cyrij followed.

"*Why did you leave?*" she asked, pulling off her shirt. Modesty be damned; she needed to get out of her blood-soaked clothes. And since chimera were technically naked all day every day, she doubted it'd be a problem.

"*Rage*," he replied, his normally sunny mind dampened and gloomy. Olivia caught another glimpse of that spotless, cream-colored chimera before it was gone. "*That rage is not for you. After this, I do not leave again.*"

"*I get that you left because you were angry.*" They reached the tide pool. It was smaller than the one next to Citadel, just outside the walls. As soon as the tides retreated, a dozen boats would be on the pool and fish out any lingering animals within a day. Sometimes the soldiers in training would have swim lessons there, a useful skill for when they had to go out and rescue lost or hurt fishermen. When Olivia was a child, she'd been enchanted by the act of swimming, one of her random fixations. Peterson and Sarai had obliged her and taken her out to the tide pool to teach her how to swim. Whole afternoons would be spent splashing in the cool water, diving to the bottom to collect whatever treasures the tides had brought in from the freshwater sea.

This far from the wall, there was no backup in case a menziva was lurking in the depths or someone struggled and risked drowning. But having Cyrij nearby was a comfort. After a quick look to make sure there were no predators around, Olivia stripped off the rest of her clothes and dove into the tide pool. It being summer, it wasn't freezing. But it was cool enough to send goose bumps across her skin, a pleasant jolt to her system as she swam. Being able to talk while underwater was nice: "*I just want to know* why *you were angry. Who's that chimera you keep thinking of?*"

One by one, Cyrij's memories unfolded. His earliest memories, always having the cream-colored chimera at his side. Learning to fly together. Learning to hunt together. Learning their packs' history together. Until one day the cream-colored chimera left, and the link in Cyrij's mind was filled with terror until it shattered—

Olivia's breath came out in bubbles. She rose to the surface. "*He was your brother. We killed him.*"

"*His name is Takkaz,*" Cyrij confirmed.

Olivia grimaced. At least Takkaz's death had been quick. She didn't recall ever seeing him being tortured to death in Citadel.

She didn't say *I'm sorry for your loss.* She'd never understood the sentiment, even when it'd been said to her after Sarai, and then Elias. The well-wishers had had nothing to do with their deaths, nothing to apologize for, and their words did nothing to bring her dead loved ones back.

Instead she said, "*That shouldn't have happened. I've lost someone to this war too.*"

"*Who is your pain?*"

Olivia washed her hair, getting the oil and grime out of it, letting the methodical movements calm her. "*My boyfriend, Elias.*"

"*Boy-friend?*"

It hurt. It still hurt. But Olivia could still remember her favorite moments with Elias: him teaching her how to use a bow, their first kiss, him telling her that he loved her and realizing with both elation and terror that she loved him back . . . She bundled those memories up and sent them to Cyrij.

"*Oh, your mate,*" Cyrij realized. He drooped. "*Warrior. He fights us.*"

"*Not willingly,*" she said. "*Citadel makes all able-bodied men go through military training and go on a hunt. He didn't want to go, but deserters are punished by death.*"

"*They* force *him to fight?*" Cyrij growled. "*If warriors do not want to fight, there should be no fight!*"

She hummed in agreement. "*I just want to know why. Why did he and Takkaz and everyone else have to die?*"

"*As I say before: humans start it.*" His ears twitched. "*Mek'tay is here.*"

Olivia got out of the pool and hastily cleaned her clothes. She didn't bother wringing them out; she had a spare outfit back at camp. The wind chilled the water against her skin, and by the time they'd made it back to camp, she was half jogging to stay warm, ready to put on dry clothes.

"*Humans need fur,*" Blue said, and Olivia couldn't argue with that.

Mek'tay sat a respectful distance from Blue. After donning her spare outfit, Olivia started a hardwood fire to keep everyone warm, pulled out her little iron pot, and began the arduous process of removing the tough scales from the menziva leg and stripping the meat from the bone so she could smoke it over the fire.

"*Before, no human comes into the forest alone,*" Mek'tay said. "*You do. Why?*"

She tossed a chunk of meat into the pot and studied him, narrowing her eyes. Something had changed in his mind between now and when he'd rescued her from the menziva. There was an agitation there, like an insect caught in a trap. It was faint, but there.

She decided to ignore it. If he had a problem, he could tell her. It wasn't like she knew how to help, anyway.

One of her favorite advantages of chimeric telepathy—other than the obvious ability to talk—was being able to quickly convey information through images and memories. But it was hard to condense the entire experience of growing up in Citadel believing only one story about "demons" and then suddenly coming to the realization that it wasn't true at all and that there was only one way to be sure.

She did her best: recalled lessons from her books and teachers, the religious and historical texts that all claimed chimera were unholy abominations who attacked humans as soon as they arrived, her meeting with Cyrij, and the research she did after that.

"*You have questions,*" Mek'tay said.

"*Why* are *you attacking us?*" Olivia asked. "*I can understand fighting the soldiers coming in to kill you, but the hunters and gatherers? And were the historical texts accurate: Did you strike first or was it us? Also, why was Cyrij the first to suggest giving us the green flower instead of when we first arrived four hundred years ago? Oh, and—*"

"*Too many questions,*" Mek'tay said.

Olivia winced and focused entirely on stripping the next bit of menziva meat. "*Sorry.*"

"*That is not bad,*" he replied, his tone gentle. "*I can answer. I can show you memory, from long before.*"

"*Long before . . . You mean one of your ancestral memories?*"

"*From first chimera.*"

She dropped the knife and menziva limb entirely. "*Yes! Please!*"

"*Me too,*" Blue said.

"*I can show you,*" he said. "*But first, you do something for me.*"

Olivia narrowed her eyes. "*What?*"

"*The Kimuud pack is friend of my pack. One sunset before, Kimuud*" *cub falls into a hole that leads to cave and breaks his wing. The hole is too small for grown chimera to go in."*

She jerked her chin to Blue. *"What about kizaba?"*

"Kizaba can only move what they see and what is close. It does not work here. I hear about this problem after we kill the menziva. I tell them about you, that you are skinny like twig and may fit in the hole."

She had been called many, many things in her life. "Skinny like a twig" was not one of them. "Freakishly tall" and "ugly like a grandma" and "built like a man," sure. Only a handful of people had ever complimented her looks, and she was skeptical as to how genuine they had really been. Elias's favorite word for her had been *striking*, but boyfriends were supposed to say nice things.

There was no emotion in Mek'tay's description of her, though. No malice or awe. It was just a fact. She was skinnier than the adult chimera, which made her ideal for the job.

Somehow, that stark statement of fact—no attempt at flattery or command—made her a lot more willing to go through with this.

"So you want me to go into a cave to rescue a cub, and then you'll tell me what I need to know?"

"Yes."

She wanted to tell him that this was a bad idea. She'd never been on a rescue mission before. She wasn't trained for it like the soldiers. And he'd said the cub was hurt; she was no medic. It'd be much better to bring someone like Peterson or Asiya who would at least know what they were doing.

But Citadel was days away. By the time she got there, the tides would come in. That cave would fill with water. The cub would drown, assuming they hadn't starved to death first.

She mournfully looked at her menziva leg. It wasn't getting smoked anytime soon. Depending on how long she was gone, it could even get spoiled.

With a sigh, she offered it to Cyrij and got to her feet. *"Where is this hole?"*

CHAPTER TWENTY-EIGHT

Mek'tay offered to give Olivia a ride to the Kimuud pack. As if Olivia weren't already willing to hold up her end of the deal.

Because of the placement of the chimera's wings on their backs, Olivia couldn't relax her legs without restricting their movement. She had to bend her knees almost to the sides of her torso while pressing her chest against Mek'tay's black fur so the wind resistance wouldn't slow him down or mess him up. And she couldn't clutch the fur too tightly, no matter how much she wanted to when Mek'tay launched them into the air. That would hurt him.

But once they were in the air, it was *amazing*. The lurch of her stomach when gravity tried to pull them back down, the way the trees and ground shrank beneath them the higher they got before they burst through the fire-colored leaves, the sharp knowledge that one slip and she would plummet to her death—she loved all of it. She laughed, the sound startling a flock of birds. She felt more free and powerful than she had in months. In years.

As they flew southwest, she noticed the elevation getting higher. The trees went from the tall blue monsters to smaller, greener things. *"Do the tides reach this part of the forest?"*

"Yes. But it is shallow."

Excellent. She probably wouldn't have to worry about the cave being flooded by a tide pool.

The sun neared its descent by the time they reached the cave, with two chimera at its entrance. Mek'tay landed and collapsed, panting. Olivia climbed off him. "*Are you all right?*"

"*Fine,*" he said. "*Humans are* heavy."

"*Sorry.*"

One of the chimera approached Mek'tay and pressed the top of their head into him, like how Cyrij sometimes did to Olivia. She decided that meant they were friends and knelt in front of the cave. It was little more than a hole in the rock, and a tight squeeze, at that. "*The cub fell down here?*"

"*Yes,*" the other chimera said. Female, with indigo fur and pale-blue feathers. Blood was dried on her front paws, and there were deep scratches in the rocks. "*But before, he is scared and moves further in. We do not know why.*"

"*Can't you ask him?*"

She snarled. "*He is too young for our bond to be that strong, and too far.*"

Right. Cyrij had explained that to her: the reason her bonds with him and Blue were stronger than the ones with Mek'tay and the medic Ukurf was because she regularly spent time with and communicated with them. But if Cyrij went too far away, she couldn't talk to him, could just faintly feel his emotions.

Olivia dropped her head. This was going to take much longer than she'd thought. She had brought her bow and quiver on the off chance that she'd have to defend herself but took them off now. She was barely going to be able to squeeze through that hole without the weapons strapped to her back.

"*How deep is it?*" she asked.

"*Deep,*" the blue chimera said. "*Ta've says there is long tunnel that goes to large cave.*"

"*I can work with that.*" She took out her rope. "*I need a branch. The straighter the better. About the width and length of my arm, maybe a little shorter.*"

"Why do you need stick? Get my cub!"

"I can't see in the dark," Olivia explained, finding a skinny enough tree to tie the rope around. *"The stick is to make a torch so I can* find *your cub."*

The other chimera, the one who had greeted Mek'tay, spoke. *"Sorry. She worries for her cub. I am Acmare, iyi'ke of the Kimuud pack. This is my littermate, Idavi. Ta've's mother."*

It was a strong family resemblance. Acmare had the same dark-blue fur as Idavi, with the only discernible difference being that his wings were darker.

Olivia tied the rope around the tree and used her foot to brace herself as she tightened the knot. *"Can I get that stick?"*

Acmare flew off and came back a few minutes later with a few sticks and small branches in his mouth. Using the straightest of the bunch, her socks, and the alcohol from her medical kit, she readied a sturdy torch but didn't light it yet.

Idavi watched her in silence. It wasn't until Olivia pulled her hair back in a ponytail, ready to go, that she asked, *"Why do you do this? Humans kill cubs."*

"This human doesn't," she replied. *"I made a deal with Mek'tay. I'll be right back. Don't touch my rope."*

Rope secure, medical kit in her pocket, and torch in her belt loop, Olivia crawled into the cave. The sunlight quickly expired, and she had to grope her way down the pitch-black crevasse. It was carved into the rock at an angle, gradually turning to go straight down. She gripped the rope with one hand, bracing her back against one stone wall and feet against the other, feeling the blood rush to her head as she became more and more upside down.

Until the cave suddenly opened up. Olivia was able to twist herself so she skidded down the rope feet first and hit the floor.

She had thought the Flooded Forest at night was the epitome of darkness. But down here, when she turned away from the light above, there was no difference between having her eyes open and having them closed. It was as if she'd been swallowed by some great beast. She hastily lit her torch.

The cavern was about the size of her living room, tall enough for her to stand on someone else's shoulders if she wanted. The rock walls were surprisingly rough and jagged; that meant the floods didn't come here often enough to smooth them down. A tunnel led into that impenetrable blackness. She started walking.

Several long minutes passed in dark silence, the only sound being the scuff of her boots on stone and the flicker of fire. Eventually the tunnel opened up again, half of the area filled with water in an underground pool. Stalactites dripped more water from the ceiling, their teeth inching closer to the water's surface. The other side of the room had stalactites and stalagmites both, creeping closer to each other over the millennia, a stone monster slowly closing its mouth.

She lowered her torch and smiled at the blue feather she found by the pool's edge.

The smile dropped when she saw the rather large pile of feces nearby.

She knelt next to it to get a better look. The pile was a few days old, which automatically ruled out Ta've's doing it. And frankly, it was far too much for a baby cub to excrete in a single session.

She wandered over to the stalagmites, wondering if the cub had decided to make a home in the relative cover. She found another blue feather, next to claw marks carved into the stone.

She tugged on her thin bond with Mek'tay. "*Problem.*"

"*What?*" he asked. His voice was faint in her mind from the distance.

She showed him the claw marks and feces. "*This cave is something's home. Some kind of predator, I'd wager.*"

Mek'tay's mind did a little worried wobble before returning to stability. "*Idavi cannot talk to Ta've, but she says their bond is still there. He lives. Keep looking. Be careful.*"

"*Is there any way I can connect with him telepathically?*"

"*Reach out with your mind as you do when you meet new chimera.*"

"*I never reached out to you. You formed the bond with me, first.*"

"*Hmmm . . . it is sometimes easier for cubs to form their bonds when they close their eyes.*"

Olivia did as she was told, trying to search the cave with her mind and nothing else.

Something flickered on the edges of her psyche. Like a candle lit in the distance.

"*I think I got something!*" she cheered, opening her eyes and almost jogging down the cave. She slowed when she saw more claw marks.

Right. Unknown predator lurking in the shadows. Best to keep quiet.

She didn't know how long she walked—how deep was this damn cave?—before the tunnel forked in two different directions. Closing her eyes again, she looked for that other mind. It pulled her left.

She followed the tug, homing in on the mind, until she turned another corner and it abruptly stopped.

Olivia raised her torch, illuminating the indent in the cavern hall that was filled with stalagmites and stalactites. With the dark shadows flickering, she almost missed the chimera cub hidden behind the stone.

"*Found him!*" she cheered.

No response.

She frowned. "*Mek'tay?*"

Nothing. She could feel the bond between them, but it was a thin thread, not strong enough to carry messages through this distance.

She was on her own.

Slowly approaching the cub, she formed a new link. "*Ta've? My name's Olivia. Your mom sent me here to find you.*"

He skittered back, deeper into the twisted maze of stone. His mind trembled. "*Human. Human is bad.*"

"*Not me,*" she said. "*I won't hurt you, I promise.*"

He didn't budge.

Olivia sighed and sat against a particularly large stalactite. She could conceivably try to reach in there and grab him, but . . . "*They said you broke your wing on the way down?*"

"*Hurts,*" he admitted.

And that was the problem. If she tried to grab him, she could easily make his injury worse, even life threatening. If it wasn't already.

"*I broke my arm once,*" she admitted, sharing the memory in his mind. She was eight, maybe nine years old, and had decided to climb to the roof of her house. Riley was there—they often spent time together after he was done with school—and warned her not to. She didn't listen, climbing anyway. Getting up wasn't an issue, and when she was there, she could see almost all of Citadel and the tops of everyone's heads. She thought if there was a Hundred-Faced God judging them from the sky, this was probably how He felt. Being up high made everything below seem insignificant.

But when she tried to climb down, her foot slipped, and she fell. The break hurt worse than anything in her life, making her a sobbing, inconsolable mess. Riley panicked and ran off, and that was worse. Because now she was alone and scared and didn't know what to do. She just wanted to stop hurting.

Eventually Riley came back with an adult, who took her to the hospital. Sarai was livid. Recovery was difficult. But the good news was her arm was all better now; she was able to fully use it after a couple of months.

Ta've stayed quiet after the memory was done. He tentatively shared one of his own. It was his first time leaving the den, being allowed on the ground. His mother kept a close eye on him as he sniffed the forest floor, the rich, earthy scent almost overwhelming him. He found a hole and wanted to know where it went. He stuck his head in, trying to smell it. But then he lost his footing and tried to fly out, but his wings caught on the stone, and one of them exploded in pain as he fell and fell and just barely managed to glide as he hit the ground.

"*That was some good gliding,*" Olivia said. "*Probably saved your life.*"

"*I cannot fly now,*" he moaned.

"*No, but once we get you out of here, we'll get that fixed.*"

He hesitated.

Olivia tried a different tactic, pulling a slice of jerky from her pocket. "*Hungry? You've been down here awhile.*"

"*Humans poison meat.*"

"*This isn't poisoned. Look, I'll prove it.*" She took a bite, chewed, and swallowed. She even stuck out her tongue so he could see that she'd really eaten it. "*See? Tasty. Not poisoned.*"

She held the piece out. Ta've poked his head out of the shadows to sniff, and Olivia desperately tried not to melt at the sight of him. Baby chimera were *adorable*, with tiny snouts and big yellow eyes and fluffy wings.

He carefully took the meat in his (cute) snout and ate it. Olivia offered him another, and one more for luck.

"Want me to take a look at your wing?" she asked. *"I can try to make it stop hurting."*

"But the monster!"

She stiffened. *"Monster?"*

Another memory. He was in the cave, cold and scared, but so thirsty. He followed his nose to the smell of fresh water. As he drank from the pool, he noticed something moving in the water. Scrambling away, he ran for the first cover he saw: the pointy rocks that looked like teeth. An unfortunate bump made him yowl in pain, the movement sending shock waves through his broken wing.

Something burst out of the water. Ta've squeezed himself between the rocks as the monster charged, its claws scraping against the rocks as it tried to get him. Its snout alone was longer than Ta've's whole body, and it had a stinger on its tail that bashed against the rocks inches from the cub's fur.

Olivia blinked, back in the present, and cursed herself for not bringing her bow. That was an antrebull, a semiaquatic carnivore that had only been sighted during high tide. The common theory was that it lived in the ocean and came with the tides. Maybe it was trapped here too? Or perhaps all antrebulls lived in caves in a sort of hibernation during low tide and came out when the waters rose. Or maybe since it was summer, it was laying eggs, like the ingencis.

She shook her head. *"Don't worry. I'll protect you from that."*

He still hesitated.

"I'm a big scary human, remember? I think I can handle one cave monster."

His mind bubbling, Ta've crawled over the rocks until he was out of the mess of stalactites. He had some of his mother's blue coloring on his belly, paws, and wings, but the rest of him was dark brown, his ears tipped black. His left wing hung at an angle, almost touching the ground. Olivia moved her torch to get a better look. If the wing could be divided in half—the part of the fold closest to the back, and the part of the fold that led to the wing's tip—then it looked like the break had happened closer to the tip, where the bones were smaller and more delicate.

"*Okay, the good news is I can help. Bad news is it's going to hurt while I work with it, then get better when I'm done. Does that make sense?*" she asked.

"*Can we make it all stop hurting?*" he pleaded.

"*Sorry, cub. Broken bones are the worst.*" She pulled out her medical kit. "*I take it you've bumped that wing against a lot of rocks while down here and it hurt a lot, huh?*"

"*Yes,*" he admitted, looking down.

"*Well, I'm going to bandage it so it doesn't do that anymore, and then hopefully it'll start healing. Lie down.*"

Ta've did. Olivia carefully folded the broken wing in a rest position, apologizing every time the cub yipped or whined in pain. She made sure the bandage wasn't too tight, smoothing feathers and fur that trembled beneath her hand, whether in pain or fear, she wasn't sure.

Finally, she was done. She gave Ta've another piece of meat and packed away her kit. "*All right. Let's get you back to your mom. Do you want me to carry you?*"

"*Yes,*" he said.

Olivia picked him up, careful not to jostle the wing any more than she already had. His fur was softer than anything she'd ever felt, taking Herculean effort not to bury her face in it. She scooped up her torch and started the trip back.

They traveled in comfortable silence. Ta've seemed happy enough to snuggle against Olivia and doze, probably relieved to have an adult do the heavy lifting now. The fact that *she* was that adult was . . . not something she wanted to contemplate. Even though she was nineteen and had thus been an adult for over a year now, she'd always seen true adulthood as freedom from the Claudes and being able to provide for herself. She hadn't considered that it *also* included younger people turning to her for help.

Well, since I'm the responsible one, I'd better make sure we don't run into trouble, she thought, taking extra care to avoid the antrebull. She hadn't seen any more signs of it, but it could still be down here. She kept her ears open, trying to pick up any other sounds besides the crackling of her torch and distant drip of water.

After some distance, she poked the telepathic bonds. "*Mek'tay? Can you hear me now?*"

"*Yes,*" he said, very faint.

"*I got him. We're on our way back.*"

Relief flooded from him like water. "*Thank you.*"

As they passed the part of the cave where the tunnels forked, Ta've's ears perked up.

Olivia heard it a second later: a snarl.

She raised her torch.

The antrebull stalked out of the shadows, blocking their escape.

CHAPTER TWENTY-NINE

Antrebulls were primarily evolved for life in the water, but they'd been known to climb trees in search of prey, paralyzing larger creatures with their stingers before devouring them, shredding the flesh with long claws and needlelike teeth. They didn't have much in terms of armor, having thick scaly skin rather than the platelike armor of the menziva, which would have been great if Olivia had any weapons besides one little knife.

"*Silver?*" Mek'tay called. "*What is wrong?*"

She sent him an image of the antrebull prowling closer.

Ta've trembled in her arms. Olivia waved her torch at the creature, wordlessly shouting and making herself look big. The antrebull snapped, and she didn't think it was bluffing, unlike her. This wasn't a random encounter in the middle of the woods; she was in this creature's home.

Fuck. They needed to make it past this thing. It was the only way out—

Wait a minute.

Olivia studied the antrebull. It wasn't huge, being about the size of Cyrij, with its head up to her shoulder. But it was still too big to have squeezed through the same hole she had.

Which meant there was another way out of the cave.

"*Ta've, that passage we were just in. Did you go down all the way?*" she asked.

"Yes. It goes to a wall."

"What about the other one?"

"Other one?"

The antrebull snapped. Olivia held her ground, showing Ta've the fork in the tunnel. *"The one on the right!"*

"It stinks of monster. I do not want to go there."

Perfect.

"Mek'tay, there's a back entrance! Follow our links!" she called, slowly backing away. The antrebull prowled after her, eyes on the torch. Olivia kept it directly between them; it was the only effective weapon she had. She carefully set Ta've on the ground. *"I need you to run. Follow that tunnel on the right; you should be able to find an exit."*

"And you?"

"I'll be fine," she lied.

The cub ran off.

As if that were some kind of signal, the antrebull lashed with its stinger. Olivia jerked back, stabbing with her torch. With one hand now free, she unsheathed her knife.

The antrebull stepped closer. Olivia stepped back, trying to block with her torch whenever it stabbed with its stinger. She gladly gave up ground, letting the antrebull push her deeper down the tunnel.

"There is no exit!" Ta've cried.

"What?"

The distraction cost her. The stinger pierced her thigh, pumping fire into her blood.

Olivia screamed, burying her knife into the tail. The antrebull's shriek deafened her, echoing off the walls. She pulled it closer with her blade, pressing her torch against its skin, driven by panic and rage. This thing was trying to kill her; she was going to make it *hurt*. The stink of burning flesh permeated the air. It scrambled away from her, disappearing down the cavern tunnel.

She groaned, leaning against the rock wall. The wound on her thigh wasn't that serious, but the poison was a concern. Antrebull venom hadn't been properly tested in Citadel, but they didn't *think* it was deadly except to smaller animals. It would paralyze her, though, and if she wasn't out of this cave before then, the predator would return for its meal.

And it had just run in the direction of their original entrance.

"*What do you mean, there's no exit?*" she asked, limping down the hall.

"*There is just water.*"

Water?

She hurried, almost running over Ta've. Her entire left leg was numb.

The cave ended in another pool. But there was light coming from below.

"*That* is *the exit,*" she said, grinning. "*Can you hold your breath?*"

"*Chimera do not go in water!*"

The numbness spread to her hip. She didn't have long. "*I'll carry you. Just hold your breath.*" She scooped him up and dove.

The water immediately extinguished the torch. She was guided only by the dim light coming from a hole in the rock wall. She used her free hand and nonparalyzed leg to scramble beneath the rock, not so much swimming as dragging herself along the bottom of the rock wall.

Neither of her legs would move.

Something splashed in the water behind them.

No! You were supposed to stay hurt until we were out!

Olivia shoved Ta've forward, out of the hole. He dog-paddled up to the surface.

Something sharp and strong tugged on her leg, pulling her back. The shock of it, despite not being able to *feel* it, made her gasp. Bubbles floated up to the rock ceiling and popped.

"*Where are you?*" Ta've called.

"*Get to land. And call your mom!*" She clutched the rock wall, her lungs squeezing as they slowly lost air. She was just a handspan from the exit. If she could get enough of a purchase, she'd be out.

The numbness spread to her chest.

She pulled herself forward, her arms burning with the strain. The antrebull yanked on her again, almost pulling her back entirely. Only the fact that her arms were out of the hole, granting her more purchase on the wet rock, saved her.

She launched herself out of the hole completely, toward the surface. Her arms and head were the only parts of her that could move.

She breached the surface, gasping for air. Three shadows flew overhead, howling with joy. Ta've howled back.

"*Antrebull in the water!*" she warned, trying to half swim, half float to shore.

Something grasped her other leg and *pulled.*

She went down, the water swallowing her.

Through the blurry water, she could see the shape of the antrebull, its teeth in her calf. Tendrils of blood floated up, and it was bizarre to see it but not feel it.

She tried to reach for her knife, but her fingers wouldn't cooperate. The paralysis had affected her entire body.

She couldn't move. She couldn't defend herself. She was going to be eaten alive by this thing.

No, I'll just drown first, she realized.

Something *splooshed* above her. Talons gripped her shoulders and pulled her away from the antrebull, her leg yanked out of its jaws.

She breached the surface again, wheezing and coughing. Mek'tay flew her to the end of the pool and gently set her on the ground.

"*We cannot stay*," Idavi said. Olivia managed to turn her head to see Ta've nestled between her bloody paws. She smiled, despite the fear still coursing through her. *Mission accomplished.*

"*We cannot leave Silver here*," Acmare retorted. "*That is not* psikar."

"*Psikar?*" she asked, her mind latching on to that and not the very angry predator who wanted to eat her alive.

"*I do not want to carry her if she cannot hold on*," Mek'tay said.

"*It's okay*," she said. "*Maybe just far enough away that the antrebull can't find me and eat me?*"

"*You can stay in Kimuud territory*," Acmare said. He moved into Olivia's field of view and bumped the top of his head against her chest. "*Thank you.*"

"*You're welcome. Ta've?*"

He poked his head out from his mother's legs.

"Keep your wing still so it heals. And don't fall down any more holes, would you?"

"I do not fall," he promised.

Idavi used her teeth to pick up Ta've by the scruff of his neck and flew off, Acmare right behind them. Mek'tay picked up Olivia with his talons again and flew them back to the cave's original entrance, where she'd left her bow and rope. He set her down so she was lying on the ground, facing up. These smaller, skinnier trees looked bigger than the blue giants from this angle.

"How bad is my leg?" she asked.

"Small wounds," Mek'tay said. *"The teeth do not go too deep."*

"The bones don't look broken?"

"No."

"Yay." She closed her eyes. She needed a nap.

He settled down next to her head, black fur and feathers dripping water. They were in a warm, sunny patch. Too bad Olivia couldn't feel it, with how all of her skin was coated in cold numbness.

"When I tell you to save Ta've, I do not think you do it," Mek'tay admitted.

"Why not?"

"Humans hurt and kill chimera, not save them. They do not see us as people. Someone who does not see us as people does not risk her life to save us."

"I didn't see you that way, at first," she admitted. *"Everyone in Citadel is taught that you're demons, beasts, dangerous animals that need to be killed so we can survive. And while I never bought into the whole 'demon' aspect, I did think you were just creatures. It wasn't until Cyrij gave me the flowers that I realized there might be more to it. I'm sorry."*

Mek'tay nudged her with his snout. *"It is all right. Before, when Cyrij first meets you and tells us what he does, his parents and I are furious. We yell at him until the sun goes down. He tells us that you are not threat, but I do not believe it. So we follow your scent to make sure."*

Olivia remembered her father shooting at Mek'tay as soon as he saw him and winced. *"Well, you were sort of right."*

Mek'tay shared a memory: watching the silver-haired human pick berries. She clearly saw him but made no move to attack him. Or even defend herself. She just kept picking berries and, when she was done, slowly approached him. Perhaps the humans knew better now. Perhaps Cyrij was right to extend a flower rather than a claw.

But then one of the other humans attacked him, and the silver female ran back to them.

"*Good thing he missed,*" Olivia said. She tested her paralysis. She could move a toe, and there was a certain tightness around her lower leg that she knew was going to turn to pain soon.

But just because she couldn't move didn't mean she didn't want to. She felt an itch in her mind, that pressing need to *do something*. Draw, go for a walk, pick a fight. Something! But she couldn't. She was trapped in her body until the venom wore off.

She needed a distraction.

"*So, that memory . . .*" she prodded.

"*The memory I can show you is from first chimera, passed down from litter to litter,*" Mek'tay said. "*It is not happy.*"

Olivia snorted. "*Never thought it would be.*"

He dropped the memory in her mind.

CHAPTER THIRTY:
MAMA

She's born wrapped in metal. Metal bars within a metal room within a metal den. There is no other like her. On the other side of the bars is what she assumes is her mother: a furless, wingless creature who stands on her hind legs and has little, flat teeth. At first, Mother is with her a lot: stroking her feathers, feeding her milk from plastic, cooing at her.

She doesn't have a name. Mother doesn't give her one.

Mother talks a lot, forms sounds with her mouth that she can never hope to replicate with her snout and sharp teeth. But she learns, through what Mother says and what other, similar-looking creatures say, what they mean. Before she can even wobble on her two front paws and hind talons, she knows the basics of their language. She knows she is something called a chimera. She knows she is the first.

"With you here, we can finally leave this damn ship," Mother says.

She's never allowed to leave her cage. It's just big enough for her to walk, eat, and sleep in the pile of blankets in the corner. The bars separate her from half the room, where the other creatures sometimes visit and watch her. Mother calls one George and the other Lieutenant Bevill.

There is a red light on her cage that turns greenish white whenever Mother or someone else enters. But every time she tries to push out, the red light stays, and the bars don't budge.

It's nice, at first. Not great. She wishes she could go beyond the bars. She can't tell Mother that, no matter how she contorts her jaw, but she tries to communicate it by gnawing at the metal. Mother shushes her and pulls her back. "Not yet, dear. You're not ready."

The cage is big enough that she can spread her wings, but she can't fly. She does not understand why she has them yet cannot use them.

A new set of teeth grow in. As they do, Mother gives her toys and treats to chew on, moves her from milk to brown, crunchy pellets. She teaches her commands: sit, stand, stay.

"You've made a fucked-up dog," Lieutenant Bevill says, glaring down at her after Mother has her follow her commands.

"She's still a puppy," Mother replies. "And even if she's never able to defend us, it's still a massive achievement."

Mother teaches her a new command: attack. George comes in wrapped in thick, soft stuff that protects him from her teeth. She can't do more than tug on it and shake his arm a bit, but Mother is pleased.

"It won't be any good if the Nostrians can get in her head," George says, shedding the soft stuff.

"We used some of their DNA to create her," Mother argues. "She'll be fine."

"She's just a dog, Joyce. A smart one, to be sure. But still."

She doesn't know what a "dog" is, but she knows she's not it. She tries to tell them that, tries to make the words form. They don't come.

As she grows, Mother has fewer smiles, fewer words of praise. She spends more time on the other side of the bars. By the time she's grown, Mother hasn't come into her cage for a long time.

"Come on, *talk*," Mother growls, holding a long metal tube someone calls a taser.

The chimera whines. She can't.

Mother jabs the taser at her. Sharp pain jolts through her entire body. She jerks away, yowling.

Mother does this multiple times, trying to get her to talk. She can't.

Mother withholds food, says she'll feed her if she asks for it. She can't.

"They're supposed to be telepaths," Mother tells George, after once again refusing to give her food. Her stomach stopped growling a while ago. She's tired. "But we haven't heard a peep from her."

"Probably a good thing. Wouldn't want her jerking us around."

"We can't declare this a failure yet. There's only one of her."

George sighs. "I don't know what world you're living in, Joyce, but we're on a spaceship. Our resources are limited."

"If the Nostrians ever find us, it won't matter what resources we have. We need to be able to defend ourselves."

When they finally feed her, the usually bland food tastes odd.

She sleeps for a long time.

When she wakes, she knows something's wrong. Everything hurts. After the pain, she feels . . . different. Strange. Eventually her belly swells, and she realizes she's carrying cubs.

Mother is very pleased, but the chimera can't stop worrying. This is no place to raise cubs. There's hardly room in this cage for herself, never mind a pack. And while Mother hasn't used the taser on her in quite a while and has made sure she has plenty of food, that trust is broken. The fear is there. Will it happen again? Will she hurt her cubs?

Mother watches her closely, coming into her cage for the first time in ages. George tsks from the other side of the bars. "There are so many ways this can go wrong . . ."

"Shut up, George."

"She's part wolf, part owl, part human, part Nostrian. Is she supposed to lay eggs? Go into labor? Do whatever the hell those aliens do to reproduce?"

"Her reproductive system is entirely canine. It'll be fine."

Mother's right. She gives birth to two healthy cubs.

As she nurses them, she feels something tickle the back of her mind. On instinct, she forms a link.

She doesn't realize what that means right away. But gradually, she'll feel hungry even when she's eaten, feel confusion over things that make perfect sense, feel happy and content even when her mind swims with worries.

They aren't her feelings. They're her cubs'.

Words soon follow. They call her Mama.

"*My cubs*," she says, nuzzling them both.

She tries to make the link with Mother and George and Bevill. But it's like running into the walls of her cage.

Mother finally gives all of them names. She is Subject Zero. Her cubs are Subject One and Subject Two.

She doesn't like those names. She doesn't know how to find better ones.

Her cubs begin to walk and stretch their wings.

"*Why no fly, Mama?*" they ask. She doesn't know. She tries gnawing on the bars again, pleading with the humans to let them out, just for a little while. They don't.

Her cubs are old enough to move from milk to pellets. And Mother takes them away.

As soon as she realizes what's happening, when George takes one cub and Mother takes another, she attacks.

For the first time in her life, she bites.

The taste of human blood is thick, like liquid metal. She likes it.

She tears off George's arm and digs her claws across Mother's face. Her cubs hide behind her. More humans enter the room, on the other side of the bars. They have strange metal tubes and they shoot something at her. Everything goes dark.

When she wakes, her cubs are gone.

But not entirely.

"*Mama?*" they ask. "*You wake?*"

She whines, looking around. "*Where are you?*"

"*Do not know.*" She sees a cage, but a different one, in her mind. Her cubs are separated. But they're there.

She never sees George again, and Mother never comes into her cage again.

Mother makes her give birth to five more litters. She's afraid to sleep. When she sleeps, Mother takes her cubs away. And even though they are bonded through the mind, it's not the same. It's worse, because she can feel her cubs' suffering. When they get shocked with electricity, starved, drugged. When they die. Mother wants them to talk to her, the way the humans can talk to each other. But no matter how many times the chimera try, they can't. They can only talk to each other.

Some of her cubs are forced to give birth, too, when they're grown. She tries to comfort them when their litters are taken away.

This goes on for a long time.

All of the chimera call her Mama, even if she's not their mother. Even the chimera who are not born but made, like her. She does not feel like a mama.

By the time Mama's muzzle is white and Mother's hair is gray, there are enough of them that they're not all separated. Some of the littermates get to stay together.

It's a cold comfort. There are broken links in their minds where chimera once were. The humans have killed many of them, one way or another. Mama is still alone in her cage.

Mother is watching her pretend to sleep, taking notes. The sickly white light shines on the scars on her face that never went away. She's joined by Bevill. They've stopped calling him Lieutenant and started calling him Captain a while ago. Mama doesn't know why and doesn't care. She doesn't care about a lot of things, lately.

"We've found a planet," Bevill says. "EDL-9. We still need to do some tests, but it should be completely habitable."

"What happens to the chimera if we make landfall?" Mother asks.

"You said they're supposed to be our bodyguards, but I haven't seen much progress."

"They're immune to mind control."

"Theoretically. You've just done some autopsies. We won't know for sure unless we're found by the Nostrians, and it's my job to make sure that never happens." He leaves, calling over his shoulder, "When we land, we're scrapping the project."

Mama isn't sure how to feel. She knows the captain means to kill her, and part of her longs for death. But she doesn't want to leave her cubs behind, and many of them still want to live. She decides not to tell the other chimera. This is one piece of dread she can protect them from.

Mother and some of the others talk more and more about this new "planet," whatever that is. Sometimes they call it EDL-9. Sometimes they call it something else: Eda, Edalin, Edalide. They talk about "rings," but it's not the kind some humans wear on their fingers. Apparently it's the kind that's stopping them from landing, but that can't be right, because they're not flying. They've never flown.

"Do you think it'll be like Earth?" one of the younger humans asks Mother one day.

"I don't know," she says, her voice sad. "I was only a baby when we left. I don't even remember it."

Mama sleeps.

And then something happens.

It jerks her awake. The cage, the room, the den, it all starts shaking, throwing her around her cell. She smacks into the wall twice, bloodying her muzzle, before she manages to grab onto the bars of her cage with her talons and hold tight. Her cubs scream in her mind. Outside, she can hear several humans scream as well.

The crash yanks Mama away from the bars, slamming her into the wall. When she shakes off the dizziness, she realizes two of her cubs are dead, the gaps in her mind raw and black.

She has no time to mourn them. All the other cubs are alive, many of them hurt. Her den is sideways; the wall is the floor now. The lights are broken, flickering. Except for the red one on the bars of her cage. It's green now.

Carefully, she pushes the door open with her wing.

She shares the discovery with her cubs.

Her first steps of freedom take her out the door to a hallway. It's sideways, like her den: the floor is the wall and the wall is the floor. On the "ceiling" and "floor" are doors, many of them leading to more chimera, stumbling out into the den. Some have broken wings. Bloody noses. Twisted talons. But they're alive, and they're free.

"Mama!"

She sees her cubs for the first time in so long, right next to her cage. They've grown so much! The two eldest already have flecks of white on their snouts. They nuzzle for a long moment, pressing their heads against the others' heads and chests, hearing their heartbeats, assuring each other and themselves that they are here and alive and well before going out to search for more.

There are more halls, more rooms. There are almost no humans here, and the few she finds are all dead, bashed against walls during the commotion. They find more cubs, cubs that Mama has never met or seen but has been connected with all their lives.

"*Stuck!*" a younger cub cries. They show images of a smaller room, with much tighter cages made of intertwined metal squares that won't budge. An older chimera tries to pull the cages apart with tooth and claw. It's not working. Many young cubs are trapped.

Mama tries to find a solution. They have to leave this metal den before the humans rouse and shove them back into cages. She knows that if she returns to her bars, she will bash her head against the wall until she dies.

One of the doors on the "floor" opens. Mama stiffens when she recognizes Mother's scent.

Mother climbs into the hall, leaning against the wall that was the floor. She's holding her head, blood dribbling down her temple.

Hot rage unlike anything Mama has ever felt consumes her. The cries of the little cubs prevent her from killing Mother just yet. But now she has a solution.

She charges Mother, tackles her to the metal before she realizes what she's done. Mother's eyes widen. She reeks of fear.

Mama gets off her. She grabs her white coat by one of her talons and drags her down the hall in a three-legged limp, following the mental tug of the little cubs. Her older cubs surround them, making sure Mother doesn't try to run, growling at her when she moves.

They get to the room where the little cubs are held. They're each in their own cage, barely big enough to spread their wings. The older one who found them first has been gnawing at the metal mesh and managed to make a small hole. It's slow going, and already his gums bleed.

Mama orders him aside and drops Mother in front of the cage.

The human scrambles to her feet, looking at all of them. Even the cubs glare at her, recognizing her from their torments. By now all the other chimera have found them and are in the room or looking in from the hallway. Mama does a quick mental count but doesn't know any number over ten. She just knows they have over three sets of ten, more than enough to dispatch Mother if she tries something.

She looks at Mother, then at the cage with the cubs.

Mother stares at her. "You . . . want me to . . ."

Mama waits.

Slowly, Mother presses a few buttons on the side of the cage. It opens.

She does this for all of them. The cubs tumble out and go to their parents. One of them even manages to fly a little ways, to the utter delight of all the chimera.

"You're sentient," Mother breathes.

Mama's ears flick in annoyance.

Mother laughs. "Of course! I was so focused on turning you into guard dogs I didn't even realize—but of course you're sentient; you have human and Nostrian in you! Oh, this is fantastic. Once we've got everything under control here, we'll—"

Mama tackles Mother to the floor again. This time, instead of biting her clothes, she tears into Mother's throat and torso.

She licks blood from her chops after Mother stopped moving. The other chimera patiently wait for her.

"*We leave now,*" she says.

It takes some time. The metal den is huge and nearly impossible to navigate. They try following scents, but it's as if the humans never left this place, for there aren't any immediate exits. Whatever living humans they come across are quickly killed.

They notice the air becoming colder and follow it. It leads to a massive hole, just big enough for them each to squeeze through one at a time.

There is no metal out here. There's cold, fluffy white stuff on the ground. Above them the sky is dark, with only snippets of light peeking through. For the first time in their lives, the chimera inhale the smell of fresh air, dirt, and snow.

Mama likes it.

"*What is it?*" one of her cubs asks.

"*Edalide*," she says, remembering all the conversations she's overheard. She thinks, *So this is a "planet."*

What she says is, "*It saved us.*"

Something shuffles inside the metal den. There are footsteps, people talking and running about.

"*We move*," Mama orders.

CHAPTER THIRTY-ONE:
ORMUS

After his morning workout (a holdover from basic training that he'd never let go of), Ormus took a carriage to work. Markus Brown's house was on the way, and he watched as the front door opened, hoping to get a glimpse of suspicious activity that would put this case to rest.

Instead, Riley Thompson came out.

"Stop!" Ormus snapped. The carriage puller skidded to a halt, cursing when he almost stumbled.

Riley hovered in the doorway, looking into the house. Through the doorway, Ormus could just barely make out a woman's silhouette before the door closed.

"Riley!" he called.

The boy startled, then smiled. The black shirt of a medic in training drowned his slim frame. "Captain Claude! A hundred blessings to you."

"And to you," he replied automatically. "What are you doing here?"

"Delivering medicine. They make all the trainees do the grunt work. But at least it's sunny out."

A chill wind blew, making them both shiver.

Ormus beckoned him into the carriage. "Come on. I'll give you a ride."

Riley brightened and climbed into the carriage, folding himself with familiar grace into the corner of the seat to take up as little room as possible.

It was on the tip of Ormus's tongue to tell him to stay away from the Brown household. That the evidence against them didn't look good. It was strange. Despite Ormus having watched the boy grow up—being so close to the governor—the two of them had never really connected, had never spent any time alone together.

But Riley was his daughter's best friend. Had been there through Sarai and Elias. Ormus couldn't help but feel a little bit responsible for him.

Unfortunately, telling him anything about the Dove investigation could jeopardize it. So Ormus decided to focus on the other matter: "Have your parents tried contacting you?"

Riley snorted. "No. Dad's pretending I never existed, and Mom . . . Well, I imagine she hasn't been sober all week."

"It might be easier on her if she got to see you."

Riley glared at him. "If she didn't get sober while I was *living with her*, then a short visit won't change anything."

The sudden vehemence in his voice came as a surprise, and Ormus instinctively cleared his throat. Riley might have had a point, but that was no excuse to be rude.

The boy drooped, rubbing his eyes. "Sorry. The hospital has been at maximum capacity since long before I started training, and everyone's working double shifts. Even those of us who have no idea what we're doing."

"I heard about that," Ormus said, acknowledging the apology. "Asiya hasn't spent as much time there since before Evelyn was born."

"Nutritional problems from lack of food, sickness from poor hygiene, more hunting and fishing accidents as people take more risks . . ." He forced a smile. "It's very educational."

"There's no shame in changing careers now," Ormus ventured. "Plenty of young men think they want to do one thing, then find out after a week that it's not for them."

"This is for me," Riley said. "I'm happier now than I've ever been."

Ormus blinked. "Really?"

Riley nodded, his smile a lot more genuine.

"You're living in a rotten end of town and being worked to the bone."

"I've never liked this end of town," Riley said, motioning to the extravagant houses where he'd spent his childhood. Where it was clean and spacious and safe. "It's always been too confining. You *must* do this. You *can't* do that. Certain things are *expected* of you. It was suffocating. My only regret is that I didn't run off sooner. It took Olivia . . ."

His voice caught. Ormus's gut tightened.

Riley continued, "It took Olivia telling me to pursue my dreams, and watching her do the same no matter what the consequences, for me to realize I couldn't even call myself half a man if I didn't do the same."

"She ran off into the forest chasing ghosts," Ormus grumbled.

"She *never* does anything without reason," Riley countered. "Sometimes that reason doesn't make sense to the rest of us, but it's there."

They reached the hospital. The driver set down the carriage and stretched his back, enjoying his short break while Riley climbed out.

"Take care of yourself, Riley," Ormus warned. "You don't have the same protections you once did."

Riley smirked. "Those were chains, Captain."

Ormus was just finishing for the day when there was a knock on his door. He bit back a sigh. The month of Aestus was almost over, with most of the town looking forward to the big festival of gorging and celebration that happened on the last day. But until then, they still restricted themselves from eating during daylight hours. The sun was almost down and he hadn't had lunch; instead he counted the minutes to dinnertime.

"Come in," he called, as pleasantly as he could.

Ensign Gabriel Byruk entered and saluted. He'd gotten his stripes and new uniform yesterday and wore it like he'd been an officer for years. Not like Ormus, who had kept touching the stripes on his arm because he couldn't quite believe they were there.

Ormus knew what he was going to say before Gabriel even opened his mouth. It happened every time a class's two years were up and the ones with more than basic education stayed on to become officers. Especially officers who specialized in demon hunts rather than wall guard or city patrol. And *especially* officers who had so recently lost someone to the demons.

Still, no reason to be rude.

"Ensign," he greeted, leaning back in his chair. "What can I do for you?"

"Sir, I know the demon hunters for this tide already left," Gabriel said. There was an edge, a hardness to his face that hadn't been there before Michael's death. "I'd like to be assigned to the next hunt."

"No."

He blinked. "Sir?"

"You just got your station and have only been sent out once as a private. Learn your ropes, first, and get acquainted with the men you're going to lead before jumping into a death trap."

"Sir, I know that you're worried about your daughter, and that you gave the men in this hunt explicit orders to keep an eye out for any sign of her. That's why I want to join. We were friends in school," he said. "I'd like to think we still are."

Ormus wasn't so sure about that. Olivia had told him that she'd been bullied by the twins, but they were such upstanding young men—no record of mischief, excellent grades, a good family—that Ormus assumed she had made it up for attention. She'd never brought it up again and had insisted on continuing to go to school even when most girls stopped. So if there had been a problem, it obviously hadn't been that bad.

But *friends?* Olivia's social circle was extremely small and tight. He'd seen her spend hours with Riley, Elias, and Sergeant Peterson, but not once with the twins.

"If that's true, then you definitely shouldn't be a part of these hunts," he said. "Wouldn't want your personal feelings to get in the way of your responsibility to the town as a whole."

Gabriel huffed. "You said I'm inexperienced. Give me the experience."

"Not with your head clouded by grief," Ormus said. He gentled his tone. "You've just experienced a terrible loss, and you have every right to be angry about it. But rage clouds the mind, and that will get you killed faster than any demon."

Gabriel swallowed, looking down. "Michael and I wanted to be officers together. Hunt demons together, fight crime together, train the new recruits together. I just . . . I want to do him proud. I want to make them pay for taking that away from him. From me."

"You will," Ormus promised. "And I have no intention of letting you get yourself killed before your time. Not if I can help it. Take some time to grieve, first. As soon as I deem you ready, I'll put you on a hunt."

Gabriel nodded and left.

Ormus finally got to go home. He found himself craving that more and more lately. When before he'd never hesitated to spend hours past dusk at the office, now he left as soon as he could, looking forward to seeing Asiya and Evelyn.

Even when they were having a bad day.

His wife had dinner ready for him, but he knew it wasn't going to be a fun meal. Evelyn kept shifting in her seat, poking at her food.

"Evelyn, would you like to share with your father what happened today?" Asiya asked.

Ormus knew that tone. Asiya had opened several such conversations that way, but never with Evelyn. Always with Olivia. In the five years she had attended public school, Ormus had had to discipline her for her behavior dozens of times and had had more meetings with the faculty there than he cared to admit. *Your daughter got into a fight with another student. Your daughter had a breakdown today and disrupted the entire class. Your daughter got into an argument with a teacher.* How that girl had graduated, he'd never know.

But Evelyn? Evelyn had never had a problem with school in her life.

She kept her eyes firmly on her plate as she said, "One of my classmates told me it was a good thing that my sister has, and I quote, 'fucked off to the forest to get herself killed.' I . . . uh . . . lost my temper."

"You lost your temper," Ormus repeated, slowly.

"I said that I wasn't surprised he was dumb enough to believe such things, since I overheard the teachers were sending him to remedial classes. He called me a liar. I called him a pox-faced virgin not even the demons would want. He called me a bitch. I slapped him. They sent me to the principal."

It was only through very strenuous effort and several years of experience that Ormus did not crack a smile. "I imagine so. Evelyn, even when someone says something hurtful, you don't respond with violence. You know that."

"If one of your soldiers said that to you, how would you have reacted?" she challenged, dark eyes blazing with impertinence.

"I would have given him a string of very unpleasant jobs. But I wouldn't hurt him, especially since it's my job to keep my men as safe and secure as possible," he said. "Who was this boy, anyway?"

"Riley's cousin, Francis."

Oh, great. The governor's nephew. Just what he needed.

"He said some crummy things about Riley too," she added. "About him being a girl, like that's a *bad* thing!"

Asiya stabbed her carrots with a little too much force. Ever since the disastrous party last week, she kept trying to convince him to let the boy stay with them, even though Ormus had confirmed that he was staying with Sergeant Peterson. She had started making large dishes every other night—a loaf of metabread, a casserole, a container of pulled pork perfect for sandwiches—and taking them to work, returning empty handed. He never confronted her about it but would bet good money that that food was now in the Peterson house.

Well, that was fine. So long as they kept it under the table and didn't blow too big a hole in their grocery budget.

"What did the school say about this?" Ormus asked with a sigh.

"She has to stay after school tomorrow to write an apology letter to Francis," Asiya said. "If she gets into another fight, they'll suspend her."

He had half a mind to ground her on top of that but decided against it. Evelyn and Olivia's relationship had never been *great*; Evelyn would get jealous about the extra attention her sister got—even if most of it was negative—while Olivia spent the first year of living with them pretending her sister (and father) didn't exist. It wasn't until Evelyn had ended up in advanced science classes—and needed help with her homework that Ormus was, frankly, not qualified to give—that they had formed something of a bond. Strong enough that, with Olivia gone, Evelyn was acting out. She needed support, and cutting her off from her friends and normal school activities would not help her.

"If we hear anything about you fighting another student again, you'll face severe consequences," he warned. "Understand?"

She nodded, setting her fork down. "May I be excused?"

She'd barely touched her food. Ormus and Asiya let her go anyway.

They waited until she was upstairs, out of earshot, before Asiya said, "Admit it: if one of your soldiers said what that boy did, you would want to slap him too."

"Of course," he said. "But I wouldn't *do* it!"

Her chuckle was fleeting. She took his hand. "Ormus, it's been over a month. A priest stopped by today and asked if we would be doing a service."

He took his hand away. "Absolutely not. There's no evidence that she's dead. A service won't be necessary."

She gave him a worried look but didn't push. For that, at least, he was grateful.

He looked at his plate. His conversation with Peterson had been poking him for days and wouldn't leave him alone. "Asiya. Do I . . . Are you . . ."

She waited, resting her chin on the back of her hand. Ormus gathered his thoughts. "Do I support you enough?"

"Of course you do," she said, clearly startled. "Money might be tight right now, but we have savings . . ."

"That's not what I meant. I mean . . ." He grimaced. He hated bringing up his past lovers with his current wife, but he couldn't beat around this bush. "One of the reasons Sarai cut off all contact with me, even after Olivia was born, was because I wanted her to stay at home. I didn't like the idea of her trying to pursue a career while being a mother. I know when we got married you said that children always came first and that you were more than happy to go from full time to part time, but . . ."

"Are you asking if I resent you?" Asiya asked.

". . . A little?" God's Faces, he was a wreck.

"No, I don't," she said. "But Sarai and I were cut from different cloths. *I* wanted and still want a man who takes the financial responsibility of the family. With Evelyn almost graduating, I might go back to full-time work, but I can assure you that I am counting the days until I get to look after some grandchildren, either from her or Olivia. I'm no leader. I *like* following your lead. But Sarai wasn't like that. She wanted to do things her way, including raising a family. And there's nothing wrong with that. She had a powerful spirit, and she passed that on to her daughter." Asiya studied him. "So while *I* like having your guidance, I don't think our daughters do."

He rolled his eyes. "They're children, and I'm their father. Of course they don't like it."

"Olivia is an adult. She knows what she wants, and she will never fit in with Citadel. Ever. Trying to force it will only make her more miserable," she said firmly. "And Evelyn has one of the brightest minds of her generation. If she wants to put it to use instead of concentrating on raising a family, the way I did, then that's her prerogative."

"Citadel isn't built for women like that," Ormus argued. "They're going to get crushed."

"Not if their father supports them."

He didn't have anything to say to that. Asiya cleared the dinner table, putting the leftovers in a pan that would probably go to the Peterson house.

Dear Elias,

It's us. It's our fault you died.

CHAPTER THIRTY-TWO

Olivia paced around the campfire, pulling at her hair. Cyrij and Blue talked on a private link while Mek'tay cleaned his wings.

It had taken an hour for the antrebull venom to work its way out of her system, at which point Mek'tay had taken her back to her camp. Olivia still hadn't gotten over the shared memory.

"*Silver?*" Mek'tay asked, once his wings were straight and polished, gleaming black in the fading daylight. "*Share your mind?*"

That was a bad idea. Her mind was a chaotic mess, whirling with the implications of everything she'd witnessed.

Humans had created chimera. They'd created them for protection against . . . something. Something called the Nostrians. She didn't know what the threat was; Mama had never seen or heard it.

Then they—*Olivia's ancestors*, the so-called angels—spent the next several decades torturing them, because they didn't understand what they'd created, saw them as little more than a failed experiment.

And for some reason they were in a spaceship that, when they tried to land on this planet, crashed instead.

"*What happened to Mama?*" she asked.

"*Mama is old when she meets Edalide,*" he said. "*Too weak to fly more than a little ways. She comes to the forest with her cubs and dies soon after.*"

"*So she spends her whole life in a cage and doesn't even get to enjoy her freedom?!*"

"*Short time free is worth more than life in metal,*" Mek'tay said, his mind steady as stone. Through the mental link, his steadiness acted as an anchor for Olivia. Calming her. She still needed to move, do something, but didn't feel the roaring need to circle the camp like a prowling predator. She sat in front of the fire and glared at it.

"*What are the Nostrians?*" she asked. Some of the humans had called them "aliens," but she didn't understand that word either. Not in that context. It was an adjective, not a noun. When something was strange or beyond comprehension, it was alien.

"*We do not know. A dangerous predator?*" he guessed.

"*What were the humans doing in space in the first place?*"

"*We do not know.*"

Olivia hissed at the incomplete answers, even though she couldn't blame Mek'tay for not having them. She had lived through Mama's memories. Solving historical mysteries had been the last thing on her mind.

The fire grew smaller. Olivia threw another log on top. "*Captain Riley Bevill was the founder of Citadel's religion. He wrote Scripture. Or at least, wrote all the teachings that eventually became Scripture.*"

Mek'tay's ear flicked. "*Why does he lie?*"

"*I don't know. There were so few humans involved in the chimera experiment it must have been top secret. Most of the people who knew probably died in the crash or got killed by the chimera.*"

"*Humans hide their minds from each other?*"

"*What do you mean?*"

"*You know when I am angry. Sad. Lying. Because of this.*" He prodded their mental link. It had grown much stronger since before he'd shared Mama's memory. "*We can hide some, but not all. With stronger links, something always bleeds through. But humans are mind deaf.*"

"*Yeah, people lie to each other all the time, and it's easy to get them to believe it.*" Her mouth twisted. "*It's very annoying.*"

"*If I am Riley Bevill, and I lie, I do it to save myself,*" he mused. "*Ones with* sadakra *will tell the truth. But without it,* not *telling your pack 'I create the things that now kill us' is possible and keeps him alive."*

"*He lied to save his skin and accidentally made a religion out of it.*" Olivia thought about that for a moment, then nodded. "*That makes sense. What's sadakra?*"

Mek'tay couldn't put it in words. Instead it was snippets of memories and stories. Sharing food with packmates instead of hogging it all for yourself. Promising to look after a packmate's cubs and sticking to it even if they were annoying. Helping a friendly pack fight off a bunch of humans that had invaded their territory.

"*I think the human word for that is 'honor,'*" she said. "*Or maybe just 'don't be an ass.'*"

"*Honor.*" Mek'tay rolled the word in his head. "*Good word. What of* psikar *and* namsuud?"

"*What and what?*"

Like sadakra, he had to show her instead of tell her. They were all very similar, with the only difference being who it applied to.

If sadakra was acting honorably toward packs and friends, psikar was doing that for people who were neither allies nor enemies. The closest Olivia could call it was "rival-given honor." Sparing the life of a stranger that wandered into your territory totally by accident and giving them proper directions out. Playing a sport without cheating. Working with a neutral pack to find a common solution to their problems without resorting to violence.

Namsuud was acting honorably toward enemies. Sparing enemies who had surrendered. Fighting only warriors instead of noncombatants and cubs. Warning an enemy pack ahead of time that a group of humans was heading their way.

Olivia couldn't think of a single instance when Citadel's people had treated chimera with even namsuud, never mind psikar and sadakra. They barely did that with each other.

She poked the burning wood with a stick. "*Bevill shouldn't have lied,*" she said. Dull fire lit her bones, but she couldn't summon more energy than that. "*Maybe more humans and chimera would still be alive if he hadn't.*"

"*Maybe,*" Mek'tay mused. "*Chimera are still angry at humans. We have our pain, but we also carry Mama's, and all other chimera's.*"

"*Humans don't have ancestral memory, but we're still angry at all the people we've lost,*" she admitted, thinking of Elias. Thinking of the way he'd kissed her before leaving with all those other doomed men. Thinking of watching a fraction of that unit return. Thinking of staring into the forest, waiting for him to return and knowing he never would. Part of her was still waiting. "*I'm tired. Of this. Everything.*"

"*As am I,*" he admitted. "*I do not want to lose more chimera. Or see you lose more humans.*"

"*Do you think there's a way to get both sides to sit down and talk this out?*" Mek'tay studied her. "*Yes. Slowly.*"

Olivia lost a bit of time after that, diving into her sketchbook to write and draw everything she had seen in Mama's memory and the discussion of honor. There were only fleeting dimensions of the spaceship that had brought humanity here, and she had a vague sense of where it was located in the Shadowlands. Was there anything left after four hundred years? If there was, that could be a good way to prove to Citadel that she wasn't lying. But getting there and back would be a daunting task. Mek'tay, Cyrij, and Blue might help her navigate through the perils of the Flooded Forest, but the Shadowlands were a whole other monster. What little literature about it existed described it as a desolate waste plunged in eternal darkness, and that had been confirmed by Mama's memories. Given that the area was in the shadow of the planet's rings, perpetually blocking out all sunlight, that made sense. Did the freshwater oceans even go that far? Did it ever warm up, or was it always snowing?

Maybe fetching the little remains of the spaceship wasn't worth it. At least, not until Citadel was on friendlier terms with the chimera. The question still remained of how to get *that* to happen.

She could try to convince some of the others to eat the green prasina flower, but which ones? If she asked the wrong person, she'd be executed.

And if she asked someone like Riley and he had an allergic reaction to it, he could get seriously hurt. Maybe Peterson? But then what? Until Governor Thompson and the majority of Citadel were convinced that chimera weren't demons and were in fact sentient beings created by humans, they'd be stuck in the downward spiral of war until Citadel destroyed itself or the chimera. There had to be a better way, but what—

Something furry knocked into her. "*Silver!*"

"*Huh?*" She looked up. Cyrij had been the one to bump her. She studied her sketchbook. She'd stopped drawing entirely and had just been making frantic spirals on the paper, so deep it threatened to tear. She flipped to the next page.

"*All right?*" Cyrij asked.

"*Fine. Just . . . spiraled. It happens sometimes. What's wrong?*"

"*Your mind calls for help, and your stomach calls for food.*"

At that moment, Olivia's stomach growled.

"*Humans eat many times, Silver,*" Cyrij scolded.

"*I know, I know,*" she said, checking on the meat she roasted over the fire. To her surprise, it was already done. And the sun was down, leaving a patch of stars through the gaps in the leaves. She must have been sitting there for hours. But at least she got dinner now.

She offered one of the smoked slabs of meat to Cyrij, but he shook his head. "*Not hungry.*"

"*Don't chimera need to eat often too?*"

"*No.*"

She almost asked how often they needed to eat, but then remembered that they didn't even know what a year was.

Most predators only had to eat once every few days or so. Chimera were probably the same. She jotted the thought down.

"*Silver!*" Cyrij knocked his head into her again. "*Eat!*"

"*All right, all right,*" she said, looking back up. The roasted slab of meat hovered before her, held by telekinesis. She couldn't remember what it was that Cyrij had caught, but it didn't matter. She plucked it from the air and took a bite. It was tough, chewy, and probably could've used some herbs and spices. Asiya would have made it a masterpiece, but at the moment Olivia just appreciated the fact that it shut her stomach up. "*Thanks, Blue.*"

"*I am not Blue.*"

Olivia took a proper look around the camp and saw that Blue had moved to her other side, a little farther away from the fire. Mek'tay was gone. In his place was another adult chimera, this one a dark sable with near-black wings. His yellow eyes glowed in the firelight, and through the new link between them, Olivia got the sense of a calm, patient mind.

She knew this one too. He'd been with Mek'tay that day Michael had died. He'd thrown rocks at her father. For that, she liked him already.

"*Where'd Mek'tay go?*" she asked.

The new mind bubbled. "*To our den. He asks that I look after you and cubs. I am Ebevil, father of Cyrij.*"

"*You do not notice him before?*" Blue grumbled to her.

"*Ah . . .*" Olivia thought back to the last few hours lost to her sketches and notes. As usual, she remembered nothing outside of what she'd been doing at that time. "*Not a thing.*"

"*How do you survive?*"

She shrugged, taking another bite. She studied her meal. "*You're telekinetic, too, aren't you?*"

"*I am kizaba, yes,*" Ebevil said.

Blue's golden eyes narrowed. "*Mulo pack does not take you?*"

In answer, he showed them a line of memories. He was a cub, hiding behind his mother's wings when the strange chimera arrived, demanding that he come with them to live in their pack. His pack's iyi'ke said no, and when the strangers left, the iyi'ke told him and his mother to hide in a cave when the waters were low. They did. When they came back with the rising waters, the den smelled of old blood and there were fewer warriors.

He was old enough to think about getting a mate soon, and the strange chimera—he knew them now as Mulo—came again. This time *he* told them no. He knew who the Mulo were, had heard what they'd done to other packs, and would rather join the humans. Later, he went hunting with his father and they got ambushed. He made it back to the den. His father did not.

He'd met his mate, Siyet, who was carrying their first litter, when the Mulo came yet again. This time, he considered. His pack was smaller now. Siyet was willing to fight but could very well die with their cubs.

The pack's new iyi'ke, Mek'tay, told the Mulo to get out of his territory. When they left, Mek'tay reached out to other packs, other iyi'kes who were good friends of his. They each sent warriors to help guard Mek'tay's territory until one of the moons was full. The Mulo came. Twice. They were fought back each time. They lost warriors and gained scars. Ebevil thought he should have gone. As a warrior, shouldn't he spare his pack and friends this pain? But his pack and friends and the *other* packs told him he was right to stay. They gladly fought the Mulo.

"*You lost your father?*" Olivia said, blinking back to the present.

"*Yes,*" Ebevil replied.

Just like Blue had lost her mother. To the same pack, no less.

"*My mother was killed when I was younger,*" she admitted. "*I tried to save her.*"

"*We kill her?*" Ebevil guessed.

"*No, humans did.*"

He tipped his head to her, not apologizing, just acknowledging the grief.

"*Are there other packs as violent as them?*" Olivia asked.

"*No. Mulo is only pack without namsuud,*" Ebevil replied.

"*Why?*" Blue asked. She was as still as stone.

"*They think there is Edalide, like all chimera. And they think there is Mulo, too. Death. Other packs—like ours, the Isilna—say death is part of Edalide. She saves us, houses us, feeds us. But needs death for balance. All creatures die, all creatures return to Edalide. Life is death, death is life. The Mulo pack says that death is Mulo, mate of Edalide. Edalide gives life, Mulo takes it. For every gift Edalide gives, Mulo demands one, too. The Mulo pack takes those gifts from other packs.*"

Olivia held up her hand. "*Let me make sure I understand clearly:*

Their death god, Mulo, demands sacrifices for every life they get. So if three cubs are born into the pack that year, they have to kill three other people?"

"Yes."

"But instead of killing from their own pack, they decide other packs are going to pay a price that they don't even believe they have to pay?"

"Yes."

Olivia dropped her head in her hand. She'd expected this kind of stupidity from Citadel, but finding it here gave her a headache. *"Right. Continue."*

"Mulo pack starts small, before. Now, they have many, many warriors. Larger than Isilna. Many warriors are kizaba, born into Mulo or stolen from others. They say kizaba are better than other chimera. There is no mating between kizaba and nonkizaba. Nonkizaba cannot be iyi'ke, or rhubo. Rhubo is second to iyi'ke," he said, answering Olivia's question before she could ask it. *"Only some packs have rhubo. Others have elders. Others have no second."*

"Let me guess: We can't just ask the Mulo to stop terrorizing the other packs?" she said.

"Mulo wants all forest."

"Where are they? Just so I know to stay clear."

A map appeared in her mind of the northern chunk of the Flooded Forest from a bird's-eye view. Instead of kilometers, the metrics were how long it took to fly overland, the "how long" vaguely defined as "very short," "a ways," "you need to stop to sleep once," and "you need to stop to sleep twice."

Citadel was a relatively short flight to the south, according to Ebevil. Apparently, Olivia's camp was right on the border of the Isilna pack, not quite in their territory but close enough that no other packs would come sniffing around. They shared a border with the Kimuud pack— Ta've and his family—to the southwest. Farther west there was a short bit of land where Isilna and Mulo met.

That was all Ebevil showed her. Olivia quickly jotted the map down, dotting each border and labeling each territory.

"You fight Mulo and win three times," Blue said. *"How?"*

Olivia wanted to ask more about those experiences herself, but Cyrij mentally tugged her away from the conversation, to the other side of the campfire.

Until now, every conversation she'd had with the chimera had been open. She hadn't realized it at the time, but it was like talking aloud in a room. Anyone nearby could hear her.

When Cyrij spoke to her, it was just through their link. One to one, preventing any other telepaths from eavesdropping.

"Do not tell Blue, but we bring Papa to her so she can make another Isilna link."

"Okay. Why?"

"So she joins Isilna pack," he said, like it was obvious. *"If she says yes, good. If she says no, she still has links and can call for help. We hope meeting Papa brings that yes."*

"You're showing her how kizaba are treated in your pack," she realized, glancing over at the two of them. *"Would you be putting in this much effort if she didn't have telekinesis?"*

Cyrij's mind flared with fire. *"Of course! Blue is alone, and scared, and cub. Being kizaba is like . . . like . . . extra meat on menziva leg. Or spots on fur!"*

Olivia smiled and nudged him. *"Just checking, Freckles. After all we've done together, I'd hate to have to kick your ass for being a jerk."*

"Ohhh . . ." He wagged his tail. *"Good."*

The idea of forming links inspired Olivia to take mental stock of her own. It took a little experimenting—and guidance from Cyrij once she told him what she was doing—but she closed her eyes and imagined herself standing on a blue tree. Its branches connected her to other trees, each one representing a chimera. The branches connecting her to Cyrij and Blue were surprisingly strong. Mek'tay too. Ta've's, Ebevil's, and Ukurf's weren't so much branches as they were vines, given how little she'd interacted with them.

"So this is what it's like in a chimera's mind," Olivia mused. *"I wish Citadel was like this."*

"Why is it not?" he asked.

She snorted, showing him memories of trials and executions of people who had done a lot less than what she was doing.

Cyrij yipped. "*Humans kill their own packmates?*"

"*We call it 'execution' when it's done by the governor,*" she said. "*But yes. Citadel has a lot of rules, and some of them are punishable by death.*"

"*Chimera too,*" he said. "*But only very, very bad ones. In last Isilna 'execution,' one warrior murders another pack's cubs in fight. We kill her for it.*" He settled on the ground. "*After you go to Citadel, do other humans kill you?*"

"*If I tell them what I've been doing here, absolutely. I'm still trying to figure that part out.*"

"*Do not go back to Citadel,*" he said. "*Stay with chimera.*"

She blinked. "*You're serious?*"

"*We want Blue in our pack,*" he said. "*Why not you?*"

"*Oh, I'm sure there are several reasons why that won't work,*" she said.

"*You think on it,*" Cyrij said. "*I ask Mek'tay. We do not want you dead.*"

She chuckled, watching Blue and Ebevil across the fire. "*I don't want me dead either.*"

CHAPTER THIRTY-THREE

Olivia jolted awake, one foot still in a forgotten dream while the other figured out what had woken her. Everything was dark; she'd put the fire out ages ago, but dawn hadn't yet arrived. The moons and planet's rings in the starry sky gave her a little light, dusting the trees and rising tides with silver. Shadows rolled and clashed and flew; she couldn't make any of them out. But she could hear it: the snarling, howling, yelping. All the minds bleeding emotions around her.

"*What the hell?*" she demanded, fumbling for her flint rather than her bow. It was no use trying to shoot anything in the dark.

"*You lie!*"

"*Ta've?*" she asked, following the bond that was filled with fire. "*Is that you?*"

"*Humans are evil! You lie!*"

The bond broke. Olivia yelped, clutching her head, lightning crackling in her skull where the bond once was. "*Ta've? Ta've!*"

An unfamiliar mind, seething pure fire, snapped, "*Human filth!*"

"*That's impossible; I bury my filth so it doesn't interfere with— Oh, wait. That's an insult to me. I get it now.*" She finally got a fire going so she could see.

Blue's wings were out, hackles raised as she snarled at two other chimera. Cyrij stood at her back, doing the same thing to another chimera. Ebevil made them a triangle, his head swiveling to look at all three attackers. Several rocks spun above the three of them like a massive crown. The three attackers landed and snapped at them but didn't get too close. To Olivia's surprise, she recognized two of them.

"*I know you!*" she said, pointing at the beautiful gray chimera with black wings. "*You're the first one who attacked me.*" She pointed to the red one. "*And you're the one who attacked Blue!*"

The red one snarled. "*I protect her. Lone chimera is dead chimera.*"

"*Chimera who attacks me is dead chimera,*" Blue shot back.

"*You just want kizaba,*" Cyrij accused.

"*Enough,*" Ebevil said, his mind a stone amid the raging fires around them. "*Silver, this is Sima'ik, Ulcoza, and Inyetaz.*" He motioned to the gray one, the red one, and the new one, respectively. Inyetaz was female, with a graying muzzle and pale-gold fur with grayish-blue wings. "*They are Kimuud. Friends, this is Olivia, silver human.*"

"*We know,*" Sima'ik growled. "*We do not know why she is not dead.*"

"*She tells us about humans and learns about chimera.*"

"*She does not tell us about human attack on our pack!*"

"*What?*" Olivia asked.

All three of them hit her with memories all at once, making it impossible for her to trace which one belonged to who.

He was flying with Idavi, feeling the wind ruffle his feathers, when she fell, an arrow in her chest. Their link was filled with nothing but fear and pain until—

Now that they knew where they were, they could hunt them. She charged one of the humans and felt hot blood in her mouth as her teeth sank into his throat. She had to abandon the kill as the humans fired at her, and she tried to swoop back in to kill another, but there were too many, too many projectiles aimed at her—

As Inyetaz drew their fire, he tried to dart in. He pulled a human from its roost in the tree, letting it fall screaming to its death. He yelped in pain as one of the human weapons grazed the edge of his wing, and he rolled in the air, letting the darkness swallow him. One of his packmates wasn't so lucky, and he felt their mental link shatter as the humans brought him down, leaving nothing but an empty void where joy and happiness should have been—

Olivia shook her head, forcing herself back into reality, away from the barrage of men in blue uniforms. The chimera hadn't focused on their faces, so in her mind, they were all blurred to look like Elias's.

Of course a demon hunt had happened. They happened almost every low tide!

"*Before, you know this happens,*" Sima'ik says.

"*No, but I should've,*" she replied, cursing herself for an idiot.

"*They kill three chimera,*" Inyetaz said. Her mind was like ice, cold enough to burn. "*We kill two humans. Let us kill this one. Three for three.*"

Olivia tensed. Her bow and quiver were near her bedroll, less than a meter away, and she had a knife at her belt. But against three coming at her at once . . .

"*No!*" Cyrij snapped. "*Silver is not bad human.*"

"*Step aside, cub,*" Inyetaz said.

"*Mek'tay lets her stay,*" Ebevil said. "*She stays. This is Isilna land.*"

"*This is* neutral *land. Mek'tay is not iyi'ke here.*"

"*And you are not iyi'ke of the Kimuud pack,*" Mek'tay said, emerging from the darkness like a black angel. He landed in the clearing. "*You threaten my warrior and his cub. Yet we are friends.*"

"*Your warrior and cub are in our way,*" Sima'ik snarled. "*Give us the human.*"

"*Or kizaba cub,*" Ulcoza suggested, looking at Blue. His red wings flexed. "*To replace what humans take from us tonight.*"

Blue snapped at him.

"*This kizaba cub is not 'mine' to give,*" Mek'tay said. "*Silver shows namsuud, psikar,* and *sadakra. She does not die here.*"

"*You protect humans instead of chimera?*"

"*I protect* this *human to protect chimera.*"

"*How about I just leave?*" Olivia suggested.

All eyes turned to her, glowing gold in the darkness.

"*I have what I need, and I won't be able to stop the hunts from the* forest," she said. "*I need to go back to Citadel and convince them that you're not unholy abominations we need to destroy.*"

The three Kimuud chimera's minds twisted in confusion. She ignored that as she dug out her sketchbook. "*But you should stay alert. Especially if you're near the iron bog or the highlands. They're looking at building a second town in one of those areas and will want it cleared of chimera before they move.*"

Ulcoza balked. "*Another human den?*"

She stuck her torch in the ground to keep it upright. As she took out her sketchbook and flipped to the right page, she sent them memories of the situation in Citadel: the draining soil producing fewer crops, the people living in the street because there weren't enough houses, the riots that broke out more and more often as people scrambled for food.

"*It wouldn't be so bad if we could go out into the forest to hunt and gather without getting butchered,*" she added.

"*If we do not kill you, you kill us,*" Inyetaz pointed out, baring her teeth.

"*So if humans stop the hunts, then you'll let us build a second town, hunt, and gather in the forest?*"

"*Humans have no namsuud,*" Sima'ik said. "*There is no peace while you breathe.*"

She didn't reply to that, flipping to the tidal calendar. The bottom of low tide had passed two days ago. Already the lowest lands in the east were trickling with water. In another four days, they would be at high tide, and then another six days for low tide again. That was when the next hunt would occur.

She had less than two weeks to convince Citadel to stop with the hunts, or more chimera and humans would die.

"*The Kimuud pack is in the south, right?*"

"*Yes,*" Mek'tay said. "*They have hidden metal humans dig up.*"

"*The last human attack is on neutral land, between us and Kryuun pack,*" Ebevil added. "*Near tall hills.*"

They were testing the waters, sending hunts in both directions to see how many chimera were in each spot. Since they'd actually managed to kill a couple of Kimuud, they might end up going there for—

"*Wait,*" she said. "*The Kimuud pack lives right on top of the iron bog?*"

"*Yes.*"

"*Can I talk to Acmare?*" The iyi'ke had been pretty amenable when she'd saved his nephew from the cave . . . God's Faces, had that been this morning? Either way, maybe, if things went really, really well, they'd be able to work out some sort of trade.

Ulcoza snarled, his fur the color of blood in the light of the torch. "*Dead. Humans kill him in 'hunt.'*"

She groaned in frustration. So much for that plan.

She dropped the book on her bag. "*Fine. I'll leave at first light and . . . figure it out from there.*"

"*There,*" Mek'tay said. "*She leaves forest. Let her return and try to talk other humans down. No more blood.*"

Whatever Ulcoza, Inyetaz, and Sima'ik thought of it, they kept it among themselves. After a minute or so of complete silence, when Olivia could *feel* them talking to each other but wasn't a part of their link, Inyetaz said, "*She has until Edalide's water reaches its height to be back in her den. Otherwise, she is dead.*"

The three of them flew off.

The other chimera relaxed, Ebevil and Blue dropping the rocks they'd been floating in the air.

"*Oh, shoot,*" Olivia groaned. "*I forgot to ask them about Ta've. He was yelling at me earlier, and now I can't link with him.*"

Ebevil nudged her. "*Ta've breaks bond connecting you.*"

"*What? Why? You can do that?*"

"*Humans kill his mother and uncle tonight.*"

She winced. Losing a mother to violence would make even the calmest person lash out. She rubbed her temples. The lightning-like pain from the broken bond was fading.

"*How do you tell Citadel to stop killing without them killing you?*" Cyrij asked.

She snorted. "*I have no idea. The idea that you're pure-evil 'demons' is so engrained . . .*"

"*This is one sticky mess,*" Mek'tay agreed. "*Do other humans want to help fix it?*"

Olivia considered it. "*There's a group called the Doves. They still think chimera are just animals, but they don't believe we have to kill you all to get into Heaven. The problem is I have no idea how I would find them. They have to stay secret in order to survive . . . Maybe Riley would know? He knows everyone. But I don't want to risk his health with a mostly unknown plant if I can help it.*"

"*Riley?*"

"*My friend,*" she said, thinking it over. She and Riley had rarely talked about religion and thus never talked about demons outside of funerals. He knew she was an atheist—the whole town knew that—and she knew he believed in the Hundred-Faced God. They both thought the other was a little silly. But he didn't try to convert her, and she resisted the urge to point out all the flaws in his faith because that apparently made people feel stupid.

Even if he refused to help her, he wouldn't turn her in. It was as good a place to start as any.

CHAPTER THIRTY-FOUR:
RILEY

The runner burst into the hospital just as Riley directed a pair of visitors to their sick family member. Breathing hard, military uniform covered in dirt and sweat, the runner wheezed, "Hunters returning . . . officer shot . . . arrow wound . . ."

Asiya, who had been just about to leave, tore off her coat. "Where's the wound and what's his blood type?"

"Shoulder. And I don't know."

"Go back and direct them to the emergency wing of the hospital. *Do not* remove the arrow or move it at all if you can help it. Riley, with me."

The runner ran back out. Riley jogged after his mentor, having to dodge around other medics and patients. He'd been in training for about a week now and knew that every single bed was full. Where they were going to keep this new patient, he had no idea.

As soon as they reached the emergency wing, Asiya whistled so loud his ear vibrated. "Incoming demon hunt, arrow to the shoulder."

Immediately, the other medics moved. Riley felt himself adrift in a sea before Asiya turned to him. "Get me antiseptic, needle, water, and bandages."

He dashed off, grateful that he'd spent the long, boring afternoon restocking those very things, so he knew where they were.

He was gone for less than a minute, but by the time he returned, a wheeled bed was set up, blood bags had been retrieved, and Mrs. Princops called out that room three was open. He set the supplies on the nearby tray where Asiya could easily reach them.

"Riley, you're my second for this one," Asiya said.

He stared at her. Mrs. Princops scoffed. "Really? Him?"

"You have surgery in half an hour. And the more experience the trainees get, the better."

Mrs. Princops's mouth thinned, and Riley couldn't blame her. The group of fresh medics he'd joined with had already lost half their number. Gabrielle had quit after refusing to take her own notes and actually study. Bella quit the first time a patient vomited on her. Two more had gotten engaged and decided to devote all their resources to their upcoming weddings and families, while another had been pulled to help with a surgery and quit immediately after. Several more left after the first human dissection—which Riley had loved, because he could finally see and touch the veins, organs, and muscles beneath the skin. But it had proved too much for many other trainees. Even more cracked under the strain of twelve-hour work shifts as the hospital scrambled for more staff.

Riley wasn't even finished with his training, still wearing the black shirt. But he couldn't keep to just paperwork, study, and stocking shelves. Especially when even untrained hands could be better than none.

"If that soldier dies, it's on both of your heads," Princops warned. She stormed off to prepare for her own surgery.

Asiya turned to Riley. "Wash your hands, quickly and thoroughly."

He did, scrubbing hard enough to turn the skin red. He took a moment to touch his amulet of the Hundred-Faced God, sending a quick, silent prayer to the Faces of Healing and Courage. Because Mrs. Princops was right. If this person died, it would be at least partially his fault.

The runner returned, supporting an injured ensign with the help of another. The injury was, indeed, an arrow through the shoulder, piercing the front and back. His clothes beneath the wound looked like they'd been washed in a red waterfall. The two other soldiers tried to keep pressure on the wound—front and back—while also moving him, but they weren't doing a particularly good job.

Riley's instincts took over. He helped them lay the patient sideways onto the bed, careful not to jostle the arrow. As soon as he was down, Riley took over keeping pressure on the wound, adding fresh, clean cloths. The man groaned in pain, semiconscious.

"When did this happen?" Asiya asked, examining the wound.

"Last night. One of the men thought he was a serovim," the runner explained.

"We tried to keep it clean, but we didn't want to pull the arrow out," the other soldier added.

"Good. He might've bled out if you did," she said. "Help us get him into surgery."

They did, moving the wheeled bed down the hall and into one of the surgery rooms. Each was big enough for a patient and a handful of medics to work, plus a counter for tools and medicines. They were kept as clean as humanly possible, the floors and walls regularly scrubbed with citrus-smelling, bacteria-killing cleaner. That had been Riley's job yesterday, and his arms still ached. Someone had already lit the torches and lanterns around the room so they could see clearly.

As soon as they were in the room, Asiya shooed the other two soldiers out. "Riley, keep pressure on that. I'm going to start a blood line so he doesn't bleed out while we do this."

He did as he was told, eyes on the white cloth that was very slowly turning red. The patient's somewhat glazed eyes were fixed on the ceiling, so wide Riley could see the entirety of the brown iris. He didn't recognize him, but his features looked familiar.

"Ensign, can you hear me?" Riley asked.

The soldier tore his gaze from the ceiling to his face.

"What's your name?"

"J-Jacob."

Riley beamed. "Hi, Jacob. I don't know if you've noticed, but you've got a sizable arrow in your shoulder."

Jacob huffed a laugh. "You know, I was wondering why my arm was so stiff."

"You look familiar. Have we met?"

"No . . . my father's a priest. Victor?"

"Oh, Father Victor! Over at the Temple of Mercy."

Jacob nodded, then grimaced at the movement. "That's him."

"I've only managed to go to two of his sermons, but he seems really good."

"Thanks." His mouth thinned. "Medical bills . . ."

"Don't think about that now," Asiya said, coming back with an iron needle connected to a strip that led to a blood bag. "Blood line's going in. You'll feel a pinch."

Jacob winced as the iron needle went in, but didn't move the arm, letting her work.

"You got any other family, Jacob?" Riley asked, trying to keep his patient's mind occupied and calm.

"Wife. Expecting our first."

"Congratulations! When is she due?"

They kept talking, Riley alternating between eye contact and checking the status of the wound.

"Next step is giving him a painkiller, then taking off the arrowhead and removing the shaft," Asiya said. "Once that's done, we'll put a clotting agent in the wound, then stitch it up."

"What if it nicked a vein?" Riley murmured, low enough that Jacob couldn't hear. The brachial artery and basilic vein both went through the shoulders, carrying blood directly to and from the heart.

"It's been hours. If that were the case, he'd be dead," she replied, just as quietly.

Riley nodded to himself, applying more pressure to stabilize the arrow. They gave Jacob a drink made from saxum mushrooms that would effectively deaden his pain receptors. Asiya cut the jacket and shirt away as they waited for the potion to take effect, tossing the bloody scraps.

The good news about military arrows was they were relatively easy to take apart for exactly this reason. With a careful twist, Asiya removed the bone arrowhead from the wooden shaft. Jacob didn't even wince.

"Now even with the saxum, you're still going to feel this," she explained. "We'll make it quick, but it'll help if you stay as still as possible. Do you understand?"

Jacob nodded.

Riley pulled the bandages away and moved to keep Jacob pinned to the bed, as immobile as possible. Asiya put a hand on the shaft and, quick as lightning, pulled out the arrow.

Jacob gasped. Riley put all his weight into keeping him down, cursing his skinny frame. Either he proved stronger than he thought, or Jacob was remarkably disciplined, because the man stayed relatively still.

Asiya poked around the wound a bit, cleaning it with water and making sure that they hadn't nicked anything important or left a piece of the arrow behind. Then she slathered it with what, to the untrained eye, looked like brown goop. In truth it was a clotting agent made from a local plant that fought infection, honey (which was a styptic, having the ability to stanch blood flow and bind flesh), incengis wax, and oil.

"We're going to have to keep an eye on this," she murmured. "A night and half a day is a long time to spend running around the forest with an open wound. It might still get infected despite our efforts."

"You can fix that, right?" Jacob slurred.

Riley patted his arm. "Of course we can. Mrs. Claude, do you need a needle and thread?"

"Yes, I do."

He prepared that while she washed the sticky agent off her hands. He glanced at the injury again, pleased to see that only a bit of blood had managed to leak through the goop.

Asiya instructed Riley to keep holding a bandage on the front side of the injury while she stitched up the back. He did, checking in with Jacob.

"Mm . . . sleepy," he said. "Is that normal?"

"That'd be a side effect of both the blood loss and the saxum," Asiya replied. "We'll give you another bag to help replace what you've lost. And you'll be wanting a new uniform."

"Just got it."

"I'm sure your commanding officer will understand," Riley said.

"You'll likely have a scar, though," Asiya warned.

Jacob lifted his head to look at the wound, then lay back down. "Girls like scars."

"Excuse me, Ensign, I thought you were married," Riley teased.

"I c'n still show off."

The rest of the procedure finished in relative peace and quiet. Asiya stitched the back, then handed the needle to Riley for the front. "It's a bit more difficult than sewing shirts, but relatively easy."

"Now I'm *very* glad he doesn't mind getting scarred," Riley grumbled, taking the needle.

His stitches weren't as small or neat as Asiya's, but they did their job of sealing the wound. They washed the area and wrapped it all in clean, white bandages. Jacob drifted off to sleep somewhere in there, rousing only when they changed his now-empty blood bag.

Riley looked at their work with pride. This man had entered the room with a potentially life-threatening injury. He would be leaving all patched up, with a near certainty of survival. He'd get to return home to his wife and, in a few months, raise his firstborn child.

This went beyond pride. It was a feeling unlike anything he had ever felt before.

Asiya called for someone to take Jacob to one of the observation rooms—which he would be sharing with at least one other person, probably more—while she and Riley cleaned up.

As they did, standing side by side at the long sink, Riley realized his hands were shaking.

"A bit of a head rush, isn't it?" Asiya asked, smiling.

He gave a sheepish grin, completely at a loss for words.

She flicked the water from her hands and squeezed him in a hug. "I'm so proud of you. Most trainees freeze during their first big operation."

"I was just doing what you told me to do," he said, returning the hug.

"It was a big help. And you handled Jacob *perfectly*, keeping him calm and distracted so I could work." She pulled back, looking him up and down. "Go change your shirt, dear, then meet me in the cafeteria for lunch. I tried a new casserole dish, but Evelyn didn't like it. If you want it, you can take it home."

Riley bit back a snort. Almost every day since he'd started working at the hospital, Asiya would give him a loaf of metabread or pot of soup because Ormus or Evelyn "didn't like it" or "we had some leftovers that I just couldn't fit into the cold box" or even "I think I'm developing an intolerance for this kind of food."

She was not subtle. But Riley wasn't going to turn down her gifts. Partly because he knew she *wanted* to help him and didn't think she *had* to. Partly because it was very helpful to his and Peterson's grocery bill. And mostly because her food was some of the best he'd ever tasted. He was pretty sure Peterson would kick him out if he told her to stop.

He left the surgery to change. Not even Mrs. Princops's glare dimmed the smile on his face. For the first time since his eighteenth birthday, he felt like he'd made exactly the right choice.

CHAPTER THIRTY-FIVE:
ORMUS

Commander Brodsky came into Ormus's office with a slightly rumpled uniform and a broad grin on his wrinkled face. "We have Brown. One of our undercover officers convinced him he wanted to join the Doves. Only problem is the agent got a little too eager and arrested him before he could get the names of any of the others. We've got him in interrogation now."

Ormus barely looked up from his paperwork. "Good to know."

"And we've got word back from the hunt."

He set his pen down. "Yes?"

Brodsky's smile dimmed. "Minimal casualties, and we've got a couple of demon bodies to bring back. No sign of your daughter, though. Or anyone else out there."

Ormus bit back a sigh. "I see. Search Brown's house and work. I'll interrogate him myself."

Sometimes, Ormus wished he could set up his office in an interrogation room. There was no decoration on the walls, sufficient lighting, and no possible distractions from his work. But the lack of windows made the room stuffy, and he itched to get out after only an hour.

Best to make this conversation quick. He sat at the table with a book across from the only other person in the room.

Markus Brown didn't say anything, watching him rifle through his personal journal. There wasn't so much as a wrinkle in his fine suit, but there were bags under his eyes and a little more gray in his hair, both signs of stress. His hands were cuffed on top of the table.

"There is a *lot* of contraband in here," Ormus said, scanning the journal he'd already read through. "'The Faith is wrong to hide anything in the Vaults.' 'Nobody should be executed for their private beliefs.' 'R is afraid of the governor's pet Claude . . .' That's uncalled for."

Markus still didn't say anything.

Ormus flipped to another page. The journal was old and worn, almost falling apart at the seams. The city guard had had to pry up the floorboards of Markus's house to get it. An excellent hiding place, just not good enough. And while Markus wrote about his fellow Doves, he was careful to only use first initials and never give out personal details.

"What else . . ." he mused. "This looks interesting: 'Jane had to go to the hospital again. She says she wants to get back to work, that she misses teaching.'"

"Stop," Markus muttered.

Ormus continued to read: "'Though I openly support her and tell her she'll of course go back to teaching someday, in truth I fear she'll never be well enough to work again. Mrs. Claude isn't sure she'll survive the next winter—'"

"Enough!"

Ormus looked up from the journal. "Something to say, Mr. Brown?"

"My wife isn't a Dove. She has nothing to do with this."

"You're a terrible liar." He closed the journal and set it on the table. "Here's what's going to happen: You will be executed as a Dove when the waters rise. That's four days from now. Depending on the evidence, your wife might be spared. But without you to support her . . ."

"You don't know what'll happen," Markus said.

"My own wife and I have gotten into a handful of arguments about it. She's of the opinion that the hospital can and should service everyone who so much as scrapes their knees, the way it used to be when Citadel was founded. She especially doesn't like having to charge for more than the basic services. Apparently, if you can't afford to pay for even lifesaving treatment, then . . ." He shrugged. "And with your assets seized by the town because of your crimes and your wife unable to work, I'll have to agree with Asiya: she won't last long."

Markus gritted his teeth. "What do you want?"

Ormus pulled a small bundle of letters from his pocket, also pulled from the floorboards of Markus's house. "These are coded, and I assume they're from your coconspirators. Help us crack your letters and give me a list of names of your fellow Doves," he said, sliding a pen and piece of paper across the table.

"And what'll happen to me and Jane?"

"I cannot guarantee that you will get out of this," he admitted. "However. The waiting list for the women's shelter is as long as your arm. I can put her on the top. She will inherit the house from you and can sell it at a great price for her medical expenses, while still having a roof over her head and food on the table."

Markus was silent for a long moment, thinking it over.

He picked up the pen and began to write.

Ormus couldn't keep the smile off his face as he strode into Augustus's office to deliver the news himself. "Apologies for the interruption, Governor, but you'll want to hear this."

The governor's office was right across the hall from the captain's, but bigger. Augustus had spared no expense in decorations, commissioning fine art on all four walls, a one-piece bookshelf filled with Scriptural and legal literature, and even a grandfather clock.

Augustus put down his pen. "Oh?"

Ormus held up a piece of paper. "Markus Brown gave us plenty of evidence against *four* longtime Doves. I've already issued warrants for their arrest. Give me another few days, and that entire organization will be shattered."

The governor grinned, opened a drawer in his desk, and pulled out an expensive bottle of sauvib wine. "This calls for celebration. Let me see that list."

Ormus handed it over, letting Augustus skim it as he poured the wine. They clinked glasses and drank.

Looking around the room, Ormus noticed something rather odd: a blank spot on the blue walls. "You removed the portrait of Riley."

"Yes, I did."

He frowned. "Are you really going through with this disowning process? Because Riley isn't backing down."

"He's little more than a child. He'll come back," Augustus said.

Ormus sighed, setting down his drink. "I talked to him, Augustus. He's happier than I've ever seen him."

"Happiness doesn't last long in poverty."

"I think you're underestimating your son's love for his vocation." He held up his hand. "I know that it's women's work, and I think you're right in that he should pursue something like law. But it is what it is. You think I want my daughters to be as invested in science as they are, when I know the chances of their success in Citadel are slim?"

"Forgive me, Ormus, but one of your daughters is lost to the forest and the other refuses to continue your line in favor of her own selfish desires," Augustus said. "That's not a model I want for my son."

"You're *disowning* your son."

"The process can be reversed, if he gives me the incentive."

Ormus ran a hand over his face. He didn't know why he bothered. Clearly, both Thompson men were stubborn to the extreme.

"I know it seems harsh, to an outsider," Augustus said, when Ormus didn't reply. "But the alternative . . . well. Did you know my father?"

"Not well," he admitted.

"A weak man. He almost caused the ruin of our family. Let my mother waste half our fortune on gambling and the other half on illicit suitors. Allowed my sister to marry someone of weak blood—she and the baby might have survived the birth if he'd chosen someone good for her. And instead of taking every opportunity to advance his position, he let his rivals get ahead.

"If I hadn't married Mia, her father never would've given us the loan needed to save us from bankruptcy. The only real downside to the match is that she couldn't give me more than one child, and a weak one at that. If Riley knows what's good for him, he'll come to heel. If not, then I have no son." He pointed at Ormus. "If you'd done the same to your girl, she wouldn't have run off into the woods."

"Believe me, I tried," Ormus admitted. "If I'd gone any further, it would've broken her spirit."

"Break it, then," Augustus said.

Ormus blinked. "What?"

Augustus shrugged his massive shoulders. "When Mia and I first got married, she wasn't keen on the idea. Wanted to shirk her duties as wife and mother and pursue a career in music. Dressed like a harlot, too. I had to teach her that she was mine. An extension of my will. Nothing more."

". . . Your wife is an alcoholic."

"It comes with some consequences," he admitted. "But they're better than the alternative."

Ormus sat heavily in his chair, trying to imagine doing that to Asiya. Forbidding her from ever taking another shift at the hospital or even preparing a meal like a "common woman." Ignoring her advice and contribution in raising his daughters. Dictating even what she wore. Controlling her every move until she had to turn to drink to feel somewhat human.

He couldn't do it. Though she had always put her family life first, those things were as much a part of her as her curly hair and freckled face.

It was the same with Evelyn and Olivia. Their curiosity, intelligence, and independence. Evelyn's steadiness, loyalty, and sharp tongue. Olivia's impulsiveness, bluntness, and ferocity. As much as he sometimes wished that they were easier to deal with, that they would bend to his will or follow the Faith's guidelines more strictly, he couldn't take that away from them. They wouldn't be *them*.

He couldn't ever treat them the way Augustus treated his family, as if they were objects. Tools for him to use at his leisure.

He set his still-full glass on the desk. "You're a great governor, Augustus. But I don't think you'll ever be considered a good man."

By the time he got home, he felt more settled than he had in ages. Asiya gave him a guilty smile over a steaming pot of something on the stove. "My shift went late. I didn't have the chance to go grocery shopping today, so I'm afraid it's leftovers."

He kissed her cheek. "Even garbage tastes good in your kitchen."

She lightly smacked his chest. "You'll give me a complex."

"Is Evelyn home?"

"In her room. She had to work on a school project at a friend's house, so I don't even know if she's taken off her boots."

Ormus went upstairs, wincing as he passed the closed door to Olivia's room. He brightened considerably when he got to Evelyn's. It was much neater than her sister's but incredibly similar: they both had bookshelves for their never-ending libraries, closets stashed with too many clothes, and beds pressed against the wall as if sleep were an afterthought. She sat on the floor of her room, tinkering with something metal in her hands.

She looked up, wide eyed, but didn't scramble to hide her work or justify it.

"Where did you get that?" he asked.

"One of my friends' uncles is a priest. He gave it to her, and she gave it to me." She wound up the something in her hand and set it on the floor. It was a little wooden mouse with wheels. It zipped across the room, stopping next to Ormus's toe.

"It's just a toy," Evelyn said. "Not much of an Artifact, but I guess even angels were children, once."

Ormus picked up the toy and studied it. The paint on the wood had long since faded, barely leaving any trace of color. The metal bits must have been replaced a dozen times. The soldier in him wanted to melt them down for bullets. The rest of him shuddered at the thought. This toy, this inanimate object, had *moved* because Evelyn had turned a knob. If that wasn't a miracle, he didn't know what was.

He dropped the toy in her hand and kissed her forehead. "You are going to be the most intelligent nun in Citadel's history."

Dear Elias,

Remember when I first tried knitting? Half the time, the yarn got caught in this massive, tangled mess that I'd spend ages trying to undo. And when I did, I'd knit only a few more rows before it got tangled again. Sometimes, I just had to take a knife to it.

That's what Citadel is. It's one giant mess of tangles that I have to undo. And I need to do it quickly, because every day I delay is another life lost. Another you gone. But if I go too fast and reckless, the tangle just gets tighter.

I don't know how to do this.

Love,
Olivia

CHAPTER THIRTY-SIX

After the incident with the Kimuud pack last night, Olivia had immediately packed and set off at first light. Blue decided to follow her, not trusting the chimera to keep their word, even though Mek'tay and Ebevil both said they had excellent sadakra and psikar.

Cyrij wanted to go with them, too, even arguing that it was his duty since Olivia was technically his responsibility. But they were going straight to Citadel, which was constantly surrounded by hunters, armed gatherers, and military patrols. She didn't want either of them to get too close.

"*Don't worry*," Olivia said, tapping her temple. "*I'll let you know how it goes.*"

Blue took to the trees, flying from branch to branch while Olivia stayed on the spongy ground, which was still dry enough to walk, though that wouldn't last. She'd have to make her camp in the branches tonight. The early-morning light barely penetrated the ceiling of leaves, giving Olivia just enough to see the trees and terrain as pale-gray specters.

As eager as she was to return to her friends and get to work ending the slaughter, she also dreaded it. Returning to Citadel meant returning to rules that didn't make sense, people who refused to hear her, and bad memories. She tried to take her mind off it.

"*So what's your plan, after all of this?*" she asked.

Blue looked down at her from the trees, dark-sapphire wings spread for balance. "*I do not know. I like Cyrij and Ebevil. Mek'tay is fine. But I do not join packs.*"

"Fair enough," Olivia said. "*How come you won't let anyone call you Is'hav?*"

"*Memories of my pack are foggy. But I remember names are sacred. We tell others when they can use them. That makes them pack.*"

"So . . . *you tell someone when they can use your name, and that's like you saying you want to be a part of their pack?*"

"*Yes.*"

"Huh. Neat."

Blue showed Olivia her view of the forest, including the spiven just east of them. Olivia slowed her pace so as not to make any noise.

"*Cyrij says he wants you to join Isilna,*" Blue said. "*Do you do that, after?*"

"*I'm tempted,*" she admitted. "*I've always loved the forest.*"

It was more than that. For the first time in her life, she didn't feel like she was being shoved into a box where she didn't fit. Sure, the chimera didn't welcome her with open arms (er, open wings), but she was still happier here than she'd ever been in Citadel. Even when she'd been dating Elias.

She paused.

She was . . . *happy.*

Thinking about Elias still gave her a pang in her chest, but it wasn't like trying to breathe through glass. She still wrote her letters, but she wasn't constantly wishing he was here. She was just . . . enjoying the moment. For the first time. Ever.

Olivia grinned, strolling through the forest. "*Is that spiven still there?*"

"*Ye— Wait.*" Ice shot through their link.

Olivia froze, looking up at Blue. The chimera was almost invisible in the shadows between the leaves. Olivia nocked an arrow and ducked behind a tree. "*What's wrong?*"

"*Chimera,*" Blue whispered, her mind trembling.

"*Kimuud?*"

Cold terror crept through their link, images of the Mulo pack slaughtering Blue's.

"Those *chimera? You recognize them?*" Olivia verified. When Blue didn't answer, she gave their link a pull. "*Hey! Blue, breathe.*"

"*Trying,*" she growled.

Olivia ran a hand down her face. If she were Riley or Asiya, she'd know what to do to help the panicking chimera.

A shadow passed overhead. Olivia pressed herself against the tree, praying it was just a nugzuuki and not a Mulo.

She reached out through her other links. "*Cyrij, Mek'tay, Ebevil. We've got Mulo.*"

Cyrij, she could tell, had been asleep, groggily answering with dreary confusion. The other two initially sent spikes of alarm through her whole core before clamping down on it, Mek'tay before Ebevil. "*We come,*" the iyi'ke promised. "*Get out.*"

Their reactions gave Olivia an idea. She took a deep breath, forcing her mind to calm, hoping that that would serve as an anchor for the cub. "*Blue. Help is on the way. We need to get you back to camp.*"

"*I cannot move,*" she snapped, her mind little more than a high-pitched tone of panic. "*If I do, they see me.*"

"*I have my eyes on you. If anything else moves, I'll shoot them down. Now go!*"

Blue spread her wings and dove off the tree.

Almost immediately, two other chimera appeared, converging on her. "*Stop!*" one of them called. "*We are friends—*"

"*You are Mulo! Go away!*" Blue snarled.

"*You come with us now, Is'hav.*"

"*NO!*"

Olivia fired.

The arrow cut through one of the Mulo's wings, dropping him. The other one scrambled as their injured companion fell.

Olivia ducked back behind her tree, nocking a new arrow.

"*Hello.*"

An invisible force yanked her into the open. She slid across the dirt, barely keeping her feet, as a third chimera landed before her, just a few meters away.

The chimera she'd shot tumbled to the ground behind her, arrow sticking out of their wing. Where was their companion?

Blue yowled above their heads. She was trapped in a net, wings straining against the woven vines as she bit and clawed at it. But it was so tightly woven she had no luck.

For a moment, Olivia thought some soldiers had managed to sneak this far and set some kind of trap. But then she saw the second Mulo—with two others—and the fact that the net and Blue were floating in the air. They must've used telekinesis to make the net and now used it to trap her. Her panic flooded Olivia's mind. She had to grit her teeth to stop herself from letting it take over.

"*Make them leave!*" Blue shrieked. The only thing keeping her in the air was the Mulo's telekinesis. The net covered her entire body; Olivia didn't think she could see anything, never mind use telekinesis herself.

Olivia's fingers twitched for an arrow. The two Mulo on the ground with her growled, stepping closer. There were three more with Blue, bringing the total to five.

"*I can't.*"

"*Silver!*"

Tears stung her eyes. "*I'll find a way to get you out! I promise!*"

The three chimera flew away, carrying the net and Blue with them.

"*The Isilna pack is on its way,*" Olivia warned, trying to keep her eye on both of the Mulo on the ground with her. "*So go fly away now, and leave Blue with me.*"

They paused. "*You speak,*" said the one who'd pulled her with telekinesis. "*How?*"

She showed them an image of the green prasina flower. "*I can use it to get all humans to communicate with chimera. We can end the war.*"

"*So?*"

Olivia gritted her teeth. Every second she was here was another second Blue was pulled farther away. Her howls grew more and more distant. *"Don't you want to stop your packmates from dying?"*

"Edalide gives, Mulo takes. That is their price."

"It is their price," the other chimera echoed.

"Riiight," Olivia said, knowing she was failing miserably at hiding her skepticism. Mostly because she didn't try.

"I'm going to get my friend and go now . . ." she continued, slowly stepping away.

The invisible force gripped her and pulled her up, stronger than the others. It was like two people had grabbed hold of her instead of one, and it was enough to lift her off the ground. She nocked and fired an arrow in quick succession.

It didn't hit the chimera, but it got close, distracting him enough that his grip on Olivia dropped, and the other wasn't able to hold her on their own. She hit the ground and ran.

Not fast enough.

They pulled her back. While one kizaba wasn't strong enough to carry her on their own, they could slow her down.

Damn telekinetic.

She nocked a new arrow and turned to fire. But as she did, one of the Mulo threw a massive rock.

She let go of the arrow just as the rock hit her temple.

CHAPTER THIRTY-SEVEN

Olivia groaned, blinking her eyes open. *Why is the sky on fire?*

She squinted. That wasn't fire. It was the sun filtering through the orange and yellow leaves. She was on her back looking up.

The entire left side of her head throbbed. She poked it, wincing at the fresh pain. Her fingers came away wet with blood.

"*Silver!*" Cyrij's head was suddenly right above her. "*Do you hurt?*"

She blinked.

Then bolted upright. "*Blue!*"

One Mulo chimera lay dead by her feet, his throat opened with four parallel lines. The other—the one Olivia had shot through the wing—was pinned down by Mek'tay and Inyetaz, her fur shining gold in the sunlight. Ebevil stood a little ways away, a handful of rocks not unlike the one that had knocked Olivia out spinning over his body. And there was another chimera with them, one with cream fur and gray wings.

"*Blue is gone,*" Cyrij said. "*She does not answer. They make her sleep, like you.*"

She tried to reach out to her friend. The link that had been filled with panic and fear during the attack was now dead and silent. That terrified her more than anything.

"*We have to get her.*" Olivia stood, only for the ground to buck under her feet, sending her back on her bottom.

"*Your head is broken. Sit and get better.*"

The new chimera approached her, looking her over. A quick glance told Olivia this was a female. Cyrij's mother, maybe? The cream coloring was the same, though the freckles were missing.

"*We may need Ukurf,*" the new chimera said.

Olivia blinked. That voice was *male.*

"*Who are you?*" she asked. Then, remembering the manners Ormus had drilled into her, added, "*I'm Olivia.*"

"*Siyet. I am Cyrij's parent.*"

"*Uh . . .*" She gave Siyet's mind a poke just to make sure. That was definitely a man's brain in there.

Her head throbbed again. She gave it a few experimental prods and confirmed that the wound was shallow, if bleeding like a stuck pig. It stained her hair red.

She dug into her bag for her medical kit, already losing interest in Siyet's gender. It happened sometimes in Citadel too. Sarai had explained it as a person with a woman's body and a man's soul, or vice versa. Most people didn't hear about it until someone like that was on the posts for "unnatural sexual deviance." How that warranted a death sentence was yet another aspect of the Faith and Citadel governance that Olivia did not understand.

While she cleaned her wound and tried to determine whether she needed stitches, Mek'tay and Inyetaz questioned the Mulo.

"*Where is Blue?*" he demanded.

"*In our den,*" the Mulo said.

"*Where?*"

He didn't answer.

Ebevil shot a rock at the injured wing. The Mulo yipped as the arrow jolted.

"*Where is your den?*" Mek'tay repeated.

"*You cannot attack,*" the Mulo said. "*Is'hav is not yours. If you attack our territory, we have war.*"

"*Break his mind,*" Inyetaz said.

Cyrij stiffened. Siyet growled.

Olivia used a closed link with Cyrij: "*What's that mean?*"

"*We go into their mind and steal their memories. Break bonds. Some chimera go insane,*" he explained. "*There is no namsuud in breaking minds.*"

Mek'tay apparently agreed, because he ripped out the Mulo's throat with his teeth.

Inyetaz flattened her ears at him but didn't argue. She walked over the corpse to Olivia. "*Before we come, what happens to Blue?*"

The head wound wasn't too bad. She still ached, but it wouldn't need stitches. She put a bandage over it while sharing the memory of what happened.

"*We can save her,*" Cyrij declared. "*Right?*"

Mek'tay hesitated. "*If we go into Mulo territory, we start war.*"

"*Isilna and Kimuud together may win,*" Inyetaz said.

"*I cannot risk my pack for one cub.*"

"*She is kizaba.*"

"*She is cub,*" Siyet pressed. "*That is worth risk.*"

"*We ask other packs to fight too?*" Ebevil suggested. "*They do not like Mulo.*"

"*They* fear *Mulo,*" Mek'tay pointed out. "*Mulo is very powerful. We must be careful.*"

Olivia finished her bandage and gave standing another try. The dizziness remained but was manageable. "*All right. You guys distract them at the border; I'll go in.*"

"*What?*"

"*You don't want to spark war with the Mulo pack. But us humans are* already *at war with them. I can go in and find her while you draw the Mulo out. Once they're at the border, they're fair game, right?*"

Mek'tay's mind stilled. She couldn't get any grasp on his thoughts or emotions.

Ebevil wagged his tail. "*It has namsuud.*"

"*I do not tell* any *chimera to fight Mulo,*" Mek'tay decided. "*I ask.*"

Olivia nodded. "*Volunteers only, then. I like it.*"

"*I volunteer!*" Cyrij cheered.

"*No!*" Ebevil and Siyet snapped.

"*You are still cub,*" Ebevil said.

Cyrij bared his teeth. "*Silver is going to Mulo. She is* my *responsibility. It is sadakra. And Blue is my friend! I must go.*"

Mek'tay turned to the parents. "*Your cub, your choice.*"

Siyet and Ebevil silently discussed it. Siyet huffed.

"*Cyrij comes,*" Ebevil said. "*He has strongest bonds with Silver and Blue, so he* stays in the back, *out of the fight, and speaks with them.*"

Cyrij howled. "*Yay!*"

Inyetaz studied Olivia with her pale-yellow eyes. "*Why do you care about chimera?*"

"*Like Cyrij said: Blue is our friend.*" She ripped the arrow out of the dead Mulo's wing. "*And I don't have a lot of those.*"

Siyet was the largest of the chimera, so he offered to give Olivia a ride.

"*Two tens of chimera join us,*" Mek'tay said. He tipped his head. "*Three tens. Three tens and five.*"

"*They know not to attack* me, *right?*" she asked.

"*They treat you with namsuud, unless you do not.*"

She counted the arrows in her quiver. Nine, plus her knife. "*How many chimera are in the Mulo pack?*"

"*Many,*" came the frustrating answer. "*More than five tens of warriors, with many kizaba. We do not know how many cubs and nonfighters.*"

"*You must cover your smell,*" Siyet instructed. "*Rotweed tree is close.*"

That was a good idea. The pungent ivy wrapped around the tallest branches of trees. The soldiers of Citadel used it for their stink bombs in crowd control—

Olivia stopped. She turned that thought over in her mind.

"*Silver?*" Siyet asked.

She took her spare shirt and some ingencis oil out of her bag. "*Cyrij, help me stash this.*"

He took the bag in his talons and flew it up into the trees, where it would be safe from predators. All she had in hand were her weapons, water canteen, and shirt.

Mek'tay put a map in everyone's minds. "*We go to hills, here,*" he said, highlighting one part of the map, on the eastern border of Mulo territory and western edge of Isilna. "*Siyet takes Silver to cliffs, here.*" He highlighted a part of the border farther south. "*After, he meets with us. Cyrij stays behind us and tells us when Blue is out. Then we leave.*"

Cyrij nudged her with the top of his head. "*Be careful. We have good bond because you are my friend too.*"

She scratched behind his ears, trying to send a confidence she didn't feel. "*Don't worry, Freckles. We can do this.*"

CHAPTER THIRTY-EIGHT

Siyet flew Olivia to a tree that *reeked*. The rotweed spread from branch to branch like a purple-vined sickness. Olivia held her breath as she rubbed it over her skin and clothes, stuffing a few bunches in her pockets for good measure. Siyet gave her a couple of sniffs before nodding his approval. "*Stay out of water so it does not wash off.*"

"*I can't wait until I can,*" Olivia grumbled, wrinkling her nose. She tore her spare shirt into pieces, large enough to make two pouches. She took out two arrows. Then, holding her breath, she tore out several more handfuls of rotweed.

"*What are you doing?*" Siyet asked, gagging.

"*Making stink bombs. It's not just a camouflage; it's also a weapon.*" She stuffed the stinky leaves and poured a bit of oil into the pouches before tying the cloth closed around the arrowhead. It would be more pungent with rotten food or dung added to it, but this would have to do. The process gave her seven regular arrows and two stink arrows, which she held in her hands rather than put back in her quiver. Wouldn't do to activate those bombs early.

She returned to Siyet's back, and they flew. She didn't know how long they traveled, but by the time they reached the cliffs, her legs were sore from keeping them bunched up near her chest.

The forest had split, the other side revealing a large stone cliff face that rose at least five stories up. The tides had never touched the top of the cliff: tender bushes, flowers, even grass grew straight from the ground. Vines grew down the stone wall like hair, their roots at the top of the cliff and their ends reaching for the bottom. A river—an honest-to-God river—broke into a waterfall before crashing back below.

"*This is Mulo territory,*" Siyet said, landing on the top of the cliff, near the waterfall. "*We do not know their den. At bottom of cliff is neutral ground. We help you once you're there.*"

Olivia slid off his back, knees wobbling as she shook out the tension. She took a deep breath, studying the dark shadows of the forest.

This felt worse than leaving Citadel. Then, she had known there was at least one ally somewhere in the woods she could work with. And that had been a selfish mission. She'd wanted answers to her own questions. No one else had been at risk.

Here, there were consequences. Here, if she failed, Blue would suffer, and none of the other chimera would help her.

She tightened her grip on the bow Elias had made for her. It wasn't the same as having her boyfriend alive and breathing, probably swearing at the situation, but it would have to do.

"*Thank you, Siyet,*" she said, dismissing him.

Siyet jumped off the cliff and flew away. Olivia followed one of the bonds in her mind. "*Cyrij, can you hear me?*"

"*Yes,*" he replied. It was fainter than what she was used to hearing from him, probably because of the distance.

She followed another bond. "*Blue. Blue, can you hear me?*"

No response.

"*Blue?*" Did she hate Olivia for not being able to stop the kidnapping?

"*Cannot talk,*" Blue replied, her mind a combination of ice and fire. "*They try to break my mind.*"

Olivia went cold. "*What?*"

"*They want to cut my bonds—need to go!*"

She retreated back into her own mind, taking her fear and rage with her. Olivia started walking, following the bond like a trail of bread crumbs. This part of the forest was extremely strange. Rather than the massive blue trees of the lowlands, these trees were smaller, skinnier, and paler, which let in much more sunlight on the ground. The ground was absolutely *covered* in red-orange grass, spongy beneath her boots. If she squinted, it looked like the ground was made of fire while a forest grew from the flames. She wished she could sit down and draw or even paint it.

A hundred howls rose, their voices surrounding her. By instinct, Olivia pressed herself against the nearest tree, frustrated that it couldn't completely hide her. She nocked an arrow, trying to find the source of the howls. She couldn't tell how many there were or how close they were. Had they found her already?

"*That is us*," Cyrij said, mind bubbling in amusement.

She breathed. "*Right. I knew that.*"

"*You lie*," he chuckled.

She resumed walking, following the bond with Blue as it got stronger.

"*They leave*," Blue said. "*Is that you?*"

"*Most of the other chimera really don't like the Mulo pack*," Olivia replied. "*What's your situation? Can you fly?*"

"*No.*" Through Blue's mind, Olivia could feel the net still tangled around her body, wings forced tight to her back. She wasn't *in* the den itself, rather on the edge of it. Close enough that she could hear and smell several chimeric warriors fly away to investigate the howls. But two chimera stayed with Blue. One turned to look at her—

The link cut off, Blue retreating again.

Several *more* howls echoed Mek'tay's. Olivia kicked it up to a jog, not knowing how long Mek'tay and the others would be able to hold everyone's attention. It was a game of hot and cold; sometimes the bond with Blue would get fainter, and she'd have to double back and take a turn. The bond pulled her away from the river. Whenever the shadow of a chimera caught her eye beyond the leaves overhead, she ducked beneath a tree, waiting until they were gone to keep going.

"*Hurry*," Cyrij urged. "*Mulo are here.*"

Another chimera flew overhead. Olivia pressed herself against the tree. There were more of them flying around. She had to be getting close.

After a few steps, she heard high-pitched yips and the occasional bark. Two minutes later, she saw *dozens* of chimera and immediately ducked for cover beneath a bush. She waited for the attack to come.

Nothing happened.

She peeked over the bush. Some of the chimera were adults, but a lot of them were cubs, playing and napping in the sun. Underground dens and crude lean-tos made of branches and ferns were everywhere. There was even a fire in the center!

Olivia could have spent ages studying them just like this—chimera had *architecture*, they burned bones instead of wood for a longer-lasting flame, and it looked like a couple of kizaba were weaving another net—but she was all too aware that if any of them saw her, she was dead. That alone almost killed the scholarly spirit in her.

The chimera's sharp noses should have been able to smell her, but the rotweed did its job. Nobody noticed her presence.

Blue's bond pulled her south. She crept around the den, giving it as wide a berth as she could. Keeping them all in hearing, if not sight.

On the south side, without a den or lean-to, was Blue, still tangled in the net used to capture her. Despite her squirming and pressing against it with her wings, she was well and truly trapped, like a fish already put in a boat. Two adult chimera were with her, both looking at her.

Olivia could theoretically kill them both, then cut Blue free and run. But with telepathy, it would be seconds before everyone realized what was going on and hunted them down.

She'd have to cause a distraction. But she couldn't be in two places at once.

She tried to talk to Blue, to no avail. That cub was deep in her mind, protecting herself from the two Mulo guards, who must have been trying to break in.

Olivia readied a stink bomb and shot it into the firepit.

Rotweed by itself smelled bad enough. Rotweed *burning* was borderline explosive. And incengis oil was downright flammable.

A small explosion burst out of the firepit. A massive cloud of stink surged through the den.

The den exploded in movement. Olivia almost gagged at the stench twelve meters away. The chimera closest to the fire stumbled back as if drunk. More than one passed out. Cubs were picked up by the scruff and flown up and away. The howls were deafening. Olivia ducked against a large tree as chimera shot into the air, looking for the source of the explosion and smell.

One of Blue's guards left. The other put a paw on Blue's net, making sure she couldn't go anywhere. Blue looked up and met Olivia's eyes.

"*Silver, what happens?*" Cyrij demanded. "*Mulo leave.*"

"*I had to pull their attention from Blue* somehow!" she snapped. She unsheathed a knife and held it up. Blue showed her teeth.

The knife flew from her hands, like it had a mind of its own, and buried itself in the remaining guard's skull.

The chimera dropped on top of Blue, crushing her body. Olivia shoved him off and used the bloodied knife to cut Blue free.

"*Are you hurt?*" she asked.

"*No.*" Blue's mind quickly turned to white-hot fury. "*No others here?*"

"*They can't. Not without officially declaring war with Mulo. You'll have to fly out yourself.*" Olivia hesitated, then decided against asking for a ride. Blue was too small to carry her, and that would just slow them down. "*I'll cover you as long as I can. Follow Cyrij's link and join the others.*"

As soon as Blue was free, Olivia held up the knife. "*Take this in case you run into trouble.*"

The blade floated. Blue bumped her forehead against Olivia's chest and flew off.

The stink was already noticeably fading. Olivia fired her last bomb into the fire and ran off, leaving the Mulo warrior's body by the shredded net.

Shadows flew overhead. In addition to the howls, Olivia could *feel* the chimera around her, like candles in a dark room. She could only hope her own mind was camouflaged, able to blend in with the others.

"*New kizaba escapes!*" someone called on an open link. Olivia kept her mind still, refusing to acknowledge it. "*Go south.*"

Olivia saw a handful of chimera fly in formation to the south. They could easily catch up to Blue before she hit the border.

Olivia nocked, aimed, and fired.

The arrow hit one of the chimera in the stomach. They fell, crashing through leaves and branches. The others scattered. She sprinted away from the den's enraged howls. "*Blue, you have a team going after you.*"

"*Two chase me now.*" A pause. A breath of vicious satisfaction. "*Now one. I like your knife.*"

Still sprinting, Olivia dared to look up.

A chimera followed her. They folded their wings and dove. She barely had time to roll out of the way before their talons hit the ground where she'd been, leaving a deep groove in the dirt like a comet's tail. Olivia jumped up and readied an arrow. Before she could even aim, the chimera telekinetically threw half a dozen rocks at her. She cringed behind her arm as they fell on her in a shower.

The chimera charged.

Olivia shrieked and fired her bow.

The arrow went right through the chimera's chest.

They hit the ground with a thud. Olivia jumped, scrambling away. The Mulo didn't move.

She realized this was the *second* chimera she'd killed today. Third, if she included the first one Blue had taken out with her knife.

Three chimeric people. Dead.

"*Silver?*" Cyrij called. "*Do you hurt? What happens?*"

"*. . . Nothing.*" She went back to running.

Olivia kept running until she hit the river. She leaned against a tree, gasping for breath. For all the self-defense training Peterson had put her through and archery lessons with Elias, she'd never had to do much running. She understood why Elias had hated those drills. It felt like her organs were shriveling up inside of her chest and kicking her spine. *What I would give for a pair of wings.*

"*She is here!*" Cyrij cheered. "*Blue is here!*"

Olivia grinned. "*Blue, are you all right?*"

"*Nothing hurts,*" she reported. "*Are you still in there?*"

"*Not all of us have wings!*" Olivia pushed off the tree and started walking. "*I just have to follow this river to the waterfall and climb down the cliff.*"

"*You have problem,*" Cyrij said, suddenly sober. "*All Mulo are gone. When you free Blue, they know we trick them. They return to their den.*"

She winced. "*Does the fact that Blue and I killed three of them factor into that?*"

He paused. "*That makes them* very *angry.*"

"*Sorry.*"

She knelt by the river to get a drink of water, setting her bow by her knee. The urge to dunk herself in the water was almost as strong as the reek of rotweed on her skin, but she just drank two large mouthfuls and refilled her canteen. Through the thin trees, she could see the open sky. Neutral ground was close.

She tried to decide if she should feel guilty about what had happened today. The whole point of her returning to Citadel was to stop humans and chimera from killing each other, and now three people were dead because of her. They'd been trying to kill her and hurt her friend, but she had invaded their territory. If she'd just walked away . . .

If she'd walked away, Blue would still be trapped. Her mind would've been invaded, the bonds with her friends broken, and she would've been forced into a pack that had murdered her family.

Olivia might feel guilty about the bloodshed, but she couldn't regret saving her friend.

The ripples in the water faded, smoothing into a reflective surface. Like a mirror.

That showed two chimera coming down from the sky.

Olivia grabbed her bow. The chimera dove down, three more following them.

No use staying hidden now, she thought and jumped in the water.

The current swept her downstream. She kept herself as far beneath the surface as possible, trying to hide from the Mulo. The water slammed her into a rock, blowing the breath from her lungs, almost distracting her from the snap of her bow breaking.

Elias's bow.

She kicked up, working with the current rather than against it, and broke the surface. Beautiful, glorious air filled her lungs.

The current picked up speed. Suddenly remembering that there was a waterfall nearby, she grabbed a low-hanging branch that dipped into the water and looked down.

That drop was an uncomfortably close four meters away.

Something yanked her out of the water, like a set of invisible hands. Olivia found herself floating over the river. All five chimera watched her as she dangled in the air.

Her bow had broken right in the middle, the two pieces of wood dangling from the bowstring.

No shooting her way out of this.

No getting out of this, *period*.

For reasons not even she understood, she laughed.

The chimera threw her off the cliff.

CHAPTER THIRTY-NINE

Flying had been fun.

Falling? Decidedly *not* fun.

Olivia stopped laughing. She screamed as the ground rushed up to meet her. Her mind was a chaotic rush of panic, almost like a breakdown. There was nothing she could do to slow her fall or save herself. She was going to hit the trees first and end up impaled—

She stopped falling, gliding to a halt a handspan from the orange leaves.

Before she could process the fact that she wasn't going to die—not like this, anyway—she was pulled into the leaves, her body navigated through twigs and vines until she was set on her feet on a large branch. Her legs wobbled. She dropped to a sitting position, clutching her broken bow.

Ebevil and Blue stood before her, as well as Siyet, Cyrij, and Mek'tay. Mek'tay headbutted her shoulder. "*Up. We cannot rest here.*"

Remembering that the five Mulo who wanted to kill her were still close, Olivia pulled herself to her feet and shoved her broken bow in her near-empty quiver. Her knife went back into its sheath. Siyet urged her onto his back, and then they were all flying, Cyrij taking the lead.

They kept below the leaves, taking advantage of the low tide to stay close to the ground. This part of the forest was low enough that the ground already had a thin layer of water covering it, reflecting the big blue tree trunks and their ceiling of fiery leaves. Howls followed them, and within minutes Olivia saw the five Mulo coming up behind them.

"*Incoming!*" she warned.

Siyet took a sharp left around a tree, almost throwing her off. Olivia tightened her grip on his pale fur and gritted her teeth, the chill wind slicing her cheeks. Ebevil and Mek'tay adjusted their flight and speed to stay between them and the Mulo.

We're not going to make it, she realized as the distance between their group and the Mulo grew smaller and smaller.

And then she realized that *she* was slowing them down. Her weight on Siyet reduced his speed, and while Cyrij and Blue were far enough ahead that they could escape, Mek'tay and Ebevil weren't.

If her bow had still been functional, she might have at least been *useful*, shooting at their pursuers. Instead, she was deadweight.

"*I can slow them,*" Ebevil said, slowing so he was farther down their tail.

"*Ebevil, no!*" Siyet snapped. "*We are so close!*"

"*Not enough.*"

"*Just drop me,*" Olivia said. "*I'm the one slowing you down.*"

"*We leave no one!*" Siyet cried. "*Ebevil, go to Cyrij!*"

"*No, mate,*" Ebevil said softly.

Ebevil was *one* telekinetic. Going against five, he'd never make it.

Olivia was so busy looking back, trying to figure a way to get everyone out of this, that she didn't realize the two chimera cubs ahead of them were no longer there.

Just as one of the Mulo was about to overtake Ebevil, Cyrij burst from the orange leaves and slammed into them. They fell to the dirt, teeth snapping, wings pummeling, claws and talons raking. Ebevil dove down and joined the fight, trying to tear the Mulo warrior off his son. Two of the other Mulo went after *him*. Mek'tay joined the mess. They all fell to the ground, splashing in the knee-high water. Siyet veered to join, but there were still two other Mulo who followed him, their hateful yellow eyes on Olivia.

"*Silver!*" Blue called. "*Give me arrows!*"

Olivia grabbed her last handful of arrows and threw them into the air.

They stopped falling after only a couple of meters. Blue shot them at the two Mulo on Olivia and Siyet's tail. Their bodies fell, riddled with holes.

On the ground, a bloodied Cyrij raised his hackles and wings against the equally bloodied Mulo he'd air-tackled. The Mulo kept trying to get to him, cutting through the low water, but Ebevil was firmly in the way. Mek'tay was frozen, telekinetically pushed to the ground by the other two Mulo. He just barely kept his snout above the water.

As Siyet flew low to join, Olivia unsheathed her knife and slid off the pale chimera.

She fell two stories and landed on a Mulo's back.

Something *snapped* beneath her. The warrior gave a high-pitched, painful *yipe!* Olivia slit their throat, feeling only marginally guilty about it. *That's four people I've killed today.*

One telekinetic wasn't enough to pin down a pissed-off iyi'ke. Mek'tay broke free of the invisible grip and, like a streak of black lightning, tackled the other.

The Mulo attacking Ebevil and Cyrij didn't notice Siyet swooping down. That is, until the enraged parent swiped at one of their wings with his talons. Half of the massive feathered appendage flew right off, landing so close to Olivia she got splashed when it hit the water.

The Mulo froze, probably from a combination of shock and blood loss. Ebevil quickly finished them off.

The last surviving Mulo, still engaged with Mek'tay, didn't notice, still trying to take a chunk out of the black iyi'ke. Olivia readied her knife to throw it.

She needn't have bothered. All five of the arrows she'd given Blue—which, last she'd seen, had been left in two other chimera bodies—shot at the surviving Mulo in rapid succession. One hit a wing, one got the snout, and the other three landed in the torso. All of them were buried to the fletching. He was dead before he hit the water.

Olivia turned to see Blue standing behind her, glaring at the Mulo bodies.

"*Before, you should keep flying,*" Mek'tay scolded, but it was gentle. Edged with . . . it was like a golden glow. Like what Olivia felt whenever Evelyn did something really smart, or Riley asserted himself—oh. Pride. "*You and Cyrij.*"

"*You should leave me with Mulo,*" Blue retorted, mind bubbling with amusement.

"*We'll remember that next time,*" Olivia said, putting her knife away. She considered sloshing through the water to collect her arrows, but they were buried so deep in that Mulo that it would take too long. Besides, without a bow to shoot them with, they were useless.

"*Who hurts?*" Ebevil asked. "*Cyrij?*"

Out of all of them, Cyrij definitely looked the worst. His cream fur was smeared with blood, almost completely covering the brown spots. Siyet licked at the worst of his injuries, trying to clean them.

"*Just scratches,*" Cyrij said, panting heavily.

"*We need to fly,*" Mek'tay said. "*Mulo is still too close.*"

"*I can fly.*"

Siyet slowly stepped away so Olivia could get on his back. Nobody left the ground until Cyrij did, and they stayed close behind, watching his sluggish flying.

"*Mek'tay is right. Cubs stay away from fighting,*" Ebevil scolded, though he had the same glow of pride as Mek'tay.

Though Cyrij preened under that pride, his response was still mulish: "*I lose Tekkaz to humans. I do not lose parents to Mulo.*"

"*Or friends,*" Blue added softly.

Olivia felt that kill the relatively good mood of the group, especially in Ebevil and Siyet. They flew the rest of the way to safety in silence.

Olivia dropped onto her sleeping roll with a groan. All the chimera panted around her, most of them following suit on the dirt. The sun had begun to set, blanketing the ground in shadows. She should get a fire going. Eventually. When everything stopped being sore.

They weren't anywhere she recognized, not the berry bushes of her first long-term camp or high ground of her second camp. After grabbing her bag, they had gone somewhere in Isilna territory that had a tall hill and a tide pool, similar to Citadel's. This part of the forest wasn't like the Mulo's, the tides not quite reaching them yet. Come morning, it would be very different, and they'd be glad for the tall hill that gave them dry ground.

Olivia had used the water and her medical supplies to patch up Cyrij the best she could. Though the Mulo warrior had definitely gotten several scratches and even a bite in, none of the wounds were deep. He just needed to keep them clean to avoid infection. He lay on the ground, smooth fur interrupted with bandages and stitches. Both of his parents lay on either side of him, practically squishing him. Olivia tried to contain her jealousy; it looked *very* cozy. But even if she could join in, the amount of effort it would take to leave her cot seemed monumental.

Her empty quiver dug into her back. She squirmed and slithered until it was off and turned it upside down. The broken bow fell on her chest.

She held it up to the light. It hadn't been anything ostentatious or with unnecessary decorations. Beautiful in its simplicity. It had been Elias's last, most meaningful gift to her and had saved her life countless times in this forest.

She would always carry the weight of Elias's death with her, the same way she carried Sarai's. But now, she felt free from the suffocating grief. Maybe it was finally having the answers she'd set out to get, or making new friends to help her carry the burden, or just the slow healing power of time. But it felt good to let go.

Olivia kissed the wood. She tossed the broken bow into the water.

She hauled herself upright, started a fire from the nearby kindling, and dug into her bag for some food. Without a bow or arrows, she couldn't hunt. Going back to Citadel was no longer a matter of principle but one of survival.

Mek'tay raised his head. That was the only warning Olivia got before Inyetaz landed in the camp. The light reflected off the water to give her a golden glow, like sunlight reflecting off a knife.

"*You are not dead*," she praised.

"*No. Your pack?*" Mek'tay asked.

"*Unhurt. Mulo retreat before we can fight.*"

"*That was my fault,*" Olivia said, not sure if Inyetaz was happy or disappointed by the lack of fighting. She kept her emotions sealed in her mind.

"*Mulo are very angry,*" Inyetaz continued. "*After this, they watch neutral zones closely. They kill any chimera and steal kizaba. Unless they are in pack.*" She looked at Blue.

Blue growled. "*If I am not kizaba, do you help Mek'tay and Silver get me?*"

"*Of course,*" Inyetaz said. But there was something in there that was different. A hiccup in what should have been a smooth link.

"*Lie.*"

Inyetaz huffed. "*Our pack is much stronger than Isilna pack. You are safer with us.*"

"*Leave me,*" Blue growled.

"*We risk our lives to save yours,*" she snapped.

"*So do we,*" Ebevil growled.

"*LEAVE ME!*" Blue roared.

Inyetaz glared at them. With a beat of her golden wings, she was gone.

Blue turned to Mek'tay. "*Well?*"

He lay back down. "*Well what?*"

"*Do you ask me to join* your *pack now?*"

"*You join Isilna if you want,*" he said. "*Cyrij and Ebevil like you, and I think you are good for the pack.*"

"*If I am not kizaba, do you rescue me from Mulo?*"

"*Yes. We do not like Mulo.*" There was no hiccup in that statement.

"*I have to tell Cyrij not to go himself to get you,*" Ebevil grumbled, showing the memory of Siyet literally holding Cyrij back by the scruff as soon as he'd heard about the attack.

"*You worry for her too,*" Cyrij complained.

"*Shush.*"

Olivia chewed on some jerky between yawns and, when it was clear the conversation was done (at least to her), she asked, *"Can I get some of those green prasina flowers before I leave tomorrow?"*

"Why?" Mek'tay asked.

"I think it's the best way to handle Citadel. We give them telepathy just like you gave it to me. Then they'll be able to hear you. They won't be able to call you 'demons' after that."

"Pale flowers stop working after a time," Siyet warned.

"How long?"

He showed her an image of the green flower wrinkled and dry. *"Until this."*

Days, then. *"Maybe I can try growing them,"* she mused.

"I can give you flowers, and maybe seeds for growing," Mek'tay said. *"After sunrise?"*

"After sunrise." She finished her meal and went to sleep.

Dear Elias,

   I broke your bow. Sorry.

   But I'm still alive? That's probably better. I think so, at least.
That's the second (third?) time Mek'tay has helped save my life. I
think you'd really like him.

   I still don't know what I'm doing, or how I'm going to do this
with Citadel. But I think I can figure it out.

                            Love,
                            Olivia

CHAPTER FORTY

At sunrise the next day, Olivia packed. She felt naked with only her knife as a weapon, but it was all she had.

Mek'tay flew off to get her the flowers. Siyet, Ebevil, and Cyrij got ready to return to their den. Olivia checked over Cyrij's injuries, annoyed that she didn't have Asiya or Riley here to help. Blue watched silently.

The bandages were still white, nothing bleeding through. She told them at what point they should remove the stitches, then leaned back on her heels with a smirk. "*You know, approaching an armed human by yourself with only a mouthful of flowers was probably really stupid.*"

"*We know,*" Siyet grumbled, while Cyrij whined. "*We yell at him.*"

"*Going into the forest alone is also 'probably really stupid,*'" Ebevil noted.

Olivia grinned. "*Absolutely.*" She rubbed Cyrij's head. "*Thanks for bringing me here.*"

"*Come back soon,*" Cyrij said, headbutting her.

She looked at Blue. "*Are you going to be all right?*"

Blue scoffed. "*Of course.*" She hesitated. Then, on a private link, said, "*You can call me Is'hav.*"

Olivia beamed. "*You got it.*"

"*Ebevil. Siyet,*" Is'hav said. "*Is there room in your den for me?*"

Cyrij howled. Ebevil made a sound that might've been a scoff. "*Of course!*"

Olivia hoisted her bag onto her shoulder, waved goodbye, and started walking.

The first evening, as she made camp on a tree branch above the rising water, she spotted a chimera. A stranger. He clearly saw her too. But Mek'tay must have already told the others to back off, because he left her alone. She snuggled into her tiny tent and went to sleep.

It was midmorning the next day when Mek'tay tugged on her mind, showing an image of a basket full of green flowers. "*Where are you?*"

She gave him a mental pull. Moments later, he landed on the branch in front of her with a basket hanging from his neck, stuffed full of prasina flowers.

"*Did you* make *this?*" she demanded, pulling the basket from his head. It was woven from plant fibers, with simple, tight knots to ensure nothing fell out. It wouldn't be able to hold water, but it could definitely hold plants.

"*Ebevil makes baskets.*"

"*Does he give lessons?*"

Mek'tay's tongue lolled. "*Maybe after.*"

It took more effort than she was willing to admit, but Olivia managed to tear her attention away from the basket itself to examine the contents. There had to be at least twenty flowers stuffed inside. They reminded her of the time she and Elias had woven flower crowns in spring. At least, Elias had tried. The crown had crumbled around her shoulders within ten minutes, leaving purple and yellow petals in her hair. Hers had stayed intact for at least an hour, which he never stopped grumbling about. The memory made her smile.

"*Thanks, Mek'tay. This is perfect,*" she said.

Mek'tay hesitated. "*Who is human in your memories?*"

"*That's Elias,*" she replied, half-distracted as she put the basket over her shoulder, wearing it like a bag. The fibers would've irritated her skin if not for her sweater. "*The chimera term for him is 'mate.' He died on a demon hunt. Uh, sorry.*"

The chimera's mind was stone, carefully still as he thought about something, just beyond his mental barriers where Olivia couldn't get a feel for it. She shrugged it off. If it was important, he'd tell her.

"*I'll be sure to contact you and the others as soon as I make headway in Citadel,*" she said. "*But fair warning, I might be chased out or have to hide in the forest to avoid being killed.*"

He flexed and relaxed his wings. "*I must show you memory, Silver. It is not good.*"

"*. . . All right?*"

She braced herself for an imminent attack from the Mulo pack, or perhaps a fresh wave of "demon hunters" coming into the forest. Or maybe the Isilna pack wouldn't let her back into the forest if this went wrong, and she was completely on her own.

And then Mek'tay dropped a memory in her mind, and—

He watches the human kneeling at the edge of the small tide pool, having followed the scent from the fight. He, Ebevil, Sima'ik, Ulcoza, and several other warriors from the Isilna and Kimuud packs have scattered the warriors from where they were clustered before, and now they need to pick them off one by one so they do not come back stronger. Every human they kill now is one less human to fight later.

The human buries his face in a piece of gray cloth around his neck, probably meant to keep him warm. Mek'tay creeps closer, not quite close enough to charge.

After a deep breath, the human drops the cloth and looks up, squinting at the sky. Mek'tay realizes that he's navigating by stars, just like chimera do. Probably trying to find a way back to the human den, since human noses are particularly weak. There are spots on his skin like Cyrij.

He pities the human. Doesn't really want to kill him. He's alone, away from his pack, scared. He's young. He might have a mate or cubs.

But he's wearing the blue cloth of a human warrior. He's in chimera territory. He is here to kill chimera with arrows and poisoned meat. And

Mek'tay is an iyi'ke. He promised to protect his pack from all threats, and there is no greater threat than a human warrior. They have no namsuud, so Mek'tay can't afford it either.

He shifts closer.

The human stiffens. His hand drifts toward his bow.

Mek'tay lunges.

They roll into the shallow water, Mek'tay's claws digging into weak human skin. The human gasps in pain and manages to kick Mek'tay off him.

Mek'tay spreads his wings to keep his balance. The human pulls out a knife, but if Mek'tay is careful, it shouldn't make much of a difference.

Mek'tay bares his teeth, and the human . . . chuckles. A broken, hysterical sound in the otherwise still night.

Humans are mind deaf. They cannot hear chimera. But for a moment, Mek'tay thinks he can hear him, crystal clear.

The human knows he is going to die.

He doesn't want to die. Not here, not now, not like this.

But he does not beg.

Mek'tay prowls closer, looking for a good angle for his next attack. Humans may not have namsuud, and chimera cannot afford to spare a human warrior's life. But that doesn't mean Mek'tay has to prolong his suffering. He will make this quick.

The human flips his knife for a better hold and braces himself. "Let's go."

Mek'tay charges.

The memory ended before Olivia could see any more, but it didn't feel like much of a mercy. She knew how it ended.

The relief she'd felt at letting Elias go vanished. The grief that had been lifted from her shoulders crashed back down around her, along with a thunderous rage.

Before she consciously knew what she was doing, Olivia punched Mek'tay across his snout.

Her entire body was on fire. For the first time, she understood the appeal of torturing chimera to death. She wanted to tear Mek'tay apart limb from limb. "*Why did you show me that?!*"

"*Namsuud,*" he said. "*Honor. You deserve to know.*"

Blood dripped from his mouth. He spat out a tooth. Olivia distantly registered a sharp throb of pain in her knuckles.

One part of her mind—the small, rational part—did process the fact that Elias had been an invading soldier, and that she had always known a chimera had killed him. There was every chance she would have run into his killer.

The other part calculated how many times she could stab Mek'tay before any other chimera noticed.

Something must have come through the link. Mek'tay very subtly shifted his posture for defense. "*Now, you are friend to Isilna and chimera. Do not become an enemy.*"

Olivia gritted her teeth so hard her jaw ached.

"*Silver?*" Cyrij called. "*Your mind . . . What happens?*"

She blocked him out, a hand on her knife. She didn't know whether she was going to draw it or not.

Mek'tay didn't give her the option. He jumped off the branch and flew away.

She closed her eyes and saw the link between the two of them. A branch strong enough for ten men at once.

She snapped it in half. Mek'tay's thoughts were gone from her mind.

CHAPTER FORTY-ONE

She lost much of the day to a breakdown. Falling in that endless black tunnel.

All that grief and rage that she'd thought she'd left behind returned with a vengeance. Only now it had a clear target. Mek'tay's kindness in the last few weeks, the fact that he had saved her life twice, meant nothing. She wanted him erased from her mind, from her very existence.

And yet, when she tried to tear the drawings of him out of her sketchbook, she couldn't.

Cyrij's thoughts burned through her mind: "*You try to hurt Mek'tay?!*"

"*He killed Elias,*" she snapped.

"*You are supposed to be different.*"

The link between them shattered.

Olivia screamed at the pain. One of the strongest bonds that covered over twenty kilometers, suddenly ripped from her mind. She almost didn't notice Ukurf, Siyet, and Ebevil retracting their bonds. Only Is'hav stayed.

She spent the rest of the day dreading when the blue-eared chimera would break it. The holes in her head from the others throbbed, leaving her with nothing but pain and sharp, bitter loneliness.

When night fell and the one bond still remained, she demanded, "*Well?*"

"*Well what?*" Is'hav asked.

"*Aren't you going to break this? Everyone else has.*"

"*Everyone else is stupid. Mek'tay hurts you. You snarl. He leaves.*" Something smug slithered through the link. "*He yells at others for breaking their bonds with you.*"

Olivia deflated, sagging against a tree. The gaping holes in her mind throbbed, echoing Cyrij's anger. She'd become the very monster they thought humans were. "*I shouldn't have punched him.*"

"*No.*"

"*I am so* angry . . .*"

"*Then be angry. Mek'tay stays away. Come back when you stop hurting.*"

She laughed out loud. "*I don't think that's ever going to happen.*"

"*Then do not come back. Our link stays. I like it.*"

Olivia smiled, tears dripping down her face. "*Thank you.*"

The water rose higher, streams and brooks appearing where none had been yesterday, the valleys and lowlands flooded with waist-high water. She climbed higher in the trees, poked her head through the mass of orange leaves, and quickly located Citadel, probably a two-day walk, maybe more with the rising water keeping her to the branches. If she was careful, she could make her food last that long.

A few chimera flew in the sky, little more than dots against the clouds. She ducked back below the leaves and climbed down to the larger branches.

Someone screamed.

It had been so long since Olivia had heard a human voice, thirty-six days, that for a moment, she didn't recognize the sound.

When she did, she jumped from tree to tree, getting closer to the sound of human swearing and shouting. They weren't in any chimera territory; this was neutral ground. Maybe they'd run into some sort of predator.

She jumped onto the next branch and looked down. Three men stood in a splintered rowboat floating between the trees. Given the bows, nets, and ropes, they were probably hunters or fishermen. None of them wore the blue military uniform.

Three chimera flew around them, dodging arrows and snapping their teeth. Olivia didn't recognize any of them. She whistled as loud and shrill as she could and cried, "*What are you doing? Those are hunters, not soldiers!*"

The chimera landed on nearby branches and looked at her. The humans gaped. "Isn't that the Claude girl?"

"*You are Silver?*" one of the chimera clarified.

"*What are you doing here?*" she asked. "*These men didn't attack you; they're looking for dinner to bring home.*"

"*They are humans.*"

"*So?*"

One of the hunters slowly nocked an arrow. She whistled sharply at him and glared, even though she wished she had her own bow and arrows.

"Is she . . . talking to these things?" one of the men said, probably not as quiet as he hoped to be.

"How? They're not saying anything."

"*Humans starve in their den,*" the chimera said. "*If we kill hunters, then humans die.*"

She wanted to scream at them. "*Can you at least wait until I try to tell Citadel to stop sending hunts?*"

"*You go,*" he said. "*Mek'tay asks it. They die.*"

"*Don't——!*"

The chimera descended. The hunters released their arrows, but only one made contact, slicing through a chimera's chest. The other two tore the men apart with tooth and claw. By the time Olivia climbed down far enough to jump into the fight, the two surviving chimera had flown off. The third chimera's body floated in the water. The boat was full of blood and the shredded corpses of three men.

Two days later, Olivia still couldn't get the scene out of her head.

They had torn each other apart. And she hadn't been able to stop it. How was she supposed to convince *all* packs and *all* of Citadel to stop killing each other if she couldn't do that with a handful of people?

Should you? a part of her whispered. *Don't you want to hurt Mek'tay for what he did to Elias?*

Maybe. But she didn't want Is'hav to get hurt. Or Cyrij, even if he was no longer connected to her.

But what good were wishes if she couldn't act on them?

Ormus could've stopped them, she thought. *Or Peterson. Evelyn would've thought of something clever. Asiya would've patched up their wounds and made everyone talk it out over dinner. Riley would've made friends with all of them.*

This was a people problem. She was no good with people.

She almost walked off the branch and into the water, so caught up in her head. She blinked, looked around, and realized she was at the edge of the trees. There was nothing but water between herself and the walls of Citadel.

"What in the hundred *fucking* hells?"

Peterson's cry pulled her attention to the top of the wall. He must've been doing some basic wall training for new recruits, or maybe just chatting with some officer friends. He gaped at her. She waved.

"Don't move!" he ordered. "I mean it. Boys, get me a boat and lower me down. Now!"

She sat on her branch and waited.

Some minutes later, Peterson pulled her onto the boat and hugged her. She hugged him back, sniffling into his coat. God, she had missed him.

"God's Faces, you scared us. Are you hurt? You're covered in cuts and bruises. We're going to the hospital."

She huffed but let him row her to the wall and follow her up the rope ladder into town.

The smell hit her first. Even with the tides washing through the sewers, the stench of human sweat and filth almost drove her to her knees. People still lived on the streets, begging for food scraps and banknotes. New recruits did their exercises in the barracks yard. Despite

Olivia's and Peterson's best efforts, over a dozen people brushed against her as they walked, making her grit her teeth at the pinpricks spreading beneath her skin.

Is it too late to go back to the forest?

The only change was the prices. The tags on several food items in the marketplace had skyrocketed. Iron tools too.

Peterson saw her looking and said, "The demon attacks have gotten worse. Much worse. Gatherers require a full escort now."

Olivia cringed. *My fault.*

More than one person stopped to stare as they passed. That in and of itself wasn't new. People had always watched and gossiped about her. First it was the scandalous circumstances of her out-of-wedlock birth, then her mother's death, then her "blasphemous" behavior. An older woman had once called her a harlot for refusing to put her hair in a scarf, a reputation only somewhat deserved.

(Ugh, her poor hair. She really needed to take a proper bath and give it a good scrubbing. She'd done her best in the forest, but it was limp and greasy to the point where she had to pull it back in a tail so she wouldn't think about it.)

Now, the whispers she caught at the edges of her hearing were "thought she disappeared" and "the crazy Claude girl's back."

They caught a carriage to pull them the rest of the way to Central Hospital.

The elderly medic at the front desk managed to keep it professional, at least. Olivia leaned against the blue wooden wall, drumming her fingers against the strap of her bag. The woven basket of green flowers hung from her other shoulder. A portrait of the Fall from Heaven hung on the wall across from her. She smirked at it. *I know the truth now.*

The medic led them to a room and told them to wait. Peterson huffed. "I need to report to your father. He'll probably chew me out for making him wait this long." He hugged her again. "I'm glad you're safe. Don't ever do that again."

No promises, she thought but couldn't say. Every time she tried to form a telepathic link with him, it bounced against his mind like rubber.

Peterson left. Olivia put down her bag, basket, and empty quiver on the floor and sat on one of the two chairs in the otherwise bare room. She put her head in her hands, trying to think.

If she couldn't use telepathy, she'd have to go back to writing. Writing left a trail. Sarai had taught her that.

The door burst open, loud enough to make her jump.

Riley stared at her. "What in the *hundred hells*, Liv?"

She grinned, standing.

"Uh-uh. No. I am *furious* with you. Relieved, and happy beyond belief that you're all right—I'll be doing several prayers of gratitude tonight—but I'll repeat myself: What the hell?"

She ignored the question and poked at his collar, right over his Hundred-Faced God amulet. He was wearing the black shirt of a medic in training.

Riley sighed, closing the door behind him. There was a little smile on his face. "I took your advice. Mom and Dad weren't happy, but I am."

She grabbed him in a hug. He was still an inch shorter and quite a bit skinnier than her, his curly red-brown hair tickling her nose. He hugged her back. "We still need to talk, but I'm glad you're here."

He pulled back and motioned for her to sit before going through the physical. Olivia had never liked going to the doctor's office. They'd been poking and prodding her from her earliest memories, trying to figure out why she couldn't talk, why she had breakdowns, why she acted the way she did. But Riley was different. As he went through the examination, it didn't feel like he was judging her—even if he'd said he was angry—but like he really wanted to know that she was all right. He grumbled when he found the antrebull bite on her leg and redid the bandage.

"Well, you've lost a little weight, but nothing to sweat about," he said at the end. "I'm still in training, so an actual medic is going to have to sign off on this. They'll probably just tell you to rest up, eat well, and go easy on the exercise. But since exercise helps you control your breakdowns, you can ignore that last part. And take a bath too. God's Faces . . ."

His mouth thinned as he read her chart, staring at it long after they were done. Olivia recognized the look as anger but couldn't figure out why. She used the pen and pad they'd been using for her to answer his questions and wrote, *Why angry?*

He glared at the note. "Ignoring the fact that you went into an extremely dangerous place without any backup or warning, you . . ." He ran a hand over his face. "You didn't say *anything*. You didn't tell *me* anything! Sergeant Peterson, your family, they were all looking to me for answers because we're supposed to be best friends, and I couldn't tell them anything because *you told me nothing*. I found out you left when your father burst into my house and demanded I tell him what was going on. You didn't trust me."

Olivia grimaced. She wrote, *Execution highly likely.*

"So?"

Needed to be sure.

"Of what?"

She looked meaningfully at the door. Could the passersby hear them through the wood?

He studied her, then the pad. "Does it have to do with our . . . furry neighbors?"

She nodded.

He dropped in the other chair. It was like all the energy and air in his muscles deflated at once.

"Did you find what you were looking for, at least?"

She nodded. *It's big,* she wrote. *I need your help. Please.*

Riley looked at the page. Olivia held her breath.

"I will," he said. Olivia let go of her breath, scolding herself. How could she ever doubt Riley?

"But this isn't the place to talk," he continued. "Come by Peterson's as soon as you can."

She frowned. Peterson's?

Riley grimaced. "Like I said, Mom and Dad weren't happy. They disowned me."

Olivia gritted her teeth. If she saw Augustus, she would not be held accountable for her actions. Not even Mek'tay enraged her as much as that pathetic excuse for a human.

"It's not too bad. Peterson's taken me in. I make enough to cover the groceries. And your stepmom's been pushing plenty of her food at me." He stood up, cracking the door open. "I'll get your chart to the medics, and then we can get you out of here."

She made the sign for *thank you*.

He grinned. "Oh, don't thank me yet." He opened the door all the way. "We're done. You can see her now."

She frowned, wondering who he could possibly be talking to.

Right before the Claude family came in.

She was going to murder her best friend.

CHAPTER FORTY-TWO:
ORMUS

It was like a weight had been lifted from Ormus's shoulders when Olivia returned home. He barely let her out of his sight after hugging her in the hospital, and he only eventually did because Asiya pointed out that she should probably get properly cleaned in the bathhouse.

Now she sat in the living room of their house with her sketchbook like any other day, speckled with bandages and smelling of soap. He could barely take his eyes off her. He'd even taken the day off from work to sit on the sofa and just . . .bask.

"Did you make this?" Evelyn asked, examining the basket her sister had brought with her. "Why'd you fill it with flowers?"

Olivia plucked the basket from her hands and set it aside, still drawing.

"I need to go to the market," Asiya said, getting her purse. "We're having a special dinner tonight!"

"Take some extra banknotes," Ormus said. The amount of demon attacks on hunters and gatherers had shot up in the last week. Combined with the official end of Aestus, when people no longer had religious incentive to stay thrifty, it meant food was even more scarce and far more expensive. He tried not to think about how having an extra mouth in their house was going to cause more problems.

Olivia still hadn't looked up from her book.

"Take Evelyn with you too," he added. Probably best for this conversation to be private.

Evelyn grumbled a bit but followed her mother out of the house, after Asiya squeezed Olivia in another hug and kissed the top of her head. "Good to have you back, dear."

The door clicked shut behind them.

Ormus pinched the bridge of his nose, trying to find the words. How did you address a situation like this? She'd gone into the forest for seven weeks and come out with nothing but a basket of flowers. Was that what all of this was about?

He settled on, "What theory were you testing in the forest?"

She finally looked up, studying him with an unreadable expression. Ormus had always struggled with that. When he was younger, he'd been an open book. Everyone had known exactly what he thought about everything. His emotions had been laid bare for all to see, and it had been almost impossible for him to climb the ranks by convincingly kissing ass and putting on a face of confidence to hide his naked fear.

Olivia did it all without even trying. He envied that.

After a beat, she flipped through her sketchbook to a blank page—one of the very few at the end—and wrote: *Is there a hunt scheduled this cycle?*

"Yes, of course. It's low tide. And we need to fight back, given how hard they're attacking us."

She looked down, back stiff.

"You don't seem happy about that."

Do you believe we need to kill every "demon" to get into Heaven? she wrote.

He hesitated. Asiya was a devout believer in the Hundred-Faced God and Scripture, having considered becoming a nun at one point. His relative lack of faith still prickled at their relationship sometimes.

"I have my doubts about Heaven and God," he admitted. "But I know that we cannot survive with the demons still alive."

She slowly wrote out her response, the words clear and bold. She was putting an unusual amount of thought into what she was trying to tell him.

What if we could? If we could communicate with them. Hear them.

Ormus frowned. "They're animals. Formerly holy or not, there's nothing to hear."

She shook her head.

His frown deepened. "This demon talk is skirting dangerously close to treason territory."

She rolled her eyes and scribbled, *So arrest me. Stop killing the chimera and try talking to them.*

"Chimera?"

She pointed to the word *demons.*

"Those *animals* have killed hundreds of us. You know this better than most."

Her pencil snapped in her hand. She glared at him.

He slid a hand down his face. Unpleasant though the conversation was, he was glad they'd had it. He shuddered to think of what could happen if she tried telling this to anyone else.

"You will not say another word of this, for your own protection," he said. "How you managed to survive as long as you did out there . . . Let's not push our luck."

I survived because of the chimera.

He blinked. "What?"

A knock on the door interrupted whatever Olivia might have written in response. Ormus stood and opened it. "Commander?"

Brodsky saluted. "Sir. Sorry, I know you took the rest of the day off. Might I say, congratulations."

"Thank you." He stepped aside so his commander could come in. Brodsky didn't move.

"It's about the Dove case."

Olivia perked up at that. Ormus stepped outside and closed the door on her. "What about it?"

"The four suspects have been arrested. We just need to start interrogations."

So much for spending time with family. "I'm on my way."

Dear Elias,

~~*I want to hurt them for what they did*~~
~~*I'm so angr*~~
~~*I'm confus*~~
~~*They deserve to di*~~
~~*They don't deserve to die for*~~
~~*Why should I help*~~
~~*If I don't act, how many others*~~
I don't know what to do.

CHAPTER FORTY-THREE

Olivia stayed home while her father spent the rest of the day persecuting her potential allies. She couldn't go anywhere even if she wanted to. Ever since the hospital, where Olivia had gotten hugs from her sister, stepmother, *and Ormus*, she hadn't been left alone. They wouldn't let her go to Peterson's, insisting she spend time with family instead. As if he wasn't. Evelyn followed her like a lost chimera pup, even going to the bathhouse with her while she had washed the forest from her skin, and now sat in her bedroom.

The attention made Olivia itch. In order for her to put an end to the chimera/human war, she'd have to start an underground revolution to change the very fabric of Citadel's culture so the two species stopped tearing each other apart. How was she supposed to do that if she could barely get away long enough to take a piss?

"How did you make this?" Evelyn asked, examining the basket Mek'tay had given her. She took one of the prasina flowers from it. "And why did you fill it with these things?"

Olivia plucked the basket from her hands and set it on her bed, on top of the quilt she and Elias had bought together. Some of the petals were already beginning to curl. She'd need to get them into the stomachs of people soon.

The quilt glared up at her, as if in accusation. How dare she let something Mek'tay had given her touch something Elias had given her?

All the little wooden figurines Elias had bought for her, she could feel their eyes on her back. She ought to toss those flowers in the trash.

Evelyn fiddled with the flower in her fingers, pale petals fluttering around dark skin. "What happened in that forest, Olivia? What were you looking for?"

Olivia considered her next move very carefully. She and Evelyn had never talked about religion and demons on more than a surface level. She had no idea what her sister truly thought of this conflict. Evelyn had said she wanted to be a nun, but that was specifically to work on the Artifacts, which Olivia now knew were the remains of old technology from their spaceship and home planet.

Hmmm . . .

Olivia picked up her sketchbook and wrote, *I found where Artifacts came from.*

Evelyn frowned. "Uh . . . they come from Heaven. Our time as angels?"

Olivia shook her head. *Spaceship in Shadowlands. We're from another planet.*

Evelyn's frown deepened. (Trying to read Olivia's handwriting? Realizing the implications of this discovery? Suddenly remembering that she had a massive school project due tomorrow?)

"Are you feeling all right?" Evelyn asked. "I know you're . . . odd, and don't really think the way normal people do, but this is strange even for you."

Olivia slumped. She didn't know why she bothered. She was the town freak. Why would anyone listen to her?

Olivia realized that all the food the Founders had brought with them from "Heaven" must have come from their home planet. She had no idea how they'd managed to keep goats, pigs, and chickens in the spaceship, but they were all nearing the point of endangerment. That didn't stop Asiya from making them lamb chops, with vegetables as a side and apiberry pie for dessert. As a "special celebration" for Olivia coming back. It was supposed to be yesterday, but she'd wanted the lamb chops to marinate in her special sauce overnight. And it had absolutely been worth the wait.

As much as Olivia loved the taste and wanted to gorge, her stomach twisted itself in knots. She couldn't stop thinking. Weighing the risks. The drowning posts called to her if she moved forward. And for what? To spare the life of Mek'tay, who had killed the man she loved.

Across from her at the table, Evelyn shifted her head as she reached for a glass of water. Her headscarf was draped around her shoulders, letting her black curls free. Today's scarf color was blue.

Pale blue, like Is'hav's ear.

The link connecting Olivia with her friend pulsed in the back of her mind. Not strong enough at this distance to convey actual messages, but enough to remind her that it was there. That Is'hav was alive, and so was Cyrij.

For now.

. . . *Ah, hundred hells.*

As they finished, Olivia scribbled in her book, *Visit R&P?* and slid it to Ormus.

CHAPTER FORTY-FOUR

The setting sun turned the planet's rings silver in the orange sky. Olivia wondered what they were made of. Theories ranged from ice to rock to Heaven itself. If it was ice or rock, then it was no wonder their spaceship had had a hard time getting to the planet's surface.

She and Ormus sat side by side in the carriage in total silence. He had insisted on escorting her to Peterson's house. Maybe it was just her imagination, but Olivia thought the smell of human filth was stronger in the streets, especially as they got closer to Peterson's. More people out here. The buildings closer together.

"You've lost your job at Franklin's lab," Ormus said.

Olivia didn't know why that fact surprised her. Of course seven weeks gone would cost her position. It still felt like being shot in the gut.

If she didn't have a steady income, she'd be stuck in the Claude house for the rest of her life.

"He lost the labs to the Faith a few weeks ago," he continued. "So unless you plan on converting, you're not getting it back."

She had never liked Franklin. He was partially responsible for Sarai's death. But he'd owned the only research facility outside of the Faith's control. She'd always respected that.

"It might be time to consider looking for marriage."

Olivia stared at him.

"Most girls your age are already married and have at least one child. And Elias died almost a year ago. It's time to move on."

She'd thought she *had* moved on. But coming face to face with her boyfriend's killer had reopened the wound. She wanted to get married and have children eventually, yes. But not anytime soon! It was the last thing on her mind right now.

"I'd say you should consider Riley, but with his salary as the sole source of income, I can't see any financial stability in that."

She snorted. Like she'd ever truly cared about that when it came to relationships.

"Having said that, I don't think any other man in town would be willing to have you as a wife," Ormus continued. "And few women these days are considering him, putting you both in very similar boats."

Olivia mulled it over as they watched the buildings drift by, odd mismatches of materials even in the same home. She had never looked at Riley romantically before. They'd always been friends. But it wasn't the first time Ormus had suggested it. He'd been looking to match his daughters to other prominent families for years, and who better than the son of the governor? Augustus had shot it down. "Tainted blood," he'd cited.

She didn't care what Augustus thought. Or her father. But she *did* care about Riley. The idea of a loveless marriage had always been a possibility before Elias. Though the chances of marriage itself were slim, because finding a man who didn't care about her mother's treason, Olivia's genetic oddities, *or* her career goals had proved very difficult.

Riley didn't care about any of those. Had always encouraged her pursuits. And she cared about him, probably more than anyone else in the world. But was it fair to marry him if she didn't romantically love him? The idea of being with *anyone* right now made her want to throw up. Like she was spitting in Elias's face.

Ugh. Emotions were hard.

So as they reached Peterson's house, she decided not to think about it. At least not until she'd handled the much more pressing concern of humans and chimera killing each other.

Peterson opened the door at Ormus's knock and immediately straightened. "Sir. Olivia."

"She asked to see you and Riley," Ormus said.

"Perfect. I'll walk her back if you want, sir. Unless you'd rather come in?"

Olivia stiffened. *No, no, he can't stay here. He'll ruin everything!*

"I think I can trust her with you, Sergeant. Thank you."

She relaxed. Ormus gave her a stiff side hug and left.

Peterson's house was the same as always, with the notable exception of extra blankets and a pillow on the straw sofa. Riley sat on the far end of the sofa, folding the blankets with a strange intensity. He'd changed out of the black medic-in-training shirt, opting for an oversized sweater instead. He finished and set the pile of blankets aside. "Tea?"

She nodded.

Peterson got the tea going and filled everyone's cups. They sat around the kitchen table.

"All right," he said. "Tell us what happened."

It was her last chance to back out. She could tell them what she'd *hoped* to accomplish, and ultimately tell them it was a failure. She could keep the chimera's telepathy a secret, sever her link with Is'hav, and forget the whole thing ever happened.

Instead, Olivia dropped her sketchbook in front of them.

She sipped her tea as they flipped through the book, wishing there were some cream to put in it. Peterson sucked in a breath when he saw the close-up sketches of the chimera. Riley spent a little extra time on the pages detailing the properties of the green prasina flower. There was a lot of swearing at the part about the spaceship and first chimera.

By the time they were done, Olivia had pulled the slightly crumpled prasina flowers from her sweater pocket and laid them on the table.

Riley's chin rested on his palm as he slumped over the table, staring into space. Peterson ran a hand over his face, mumbling about how he wished he hadn't decided to go sober.

I'm sorry, she wrote in one of the few blank pages near the back. *I can't do this by myself.*

"You shouldn't have done it by yourself at all," Peterson grumbled.

"Dad knows," Riley said suddenly. "About the first chimera, at least. He has to. It's probably in the top level of the Vaults."

"So why not open negotiations with the chimera so we can build a second Citadel and stop suffocating here?" Peterson demanded. "Why play this game for *centuries?*"

Olivia shook her head, flipping back to the part about the first chimera memory. She found a small blank space and wrote, *Govs & high priests know we created them, not that they're sentient. "Mother" died before telling anyone.*

Riley took one of the flowers and studied it in the candlelight. "So we eat this, suffer some nasty side effects, and get telepathy. We then repeat with as many people as possible before the flowers dry out and lose their medicinal qualities, maybe use the seeds to try to grow a domestic source. Is that about right?"

Olivia nodded.

"And all of this to try to negotiate peace with the people who killed your boyfriend."

She glared at him.

Riley held up his hands. "I don't want to put you in a bad position. What happens if we meet the chimera who killed Elias?"

She flipped through the sketchbook again, opening it at a drawing of Mek'tay.

"*He* killed Elias?"

She nodded.

Peterson swore again. "Of course it's the leader of the sanest pack. Why would it be anyone else . . . ?"

"And you're fine with working with him?" Riley pressed.

Olivia squirmed. She picked up the pencil again. *Cyrij & Is'hav might die.*

If she focused on that, on the idea of the two of them getting killed or dragged back to town to be tortured to death, she could ignore Mek'tay. Cyrij had already lost his brother. Is'hav had lost her entire pack. She wasn't going to be responsible for them losing anyone else.

Peterson nudged Riley. "If we get enough support, we can find a gifted negotiator. Someone with clout around here. Olivia won't have to go anywhere near him."

"And what about you?" Riley questioned. "Your son was killed by chimera. You've been a soldier for decades!"

Peterson nodded. "And I did it gladly, thinking I was fighting against pure-evil creatures. But that's not true. They're people. And plenty of them have lost their sons to this fight too."

He looked right at Olivia. "Besides, Jason never wanted to fight them. He would've jumped at the chance to do this. If I don't reach a hand out today, however hard that is, I'd be spitting on his memory."

Olivia swallowed around the lump in her throat and had to turn away. Elias hadn't wanted to fight either. The law had forced him to.

The feeling of betrayal ebbed, just a little, with the knowledge that Peterson was in the same boat as her.

"What about you, son?" Peterson asked. "Do you have an issue with this?"

"I'm a Dove, so, no."

Olivia whipped around to look at him.

Peterson laughed. "Of course you are! Oh, I did *not* just hear that. The boys at the jailhouse would have my head."

Riley smiled, but it was tighter than what Olivia was used to seeing. (Didn't like the sound of Peterson's laugh? Didn't like a soldier knowing he was part of an illegal organization? Trying to hold in a burp?)

Peterson put a hand on Riley's shoulder. "Don't worry about it. We're all about to turn traitor here, anyway."

Riley relaxed. Olivia found another patch of empty space in her sketchbook to write, *How long?*

"About three years," he said.

She dropped her pencil. She didn't know if she was more shocked at the fact, hurt that he hadn't told her, or impressed.

He studied one of the flowers. "I wonder if we could turn it into a tea. That might produce the same result while diluting the nastier side effects."

"That takes days. Do we have that kind of time?"

Olivia wrote, *Maybe for the others?* It was a solid idea. Siyet had said that they lost their properties after a while, but if they managed to preserve them . . .

"Do you have anything planned for the next two days?" Peterson asked.

"Nothing important," Riley replied.

They both ate their flowers.

Olivia put Riley on the couch and Peterson in his bed before they both got too dizzy and nauseated to move. Then she pushed a link on both of them. It was like pushing against a stone wall that slowly turned to mud. By the time they were both unconscious, Olivia had two new links in her mind.

Dear Elias,

I've realized something.

Mek'tay killed you because you were a soldier invading his lands. I don't think I'll ever be able to forgive him for that.

But if you hadn't met Mek'tay, if you'd instead met Freckles or Is'hav, you may have survived, but you would have killed them. And I never would have met them. And Ebevil and Siyet would have lost another child.

And I know that never happened and it's dumb to go into hypotheticals, but I don't think I can forgive you for that. Even though you didn't know that they were chimera, that they were sentient, that Freckles's mind feels like sunshine until he gets angry and burns and that Is'hav snores when she sleeps, you would have killed them. And celebrated it. We all would have celebrated it.

And I hate that. They're my friends—or at least Is'hav is—and you were my lover, and I wish this dumb war had never happened but it did and you tried to kill them and Mek'tay killed you to prevent that.

I can't fix that. I don't even know if I can stop it from happening again, from happening to someone else, but I have to try. Because no one else should lose an Elias or a Freckles or anyone. Not to this.

Love,
Olivia

CHAPTER FORTY-FIVE

"Well, it looks like the migraine's begun to abate," Asiya said, looking over Riley one more time. "Do you think you'll be ready to come to work tomorrow, or do you want another day?"

"Let's give it another day. I don't want to make a mistake and cause problems," Riley replied.

Olivia watched, leaning against the wall. She had spent the night at Peterson's to make sure nothing happened and woke the next morning to Ormus banging on the door. She'd forgotten to return home. Oops.

"He was fine last evening," he'd said, when Olivia had lied, saying that Riley had a migraine. She'd shrugged in response, and Ormus had brought in Asiya.

"I'll go to the market to stock up your shelves, and then Olivia and I should get going," Asiya said.

"You don't have to do that, ma'am," Peterson said, nursing a cup of tea from the kitchen table. Hunched over the counter and swaddled in a blanket, he looked like an oversized salt-and-pepper chimera cub. He was claiming stomach pains, "perks of being this ancient."

"Nonsense. You're both family friends. It's the least I can do." She took her purse and smiled at Olivia. "Look after the boys while I'm gone."

She nodded and watched her stepmother go.

"*Doesn't feel right, lying to her,*" Peterson said through telepathy. His mind felt like the ground after the tides: gritty and soft.

"*We have to be careful who we share this with,*" Olivia reminded. "*Otherwise we're dead.*"

Riley's mind bubbled as he chuckled. "*This is so amazing. Olivia, you're talking!*"

She smiled. It was very nice to be able to communicate long thoughts without getting a cramp in her hand.

"*I get how the chimera have this trick, being part 'Nostrian,' whatever that is,*" Peterson mused. "*How does that work with us?*"

"*It could be a unique biological response to the prasina flower,*" Riley guessed. "*The way some other plants can heighten or lessen certain senses.*"

"*Or humans might've always had the possibility of telepathy, but because of a lack of evolutionary pressures, we never developed it,*" Olivia added.

Peterson grunted. "*So long as it doesn't boil my brain, I'm happy.*"

"*I can't wait to try it with the chimera,*" Riley squealed.

Neither could Olivia. She had wanted to connect with Is'hav to verify that Peterson's and Riley's symptoms were normal and that she'd done everything correctly. But because of the distance between them, she couldn't. All she got was a longing for her chimeric friends and the forest. Yes, it had been dangerous. And yes, Mek'tay was there and she still didn't know how to handle him yet. But already she missed it. Citadel was just so confining, and the dangers of the city were a lot more insidious than those of the wild. At least a menziva would kill her for a straightforward, understandable reason like *food*, rather than ideology based on centuries of lies.

Riley sat on the couch with his elbows on his knees, steepling his fingers. "*Five Doves have been arrested, but there are several more still in hiding who'll be able to help us. That's our best bet.*"

"*I still can't believe you've been doing this for* years," Peterson grumbled, refilling his teacup.

"*You're not going to arrest me, are you?*" Riley asked. It was only because he was using telepathy, allowing Olivia to pick up on his complete lack of worry and total humor, that she knew he was teasing.

"Nah. Bit hypocritical if I did, seeing as we're all in this together now."

"Why didn't you tell me?" Olivia asked, unable to hide her hurt. She would've kept it a secret.

Riley winced. *"Some of them wanted me to. 'Get the captain's daughter on our side. We could get her to spy for us.' But I didn't want to endanger you. Especially if you weren't going to join. And since you're an atheist and we're a religious group, I didn't see that happening."*

Her mouth thinned. *"I see that. But I'm still very annoyed at you."*

"That's fair." He grinned. *"And now you know how I felt when you ran into the forest by yourself."*

She ducked her head, face turning red.

"I think we should tell your father," Peterson said.

"That is the worst idea you've ever had," she scoffed.

"He's hunting every Dove down and giving them to my *father for execution,"* Riley agreed, normally tranquil mind freezing at the edges. *"And we've all agreed that the Doves are our best chance at ending this as soon as possible."*

She winced. The lowest point of the tides was two days away. That was when the next hunt would go.

They wouldn't be able to stop it. She'd have to find a way to warn the chimera.

"Think about it," Peterson urged. *"He's the captain, so he has a lot of political and military power. He's ambitious; everyone knows he wants to be governor. He could use this to his advantage. And he'll need to know eventually."*

"Right: eventually. You're forgetting something very important: he's law and order personified. And this is all extremely illegal," Riley argued. *"We need to wait until we're in a more secure place before bringing it to him."*

Olivia nodded in agreement.

Peterson shrugged. "All right," he said aloud. "It's your show, Olivia. Why don't you give your basket to Riley? We'll play around with turning these plants into tea leaves to buy us more time. Riley, you let us know when you're ready to bring more people on. And if anyone runs into problems, we tell the others."

"Sounds like a plan." Riley hiccuped. ". . . Tomorrow."

CHAPTER FORTY-SIX

Tomorrow, the tides were low enough for a hunt.

Olivia stood next to the Claude family in front of the Temple of the Hundred Faces in the center of town. They were hardly alone: half of the town came out to say farewell to soldiers when they left for hunts, crowding the sides of the streets, even climbing onto rooftops to get a better look. The soldiers themselves stood in rows before the temple, staring straight ahead in their dark-blue uniforms as they listened to the priest's blessing, blinking against the sun in their eyes.

Olivia remembered standing in this exact spot last year—a lifetime ago—watching Elias's troop get blessed. He'd met her eyes and given her a discreet wink, even though the night before he'd admitted that he was terrified of going into the Flooded Forest.

"Honestly, Liv, I don't know how you do it. I want nothing to do with that place."

She wondered how many soldiers were going to die this week.

Asiya and Evelyn each stood next to her, Ormus on Asiya's other side, everyone dressed in their best clothes. Every now and then she felt them looking at her. She usually didn't come out to see these send-offs, but this one felt different.

Peterson stood off to the side, eyeing the young men. He had said he still felt a little off, but he wasn't going to miss this. He spoke in her mind: "*Any luck?*"

"*Nothing yet,*" she said, heat simmering in her chest with frustration. She'd tried to contact Is'hav twice now, but the chimera was too far out of range.

Peterson hummed. His mind was much like Mek . . . like the chimeric leaders she'd met, solid and steady. But as she focused on it, she sensed trepidation.

"*Are you all right?*" she asked.

"*These are my boys, Olivia. I trained them. I don't want any of them to die.*" He hesitated, then added, "*I don't want any of them to have to kill a chimera either.*"

"*Me neither.*" Closing her eyes, she reached out to Is'hav again. She strained as far as her mind would allow and—

"*Silver!*" Is'hav called, faint. "*I am here! What happens?*"

Olivia let out a quiet sigh of relief. "*You're not too close, are you?*"

"*I see human den. They do not see me.*"

Best to make this quick then. "*Hunters. They're leaving for the forest now. Almost twent—er, nine-and-ten. They're aiming for the highlands.*"

Because as valuable as iron was, food was the necessity. They needed those highlands to grow crops. Which would put them perilously close to Isilna territory, though thankfully farther from Kimuud.

"*I tell Mek'tay,*" Is'hav said.

"*Please don't kill them,*" Olivia begged.

"*Then how do we defend the pack?*"

Good question.

"*Maybe . . . just scare them?*" Olivia suggested.

"*You do not scare easily.*"

Olivia smirked, just a little. "*They're not like me.*"

"*I tell Mek'tay,*" she said again. "*Do you still hate him?*"

There was no suspicion, nothing but raw curiosity in that question that Olivia had no idea how to answer.

"*It's . . . complicated,*" she said. "*While you're passing messages, tell him two other people have telepathy: my friend Riley and Uncle Peterson.*"

We're trying to find more, but our potential allies are in a really tight spot right now."

Markus Brown's arrest had raised several Doves' hackles, according to Riley. They had survived so far by lying low and staying disorganized when one of them was caught, refusing to meet in groups until days if not weeks later.

Every day that passed grated against Olivia's skin. They didn't have time for this!

"All right," Is'hav said.

"How's Cyrij?"

"Alive." She dropped a memory down the link, and Olivia had to bite her tongue not to coo out loud. Cyrij held a stick in his teeth, practicing the writing she'd taught him on the dirt.

"His e's are a little off, but otherwise, well done," she praised, a hole in her chest. She cared about Freckles, but she'd ruined their friendship when she struck Mek'tay.

She didn't regret being angry. But she did regret that.

"I leave now. Stay alive. Do not be dumb."

"You take care of yourself, Is'hav."

Olivia felt her friend fly away, the distance too great to carry a conversation. She linked with Peterson: *"Is'hav knows. I asked them not to kill any of the humans."*

"Will they?" he asked.

The priest finished his speech. The soldiers saluted and began marching down the street, toward the wall.

"I don't know."

CHAPTER FORTY-SEVEN:
ORMUS

The next few days, as the tides reached their lowest point and started a new week, was one long string of trials for all five arrested Doves, including that of Markus Brown. Augustus was judge over all of them. Ormus had to attend to present his evidence. Near the end he'd memorized every detail of the Scriptural paintings on the walls: every face on every angel and prophet, the exact position of someone's sword or the angle of an arrow as it pierced a demon's heart.

The fact that they were sending another team of soldiers into the woods to hunt demons only increased his paperwork load. Olivia refused to look at or talk to him.

I survived because of the chimera.

Ormus pushed it out of his mind. His daughter had mental issues. That was likely a fabrication, a fantasy brought on by grief and loneliness.

Only Brown was able to afford a lawyer, not that it made much of a difference. Three out of three had been sentenced to death, the fourth standing trial now.

The girl—Mary Smith—younger than Evelyn, stood before Augustus in the standard prisoner's white dress and chains. Her parents anxiously sat on the chairs behind her.

Ormus recognized her. She was the girl who worked at the bathhouse.

Always studying or reading something during her shift. He'd walked by her for months and never known.

"You're charged with treason and affiliation with the terrorist group known as Doves," Augustus said. "How do you plead?"

Mary met his eyes. "A terrorist group uses fear to control the masses. The Doves don't."

"How do you plead?"

"And they usually murder people, too."

"How do you plead?"

"To the terrorism? Not guilty." She snapped her fingers. "Oh, you mean thinking that we shouldn't waste our soldiers in a pointless fight against animals! Well, I'm definitely guilty of that."

Her father stood. "Governor, what my daughter did was wrong—"

"Order in the court," Augustus said, banging his gavel.

The father trudged on: "But given her age and gender, maybe we should show leniency—"

"Order in my court!" Augustus snapped.

"Dad, sit down," Mary whispered, so quietly Ormus almost missed it. Her father sank back down.

Ormus didn't blame him for speaking up. He even agreed with him. The girl acted brazenly disrespectful, but she could still get married and have children. She'd probably just joined the Doves as an act of teen rebellion. He'd give her community service: going out with the other gatherers to collect food from the forest.

"Normally I would agree with you, Mr. Smith," Augustus said. "However, these times are dangerous. And there is nothing more dangerous to our fine city than these radical terrorists. Mary Smith, you are old enough to know the difference between right and wrong, good and evil. Your sin has caused the wrath of the Hundred-Faced God Himself. How else do you explain the surge of demon attacks? As such, you are hereby sentenced to death."

The girl's father went white. Her mother wailed. Mary herself stiffened. Then she forced herself to relax and smile. "When you finally keel over, I'm going to enjoy watching you explain yourself to God."

Augustus waved for the guards to take her away.

"Recess," he called. Ormus joined him in his office, taking the moment to stretch his legs.

"Was that really necessary?" Ormus asked, closing the door behind him. They hadn't talked much recently. Not since their "you're not a good man" conversation. But the governor didn't act any different toward him. Riley's portrait was still missing from the office wall.

"What? The Smith girl?" Augustus snorted. "You have a kind heart, Ormus. It'll get you in trouble someday."

"She's a child!"

"She knew what she was doing when she joined the Doves."

Ormus shook his head, trying to forget the poor mother's wail at her daughter's sentence. "At this rate, we're going to need a dozen more posts."

"We're in a forest. Wood is easy to come by. As you'll soon find out," Augustus said, gripping Ormus's shoulder. "You're going to need a lot of it when you start building the second city."

Ormus blinked. "When—when *I* start . . . ?"

"Who else can I trust to oversee a second Citadel?"

He brightened, imagining it. Fresh, fertile fields for farming. Enough food to go around. Space on the streets to move without bumping into a hundred other people. Air that didn't reek of human filth and fear.

Medics would be invaluable out there; Asiya could really advance her career. Many of the water tanks and sewers beneath Citadel came from blueprints in the Vaults, which meant Evelyn could see them modified and re-created in the new city and, if she was serious about being a nun, could actually work on it. Olivia might even be able to restart her career in science. A new place to heal her grief, away from the memories of Sarai and Elias.

And of course, this was a huge step for Ormus himself. This would be a true test of his abilities, and if he passed, he could easily be elected governor when Augustus stepped down. He'd have control over *both* towns.

"You've earned it." Augustus checked the time on his grandfather clock. "Let's take lunch before going back into the fray. Just a few more of these left, and we're the heroes of the town."

Ormus didn't think they deserved the title of heroes, but he ate his lunch, anyway, and returned to the courtroom. The Smiths were thankfully gone. Most everyone else remained, watching the trials continue to unfold.

The next defendant was an older woman, dressed in the same white cotton as all the others. Benjamin Novak's mother, Bella. Ormus hadn't seen her in anything other than black since her son's execution. Seeing her in the white prisoner's dress was surreal.

The evidence was presented, she had no defense, and everything proceeded as usual. But as Augustus was about to pass his standard sentence, she cleared her throat. "You would give mercy if I gave you names, yes?"

Augustus paused. "Perhaps. If you repent and return to the true faith, giving up the other traitors so they have a chance to seek forgiveness, then you may be shown mercy."

Ormus bit back a snort. Those who turned in other Doves were spared the posts—depending on the extent of their crimes—but their assets were seized by the town. Most ended up on the street. Not much of a mercy. Give him a quick, clean death any day.

Bella smirked, the glint in her eye immediately making Ormus wary. "I have a name for you, sir. But you're not going to like it."

"I rarely do. Who is it?"

"It's the young man who introduced me to the Doves," she continued. "A polite, upstanding citizen. So kind and compassionate."

"His name," Augustus ordered.

"I'm not sure what it is now. Seeing as you disowned him."

For a moment, the only sound was the blood rushing in Ormus's ears.

Then the courtroom exploded in gasps, whispers, and accusations. Augustus banged his gavel for order.

"Do you have any evidence to back this claim, madam?" he asked, when it was quiet enough for him to be heard.

"I'm sure you'll find something," she said dryly.

He sighed. "We will detain you until we can verify the truth of this. Next case!"

Ormus sank into a meditative state as Bella was taken away and replaced by someone else. It was the only way to strangle his rage and fear into submission.

If Riley was a Dove, he endangered everyone around him. Including Olivia.

CHAPTER FORTY-EIGHT:
RILEY

"That form goes in the other folder," Asiya corrected.

Biting back a grumble, Riley fixed his mistake. The hospital had been relatively quiet, giving him and the other trainees more time for study and background tasks.

He hated it. It gave him too much time to think and worry.

"Are you all right?" she asked. "You've been distant today. It's not a migraine, is it?"

"Just a regular headache," he said, feeling only slightly guilty for the lie. A migraine would have been preferable to his friends being arrested and put on trial for treason.

He knew what would happen. Even though he couldn't attend the trials because of work—he *shouldn't* attend, to keep suspicion off him— he knew exactly how his father would punish them.

His mental links to Olivia and Peterson gave him little comfort. They sympathized with him, but these weren't *their* friends being sentenced to death. People he had gone to meetings with and told some of his deepest, most private thoughts about God. Markus. Mary. Mrs. Novak . . .

He hadn't even been able to escape troubles at the Temple of Mercy, where he'd gone last night for a little prayer and peace. Father Victor had limped over to him and sat next to him on the pew. "Thank you for saving my son," he'd said, but he'd been troubled even in his gratitude.

After a bit of prodding, Riley had learned that the hospital bills for removing the arrow from the ensign's shoulder were monumental. Victor's son was a first-generation officer; he didn't come from a wealthy family like other officers, which meant he didn't have the money to pay for it. He and his pregnant wife were going to lose their house and have to move back in with Victor in the slums.

"I'd take a second job, but no one is hiring me with this," he'd lamented, motioning to his weak leg.

"We'll find a way," Riley promised, though all he could do was pray for it. For Victor, for the condemned Doves, for Olivia's and Peterson's peace of mind, for the chimera facing an attack of soldiers and the soldiers themselves with no idea of who they were truly fighting . . .

Everyone around him was in danger, and he could do nothing.

He was about to ask for a five-minute break—a bit of prayer would help get his head back on straight—when three soldiers came down the hall, led by Captain Claude himself.

It was only through years of practice that Riley bit back his cold anger and kept his face blank. Augustus might be the one passing the sentence on his friends, but Ormus had made that possible. As far as Riley was concerned, the upcoming deaths of the Browns, Mary Smith, and Bella Novak were as much Ormus's fault as the governor's.

"Sweetheart!" Asiya cheered, kissing his cheek.

"Darling. Riley," he greeted, his face like stone.

"Is someone injured?" Riley asked, forcing his voice to be calm and level. *Did my father keel over of a heart attack before he could sentence anyone to death?*

He felt guilty at the thought. He didn't *like* his father, but that didn't mean he should actively wish death on him.

"You need to come with us, Mr. Thompson," Ormus said.

Riley frowned. "I'm in the middle of a shift."

"Is there something I can help you with?" Asiya asked, butting in between them.

"Asiya, dear, this doesn't concern you."

"You're trying to take my trainee away while we're understaffed, so it very much does."

He lowered his voice so others wouldn't overhear. "Riley's been accused of being a Dove. We need him to come with us for questioning."

Riley's heart hammered in his chest, almost drowning out Asiya's laugh. "*Riley?* He's a sweet young man. He knows to stay away from them."

"Nevertheless, the accusation has been made. And we need to question him."

Question him. Riley seized the thought. *If they had any substantial evidence, they'd be arresting me. Not questioning me.*

"Mrs. Claude, are you all right if I leave for a bit?" Riley asked.

"Frankly, no," she said. "I'd much rather this wait until after your shift."

Ormus put a firm hand on Riley's shoulder, pulling him away. "I'm sorry, Asiya. This can't wait. If the accusation is false, it's better to reveal the fact now before the rumors start flying."

Riley snorted. "Captain Claude, if you're just here to save my reputation, you're several weeks too late. Let me get my coat."

Riley ducked back into the staff closet, getting his shaking hands under control. He muttered the Prayer of Courage: *Hundred-Faced God, loan me your Face of Courage so I may find the strength to follow your path . . .*

"*Riley? What's going on?*"

Olivia's sudden voice in his head made him jump. The telepathy was still taking some time to get used to. He couldn't tell if the guilt he felt was his own, or hers for not being able to move fast enough to prevent the latest hunt.

He breathed out slowly. "*Someone's accused me of being a Dove. Captain Claude's taking me in for questioning now.*"

"*What?!*"

"*All right, all right, this is bad,*" Peterson called. "*But it's not necessarily the end. If they had any solid evidence, you'd be arrested, not questioned.*"

"*That's what I thought.*" It was still nice to have confirmation from a professional.

"*I'm coming over there,*" Olivia declared.

"*You are not,*" Peterson ordered. "*This is something Riley has to handle himself. Son, keep me up to date. I'll go on break and coach you through it.*"

Riley swallowed. "*Thank you.*"

His hands had stopped shaking. He tugged on his coat and went back into the hall, finding Ormus and Asiya in whispered conversation. His face was tight. Her hands were on her hips. Someone was at risk of sleeping on the couch tonight. They stopped as soon as they saw him. "I'm ready."

Everyone noticed as they passed, stopping to gape and stare. Mrs. Princops smirked. Riley focused on keeping his head high, hands in his pockets.

The walk from the hospital to the jailhouse was both too long and too short. They walked through muddy, crowded streets as storm clouds threatened them overhead. Riley could feel more eyes staring as they marched and wanted nothing more than to get this whole thing over with rather than having the blade of uncertainty loom over his neck. At the same time, he dreaded the interrogation itself. Would he give himself away? Would he give someone *else* away?

It was funny. Almost everyone in Citadel—Riley included—believed in a blissful Heaven for the righteous after death. There might be a boring Purgatory to deal with before actually getting there until humanity as a whole was cleansed of sin, but that was nothing to be afraid of. And yet, when it came down to it, humans did not want to die. They fought against it tooth and nail. Riley had done it himself whenever he'd gotten sick, taking comfort in the knowledge of a pleasant afterlife while simultaneously refusing to go there anytime soon.

Hundred hells, I am a coward, he thought. Sarai Hall and Mary Smith had both gone into this building with the grace and dignity of angels, alone, without a friendly sergeant in their heads helping them through it. The least he could do was not soil his pants.

They went down into one of the underground interrogation rooms: no windows, nothing on the wooden walls, just a table and a couple of chairs.

"We'll be with you shortly," Ormus said, motioning for Riley to take a seat.

He forced a smile. "Please, take your time."

The captain closed the door behind him.

Riley sank into the chair, taking deep, meditative breaths. "*I'm here. Claude's left me alone in the room.*"

"*He wants you to sweat,*" Peterson said. "*People think up the worst-case scenarios all on their own without us having to say a word. Assume that they have nothing on you until they physically show you the evidence.*"

"*I feel like I should have a lawyer,*" Riley chuckled. He'd memorized the legalities of citizen rights when Augustus had prepared him for a career in law, and having a lawyer was one of them. Though they were never offered by the city, instead paid for by the client out of pocket.

"*Probably. But we can do this. Don't say anything unless you have to. Don't fidget or move unless you have to. Your body language gives away more than your words.*"

"*We're both right here with you,*" Olivia added.

Riley wiped his eyes. "*I'd like to pray if you don't mind.*"

"*Of course,*" Peterson said. "*You tell me the minute they come back.*"

With nothing better to do, Riley folded his fingers on the table and prayed. He wished he had a copy of Scripture, if only to spare the Hundred-Faced God an hour (or however long Ormus planned to keep him here) of his internal rambling.

Eventually, the door opened, and Ormus came back with Ensign Gabriel. Riley alerted Peterson.

"Gabriel," he greeted civilly.

"How the mighty have fallen," Gabriel goaded, sitting on the table a handspan from Riley's arm.

"I have *never* heard anyone call me 'mighty' in my life."

"At least then you weren't wearing women's clothes."

Riley looked down at his clothes. "It's a black shirt."

"A *medic's* shirt."

"Ensign, that's enough," Ormus huffed, sitting in the other chair across from Riley.

"*Good soldier, bad soldier?*" he guessed, showing Peterson what was happening through his eyes.

"*That's exactly right,*" Peterson agreed.

"*I can play along with that.*" Riley smiled at Ormus. "I believe you have some questions for me?"

"Not really," Gabriel said. "The others confirmed Novak's accusation."

Riley turned sharply to the captain. Ormus nodded. "Both of the Browns and Mary Smith confirmed that you've been a member for a while now."

He couldn't breathe. He couldn't *think*. He could see Mary turning on him; they'd only just met. But Markus and Jane? They'd been friends for years!

"If I were you, I'd start begging," Gabriel said in a conspiratorial whisper.

"*Riley? What's going on?*" Peterson demanded.

"*Whatever they're saying, it's a lie,*" Olivia added.

She was right: Gabriel was a liar. A good one. He and his brother had had plenty of practice.

"Augustus is your father," Ormus said. "I can probably persuade him to spare you from the posts, but you have to give me something to work with here."

Riley almost laughed, thinking of all the times Augustus had threatened to throw him over the wall.

He resisted the urge to fidget with his amulet, heeding Peterson's warning about body language.

"*Riley?*" Peterson prodded.

"*Just some lies,*" Riley said. Out loud, he told Ormus, "You know, when Olivia and I went to school together, she got bullied. A lot. By Michael, too, but mostly by him."

He tipped his head to Gabriel. The ensign's face darkened. "Don't you dare say his name."

Riley ignored him. "They were both very, very good at hiding their true intentions from the adults. They'd torment Olivia, push all of her buttons, use all of her triggers, and then as soon as a teacher or janitor arrived, they'd put up their masks and lie through their teeth, insisting that they were only trying to help her and that she attacked unprovoked or had a breakdown all on her own."

Ormus glanced at Gabriel from the corner of his eye before focusing back on Riley.

"You're almost as good of a liar as he is," Riley continued. "Markus has been here for days. He gave you four names. If I were a Dove, wouldn't I be on that list too?"

He buried the stab of guilt that came with the words. Most of the people Markus had turned in were relatively new to the Doves and didn't know nearly as many people, except for Mary, who he wasn't particularly close to. Riley didn't know if the Browns protected him because of his status as a long-term member or their friendship.

He didn't want to die. But he didn't want to be spared while everyone around him died either.

"*Don't feel guilty,*" Peterson said.

Damn, those feelings slid right down the link, didn't they?

"*You have nothing to feel guilty for,*" he continued. "*Someone's accusing you; you have every right to defend yourself.*"

"He held out on us," Gabriel said with a shrug. "That Smith girl, though? Didn't take much to get her to turn on you."

She's converted eight other people. If she was giving names, you'd already be on the streets arresting them.

"I barely know her," Riley replied evenly.

"You go to the same temple as her, now that you're staying at Peterson's house," Ormus said. "And you've been close with the Browns for years. It's not that hard to figure out."

"I'm also the son of the man whose mission in life is to execute them all," he snapped. "Why would *any* of them ask me to join the Doves?"

Great. Now he was angry.

He'd never liked being angry. It wasn't hot and explosive but cold and apathetic. Freezing out all other emotions, all sense of compassion and empathy.

Peterson reached through the link but didn't say anything. He was just there, a calm, grounding presence. Olivia's mind was the opposite of calm, a constant hum of movement and thought, like a school of fish or a planet in orbit. But it helped, knowing she was there.

"I don't think they asked you," Ormus said softly. "I think *you* asked *them* if you could join. And given the way your father treats you, I understand why you'd want to rebel against him."

"Interesting theory," Riley mused. *Spot on, actually.* That *had* been one of the main reasons he'd initially joined the Doves. But he'd stayed because he truly believed in their mission. Augustus had nothing to do with that.

"One minor problem," he continued. "As soon as I realized that my father would rather have me dead if I was anything less than a miniature version of himself, I stopped caring what he thought."

Gabriel snorted, turning to Ormus. "And he calls *us* liars."

Riley ignored him, keeping his focus on the captain. "I actually have your daughter to thank for that. I don't think she's ever cared for you or your opinion since you let her mother die."

"Sarai broke the law," Ormus immediately replied.

"Oh, well, I'm sure that makes it all better. Olivia's mom, my friend Markus, the teenage daughter of the Smiths, it's fine to drown them while the city cheers because they broke the law. We feel *so much* better now."

Ormus clenched his jaw.

"You sympathize with criminals?" Gabriel scoffed.

"Of course I do. Executions go too far." He gave the ensign his chilliest smile. "But last I checked, such sentiment wasn't illegal."

"You've been spending too much time with women."

Riley shrugged. "Are either of you two going to show me actual evidence that would call for a trial, or are we done here?"

"We're done when we say we're done," Gabriel snapped.

Ormus stood. "We're done."

Gabriel sputtered. "What?"

"We have no solid evidence against Mr. Thompson, except the word of a woman who has every motivation to lie. I'll report that Mrs. Novak's claims are untrue, and as such she will be executed with the others."

All of Riley's anger vanished.

"*What now?*" Olivia demanded.

"Mrs. Novak accused me. If I don't confess, she dies. If I do, she's spared."

"*Don't do it,*" Peterson ordered.

"Sorry we wasted your time, Riley," Ormus continued. "Do let us know if you hear anything."

Saving Mrs. Novak's life was the right thing to do, wasn't it?

"*She accused you, threw you under the carriage to save her own skin,*" Peterson snapped. "*You don't owe her your life.*"

Didn't he? He'd been the one to convert Benjamin. Her son was dead because Riley had introduced him to the Doves.

"*I need you alive, Riley,*" Olivia pleaded.

He swallowed and stood. "Will do, Captain."

He walked out of the interrogation room on stiff legs.

CHAPTER FORTY-NINE

Olivia followed Riley's link to one of Citadel's many, many temples. She never understood the need for so many. Couldn't they use those buildings and resources for schools? Or food banks?

This temple was much smaller and more humble than what Olivia usually associated the Faith with. It was just on the edge of the Farmers' Ring, maybe a five-minute walk from Peterson's house. The blue wooden walls kept the chill air out, there were enough pews for maybe a couple dozen people, and the small statue of God on the altar was surprisingly feminine, with four arms, each holding a Face: Healing, Justice, Humility, and, held up in front of the deity's head to act as Their primary aspect here, Mercy.

Olivia could hear someone in one of the back rooms beyond the altar, probably a priest or nun going about their duties. Riley sat in the front pew, his brownish-red, curly-haired head bowed. Other than that, the temple was empty.

Olivia slid next to him. *"Really? After hearing that all of Scripture is a lie."*

"That doesn't mean the Hundred-Faced God is a lie," he replied, not even twitching. He responded with telepathy, enhancing the small temple's air of reverence with the quiet. *"And I think we could use the prayer right now."*

She resisted the urge to snort. "*It's never helped before.*"

"*It's always helped me.*"

"*How?*"

"*It gives me hope that, wherever their souls are going to go, they'll be happier than they were here,*" he said.

"*The living need hope far more than the dead.*"

"*I pray for that too. And you.*"

This time she did snort. "*Really.*"

He cracked open an eye and smiled. "*Every day you were in the forest—even for a short expedition—I prayed for your safe return. It worked.*"

She almost told him that it probably had more to do with her skill and the friendly chimera than a nonexistent deity, but couldn't bring herself to do it. Riley's dark, frozen, guilt-ridden mind was beginning to calm for the first time all day, and she didn't want to ruin that. Sarai had always said it was rude to interrupt someone's prayers, even if you didn't believe in them. This was why. Riley's prayer was like her drawing: it centered him.

"*Your friends shouldn't have to die,*" she said. "*Not even that Novak woman. Maybe we can smuggle them into the forest?*"

"*The jailhouse is in the center of town, guarded twenty-four hours a day by hundreds of soldiers, and everyone knows their faces and wants them dead.*"

"*. . . Dress them up as angels and have some kizaba fly them away?*"

Riley giggled wetly. "*If you can find enough chimera to pull that off from miles away, let me know.*"

"*Damn.*"

He went back to praying. After a beat, Olivia sat cross-legged next to him, letting her knee press against his leg. Not interrupting, just letting him know she was there. She took out her sketchbook and drew. She expected her patience to wear thin and to leave in moments. But to her surprise, that didn't happen. There was no urgency here, no rush. Riley had created a little bubble of peace, a shelter amid a raging storm. The lit candles on the altar lighting the wooden statue, the pews, and

Riley's face and hands presented a unique drawing challenge that she indulged in for several pages.

All of her life, she'd associated the Faith and the Hundred-Faced God with Augustus, executions, and the invisible chains that chafed against her every day. But while she wasn't going to be converting anytime soon, if this was how faith was for some people—especially Riley—she could see why they liked it. Could even support it.

Eventually the door opened, disrupting the peace. Olivia relaxed when she saw who it was. "*Hey, Uncle Peterson.*"

"Sorry I'm late," he murmured, sitting on Riley's other side. Riley leaned into him, just a little. "Training recruits doesn't stop even on bad days."

"It's all right," Riley said. "Thank you for coming. And helping me back there."

"Are you sure you still want to do this?"

He snorted. "You really think they're going to stop persecuting our kind *now*? It's only a matter of time before my father finds more of us."

"Fair," Peterson muttered. "I do have some good news: The hunters came back. No casualties on any sides."

Riley and Olivia both slumped in relief. At least no one else was getting killed this week.

"They reported plenty of sightings," he continued. "In fact, one of the chimera even grabbed a recruit by the shoulders and flew off. But instead of dropping him on the ground and killing him, just dropped him in a tree. Took them half an hour to get him down. That poor boy pretty much soiled his pants."

Riley chuckled. "I'm glad."

"The officers couldn't make heads or tails of it. The theory is that the chimera just missed or made a mistake."

Olivia glanced at the closed door beyond the altar, where she could still hear the odd shuffle of footsteps. "*Maybe we should discuss this else-where. Or quietly.*"

"It's okay. We're safe here." Riley raised his voice: "Father Victor, are you in?"

A head poked out of the back room, long dreadlocks swishing with the movement. "Mr. Thompson. Sergeant Peterson. Ms. . . . Claude?"

He smiled. "Long story. But we have another one and a half Doves."

The priest—Victor—limped over. There was only one stripe on the arm of his robes, marking him as the lowest type of priest.

"One and a half, eh?" he asked, smiling.

"I didn't know you were a Dove," Peterson gasped.

"Sergeant, you are sitting where the organization was started. I'm surprised a military man such as yourself wants to join, never mind a . . ." He trailed off as he looked at Olivia, an odd expression on his face. (Confused about what to do with an atheist? Wishing this conversation were over so he could get back to whatever he was doing in the other room? Remembering today was laundry day?)

"Strange circumstances," Peterson replied.

"I know we're laying low right now," Riley said. "But we have some game-changing news. Olivia's found a way to communicate with the 'demons.'"

Victor opened and closed his mouth like a ruzina fish.

"The problem is it needs to be activated with a medicinal herb that . . . How long do we have?" Riley asked her.

"*No more than a week,*" she said. "*Assuming the tea doesn't work.*"

He relayed that to Victor. "Do you think we can get at least a handful of people together to talk about that? Maybe after the executions when the heat is off?"

"I'll send the message along," Victor promised. "Though I'm not sure how many of them will be keen to work with the sergeant. They'll think you're a spy."

Peterson snorted. "I can't even keep a straight face playing cards, never mind for spy work. I'll just stay out of everyone's way."

"I'll send the message out this afternoon," Victor said.

Riley stood and shook his hand. "Thank you, Father."

"You take care of yourself, Riley."

Olivia breathed out as the conversation shifted around her. Something about Victor's son and medical bills. In a few days, they'd have more people on their side and could start making progress. They could do this.

CHAPTER FIFTY

The Doves' executions were two days after Riley's interrogation.

Olivia had every intention of skipping them as she'd done so many others. But there was a sunken darkness in Riley's mind that she couldn't ignore.

"*What's wrong?*" she asked, watching the Claude family get ready to see the executions. She'd gone to Peterson's house earlier that day to dry more prasina flowers, using the spare key to get in as both men were already out and about town by dawn, and had returned to the Claudes' house soon after. Her boots and coat had gone off five minutes ago, and she intended for them to stay off.

Riley gave a humorless laugh. "*Two of my friends and a woman I condemned are going to die today.*"

She shifted on the couch. No one should be alone for that. "*Where are you?*"

"*At the wall.*"

"*You're* watching *it?!*"

"*It's the least I can do.*"

Olivia sighed. He'd said the same thing about Sarai's execution: that it had been horrible to watch, but he'd feel even guiltier if he missed it.

In a way, she understood. Executions were the worst, but they also prolonged the amount of time the survivors got to spend with their loved ones.

Before she could talk herself out of it, she grabbed her coat and ear-muffs and joined the family.

Ormus raised both eyebrows at her but didn't question it. They hailed a carriage and crammed in.

"What brought this on?" Evelyn asked.

Olivia pulled one of her smaller books from her coat pocket and wrote, *R's there.*

Evelyn gave her an odd look. "How do you know?"

Olivia didn't reply.

The carriage ride was a long one, the streets clogged with people trying to make it to the walls in time. She saw more people with sunken cheekbones, bags under their eyes, and clothes hanging off their thinning frames.

They climbed out of the carriage and jostled through the crowd at the base of the wooden wall. Olivia cringed at every brush against her body, trying to stay between Evelyn's and Asiya's thicker forms and use them as shields. It was only partially successful. Was it her imagination, or were there more people out here than normal?

Finally, they made it to the top. Riley stood next to a rusted bal-lista, far from his usual spot by his father on the dais. His knuckles were white against the blue wood of the wall.

Though he smiled at her, she was now able to feel how fragile and delicate his mind was today. Why he bothered to smile was beyond her.

"*I wish I could talk to them like this,*" he said. "*I think that would've been comforting.*"

Olivia remembered how painful it had been when her friends had shattered the link between them, and when she had broken her own link with Mek'tay, and shuddered. "*Maybe for them.*"

"*That's all that matters right now.*"

They had dug out the pit, making it much longer and reinforc-ing it with stone. Three more posts had been added to the original two. Rather than have one person strung up spread eagle between two pillars, they tied one person to each post. Already the waters were at their chests.

"*That's Mary*," Riley said, still using telepathy. There were dozens of people around the two of them, breathing down their necks. Olivia had to pull up the hood of her summer coat to not squirm. "*She's only sixteen.*"

"*She's very brave*," Olivia replied. When she'd been that age, she'd been nothing but a ball of grief, rage, and stubbornness. She still was that at nineteen, but then she hadn't been *actively* going against Scripture . . .

"*There's Markus. He and I did study sessions with his wife for three years. And that one's Mrs. Novak.*" He motioned to the woman next to Mary. Guilt curled around the link. "*I converted her.*"

Olivia remembered seeing her son executed a couple of months ago. She gritted her teeth, all sympathy for that woman shriveling up and dying. "*She knew what she was doing. And she tried to send you to those posts to save her own skin.*"

"*That's not what it was*," Riley said. "*She was angry at Dad and wanted to lash out at him.*"

"*It still put you at risk.*"

"*It did*," he agreed. His mind darkened. "*Maybe I should've confessed.*"

She glared at him. "*Riley.*"

"*It would've saved her life. Instead I'm letting her die. What kind of person does that make me?*"

"*It doesn't make you anything. It makes* her *a bitch*," she snapped. "*I told you: I need you alive.*"

He swallowed, looking away.

Olivia gripped his hand. "*You're my best friend. You don't get to sacrifice yourself to save some jerk who tried to kill you. Leave the stupid stunts to me.*"

He gave a weak, watery laugh. "*I'd rather you didn't do any stupid stunts.*"

"*Then you'd better stay alive to keep an eye on me.*"

He studied her. She could feel him thinking, though he kept his thoughts deep enough in his mind that she could only sense their vaguest shapes.

Finally, he nodded.

Everyone around them quieted. Olivia craned her neck to see that Augustus had risen from his chair on the dais. He hadn't changed at all in the weeks she'd been gone, except maybe a little more gray in his hair. Riley's mother, Mia, sat next to him, still as stone in a modest but intricately dyed and patterned dress. She stared straight ahead, like a painting.

Sunlight glinted off Augustus's golden rings as he raised his hand. "It is with heavy hearts that we execute five citizens of Citadel for their treason. May the waters cleanse them of sin as it cleanses our town."

Olivia used her free hand to awkwardly put on her ear coverings, letting the thick wool muffle the people's responding cheers. Riley's grip on her other hand tightened. She squeezed back.

The bells rang on the wall to mark the first death: Mary, who was shortest and swallowed by the water first. Then Markus. And then Mrs. Novak. One by one until all five people were submerged under the water and drowned.

Riley let out a deep breath, quickly wiping away a tear before anyone else could see. Olivia tugged him away from the sight of the underwater corpses. "*Where do you want to go?*"

"*The temple.*"

Right. He had that weird power to feel *better* after prayer, rather than worse.

Riley's mind suddenly turned burning cold, like touching a hunk of meat that was so frozen it tore the skin from the hand that touched it. Olivia whipped around to look at him. He stared right at Ormus.

Olivia cursed herself. Ormus had arrested those people. Had built up the cases against them. Had gotten them all killed.

Riley breathed. Once. Twice. She caught snippets of Scriptural verses along the edges of his mind, said in rhythms like a mantra:

. . . he who raises a hand against his enemy in rage condemns himself . . .

. . . trust not the blind eye of anger . . .

. . . the virtuous shall be greeted by the Faces of Mercy and Love, the wicked by . . .

He's Olivia's dad. Don't do anything stupid.

She tugged him down the stairs, away from her father.

CHAPTER FIFTY-ONE:
ORMUS

Olivia didn't return home after the executions until hours later. Asiya was gone for a shift. Evelyn was spending time with friends. It was just Ormus in the house, trying and failing to read a book from his spot on the sofa. The living room fireplace burned low, a lantern on the end table by his elbow lit the pages with a dim glow, and Olivia's trampling through the door sounded like thunder.

"I saw you with Riley at the wall," he said as she took off her coat and boots. "He seemed distressed."

Suspiciously so. There was still no evidence that Riley was a Dove, but Ormus's suspicions mounted with every day.

She glared at him.

"Don't give me that look. Blame the criminal for doing the crime, not the soldiers for bringing them in."

She scribbled something in her sketchbook and dropped it on his lap. Barely legible were the furious words *If the law is unjust, the people breaking it aren't the criminals.*

"There *is* no unjust law. The sentencing may have been harsh, but at least it'll deter future criminals, which makes Citadel a safer place. For everyone. For *you.*"

She laughed at him.

It was such a rare sound, coming from her. And tinged with so much bitterness.

She scooped up her book. *This hell destroys a piece of me every day.*

"I'm sorry you feel that way," Ormus said. He was. He wasn't an idiot; he knew Citadel was cruel to people like Olivia. "But there are no other options. Unless you want to live in the forest with the demons who killed your boyfriend."

It was a low blow, he knew. But he needed her to understand. She'd become more unhinged, more reckless, ever since returning from the forest. He didn't want to see her on those posts.

Olivia's face shut down. Whatever small emotion had leaked through was gone, invisible to him. She marched upstairs to her room.

The next day was full of paperwork. Executions came with a surprising amount of bureaucracy. He kept his eyes on his desk; the artwork from his daughters—from Olivia—that surrounded him on his walls was impossible for him to look at right now.

His pen hovered over the form for Mary Smith. Age sixteen.

He remembered interrogating her just last week. He'd walked into the room and stuttered for a moment, shocked at her age. Surely his men had gotten it wrong.

When he'd placed the letters Markus Brown had decoded, explicitly naming her as a Dove, she had sighed and said, "That jerk. What'd you threaten him with?"

"There is no evidence against his wife. She'll now inherit all of his assets and be cared for."

"Smart," she had muttered. "Cruel and soulless. But smart."

Ormus had come prepared for his usual interrogation mind games, the tricks he'd been taught and picked up over his years as an officer. He tossed them all out the window, unable to wear a mask over his own grief at this situation. "Mary, you're younger than my daughters. I don't want to see you executed. Give me something that will convince the governor to let you go. A single name, a scrap of a lead, anything."

She had looked at the letters for a long moment. Then she had straightened her back and said, "You want me to get someone else killed to save my own skin? Fuck you."

Stupid girl, Ormus thought, filling out her death certificate. Her bravery would be cold comfort to her parents.

A knock on his office door jolted him out of his thoughts.

He stretched his back, feeling several interesting pops along his spine, before calling, "Come in."

One of his ensigns poked his head in. "Sir, Governor Thompson is here to see you."

"Send him in."

The ensign disappeared, soon replaced by the governor.

"Augustus," Ormus greeted.

"Captain," he replied, unusually stone faced. "I believe you have a warrant for Riley Thompson's arrest."

"I tossed that order."

Augustus glared at him. "Why?"

"Because I have yet to see any true evidence that would require such an arrest. We interrogated him; he gave us nothing."

"Clearly your interrogators need work." He turned back to the door. "Send him in."

Two soldiers dragged a chained priest into the room, a somewhat difficult task, as he walked with a limp. His eyes were glued to the floor.

"This is Father Victor," Augustus introduced. "One of the original founders of the Doves. He came to me earlier today to deliver the names of three members in exchange for a pardon of his crimes and to waive the medical bills for his son's recent injury. You two, release him and get out."

The soldiers removed the chains and left the room, closing the door behind them.

"Tell him what you told me," Augustus ordered.

Victor licked his lips. "Riley Thompson's been a member for some time. The first time he came to my temple, we recognized each other with the coded signal and phrase. He said he's been a member since he was fifteen."

Ormus closed his eyes. "Fool boy."

"Keep going," Augustus prodded.

Victor looked between the two of them, shoulders hunched. "He brought two new recruits into my temple today: Sergeant Peterson and Olivia Claude."

"That's a lie," Ormus snapped. "Olivia's an atheist. She'd never join an extremist religion."

"She didn't come to us for the faith," Victor said. "She says she's found a way to communicate with the demons, and that she can activate that ability in the rest of us with the use of a medicinal herb."

Ormus's blood ran cold. He couldn't think. He could barely breathe. *Olivia, what did you do?*

"I'm willing to overlook a lot of things, Ormus," Augustus said. "This, though. I don't think we can sweep this under the rug."

"She doesn't know what she's saying," Ormus whispered. "She's always been mentally unstable. Her time in the woods just tipped the scales."

"Perhaps," Augustus mused. "She still needs to be arrested. Same with Peterson and Riley. You're the captain. Draw up the order."

Ormus didn't move.

"Claude."

"She's my daughter," he protested. "And he's your son!"

"I have no son. And you should've disposed of that girl years ago." He leaned over the desk. "Draw up the order. Or see yourself out. I'm sure Commander Brodsky would make a fine captain."

Arrest Olivia or get fired.

If he lost his title as captain, he lost any power he might have to save her life.

He wrote the order.

CHAPTER FIFTY-TWO

Someone knocked on the front door.

Olivia and Evelyn were the only ones home, sitting quietly in the living room: the elder sketching while the younger made a black blanket stitched with white stars and the planet's rings. They both frowned at each other.

Ormus was working late (again) while Asiya had picked up another hospital shift, forcing the girls to heat up leftovers for dinner. Neither of them would knock to enter their own home.

"Who's there?" Evelyn called as Olivia silently stood. Maybe it was her time spent in the forest, or the extra danger she'd put herself in these last few days in Citadel, but she was immediately on edge, thinking up several worst-case scenarios. Just a few days ago, a house down the street had been invaded by robbers.

Ormus has his gun in his office, but I don't know how to use that, Olivia thought. *He has his bow in there, too, but that's not good for indoor fighting. Knives in the kitchen, though . . .*

"Military police. Open up."

She upped the threat level in her head. The police would come to this house for one reason only.

Evelyn stood to get the door, pulling up her scarf to cover her black curls. Olivia grabbed her before she could open it and shook her head.

"What?" Evelyn whispered.

Olivia pointed to herself, then pressed her wrists together as if they were cuffed.

Evelyn's eyes widened.

They knocked again. "Open up! We have a warrant for the arrest of Olivia Claude."

That's Olivia Hall, she thought.

Evelyn swallowed. She lowered her voice. "Sneak out the back. I'll distract them."

Olivia kissed her (brilliant, sneaky, amazing) sister's forehead and went to the back of the house. She peeked out the window.

Four guards waited for her beyond the back door.

Evelyn cracked the front door open. "Sorry, sir, but my father always said to read the warrant before letting the police in. May I see it?"

Staying low and in the shadows, Olivia crept up the stairs. If she could squeeze out one of the windows, maybe she could climb down when no one was looking. Or even hide on top of the roof until they went away. The sun had set a while ago, making the streets dark enough for her to vanish.

"*Riley, Peterson,*" she called. "*Police are here. I'm under arrest.*"

"*What?*" Riley demanded.

"*I'm going to try to sneak away. But they might be after you too.*"

"*Oh, they are,*" Peterson said grimly. "*I just tried to leave work, and a couple of ensigns put chains on me. I'm under arrest for associating with the Doves.*"

Olivia's spine turned to ice. Or maybe that was Riley, his mind freezing over.

"*Victor,*" Riley growled. "*He's the only one who could've reported you two.*"

Peterson swore. "*He probably turned you in, too, son. Get out.*"

She could just barely make out Evelyn still talking to the officers downstairs as she reached her bedroom and peeked out the window. She scanned the darkened street for soldiers. Nothing.

Evelyn shouted, "Hey!" as the door banged open. Time was up.

Just like the night she'd left Citadel, Olivia slid through her window and scaled down the side of her house. She wished she'd had time to grab at least a sweater as the night air kissed her skin.

She also wished her neighborhood were similar to that near the Farmers' Ring, with all the buildings close together. Then she could jump from rooftop to rooftop, the way she'd done with tree branches in the forest. But in this part of Citadel, the houses were given enough room to breathe, placed several paces apart from each other. She *might* have been able to make the jump, but she definitely would've been seen in the attempt.

"There she is!"

Damn.

She dropped the rest of the way, the bones of her ankles rattling as she hit the ground, and sprinted from the house. The guards from the back door gave chase. The cold summer breeze raked across her skin. She ignored it, chancing a quick look over her shoulder. The four guards from the back, plus a few more that must have been stalled talking to Evelyn, were on her heels. She wasn't going to be able to fight them off.

Riley sighed in her mind. "*I'm caught. They were waiting for me at the back entrance.*"

Olivia veered toward Central Hospital, a few blocks away. Maybe she could distract those guards with the chase long enough for Riley to—

Someone slammed into her side, sending them both tumbling to the ground. Half-frozen dirt scraped off her skin. Olivia instinctively rolled with the motion, trying to get on top, grappling with the soldier's blue uniform. But he had the same training and made it difficult.

The other soldiers caught up to them, one of them joining the tumble and grabbing Olivia by the shirt. Another pinned her arm behind her back and used the motion to bring her all the way to the ground, facedown. She could barely move, never mind fight.

She dropped her forehead to the dirt. "*I'm down.*"

Olivia curled into her wooden chair. After their arrest, she, Riley, and Peterson had been taken to the jailhouse and thrown in different interrogation rooms. All three of them had been left alone to "stew," as Peterson said.

The old sergeant sighed. "*I'm not seeing a way out of this for any of us.*"

"*I knew the risks,*" Riley said. "*It's all right.*"

"*It's not,*" Olivia grumbled. She knew what fear felt like, the cold creeping into every pore. Riley struggled to keep it out of their bonds. He wasn't doing a good job.

She wondered if she would have to watch them execute Riley and Peterson. She was taller than both of them; it'd take longer for the tides to drown her.

An eternity later, right as Olivia contemplated who she'd have to murder to get her hands on a pen and piece of paper, the door opened. Gabriel sauntered in, sitting in the chair opposite her. He grinned, showing the gap between his two front teeth. "Good morning, freak. I think that's a *very* accurate title now."

He dropped her sketchbook on the table.

"Anyone who gets arrested gets their house searched."

She kept her eyes on her book, reaching out to Riley and Peterson: "*Problem. They have my sketchbook.*"

"Even more interesting," Gabriel continued, "is that a whole basket of those green flowers you detail in here were found in the old sergeant's house, where your boy toy, Riley, is staying. Now, you're a scientist's assistant—well, you *used* to be—so we're going to do an experiment."

From his pocket, he pulled out a red kerchief. "You are going to tell Riley and Peterson through that demon mind magic you have what color this kerchief is. They are then going to tell the men interrogating *them* what the color is. Understand?"

She crossed her arms.

"*Liv?*" Riley asked. "*Did someone give you a kerchief?*"

"*That's what I was about to ask,*" Peterson said.

"*We're not doing it,*" she declared. "*If we don't prove the facts of the sketchbook, they won't be able to use anything against the chimera.*"

Gabriel drummed his fingers on the table, glancing between her and the door. "Come on, now. I know you can do this."

She didn't move.

"Fine," he huffed. "We do it the hard way."

He stood and knocked three times on the door.

Two other soldiers barged in. Olivia jumped to her feet but was quickly pinned to the table. One of them had his hand on the back of her neck, pressing her against the wood surface while grabbing her left arm. The other soldier twisted her other arm behind her back.

Gabriel pulled a knife from his boot. Olivia couldn't stop the spike of icy panic.

"*Liv? What's going on?*" Riley demanded.

"*It's fine!*" she assured him.

With his other hand, Gabriel petted Olivia's head, tangling his fingers in her hair and sending the sensation of bugs every time he touched her skull. He grabbed a handful and *yanked.*

She couldn't stop the whine that slithered out of her throat at the shocks of pain pulsing through her scalp. She tried to kick herself free, but with two other men keeping her down, she wasn't able to move a centimeter. Already she could feel herself spiraling into a breakdown.

"*Olivia, what is going on?*" Peterson demanded.

"*Nothing!*"

"You know, if there's one thing I hate more than demons, it's people who sympathize with them," Gabriel whispered.

She kept her eyes on the knife, a finger's length from her head.

"I was planning on giving you a haircut, finally get those ugly locks off you. But then you'd be able to grow it back. That just seems like a wasted effort to me, don't you think?"

He brought the knife up, just on the edge of her vision. He pressed the edge into her skin and dragged it across the top of her forehead. She screamed at the agony of the blade carving through her flesh.

"*Liv, tell us the color!*" Riley cried.

"*NO!*"

Someone knocked on the door. Gabriel stopped. Blood dribbled down Olivia's face, into her eyes.

Another soldier poked his head in. "Ensign. They couldn't tell us the color, but . . . they know exactly what you're doing. They both flinched when you made the first cut."

From his spot behind her, Olivia couldn't see Gabriel's face. But she could hear the sound of steel cutting through her hair. The pressure on her head vanished, almost as painful as the initial grab.

"Good enough," Gabriel said. He dropped the handful of Olivia's silver locks on the table. The other two soldiers let Olivia go. She scrambled back against the wall, blinded by the blood in her eyes. She heard nothing—not Gabriel's orders or the growing concerns of her friends— as she fell into darkness.

CHAPTER FIFTY-THREE

"*So that's a breakdown, huh?*" Peterson asked.

She was, blessedly, alone in the interrogation room. She leaned the back of her head against the wall. "*You shouldn't have done that.*"

"*They were torturing you,*" Riley defended. "*You'd have done the same thing.*"

She wiped the blood and sweat from her face, wishing she had a sink to properly wash up. And a blanket. And a bed. And probably some medical equipment. Gabriel hadn't done much more than give her that one cut, but it was deep. He'd been ready to scalp her head completely.

She touched her head. The hair that she was so proud of, that had fallen over her shoulders like molten silver, was sloppily, unevenly chopped. Her longest strand was less than a finger's length.

She knew that it was just hair. That it would grow back. That it was foolish to mourn the long locks strewn over the table like corpses. But it felt as if the last connection she'd had with her mother was gone, cut clean through with a knife.

She used her forearms as a pillow and cried herself to sleep.

The door slamming open jolted her to full awareness. Gabriel jerked his head to the hallway. "We're moving."

She considered resisting. Wherever it was he planned on taking her couldn't be good.

But she wanted to get out of this room and its memory of blood, and she could already feel Riley and Peterson moving with curiosity and trepidation. She let Gabriel grab her arm and pull her into a hall, to another interrogation room with Peterson, Riley, and a handful of other soldiers. The only light was the two torches on the wall, casting everyone's face in angry orange and black shadow. Augustus Thompson sat behind the table, reading Olivia's sketchbook.

Peterson swore when he saw her. Riley gaped. "God's Faces, Olivia! Didn't anyone give you medical attention?"

"It's just a scratch," Gabriel scoffed.

Riley examined the cut. Olivia let him poke and prod, wincing as one part of her forehead moved and the other didn't. Peterson glared at the other soldiers in the room. Gabriel didn't react, but a couple of the others looked down.

"She needs stitches," Riley said. "And something to clean the wound and fight off infection."

"If the ensign says it's just a scratch, then it's just a scratch," Augustus said, flipping a page in her sketchbook. "You should've been an artist, Ms. Claude. These are better than some of the illustrated copies of Scripture."

Riley opened his mouth. Augustus held up a jeweled finger. "Right now, your job is to keep your mouths shut and listen. Understand?"

Riley did not understand. "You've known from the beginning that—"

The guard behind him punched him in the kidney. Riley dropped to a knee.

"Hundred hells, boys, really?" Peterson demanded, held in place by the two guards on him.

Olivia immediately knelt next to Riley. "*Are you all right?*"

"*That hurt,*" Riley silently admitted. "*Just give me a minute, and I'll be good.*"

"Stand up," Augustus ordered.

A guard pulled Olivia back while another hauled Riley to his feet.

"Ordinarily, I don't like research taking place outside of the Faith," Augustus said. "But in this case, I can admit that I was wrong. Your discoveries on the demons' intelligence and culture are riveting, Ms. Claude. I especially appreciate the fact that they live in different packs, and where those territories are. No more going in blind."

Barbed coils of guilt wrapped around her lungs. Everything she'd learned about the chimera, everything that put Cyrij and Is'hav and their families in danger, was in Augustus's hands.

"I think we can target this Isilna pack, first. Wipe them out or chase them away. Then the Kimuud. The Mulo will be the most difficult, given their propensity for magic. But once we have a second Citadel established, oh . . . here"—he pointed to a spot on the map in Isilna territory—"we should be able to push all the others in the north out. And then repeat the process in the east."

"You know that they're sentient," Riley wheezed. "They're capable of thought and reason. Why aren't we—"

A punch to the gut cut him off. Olivia tried to take a step to help him but was held in place by her own guard.

She could understand why Peterson and Riley had given in to Gabriel's demands so easily. Watching them get hurt was worse than her being almost scalped.

"Why aren't we negotiating with them?" Peterson finished.

One of the guards on him made a fist. Peterson glared at him. "Try it, boy. And then maybe you can go back to beating up the civilian and torturing the woman."

The guard stepped back, looking down.

Augustus's mouth twitched into a frown. "Sentience does not equal morality. In fact, the presence of higher intelligence in the demons means they are capable of even greater harm than we originally thought. Case in point: you three are planning on *joining* them and recruiting however many other citizens to do the same. Ensign, your firearm."

Gabriel handed him his pistol. Augustus checked the bullets. Olivia swallowed, counting them herself. Six total, plenty for the three of them.

"In the early days of Citadel, we had different weapons. Guns like this, except they shot lasers rather than bullets. Concentrated beams of heat," Augustus said. "They could not be maintained, so we switched to other, lower-maintenance Artifacts: bows and pistols." He waved the gun about as he talked, like it was an extension of his hand. Olivia watched the end of it carefully, calculating whether she could jump over the table and grab it. Maybe even put a bullet in his chest before anyone caught her. The numbers she came up with were not in her favor. Especially with Gabriel circling back around to her.

"But even by the time we had made enough pistols for the officers, we didn't want to waste the iron on common criminals. That's why we established the tides as the proper way of execution. It gives the condemned time to reflect, pray, and rediscover their connection to the Hundred-Faced God, while saving us the trouble of executing them ourselves and, more often than not, disposing of the body.

"However, the waters have already risen. And I'm not willing to wait two weeks to prove a point."

He aimed and fired. The sound exploded through the room, deafening. Peterson dropped.

Olivia screamed, trying to get to him. The guard behind her had already put her in a hold. She lifted her leg to kick him in the knee, to get him off her so she could go to her uncle, but she felt the end of a familiar knife against her neck.

"Don't try it, freak," Gabriel said.

She looked to Riley. He had some medical training; surely he could help?

They hadn't pinned him down, allowing him to kneel next to Peterson and examine the injury. The red stain on his shirt was slowly getting bigger, his breathing already ragged. "*Ow,*" he said silently.

"I think it went through and through," Riley said, carefully moving Peterson on his side to look at the exit wound in the back, then putting pressure on both. "But he still needs a hospital."

"Excellent," Augustus said, setting the gun on the table. Olivia hated it. Wanted to see it burn as much as the man who'd fired it. "I was worried my aim would be off."

"Here." One of the soldiers—the one who had backed off at Peterson's yelling—removed his coat and used it to help Riley with the injury. Gabriel and the other soldier refused to let Olivia move to help, the knife still perilously close to her neck.

"What was the point?" Riley snapped, bundling up the soldier's coat and pressing hard enough on the wound. Peterson hissed.

"Leverage." Augustus stood and came around the table. He stopped in front of Olivia. "Ms. Claude. Ms. Claude?"

She refused to look at him. He grabbed her chin with ringed fingers, forcing her to meet his coal-black gaze. "Ms. Claude, I need you to listen to me very carefully. Otherwise, I'll have to put a bullet in the dear sergeant's skull."

Peterson spat at his feet.

"You and Riley are going to lead my men into the forest, to the heart of demon territory. Use your newfound demon magic to lure them to your location. My men will handle the rest. Do that, and Peterson will be treated for his injuries. I'll even send for a medic for each of you right now, one for him and one to sew up that cut on your forehead."

He held up a thick finger. "However. If either you or Riley escape, Peterson dies. If you don't find any demons for my men to kill, we execute all three of you. If you refuse, we execute all three of you. Do we understand each other? Yes or no?"

"Yes," Riley hissed, glaring down at Peterson's wound.

Augustus smiled. "Ms. Claude?"

She gave a single nod.

CHAPTER FIFTY-FOUR:
ORMUS

Ormus stormed into Augustus's office. "Why am I hearing that Sergeant Peterson has been taken to the hospital? I ordered his arrest, not for him to be shot!"

"Because both of our children have proved to be disobedient, and I had to make a point." Augustus looked up from a book and smiled. "I was just about to ask for you. We have an incredible lead on the demons."

He wanted to punch the smug smile off Augustus's thick face. He gritted his teeth. "I'm a little more concerned about the fact that you shot my daughter's uncle to threaten her."

"She might be able to redeem herself. Did you ever read her sketchbook?"

Ormus frowned, realizing the book in Augustus's hands was Olivia's. The sight made his gut twist. "No. That's private."

Augustus handed it to him. "There's your research. The short of it is, demons are sentient. It's why we've been having so much trouble with them. Your daughter found a way to communicate with them and shared it with Riley. They'll be leading a new attack into the forest tomorrow."

Ormus stared at him. "Tomorrow . . . *Sentient*?"

"Quite. They have their own forms of government and leadership too. Quite fascinating."

"Why tomorrow? It's high tide."

"I want to throw them off their balance. We've become predictable. It's all in the sketchbook."

Ormus flipped through the book. Detailed sketches of plants, animals, and several different de—chimera stared back at him. One of the pages had an older woman dressed in odd, almost medic-like clothes. In addition to the drawings was Olivia's scratchy, barely legible writing. He winced every time he saw *Dear Elias*, then swallowed as the rest of what she'd written settled in: *The chimera have ancestral memory, able to inherit the memories of their forebears. Through this, they were able to share with me the creation of the first chimera. They were created by humans as a form of protection. Against what, we don't know. Our human ancestors were running from something called the Nostrians. Using a space vessel, they escaped their home and came here, crash-landing in the Shadowlands, probably getting damaged when they tried to get through the rings around the planet. Of course, humans cannot have originated in space. Elementary astronomy teaches that it's a void: no oxygen, no water, therefore no life. We had to have come from our own planet. The question is why did we leave?*

There was more. How the scientists thought their experiment was a failure because of the lack of communication. The first chimera's horrible treatment at the hands of her human creators. How the chimera got to the forest first, fleeing from the surviving humans.

That was the theory Olivia had been trying to test. She must have gotten some sign that there was more to the chimera than Citadel thought, and when she came back . . .

She should've shown this to him immediately. They could've taken this to Augustus together.

No, you wouldn't have let her, an insidious part of him whispered. *She could've gotten executed. You would've made her burn the evidence.*

But then why go to the Doves? She knew they were being actively targeted by Augustus and the military police.

Riley and Peterson are Doves. She took it to them because they listened to her.

Ormus took a deep breath through his nose and mentally set that aside for now. He had another problem in front of him: "We created them?"

"There will be time for that later. Right now I need you to put together a strike force for—"

"No, we're making time now. This says *we* created the de—the chimera. *We did that*, Augustus. The chimera already know this, so now I need to know."

"No, you don't," Augustus snapped. "I like you, Ormus. You're efficient, charismatic, and ambitious. If you ever become governor after me and get access to the proper level of the Vaults, then you will know. Until then, you do your job."

Ormus pinched the bridge of his nose. His failure toward his daughter made him feel sick, almost as much as the governor's callous attitude toward . . . *everything*. "Augustus, if you create something living, you have a responsibility to it. To look after it, raise it. And we've been failing that for four hundred years! We haven't even tried negotiating with them!"

"There is no negotiating. The demons are the product of human pride. You wonder why we kept them in cages, but the minute they were free, they started killing us. They should have just kept flying when we reached the forest. But now with Olivia, we can finally put an end to this. And if she's successful, I'll pardon her. All crimes will be forgiven, past and present."

He wanted to push. Augustus was hiding the true origins of humanity from him and God knew what else. He and every governor before him, all the way up to the Founders, had known about the truth of the demons—the chimera—and continued to wage this war. Doomed thousands of young men. Shattered the lives of everyone connected to them. He wanted to drag the man from his seat and toss him out the oversized window.

Except . . . the captain wasn't an absolute authority. Thompson had every legal right to strip him of his position and appoint someone else. Someone who would be a lot more careless with Olivia's life.

He forced everything back down into a tight ball in his chest and held up the sketchbook. "Looks like I have some reading to do tonight. I'll take care of everything, Governor."

"Thank you. You'll find further instructions on your desk."

"You're kidding," Evelyn said.

Ormus shook his head. He, Evelyn, and Asiya sat at the kitchen table, the sketchbook lying between them. He had intended for this conversation to be with his wife only, since Evelyn had been less than pleasant toward him after Olivia's arrest. But she had refused to leave, especially after hearing her sister's name. So after reading through the entire book of Olivia's work in his office, he came home and told them everything.

Evelyn snatched the book and flipped through it. Asiya took Ormus's hand, letting him squeeze it.

"I need to lead this expedition, keep Olivia alive," he said. "But if we do this, we'll be killing dozens of chimera. People we should be looking out for, or at least apologizing to!"

"Maybe you can 'accidentally' fail?" Asiya asked.

"If we don't bring back any kills, Augustus will execute all three of them: Olivia, Peterson, *and* Riley. If either she or Riley slips away, Peterson dies. And she'll never let that happen."

Asiya tightened her grip on his hand. He swallowed. He knew what he had to do. If he wanted to save Olivia's life, he had to kill chimera, sentient or not, friendly or not.

One of them killed Elias. Olivia knew exactly which one, too. He had seen it written in the final pages: *Mek'tay told me he killed Elias. I punched him in the face.*

Yet she still wanted to help them.

Ormus supposed he was just too selfish to show that kind of nobility.

"What if *you* had telepathy?" Evelyn asked.

Ormus frowned. "What?"

She held up the book, open to a drawing and description of the prasina flower. "If you can talk to Olivia and Riley without anyone else knowing, and also talk to the chimera, then you can at least come up with a plan, right?"

"The military's confiscated all of those flowers. They're locked down. If I go in and take one . . ."

Evelyn abruptly stood from the table and ran up the stairs, her footsteps like thunderclaps. Ormus and Asiya shared a confused look.

She came back down a few seconds later, holding a skinny clay vase with a single prasina flower in it, drooping over the lip.

"I took it from the basket," she said, setting the vase on the table. "I thought they looked pretty, and Olivia didn't object to it, so . . ."

He stared at the flower. "The symptoms last for two days. We have one."

Asiya took the sketchbook and, after a bit of skimming, pressed her finger against a passage. "I can get you the medicines you'll need to mitigate these symptoms. It won't be pleasant, but you'll be able to function, at least enough to get you onto those boats."

Ormus scratched his chin, thinking it over. "The only flaw is Peterson. He'll be in a guarded room in the hospital. Olivia won't want to endanger him, and as soon as Augustus realizes something is wrong . . ."

Asiya gave a sly smile. "You let me handle that."

"I can't let you endanger yourself."

Her face hardened. Evelyn snorted. "I'd say we're past that point now, Dad."

"You keep thinking that you alone are capable and willing to protect us," Asiya said sternly. "Olivia is our family too. Peterson and Riley are our friends too. And the chimera are our responsibility just as much as yours. We do this together."

He tried to object but couldn't find the words. Or a better solution. And as much as he hated the idea of his wife and other daughter risking arrest, he also felt a surge of pride and love, and had to swallow down tears.

"All right," he said. "Thank you."

An hour later, Ormus walked into the jailhouse. Nobody objected to the captain's demands to see his daughter.

The prasina flower was in one pocket, the medicines Asiya had given him in another. Small vials of liquid to help with headaches, nausea, and overall drunken side effects. Another vial, connected to a needle, was filled with adrenaline to keep him from passing out.

He found the correct cell and ordered the soldiers to give him and Olivia some privacy, then stepped in.

Olivia lay curled up on the cot in the corner of the stone room. A recently stitched, very long cut across the top of her forehead was red and raw. He stared at it. "What happened there?"

She glared at him, then rolled over so he could only see her back and shorn hair.

The arrest was supposed to protect you, not . . .

He took a deep breath. "I know you're angry at me, and you have every right to be. But you have to believe me when I say I'm trying to look after you."

She barked a laugh at the wall.

"And I'm sorry I didn't listen to you when you tried to tell me about . . . everything."

She didn't move.

He pulled the prasina flower out of his pocket and studied it. Such a small thing. It seemed utterly implausible that this plant could do something as marvelous as inspire telepathy.

He opened all the medicines except for the adrenaline shot and drank them, cringing at the taste. It appeared he had found the one thing Asiya couldn't make taste amazing.

"Olivia, I need your help."

She scoffed.

"It's to save Riley, Peterson, and the chimera."

She didn't move until he said that word: *chimera*. Not *demon*. *They never were demons*, he thought sadly.

She rolled back over and stared at the flower in his hand.

He took out the vial of adrenaline. "In case I pass out. We can't let anyone know what happened here. Understand?"

Slowly, she nodded.

He ate the flower and sat in the opposite corner, trying not to get too much grime from the stone on his pants and jacket.

It took a while for the effects to hit. He wasn't sure if it was because of Asiya's medicines or because the flower was a few days old. But just as he was starting to worry, he felt . . . woozy. As if he'd had one too many drinks. A pressure built against his frontal lobe, like someone pressing their finger *into* his skull. Then, *pop!*

He didn't realize he'd passed out until a jolt of electric energy passed through him. He jumped, bumping into Olivia, who was suddenly leaning over him. She put a hand on his chest and pushed him back against the wall. The other hand . . .

Oh. She'd stabbed him in the leg with the adrenaline.

"Ow," he grumbled.

"You said not to fall asleep here."

He blinked. He had heard that voice, clear as day, *inside* his head.

Now that he thought about it, there was a link, an invisible rope leading from the back of his head to . . .

"*Olivia?*" he asked, dazed.

Her lips twitched. "*Finally.*"

CHAPTER FIFTY-FIVE

"Asiya's in on this too?" Olivia gasped.

Ormus had spent the last hour getting his equilibrium back and telling her the plan he and the rest of the family had cooked up. Rather, the loose, undefined points of a plan that would only be fleshed out once they were physically in the forest talking to the chimera.

The fact that Evelyn was involved didn't surprise her; that girl was not-so-secretly vicious. But Asiya? She'd always seemed too sweet to break the law.

"She insisted on doing this together," Ormus said silently. *"She's going to break Peterson out of the hospital while you're in the forest. I don't know how, but she'll manage it."*

Olivia grinned. *"I knew she was my favorite."*

Ormus hummed. He still sat on the floor of her underground cell, probably wrinkling his fancy captain uniform. Olivia had moved back to her cot, sitting cross-legged on the thin, stained mattress. Since she couldn't sketch, she settled for wringing her hands on the ragged blanket, twisting it and then smoothing it out. Twisting it and smoothing it.

"Arresting me was a bitch move."

He didn't say anything for a long moment, until he suddenly managed to drop a memory in her head. Sitting in the desk of his office as

Augustus demanded he write up the arrest order, threatening to find a captain who would if he refused, Ormus realizing that if he gave up his title, someone far less merciful was going to take his place . . .

Oh. All right, from that stance, writing out those arrest orders seemed like the least bad of two terrible options.

"Scratch that: Augustus is the bitch," she amended.

Ormus chuckled. *"You sound like your mother."*

"Thank you."

She tried to get a feel for his mind. Cyrij had been like the sun, pleasantly warm unless angry. Riley was a tide pool, calm and nourishing, that occasionally froze over when he was furious. Peterson, Ebevil, and Mek'tay were all steady stones or some variation thereof. Ormus's mind felt like metal: she'd expected it to be cold, but it was surprisingly warm to the touch.

"I'm sorry," he said, mind heavy with the barbed tendrils of guilt. *"You tried to tell me what was going on, and I refused to listen."*

She paused in her twisting of the blanket. The words popped something inside of her, a concentration of frustration that she hadn't noticed was building until just now, when it was released. She hadn't realized how much she needed to hear that.

"You were trying to protect me. I get that," she said. *"I never understood why, though."*

He frowned. *"What do you mean?"*

She resumed twisting and smoothing her blanket. *"When I was a child, I remember you arguing with Mom over custody. After that I never saw you until her death. I figured you'd forgotten or didn't care, and when you took me in, it seemed like I caused a lot more problems than you wanted to deal with. Seems like it would've been easier for you to give me to Peterson or kick me out to fend for myself. You don't even like me."*

There was no change in Ormus's expression, but his entire mind stopped. Like the calm before a particularly violent storm.

She poked it. *"You all right?"*

"No," he said. He rested his head against the stone wall. *"I didn't argue further with your mother over custody because I knew you were happy*

with her, and that she knew how to handle you. I didn't. I could barely handle an average child, let alone you. Because of that she saw me as a threat to you. She thought I would stifle you, squash you, all in the name of loving you."

He chuckled, but there was no humor in his mind. *"I suppose she was right. During her trial I tried to talk Augustus out of executing her, citing you as the main reason for mercy."*

Olivia blinked. She hadn't known that.

"He refused. When I sued for full custody, everyone else said that wasn't necessary. Peterson was in Sarai's will. I already had a daughter. Why would I 'taint my line' with a girl with criminal's blood? A girl with such a severe disability? Some went so far as to suggest it would be a mercy if I took you to the wall during high tide."

Again, his face did not change. But she could feel the controlled inferno in his mind, a dark rage at those nameless people.

"I told them all to go to hell," he said firmly. *"Because you are my daughter. And maybe you never needed me the way I thought you did, but I needed you. I always have."*

The blanket fell from numb fingers. Olivia swallowed a salty lump in her throat. She left her cot, crumpled in her father's lap, and hugged him.

CHAPTER FIFTY-SIX:
RILEY

Riley didn't open his eyes as his cell door opened and closed, deciding the guards would have to drag him. He stayed kneeling on the floor, facing the wall, praying. He would've felt better with his little wooden statuettes and candles, but this would do.

Please help us find a way to end this without bloodshed, he prayed. *No more people have to die in this disgraceful war. Give us the courage and wisdom to peacefully—*

"Ahem."

He blinked his eyes open and looked over his shoulder. "Mom?"

She waved at him. "Surprise."

She was dressed like she was going to a funeral, with a long black dress and matching headscarf. Her usually flawless makeup was caked on with multiple layers, trying to hide the cracks on a doll's face. She carefully picked her way across the open floor to his cot, sitting gracelessly. Riley narrowed his eyes. "Are you drunk?"

"Did you expect me to handle this sober?" she asked, her grin all teeth.

One more thing: please give me the patience to deal with this. *Amen.*

"How have you been?" he asked, standing. His knees ached from kneeling on stone.

"Well, first my son decided to shirk his family title and responsibility by pursuing women's work. Then he joined a terrorist group. Now he has demon magic. You?"

Oh, she wasn't just drunk. That would've made her either pleasant or maudlin. This was blackout drunk: cheerful and *cruel*. She probably wouldn't remember anything that happened today.

Which had probably been the point.

Normally, blackout drunk meant that Riley stayed out of her way until she was asleep, then prepared some soup and a pitcher of water for the morning. Seeing as neither of those was a possibility, he sat next to her on the cot. "You know, the only time you're meaner than you are now is when you're trying to be sober."

"You're judging *my* choices now?"

He ran a hand over his face. He did not want to spend his last night in Citadel arguing. "Why are you here, Mom?"

"Maybe I'm trying to figure out where I went wrong in raising my son," she snapped. "Your father wanted to kill you when you were a baby; did you know that?"

"Yes, Mom."

"But I told him no."

"Yes, Mom."

"And this is how you repay me?"

He dropped his hand. This was the angriest he'd ever seen her.

He could see why. She was very likely losing her son; for all of Riley's prayers, he didn't think he was making it out of the Flooded Forest alive. Mia would be left all alone with her grief, trapped with Augustus, who wouldn't care.

"Do you want me to apologize?" he asked.

"It would help," she growled.

"I'm sorry I left you alone with Dad."

She blinked. "That's not—"

"I'm sorry I couldn't find a way to get us *both* away from him," he continued. "And I'm sorry I'm not enough of a reason for you to be sober."

She opened and closed her mouth. No sound came out.

He huffed, finding himself smiling without humor. "I know none of that is my *fault*. Peterson's been trying to hammer that into my head. But . . . I'm still sorry."

He removed the amulet of the Hundred-Faced God from around his neck and placed it in her hands. "If you remember anything from today, please remember that I love you and I want you to be happy."

Mia studied the necklace. She let it slip off her palm and hit the ground.

"I hope I forget you," she hissed.

Riley stood and summoned the guard by banging on his door. When it opened, he said, "Please make sure she gets home safe. She's not in any condition to walk alone."

The guard took one look at the frozen Mia and nodded. They both had to coax her to stand and walk, leading her out of the room. The door slammed shut behind them.

Riley was alone.

He picked up his amulet and put it back on. He wanted to reach out, but Olivia was talking to her father—a conversation that seemed to go surprisingly well—and Peterson was recovering from being shot.

He swallowed and tasted salt. He knew his mother didn't mean it when she said she wanted to forget him. She was drunk, angry, and not herself.

That didn't make it hurt any less.

"*Riley?*" Peterson called. "*What's going on in that head?*"

Riley jumped at the voice, then huffed out a laugh. This telepathy would be the death of him one day.

He sat on his paper-thin cot, leaning against the cold stone wall. "*You should be resting.*"

"*Bah. The medics already patched me up and cuffed me to the bed. I'm just bored now. You, on the other hand, feel like shit.*"

Riley wrapped his arms around his knees. He considered telling him, dropping that whole memory in Peterson's head. But he didn't want to talk about it. Didn't even want to think about it. So instead he said, *"Did you know we have a 'dumb injuries' list in the back room? It's a list of all the stupidest injuries we've ever treated."*

Peterson, blessedly, let him change the subject. He even perked up. *"Oh, really? Any good ones?"*

Riley grinned, settling in for the night. *"Asiya treated this one man who tried to kiss a spiven . . ."*

CHAPTER FIFTY-SEVEN

Hunts always happened at low tide, as it was easier to fight on the ground than on a boat. Olivia overheard several soldiers grumble about that as she and Riley were led out of the jailhouse to the wall.

The boats had already been lowered into the water. Families wished their men goodbye all along the wall. Rope ladders were barely needed, the water was so high.

The skin of Olivia's forehead felt tight and stretched near her stitches. Riley wrapped his fingers around her wrist and squeezed. "*We'll make it through this.*"

"Ah, there you are," Augustus said with a sunny smile. He wore rich furs against the summer chill. "Ms. Claude, have you put the demons in position yet?"

She shook her head. She had tried speaking to Is'hav through their link, but she was too far away. She said as much to Riley.

"She says they're too far. We have to get into the forest to talk to them," he said.

"No time to waste, then. The men will make sure you're properly clothed and fed for the journey. Wouldn't want an empty stomach or chills preventing you from doing your magic, now, would we?"

"So thoughtful," Riley said, his mind a mass of icy knives.

From behind Augustus, the Claudes approached. Ormus in his military uniform, a bag over his shoulder, Asiya and Evelyn both in black.

He looked better than he had in her cell last night, like he wasn't about to pass out any given second. He tugged a brimmed hat low on his head, keeping his eyes firmly shielded from the light. But otherwise he managed to hide his symptoms.

Asiya pushed her way past Augustus and squeezed Olivia in a big hug. "Be careful out there, all right? Watch over your father."

Under her voice, she added, "Don't worry about Peterson. I'll get him out."

Olivia blinked, cautiously hugging her stepmother back. Evelyn winked at her.

God's Faces, she loved her stepfamily.

Ormus handed his bag to a soldier, revealing the pistol in his holster beneath his arm. He even had his bow and quiver of arrows that were usually stashed in the back closet.

Augustus's smile thinned. "Captain, I think considering the circumstances, you shouldn't—"

"If you want to threaten your son's life, fine," Ormus said, loud enough that several other people turned their heads. "You want to send him into the woods without training or weapons to die, also fine. I can't stop you. But my daughter is making it back to Citadel alive. Good day, Governor."

He went down the ladder to his boat. Olivia, after getting a quick hug from Evelyn, was ushered to her own.

There were approximately three men to every boat: a front and back oarsman, and a man in the middle whose job it was to shoot down anything threatening. A dozen boats set off at dawn, meaning their army had thirty-six soldiers, three times the size of a normal hunting party.

Olivia was in Gabriel's boat with an enlisted soldier at her back.

Riley was in another boat, with a sergeant named Isaiah, Ormus in yet another. Augustus had ordered the arrangement himself.

Ormus had turned to Gabriel and said, in a voice so low Olivia barely caught it, "Any other cuts or bruises given to her, by anyone or any*thing*, will result in you getting shot. I don't care what happens afterward. Understand, Ensign?"

Gabriel's mouth tightened as he nodded.

They rowed for half the day before stopping for lunch, tying their boats to the tree branches so they wouldn't drift off course. They all looked like blobs of blue floating in the water. Olivia and Riley had both been given jackets to combat the summer chill. As Isaiah opened the rations, Gabriel took out a pair of handcuffs. "Hands."

"Who ordered you to cuff her?" Ormus asked from the next boat.

"The governor, sir. We know all about her hopping in the trees."

Olivia held out her hands. Gabriel tightened the cuffs until her fingers tingled.

"*Setting aside the fact that we don't want to lead anyone into a slaughter,*" Riley said, telepathically so he wouldn't have to shout, "*is it even possible to do what Dad's asking?*"

"*No,*" she replied. "*Telepaths can tell when they're being lied to.*"

"*So what's the actual plan?*"

"*I don't know. Ormus?*"

"*I'm still working on it,*" he said.

Riley's mind immediately turned frosty. Ormus gave him a flat look across the boats. "*Something you want to say?*"

"*I'm trying to understand how you can murder five people for saying chimera shouldn't be hunted, and then turn around and start preaching the exact same thing and still call yourself a decent man,*" Riley replied levelly.

"*I didn't murder anyone.*"

"*Oh, so when you arrested them, you just thought the governor would give them a strictly worded letter?*"

"*The Doves undermine Citadel authority,*" Ormus said, sounding tired and cornered.

"*So are you.*"

He winced. Olivia snorted, awkwardly eating her dried serovim jerky with cuffed hands. She and Ormus might have turned over a new leaf last night, but he still deserved this.

"*You say you don't have a plan, Ormus,*" Riley said, about halfway through the meal. "*Well, what is your goal?*"

"*Keeping Olivia alive is primary. Keeping you and the chimera alive is secondary,*" he said.

Riley nodded. "*You can make me a distant third priority.*"

Olivia glared at them. "*All of us are staying alive.*"

"*That would be ideal,*" Ormus said. Olivia could tell he didn't think it would happen.

"*We cannot kill more chimera,*" she stressed.

"*I will if they don't leave us a choice.*"

"*No, we don't give* them *a choice,*" she snapped. "*We kill some of them, they kill some of us, we find a den and slaughter a whole pack. On and on it goes. At some point it has to end! We can do that here and now!*"

"*Even if that means letting Elias's killer go free?*"

Olivia looked at the soldiers around her, nibbling on their food as they cast furtive glances up at the sky. Had Elias been like this during his hunt? Had he been like Ormus, dreading what was to come?

Or had he been like Gabriel, eagerly looking forward to the chance to kill some "demons?"

"*Elias was a soldier invading their home,*" she said at length. "*Mek'tay defended it. I can't condemn either of them. I want justice, not revenge, and that means no more of this.*"

Ormus sat in his boat for a long time. Olivia lost her appetite, pushing away the food Gabriel offered. He shrugged and ate it himself.

Ormus stood and whistled. "Attention!"

All quiet conversation ceased. All eyes turned to him.

"You're probably all very confused as to why we're doing a hunt during high tide," he said. "I was, too, when I originally got the order. That's because this isn't a hunt."

The men exchanged glances. Gabriel shook his head, glaring furiously at Ormus, who ignored him. Though his face and body were as still and unreadable as ever, Olivia could feel the way his mind trembled.

He was scared.

"Governor Thompson confided some information to me the other day that's . . . very upsetting," he continued. "We've all been taught that the demons of the forest were created by the Hundred-Faced God. A mistake that He's ordered us to correct. But this was a lie, taught and preserved by governors past and generations of clergy.

"God didn't make the demons. We did."

He let that sink in as the soldiers whispered to each other. Gabriel face-palmed.

"In the age when we had all of our Artifacts, all of our technological might, we thought to create our own personal guard dogs," Ormus said. "What we didn't realize was we created something so much more than that. The creatures we created—originally named chimera—are sentient."

"That's a lie," Gabriel called. Ormus's mind trembled harder, though he gave no outward appearance of his growing fear.

"It's true," Riley piped up. "My father confirmed the whole thing. Right before he shot Sergeant Peterson."

"What?!" Isaiah snapped. It was met with similar calls of outrage.

Olivia smirked. Sergeant Peterson had been in the military so long, he had likely trained each and every one of these men.

Ormus called everyone's attention to him again. "Peterson, Riley, and my daughter confronted Thompson about this discovery, and he did not react well. He wants us to destroy more chimera. But we created these beings—these *people*—in an environment of pain and fear, where they were tortured and starved and killed because we couldn't hear them. We didn't realize what we'd made. And they fought back and escaped to defend themselves. The original creators then lied to us—lied to *you*—for generations to cover up their mistake. They blamed their blunder on God and said He wanted them hunted down and killed.

"The reason I'm telling you this highly classified information is because Olivia and Riley have both found a way to communicate with the chimera, which they have shared with me. A form of telepathy. After centuries of silence, we can finally hear them. We can bridge the gap."

He pointed to Olivia. "My daughter spent *seven weeks* in this forest. Seven weeks. And she survived because she wasn't alone. She made allies with some of the chimera. We are here to talk to those people and begin a peaceful dialogue. Because I don't want to see any more brave young men die. I don't want to see wives become widows or children grow up without their fathers."

Everyone stared at Olivia when he pointed her out. She straightened her back.

"I know this goes against everything we've been raised to believe. Even as I tell you this, every fiber in my being is rebelling." He held up a hand, which visibly shook. "But we have to try. This time, we are not bringing back the body of someone's father, brother, or son. We are going to take the first steps toward peace so our children and grandchildren can live their lives without fear. Anyone who objects to this mission as I've stated is free to leave right now."

Nobody moved.

"Ms. Claude?" Sergeant Isaiah ventured. "Is this true? When you were gone, you talked to these . . . chimera?"

She nodded.

"She's the town freak. Don't believe her," Gabriel sneered.

"I believe her because she, Riley, and myself have been communicating via telepathy for the last eighteen hours," Ormus said. "You don't have to believe her, yet. But you do have to trust me. At the very least, trust that I will see each and every one of you return to Citadel alive."

"Right," someone drawled. "And when we return, the governor will arrest us."

"I was there on the last hunt," someone else hollered. "My buddy was the one who got grabbed by the dem—er, chimera? We all thought he was dead, but he just got dropped onto a tree. We couldn't believe it!"

"That's because Olivia asked the chimera not to harm us," Ormus explained. "If you are not willing to negotiate, to try to break bread with these people, then take your boats and go back to the city. I will not retaliate. No dock in pay, no arrests, nothing. Your hands will be clean. I'm sure the governor will even favor you. But if you want to put a stop to this, if you want to be *safe* in these woods, for your sons and grandsons to not have to fear for their lives whenever they step out of the walls, then please. Take this first step with me."

After a beat of silence, one of the soldiers chuckled and said, "That's all I needed to hear. Let's go break bread with some demons."

"Let's *not*," someone else said.

It took some shuffling. Men had to move boats. But about half of them left, rowing away from Ormus as if he had a disease.

Gabriel, for some reason, stayed.

"Augustus gave me my orders," he sneered. "He'll want to know the details of this."

"Probably," Ormus said, sitting back in his boat. "But in the meantime, uncuff Olivia. She's not going anywhere."

Grumbling, Gabriel did as he was told. Olivia rubbed her wrists, looking at the fifteen men left behind. She couldn't tell which were nervous or which were excited, but Riley and Ormus both started to feel *hopeful.*

"*That's a hell of a plan,*" Riley admitted silently. "*Will it work?*"

"*Only one way to find out.*" Olivia closed her eyes and reached out. "*Is'hav?*"

"*Silver!*" Is'hav called, her voice distant. "*Before, what happens?! I feel your hurt but cannot reach you!*"

"*Stuff.*" Olivia took a deep breath. "*I need to speak with Mek'tay.*"

She had hoped to put that off. Preferably forever. But Cyrij wasn't even an adult by chimeric standards, whereas Mek'tay was a respected leader among *all* the chimera.

And she needed to do this. She couldn't advocate peace between humans and chimera if she didn't find peace herself. She'd said she wanted justice, not revenge. Time to eat her words.

Besides, her father had just risked his career and life to give them this chance. Riley hated him for the death of his friends just *days* ago and was still willing to work with him. She could do this.

A new link connected to the back of her mind. *"Silver. You still hate me, but you ask to speak, so there is something very wrong."*

"I don't hate you," she admitted. *"I just . . . never want to see you again. But if that happens, then other people I care about are going to die."*

She dropped the memory of Augustus's meeting in his mind, wincing as she relived Peterson's shooting.

Mek'tay was silent for a moment. She could sense some flickers of fire before he squashed them down. *"You want me to give you chimera lives for your Peterson?"*

"No," she defended. *"We've got a better plan."*

She replayed Ormus's speech. Felt him consider the words.

"This can work," he said. *"I ask other packs to come and see. I want no more blood in this forest."*

Olivia swallowed. It tasted salty. *"I don't think I'll ever be able to forgive you for killing Elias. But I'm sorry I punched you after I found out. I shouldn't have done that."*

"No, but it is all right. I am sorry for killing your mate."

She felt him leave to go talk to the other packs. The link between them remained, fragile as a twig. She didn't break it.

CHAPTER FIFTY-EIGHT:
ABRAHAM

Sergeant Abraham Peterson lay in his hospital bed and tried not to go insane.

He could still feel the links to Riley and Olivia in the back of his mind. But whenever he tried to reach out to them, he couldn't quite get through. She had warned him that would happen, that distance was a factor in newer bonds. That didn't make it any less irritating. He didn't know what was going on, if any chimera had been killed, if any of his boys had been killed, or when they were coming back. Just that they were alive. For now.

Abe lay back and tried to clear his mind. *Just treat this like a hunt. You can't control what happens out there, but you can control your response to it.*

Right now his response was that he really needed to take a piss.

Which was difficult, being handcuffed to the bed.

He shared his hospital room with another patient, a much older man fast asleep in another bed across the room. That man unfortunately had to wear a hospital-issued smock. Abe had managed to avoid that fate by getting shot through and through, no major veins or organs hit. He still felt naked in the pale-blue pants and shirt that weren't his uniform.

The soldier in charge of making sure Peterson didn't escape—a sour-faced boy in his twenties named Vincent—hadn't been happy with the shared accommodations. It made his job harder. But even Central Hospital was a crowded mess, and the medics had been unwilling to clear out a whole room even for a man who was still recovering from a bullet wound. The young soldier stood just outside his door now, in the hallway.

Abe gingerly moved out of bed, testing the movement of his torso. The stitches tugged at his skin, and his insides weren't happy to be jostled around even a little bit. But he could function and do his business, even with his left hand cuffed to the bed. He had just finished sliding the chamber pot back under the bed when his door opened.

Mrs. Claude beamed at him. "Sergeant Peterson! Good to see you. Unfortunate circumstances aside, of course."

Abe dipped his head, remembering the last message Olivia had sent to him: *Asiya says she'll get you out.*

"Mrs. Claude."

Vincent followed her in. She huffed, hands on her hips. "Really, soldier. A little doctor-patient confidentiality?"

"The sergeant's a condemned criminal and very dangerous, ma'am. I need to be here," he replied.

As annoyed as Abe was at the intrusion, he respected the boy's commitment and professionalism. He remembered when Vincent had first been enlisted, right after his eighteenth birthday. He'd still had acne and shied away from almost anyone who looked at him, never mind outright confrontation. Now, he stood at parade rest by the door, meeting the medic's and sergeant's eyes without flinching. Abe couldn't help but feel a *little* proud. Even as he tried to think of a way to lift the keys to his chains out of the boy's pockets.

Mrs. Claude sighed but didn't protest further. She opened the window, letting in a cool, pleasant summer breeze. "How are you feeling, Sergeant?"

"Considering the fact that I was shot the other day? Right as rain."

She had him lift his shirt—he couldn't remove it entirely with the cuffs—and leaned over to examine the stitches. "I'll get you the keys," she whispered.

Louder, she said, "Those stitches are another day or two from being removed, I think. Are you having any issues with . . . digestion?"

"Besides being a fifty-two-year-old man, no."

He had no idea how Asiya planned to get those keys. She was a medic, not a thief.

She gave him a sharp look. "Are you sure? No need to be embarrassed, Sergeant." And she gave a barely veiled glare to Vincent.

Oh.

He cleared his throat. "Ah, now that you mention it, I have been having some . . . trouble."

"Too much going out at once?" she prodded.

"Yes, ma'am."

She nodded and sighed. "It might not have anything to do with the bullet and more to do with your age. Either way, those are fluids you can't afford to miss. I'm giving you some blood. Wait right here."

Abe jiggled his cuffs.

". . . You know what I mean."

Honestly, he didn't know why Citadel forbade women from combat. If he'd had a unit of women like Asiya, no human or chimera force would stand a chance.

She went out into the hall. Abe's roommate snored from his bed. Vincent stayed where he was.

"How's your brother, Private?" Abe asked, for lack of anything better to do.

"He's good," came the stiff response.

"What is he, sixteen?"

"Seventeen."

He swore. "We're getting old."

Vincent's mouth twitched. "Well, one of us is. Sir."

"I *will* order you to do push-ups."

Mrs. Claude came back a few minutes later with a blood bag and iron needle. She set the bag on the bed frame—which had a hook for just this purpose—and took Abe's free hand.

At first, Abe thought she genuinely missed his vein. He wasn't ancient, but he had a few wrinkles that made it difficult for medics to jab needles into him with any sort of efficiency. But on the second try, she didn't even go for the vein, just poked the skin.

On the third "try," she sighed and looked at Vincent. "I need to get his other wrist."

"What," he demanded.

"I can't access any of the veins on this arm. I need to try the other one."

Vincent hesitated.

Abe leaned back, helplessly holding up his hands. It killed him to put one of his boys in this position, especially since Vincent was going to catch hell if he did manage to escape. But he refused to be the knife held at Olivia's and Riley's throats.

Finally, the soldier pulled the keys out of his pocket and came over. "Hands where I can see them at all times, Sergeant."

Abe nodded and obeyed. Mrs. Claude stepped back.

Vincent released the cuff, his body as tense as a bowstring. He wasn't armed for a hunt, but he did have a knife on his belt, and Abe had trained him in hand-to-hand combat himself. With the sergeant lying prone on the bed and Vincent literally standing over him, he was at a severe disadvantage.

When Abe didn't try anything, Vincent relaxed, just a little, and chained his other hand to the bed frame. Abe let him.

As soon as the lock was in place, Abe punched Vincent on the side of the head. The soldier dropped to the floor.

"Sorry, son," he muttered, sitting up. Mrs. Claude quickly got the keys and unchained him. Both of them cast furtive looks at the other patient. He kept snoring.

"I have a bag of food, banknotes, and clothes in the closet across the hall," she said. "Go change, get out, and find somewhere to hide. Ormus will contact you when he gets back."

He nodded, rubbing his freed wrists. He considered taking the knife off Vincent, then decided against it. The boy would be embarrassed enough without losing his weapon.

She straightened. "You should probably hit me."

He gaped at her. "*What?*"

"To keep suspicion off me. The more damage you do, the better. Just don't give me a black eye; I need perfect vision for surgery."

While Abe hesitated, Vincent groaned on the floor.

What happened next, he wasn't sure. His eyes went straight to the knife at Vincent's belt, and all he could think of was that he needed to disarm him before he could turn on them or, worse, realize Mrs. Claude was helping him.

He felt a tug in his mind, and then—

The knife flew from Vincent's sheath to Abe's hand.

Abe and Mrs. Claude stared at the blade.

Vincent pulled himself to a knee.

Abe used the butt of the knife to knock him out—properly, this time.

Asiya stared at him with wide eyes. "What did you . . .?"

"I don't know. I . . . I'll panic about that later." He set the knife on the thin mattress that had been his bed for the last few days.

Mrs. Claude visibly shook herself. "Move quickly. I'll wait as long as I can before raising the alarm."

Abe put both hands on her shoulders and smiled. "You're a true gem, Mrs. Claude. Thank you."

She smiled back.

He slapped her across the face, just hard enough to bruise the cheek. "Sorry."

"It's fine."

He ducked out of the room and into the closet across the hall. Quickly locating the bag, he found a civilian shirt, pants, and a hooded summer coat.

Two minutes later, he walked out of Central Hospital.

CHAPTER FIFTY-NINE

"*We are ready,*" Mek'tay said, one day later at high noon. "*We come to you.*"

Olivia nudged Gabriel and motioned for him to stop.

"Captain," he called. "Your girl's telling us to stop. Do we keep going, or . . .?"

Ormus looked at her. "They're on their way?"

She nodded.

"Everyone stop. We have chimera incoming. Keep your hands away from your weapons at all times. Let me do the talking."

It took some maneuvering, but Ormus eventually got everyone to go where he wanted. The trees were close together, and most of them intertwined with each other. The branches that reached out of the water prevented more than four boats from being comfortably maneuvered side by side.

Riley was praying again, whispering with his eyes closed and his hands clasped together. His mind grew steady, calm. Olivia used that as an anchor.

"Up there!"

Olivia didn't know who spoke, but soon they were all pointing at the sky. Mek'tay's dark, blurry form came into sharp focus as he flew down, landing on an outstretched branch a meter away from the nearest boat.

She braced herself to feel anger, or hurt, or hate. But all she felt was twitchy nerves. She did a quick mental scan and felt a dozen other chimera slowly closing in, a few of whom she recognized.

"*Hey,*" she said. "*Thanks for coming.*"

"*Your fur is gone!*" Cyrij wailed. "*And you hurt!*"

"*It's a long story.*"

"*Keep your heads, cubs,*" Mek'tay scolded. "*Cyrij, you have the gift?*"

"*Yes.*"

Olivia frowned. "*Gift?*"

Ormus cleared his throat, studying Mek'tay. "Riley, I want you to repeat everything the chimera says here so the men can hear what's happening. As for our guest . . . Mek'tay, I presume?"

Mek'tay tipped his head. "*You are not mind deaf.*"

Riley repeated it. Ormus's mouth twitched. He spoke aloud: "No, I'm not. But my men are. This is for their benefit."

"*I see. I am Mek'tay, iyi'ke of the Isilna pack. Silver says your word is* governor.*"

"I am Captain Ormus Claude of Citadel," he said. "We've come to negotiate. No other chimera has to die."

"*Or human,*" Mek'tay said through Riley.

"I know you," Gabriel blurted, so loud that Olivia jumped next to him. "You killed my brother!"

Mek'tay tipped his head at the ensign. Ormus sighed. "Yes, during the last military expedition. That was *my* fault. I saw you near my daughter and fired my pistol. Gabriel and his brother, Michael, followed suit. You and yours defended yourself."

"The hell he did! They attacked first!"

"*They did not,*" Olivia snapped, not that Gabriel could hear her.

"Witnesses would disagree with you, Ensign," Riley said. "Olivia was there too."

The other men twitched in their boats, several darting glances at the sky and in the trees. While at night, the chimera would've had the advantage of hiding in the sky, they couldn't do that during the day. The branches still provided cover.

"*I am sorry I kill your littermate,*" Mek'tay said through Riley. "*He shoots arrows at me and my warrior. I fight back so my warrior does not die. I want no more fighting. No more blood.*"

"Well, I do." Gabriel grabbed his pistol.

Olivia shoved her shoulder into him before he could aim. Out of the corner of her eye, she saw soldiers reach for their bows.

"Stand down!" Ormus snapped.

The men froze and left their weapons alone.

She and Gabriel were on their feet, the boat rocking dangerously beneath them. Olivia went for the gun, grabbing his wrist. He tried to punch her, and she blocked with her free hand. For a moment, the two struggled against each other, at a standstill.

"Ensign, stand down!" Ormus ordered again.

Gabriel ignored him and kicked her in the shin, dropping her to a knee. He pointed his gun at Olivia's head.

Talons snatched Olivia out of the boat. She yelped. The tips of black wings darted in and out of her vision. "*Mek'tay?*"

BANG!

Blood sprayed across Olivia's face. She and Mek'tay dropped.

She couldn't tell if Ormus and Riley were screaming her name in telepathy or out loud as they plunged into the trees. She crashed through a dozen twigs and leaves before slamming into a branch thick enough to hold her weight and punch the breath out of her lungs.

A dozen chimeric minds bombarded her and Mek'tay, demanding answers.

"*What happened?*" she asked, coughing.

"*Gabriel fired!*" Riley said. "*Are you all right?*"

Olivia wiped the blood from her face and did a quick check. Her ribs were probably bruised from her fall, the stitches on her forehead were torn, and she had a fresh collection of cuts and bruises. But she was unhurt. Which meant the blood had come from . . .

"*Mek'tay!*" she called, frantically looking around the tree.

"*He is here!*" Cyrij cried. "*Ukurf, come!*"

Olivia scrambled to follow the link, pushing through a curtain of leaves and branches before finding them.

Cyrij whined, hovering over Mek'tay. The iyi'ke lay on his side, panting heavily as blood stained the blue wood beneath him. A massive hole punched through his chest.

She knelt next to him and sent the scene to Riley. "*What do I do?*"

Dread curled around his mind. She refused to acknowledge it.

"*Put pressure on it,*" he instructed. "*A lot of pressure.*"

She plunged both hands onto the wound. Mek'tay wheezed. "*That warrior has good aim.*"

"*Then you should've attacked him instead of grabbing me, you idiot,*" she snapped. Blood oozed from between her fingers. She pressed harder.

"*I say no more blood. I mean it.*"

Wings. More weight on the thick branch. Gray-blue fur and feathers entered her vision. Ukurf the chimeric medic licked Mek'tay's cheek. "*I cannot fix this, friend.*"

"*Then find someone who can!*" Olivia ordered.

"*Liv, even if we were in Central Hospital . . .*" Riley trailed off.

"*Shut up! We can fix this!*"

"*You can,*" Mek'tay said, his mind fading. "*We all can. No more blood . . . no more . . .*"

His mind went dark, all links breaking. He stopped breathing.

CHAPTER SIXTY:
ORMUS

Ormus glared at Gabriel as the link to Mek'tay faded from his mind. "Congratulations, Ensign. You just killed our best shot at peace."

"There is no peace while those monsters breathe," he growled.

Howls rose all around them. He could feel their minds clouding with grief. And rage. The soldiers on the boats reached for weapons.

A new mind spoke to him: "*You kill Mek'tay. You lie, and now you die.*"

"*This man does not speak for me. For any of us!*" Ormus cried. If he were talking aloud, he could make his voice sound however he liked. But with telepathy, he couldn't hide how scared he was. That he'd failed his men. That he'd failed Olivia.

"They're people," Riley shot back, barely audible over the howling.

"They're *demons!*" Gabriel raged. "They've killed hundreds of us!"

"*Let us leave now,*" Ormus said to all the chimera. "*I'll get my men out of here and deal with the ensign.*"

"*Humans lie,*" they hissed.

"And we've killed hundreds of them!" Riley shot back at Gabriel. "How many of them have lost brothers, hmm? They had the good grace to not kill us while we try to offer a way out!"

On and on it goes. At some point it has to end.

But there still needed to be justice.

"*I will leave my ensign here,*" Ormus said.

The howls stopped. All the men went rigid.

"*He murdered one of yours on your land,*" he continued. "*You decide what to do with him, and you let the rest of us go. Including my daughter.*"

Riley whipped around and stared at Ormus.

"What's happening?" Gabriel demanded.

"*Done,*" said the chimera.

"What happened," Ormus replied steadily, loudly so everyone could hear him, "is that the chimera will let the rest of us go. In exchange for punishing the murderer of their leader."

It took Gabriel a second too long to realize what he meant.

A dark-brown, black-winged chimera burst out of the trees behind him and snatched the ensign's shoulders. Before Ormus could warn him about the gun, the weapon was yanked out of Gabriel's hands with tele-kinesis and tossed into the water.

He winced at the loss of an Artifact. But not at the man.

Gabriel screamed as he was taken up higher and higher. Ormus waited for the drop, but it didn't come. Instead, a second and third chimera joined the first.

Together, they ripped him apart.

Half of the soldiers cringed and looked away. Several swore. More than one vomited into the water. Ormus watched the entire thing. He had made this happen.

He didn't regret it.

Pieces of Gabriel fell into the trees and water. But the chimera were kind enough not to do this directly over the men's heads. For that, and more, Ormus was grateful.

"*What just happened?*" Olivia asked cautiously.

"*Hopefully, the last human death to happen in this forest,*" he replied. To the chimera he called, "*Are we good?*"

"*You leave now,*" a female voice said. "*Do not return.*"

"*I'll have to return to restart negotiations. Preferably alone. Definitely with better planning.*"

"*Do not leave yet,*" a male voice called. Ormus traced it to the brown, black-winged chimera who landed on a tree nearby. Plainly visible to all the soldiers with bows and arrows. "*Cyrij, the gift.*"

"*Right.*" The shaky, shockingly young voice belonged to an adolescent chimera flying out of the trees. Ormus recognized him immediately from the sketchbook.

"Freckles," he realized, smiling.

"Sir?" Sergeant Isaiah asked.

Cyrij landed on Ormus's boat, wings spread to help his balance. He clutched a basket of prasina flowers in his jaws.

Ormus's smile grew. "This, gentlemen, is Cyrij. He's the chimeric equivalent of a teenager and has been instrumental in showing us how to communicate with each other."

He took the basket from Cyrij's jaws and held up a green flower. "These are what allow us to access telepathy."

"*It is all we can find, now,*" Cyrij said. His mind was weighed down by the fresh grief of Mek'tay's death, but there was some sunlight there. "*Come back and we give you more.*"

Riley repeated what he'd said. He added, "Be careful when you eat one, though. It knocks you down for at least a day, usually two."

Sergeant Isaiah looked at the flowers, then at Riley. "I'll take one now if you row me back."

Riley's smile was tight. "I don't think I should go back."

"Why?"

The leaves rustled. Olivia emerged, her clothes and hands stained with blood. She shared a look with Riley.

"Well, to be honest, my father said he'd kill me and Olivia if we didn't come back with a 'demon' body," Riley said. "And I'm not giving him Mek'tay."

Ormus grimaced. He'd hoped to return with triumphant news that the chimera had agreed to a cease-fire and that negotiations for a true era of peace could begin immediately. Such news would have shocked the entirety of Citadel and forced Augustus to play by his rules.

He supposed that had been too much to ask.

"*I think we're going to have to stay here,*" Olivia agreed. "*And Uncle Peterson, when he gets out.*"

"Will the chimera allow that?" Ormus asked. He was well aware that he was carrying out only half of an audible conversation, which made him look strange to his men. He didn't care.

"*Silver is friend of Isilna. We watch her and her friends. It is sadakra,*" Cyrij said. "*It is what Mek'tay wants.*"

Gabriel's empty boat drifted and bumped into Ormus's. He grabbed it and peeked inside. Gabriel's gun was lost, but not his supplies.

He hadn't brought a bow. Ormus rectified that by putting his own in the boat. "Riley. Olivia. Can you two stay safe out here while we . . . handle Citadel?"

She snorted. "*Out here is leagues safer than in there.*"

"We can," Riley said with a shadow of a smile. His mind was still frosty whenever he looked at Ormus. But it was starting to thaw, just a little, at the edges. "We'll try to get the other packs to agree to a cease-fire."

"*Augustus will never agree to it,*" Olivia warned.

"You let me worry about Augustus," Ormus said. He had no idea *how* he'd dispose of the highly popular governor who was the seat of all political power in Citadel. But he had two days to figure it out.

"In the meantime, Ensign Byruk generously left you his supplies. And it seems I've misplaced my bow on the stern," he added. He pushed the empty rowboat toward Riley. Cyrij flew up and landed while it was still drifting, using his momentum to push it the rest of the way.

Riley got in and smiled. Ormus couldn't hear what they shared on the one-on-one link between Riley and the young chimera, but he could sense it being formed.

Olivia's mind, on the other hand, was in turmoil. So many emotions: Pride at what they'd accomplished today. Lingering rage. Grief. Guilt.

"*I am so proud of you,*" he said to her privately. "*Today was a first step. We'll figure out the rest tomorrow.*"

She swallowed and nodded. "*Get back safe. And make sure Uncle Peterson gets out.*"

As soon as Riley joined her, Ormus ordered the men to row out.

When he did, dozens of chimera came out of the trees, poking their heads out of leaves and standing on exposed branches. Watching them.

Some of the men rowed faster. Ormus didn't. He could feel that there was very little malicious intent. Most of what the chimeric minds shared was a sense of curiosity, wonder, and hope.

CHAPTER SIXTY-ONE:
AUGUSTUS

Augustus found his wife pouring herself a glass of wine at the kitchen table, the dawn light cutting through the window and landing on her back. He sighed. "Mia. You know the rules."

She raised an eyebrow at him, and he almost startled. She wore no makeup. Nothing smoothed the lines on her face, the crow's-feet that had settled soon after their marriage and only gotten deeper. The wrinkles around her mouth formed from her disgusting smoking habit. Even the gray roots of her hair were showing.

"You sent our son to die in the woods. I'm having a drink."

He took the bottle and glass from her hands and poured them down the sink.

By the time he turned around, she'd procured another bottle from somewhere and drank straight from it.

"No wonder that boy was led astray, with you as his mother," he grumbled.

She shrugged.

"I should have divorced you years ago." She had given him only one son, and one with such weak blood that he turned out to be a criminal. That was grounds enough for divorce.

Mia barked a laugh. "Four years, five max before the effects of food starvation deeply affect even *our* circles, and that's assuming the town doesn't tear us apart before then. Your grandfather created his fortune by embezzling city funds. Humans created demons. And those are just the secrets I can remember off the top of my head. How much do you think they'd sell for if I were cast out on the street?"

Augustus refused to let the tiny sliver of fear he felt at those words show. "Who would believe you?"

She shrugged, taking another sip from the bottle.

Damn the woman. He really did need to get rid of her. She'd out-lived her use for him.

Someone knocked on the front door.

Problem for another day, he thought, beckoning for his wife to go upstairs and hide her shame. She took the bottle with her, of course.

Augustus opened the door to find one of the sergeants he'd sent out into the forest with Riley, Olivia, and Ormus, just a couple of days ago. "You can't be done already."

The sergeant shook his head. "No, sir. Captain Claude has decided to . . . parlay."

". . . What?"

Dear Elias,

This will be the last letter I write to you.

The time we were together was the best of my life to date, and I'll always remember it. It will always be a part of me. As much as I wish you were still alive today, you're not, and I have to accept that.

Thank you for being there. Thank you for being you.

Love, always,

Olivia

CHAPTER SIXTY-TWO

When a person died in Citadel, there was a funeral. People who knew them gathered around to talk about how they knew them, burned the corpse, and stored the ashes in one of the temples. Unless that person was a criminal, in which case they never got a funeral. Sarai hadn't had one. And Elias's funeral had been over an empty box.

Chimera followed a similar structure. As the sun set, turning the planet's rings yellow against a red sky and revealing the two moons, dozens if not *hundreds* of chimera gathered in the place Mek'tay had died. More than Olivia had thought could be in this forest. They gave Olivia and Riley a wide berth, but no one asked them to leave, so they stayed, sitting on their boat tied to a skinny branch. Mek'tay's closest friends and packmates stood around his body, now cold and stiff to the touch.

One by one, they shared their memories of the fallen iyi'ke:

Ebevil showed them all the times Mek'tay had stood up to the Mulo pack and other threats, led him and other warriors into battle, and saved chimera lives in fights. Many other warriors shared similar memories.

Siyet shared when Cyrij and Takkaz were born, and how Mek'tay had been almost as excited as him and Ebevil to meet them.

Ukurf showed them Mek'tay helping him comfort sick and injured chimera as they recovered. Or in some cases, died.

Some warriors—from other packs, Olivia figured out—shared all the times they'd fought *against* Mek'tay. How he stuck to his principles of sadakra, psikar, and namsuud. She wondered if their packs were still fighting, but even she could see this wasn't the time to ask.

Is'hav showed the memory of her rescue from the Mulo. How Mek'tay hadn't pressured her to join his pack, how he'd *meant* it when he said that she was free to choose to live how she liked, and that was ultimately why she joined.

Cyrij shared a memory of when he was barely old enough to fly, and how he told Mek'tay he wanted to be an iyi'ke just like him one day. Mek'tay had licked the top of his head and said, "*I tremble to think of mighty pack of Cyrij. After you are grown, you are fine iyi'ke.*"

"*I hope so,*" Cyrij said. His fathers pressed against him on either side.

There was a pause in the memories. Before she could change her mind, Olivia tentatively shared her own. The times he escorted Cyrij to the berry field to watch their writing lessons. When he answered all of her questions about chimera history and told her about Mama. When he admitted to killing Elias. When he apologized for it.

She thought of Elias, felt the grief of his death like a freshly scabbed wound. It would never truly go away, but it didn't drag her down, and the rage was gone.

Something in her chest popped and released, like a sudden breath or unraveling a ball of tension. She was going to miss them both. Riley squeezed her in a half hug.

A handful of chimera—mostly telekinetics—pushed Mek'tay's body off the tree branch and into the water.

"*We give him back to Edalide,*" Cyrij explained, without having to be prompted. "*Life is death, death is life. She uses dead for more life. And more life creates more death.*"

Riley squirmed, admitting (privately) to Olivia, "*Seems like a disrespectful way to handle a body.*"

"*They see their planet as their god. The being that delivered them from space and gave them a home,*" she pointed out. "*This is an offering.*"

The chimera flew off into the darkening sky. Most of the bonds

Olivia had made today broke, thin string harmlessly cut. Siyet's and Ukurf's remained even as they flew away. Eventually only Ebevil, Cyrij, and Is'hav remained on the bloodstained tree.

Cyrij bumped his head against her chest. "*I am sorry I break our bond, before. I see Mek'tay hurt and want to hurt you back.*"

Olivia smiled, feeling the bond repair itself in their minds. It was still new and thin but already rapidly growing. "*Forgiven.*"

"*You should stay out of all pack territories,*" Ebevil warned. "*The other packs still honor Mek'tay, but it does not last. Stay out of territories, stay out of trouble.*"

She stiffened, stepping away from Cyrij and Is'hav. "*Does this mean we're not friends anymore?*"

"*No!*" Is'hav snapped. "*We are still friends. Those packs are just stupid.*" She relaxed.

"*We'll figure it out,*" Riley promised. "*Thank you. Seriously. You saved our lives back there. I'm sorry we couldn't save Mek'tay.*"

Ebevil bowed his head. "*He is good iyi'ke. He defends his pack, always.*"

"*What happens to the Isilna pack now?*" Olivia asked.

"*We choose new iyi'ke. Then, we know more.*"

"*Could be good iyi'ke,*" Cyrij pointed out.

"*Could be bad one,*" Is'hav countered.

"*You're welcome to join our human pack if it gets that bad,*" Riley teased. "*We have a boat.*"

Cyrij's tail wagged. "*I do like boat . . .*"

"*Choose iyi'ke first. Then talk of boats,*" Ebevil lightly scolded.

"*Stay safe,*" Olivia said.

The three chimera flew away. Olivia and Riley moved to a different tree, groping in the dark so they wouldn't slip and fall in the water. Their current perch was large enough to hold them for the night, but . . . no. Not with the wood still wet with blood.

They found a new one and split the rations Gabriel had left in his boat. He'd also left a tent, but it was too dark to set it up. It was warm enough, and they had thick enough coats, not to worry about it tonight.

Riley let out a long breath. "So. What now?"

Olivia dropped the back of her head against the bark, looking through the leaves to the sky above. The silver-gray rings around the planet. The two moons. The endless stars and all their questions.

She dropped her gaze back down and opened her arms.

Chuckling, Riley squeezed next to her. She hugged him.

"We'll figure that out tomorrow."